THE MAN WHO WOULD BE KING

"The prophecy is fulfilled!" a woman cried. "Long live King Brandegarth, the wizard king!"

The Sage of Sare was breathtaking to behold. Every inch of him was clad in snowy white silk. His rich expanse of black hair was expertly combed over his shoulders, and he dazzled the congregation with jewels that reflected the sun streaming through the stained glass windows.

"Who comes into this hallowed place to claim the crown of Caithe and serve as her rightful king?" the archbishop chanted.

"I do," Brandegarth replied.

Then another voice sounded. "I'm afraid I'll have to object."

The Sage whirled around just as Athaya dispersed the cloaking spell that had shielded her approach. She shimmered into view directly behind him.

"How could I bear to miss such a spectacle as this?" Athaya asked. "It was rude of you not to invite me."

By Julie Dean Smith
Published by Ballantine Books:

THE
WIZARD
KING

Julie Dean Smith

A Del Rey Book
BALLANTINE BOOKS • NEW YORK

A Del Rey Book
Published by Ballantine Books

Library of Congress Catalog Card Number: 93-90713

ISBN 0-345-37153-4

Manufactured in the United States of America

First Edition: February 1994

To my grandmother, Ethel Glover,
the Upwards champ of Anna, Illinois.

If I have learned anything since my magic came to me, it is that banes can turn into blessings, enemies into friends, and impossibilities into reality, all for the simple price of faith and perseverance, which we all, wizard or no, have within our reach; and more, that to turn our back on our gifts, no matter what they are, is the only real madness . . . and one we sadly impose upon ourselves.

—*The Apologetics of Athaya Trelane*

ACKNOWLEDGMENTS

The author would like to express her thanks to Deborah Hogan and Lester del Rey of Del Rey Books, and also to Joshua Bilmes at the Scott Meredith Agency. Without their encouragement and valuable insights during the writing of *A Caithan Crusade*, the Lorngeld might have faced a far different future.

CHAPTER 1

※※※

SLOUGHING THE CLOAKING SPELL FROM HIS SHOULDERS, Couric of Crewe moved to the doorway of the shabby brewhouse and surveyed its interior with a pinched look of repugnance. Muttering a Sarian expletive under his breath, he stepped gingerly over the threshold, squinting through stagnant woodsmoke at the assortment of ragged, foul-smelling men hunched over games of dice and cards, and exchanging vulgar jokes with one another when they weren't actively picking fights. Couric ducked under a low ceiling beam and was promptly greeted on the other side by a buxom serving wench sporting a brazen, if somewhat gap-ridden, smile.

"T'ent seen you in here afore," she said, batting a pair of lashes liberally coated with dust. The tea-colored eyes beneath them slowly inspected him, brushing over the glossy black hair, down each of his muscled limbs, and finally coming to rest upon his deceptively plain but well-crafted tunic and cloak, as if rapidly trying to estimate their combined worth. "I'd have remembered one so handsome."

Had Couric been in the mood for a quick and inexpensive tumble—without her two front teeth he doubted she could charge full price—he might have found the woman's admiration mildly appealing. As it was, he had business to attend to. He answered her flattery with a noncommittal shrug and settled into a splintered chair near the door of the common room. "Bring me whiskey if you have it. If not, I'll settle for

1

Evarshot wine; I'm told it's the best to be found in Delfarham."

The barmaid sauntered away with a greedy glint in her eye, and Couric instantly knew he would be drinking the Evarshot no matter what the status of the tavern's storeroom—it cost twice what Sarian whiskey did, and these sorts of establishments always sold you the most expensive thing they had if they thought you could afford it. But he could not go elsewhere. *Keep to the meanest places*, the Sage had counseled him. *The rebellious fruit is ripest there and ready to be picked.* Even Athaya Trelane had known as much, having launched her fateful crusade in the looca-dens of Kaiburn rather than the gilded halls of the nobility.

Couric sighed his resignation; at least he would soon be free of such squalor and able to return to the more comfortable existence he had led until two months ago, when he was set upon this latest mission for his lord. Or more accurately, he would attain a far more comfortable existence than he had ever known, for once his business was accomplished, all the wealth and power of Caithe would belong to the Sage and his loyal apostles. And at the risk of immodesty, Couric knew that as one of the Sage's most talented protégés, he would earn a larger share than most.

The barmaid delivered the expected flagon of Evarshot wine and a dented pewter cup, surreptitiously flicking a roach out of the bowl with a greasy corner of her apron before setting it before him. Couric handed her a pair of silver coins for the cost of the wine, then held a third coin before her, just out of reach.

"I've another crown for you if you can answer a question for me and then forget I ever asked it."

The woman's saucy demeanor quickly changed to one of guarded apprehension. Yes, Couric had seen that look often enough since his arrival on the mainland. Most Caithans were so damned afraid of this Tribunal—this infernal inquisition of the king's—that they were terrified to tell you what day of the week it was much less anything useful.

Of course, one could hardly blame them, Couric conceded. Any agency with the power to carve out a man's intestines and set them afire before his still-living eyes does tend to intimidate people.

"Tell me, do you know most of the people that come in here?" he asked with artful candor. The wench might be nervous, but the coin was a lodestone, keeping her close by his side. "Know much about them?"

"This 'n that," she answered evasively. Although she was trying to conceal it, Couric caught her scanning his garments for some half-hidden badge of office, for some sign that he was in the employ of the Tribunal.

"Oh, come now, do I look like a priest to you?" He flashed one of his most charming smiles and, just this once, returned a measure of the wench's suggestiveness.

The ploy worked like a well-cast spell; a toothless smile broke across the woman's ruddy face. "If you're a priest, my love, then I'm gonna start goin' to church more often." Cocking her head to one side, she somehow managed to survey the common room without tearing her eyes from the silver coin in Couric's hand. "Most of 'em as come here are regular folks," she said in answer to his query. "Farmers, tanners, tinkers, and such. A few thieves, but Oren throws them out right quick if he catches them plyin' their trade in here. But once, not two years ago, the princess herself come in here. Gave Oren's daughter a whole crown, she did, and all for bringing her some Evarshot, same as you. My, yes, I remember that night right well." The barmaid propped her hip against Couric's shoulder as she gradually relaxed into her tale, eyes glowing like candles as if she recounted the most exciting event of her life. "The fellow her Highness was dicing with tried to make her pay up with something other than money, if you take my meaning, but she handed him his head in a handbasket, she did. 'Course, his friends came back to rough her up some, but they'd only just got started when the King's Guard up and hauled them off and took her Highness back up to the castle."

A covert smile crept across Couric's lips as he pictured that high-born lady swilling wine among the human dregs of Caithe's capital. But princess or no, one could sink to any depth during the *mekahn*, and more than a few fledgling Lorngeld had sought the numbing powers of wine in an attempt to subdue the magic burgeoning within them—a task they inevitably found as futile as pushing the tide back out to sea. Couric raked his eyes across the tavern with seeming indifference. Overindulgence in spirits was common enough in new wizards . . . and an easy way of locating them.

He didn't particularly need the wench's help; he could just as easily sit here all night and dip into the mind of each besotted wretch around him. But it would be far more efficient—

and pleasant—to be guided in a likely direction first. Too many such dabblings would muddle his mind almost as much as wine itself, and he could not afford to blunt his senses overmuch. He didn't have much time left; it was already the first week of May, and gathering an army man by man was no small task. The Sage would be angry indeed if he arrived in Caithe to find that all had not been prepared in accordance with his orders.

Absorbed with these thoughts, it took a moment for Couric to realize that his reverie had badly unnerved his companion; the barmaid was biting her lip with what teeth she had remaining, fearful that his silence meant something far more ominous. " 'Course, Oren's careful not to let any wizards in here—not if he knows 'em for such," she added hastily. "He's a good Caithan, y'know, and loyal to the king."

"Of course he is," Couric agreed amiably, setting aside the woman's fears with another winning and slightly lecherous smile. "Tell me . . . have you noticed that any of your patrons seem to drink a bit more than they used to?"

"Ever'body drinks more'n they used to these days," she said, the unexpected candor of her words both grim and revealing. Though not a Justice was in sight, Couric glimpsed the shadows of the Tribunal looming over her. "But Rob . . ." The woman tilted her head toward a disheveled young man slumped on a stool beneath the cobwebs rimming the underbelly of the staircase; his head was bent so low over a mug of beer that his bangs dipped listlessly into the foam. "He's the worst. Prickly as a thistle these days, and not a one of us can figure out why. That's his brother Dickon next to him." Couric's gaze shifted to the older but equally rumpled man whispering urgently in Rob's ear—whispers that Rob was patently ignoring. "At first we all thought Rob might be a wizard," the wench added softly. "They act that way sometimes, y'know, just afore they go all amuddle. But Rob only just turned eighteen, so that can't be it. Must be some girl or another that's got him low."

Couric narrowed his eyes, fixing his concentration on young Rob. True, eighteen was young for the *mekahn* to arise, but it was certainly not unheard of; some Lorngeld developed the power as young as sixteen, others as late as thirty, although either of these extremes was quite rare. Couric extended his senses and probed the boy's mind with minimal subtlety; drunk as the boy was, there was little need for caution. And there they were: the channels and caverns of newly developing paths, taking hold like the tangled roots of a willow tree inside the young wizard's mind. Already, Couric could sense the building pressure of the boy's untrained magic yearning to be channeled, and the confusion and fear of Rob himself, suspecting the malady that ailed him but not knowing which of the damning cures to take.

Death or treason, Couric reflected. Truly an unpleasant dilemma. Then his eyes warmed in anticipation. Soon the Lorngeld in Caithe would have a third alternative: wealth, power, and veneration. Which choice, he thought with dry confidence, would they make then?

"My thanks for your help," Couric muttered distractedly. He dropped the silver coin into the barmaid's grubby palm and gave a slight nod of dismissal. She murmured her thanks but departed reluctantly, as if hoping for some other sort of offer— perhaps one that involved several more coins and an hour or two in one of Oren's upstairs rooms.

Couric picked up his cup and flagon and strolled casually to the shadowed alcove under the stairs. He was met with neither an objection nor a greeting as he hooked a stool with his foot and sat down beside the young Caithan. He only managed to elicit a distracted and somewhat bewildered grunt of thanks when he handed Rob a generous serving of his costly Evarshot.

"You look bleak, my friend," Couric observed, swirling the wine in his own cup and savoring the heady aroma.

"Look, this here's a private conversation," Dickon said at last, looking up irritably once he realized that Couric had no intention of leaving. "If you—"

"I was talking to your brother," Couric replied, in the cool but civil tone of a nobleman scolding a neophyte servant. With no magic of his own, Dickon was immaterial to his purposes.

Rob lifted his chin an inch, revealing a pair of morose blue eyes framed by a mass of black curls. "We don't have enough money to play cards, if that's what you're wanting. Try one o' the others." Rob sniffed at his wine and took a sip, bloodshot eyes widening in response. "But if you've got the coin for stuff like this, ain't nobody here with the money to take a game with you."

Couric smiled indulgently. "I'm not looking for a card game, Rob. Yes, the barmaid told me your name. Yours, too, Dickon." He leaned forward, forearms resting on his thighs, and lowered his voice markedly. "I'm looking for something far more interesting than a card game." He took a thoughtful taste of wine and rolled it around his tongue for a moment, swallowing leisurely before dropping his voice down to a whisper. "I'm looking for wizards."

Couric's disclosure sobered his companion quicker than if he had lit the boy's trews on fire. Rob's face was utterly guile-less; had anyone not suspected what he was, his reaction to the accusation brandished it for all the world to see. Dickon lurched protectively in front of his young brother, eyes blazing with indignation, while Rob jerked to his feet, ready to bolt for his life. Unfortunately, Rob moved more quickly than the beer he'd drunk would allow; a wave of nausea overtook him and he crumpled into a puddle of stale beer on the floor, his eyes squeezed tightly closed as he clutched his head in abject mis-ery.

Dickon gave Couric a rude shove backward. "I don't know what you're up to, friend, but I'll be damned if I'll let you go about insultin' my brother like that." His voice was barely above a whisper, but it shook with fear-induced rage.

"What's the trouble there, Dickon?" a man at the next table called out. He scanned the subtle embroidery edging the collar of Couric's rust-colored tunic and belched his opinion of it. "This peacock 'ere botherin' you?"

Couric refrained from rolling his eyes at the absurdity of the insult; he was only thought a peacock because his clothes were not soiled and riddled with holes, his face was reasonably clean-shaven, and his nails were not crusted with a half-year's worth of grime. But the man's pointed words did not go unno-ticed by his companions at the gaming table; all five laid down their cards and turned to stare, sensing that the tension between Dickon and his well-dressed friend was the harbinger of an ea-gerly awaited skirmish. Couric didn't think the men had heard anything of importance, but the last thing he wanted right now was to draw undue attention to himself. Fortunately, it was the last thing Dickon wanted, too.

"N-no, no. He's . . . I know him," Dickon stammered. "Go on back to your game."

"And pay closer attention to it if you don't want to lose ev-ery coin you've got," Couric advised, gesturing indistinctly to the other men seated at the pockmarked table. "Somebody just tried to slip you a deuce instead of a knave."

Whipping his eyes back to the table, the man snatched up

his cards and howled in drunken indignation at the crime. In the space of a single heartbeat, Couric and his offending tunic were forgotten and a bloody six-man fistfight was well under way. Couric's thin lips curved up in satisfaction as he turned his back to the brawl. *Remarkable how easily these Caithans are duped by a simple spell of illusion* . . .

Dickon, however, was not so easily diverted and gave Couric another shove toward the door. "Now get your arse out of here before I—"

"Leave him be, Dickon," Rob murmured from behind him. He struggled back onto his stool, rubbing dejectedly at a foul-smelling blotch of grime on the knee of his trews.

"Why should I? Hell, Rob, the man's a damned liar!"

Rob's only reply was a lengthy stretch of eloquent silence.

As Dickon slowly turned to face his brother, the outrage on his face was transformed to barely concealed terror. "But you told me it was all because Belle married the saddler's son. You said—"

"It was for your own good, idiot," Rob snapped as he massaged his throbbing temples. "What was I supposed to say? That I thought I was a—" He broke off just before uttering the damning word, then continued more softly. "Thought I was one of them? That could've gotten the whole family killed. At best we would have lost what little land we've got. And at worst . . ."

The mere mention of such a fate sent Dickon's eyes darting rapidly around the common room in search of black-robed priests. "God's grace, man, don't look so confounded guilty!" Couric roughly turned him around and prodded him back into the darkened alcove under the stairs. "Just sit down and hear me out. I'm sure you'll both be very interested in what I have to offer."

Then, moving his lips only slightly, Couric laid a light spell of sobriety over the hapless Rob. It was only a temporary solution—the boy would simply feel the effects of his beer later rather than now—but at least he would remember the rest of the night's conversation. When Rob's nausea mysteriously passed, he refocused his artless blue eyes and studied Couric again. His fear wasn't gone, but it was subdued. Dickon, however, remained wary and kept his eyes securely locked on Couric as if expecting that the wizard might change himself into a flesh-eating demon at the slightest opportunity.

"How did you know?" Rob asked simply. "About me, that is."

"Your symptoms aren't very advanced, but they're far enough along so that I can tell what you are," Couric replied. The dispute at the next table had escalated, and he swiftly ducked a dented tin cup that whizzed past his ear and crashed into the wooden slats behind him. He had to speak louder than he liked to make himself heard over the shouts and curses of the combatants. "There's nothing for you to fear from me. Why would I turn you in to the Tribunal when I'm a wizard myself?"

"You—?" Rob's brows arched their surprise for a moment, then knitted themselves tightly together. "Well, I can't say as you look much like a Justice."

Couric's nostrils flared in abhorrence. "I most certainly am not."

"Justices are the only ones who come looking for wizards on purpose," Dickon pointed out. "To kill them." Every muscle in his limbs was taut as a bowstring, his whole body poised to bolt at the slightest whiff of danger.

"Oh, I don't want to kill them," Couric assured the two brothers, shaking his head. He settled back against the wall and his eyes glittered like stars in the shadows beneath the stairs. "I want to hire them."

The brothers both blinked in perfect unison, unable to believe that they had heard him correctly. Then Dickon's blank stare shifted to overt suspicion. "You one o' the princess' men?" he challenged brusquely. "Folks in the city don't hold kindly to her these days. Word is she tried to kill the king. Done it by witchin' her other brother, Prince Nicolas."

Couric fought to suppress a bubble of contented laughter. The Sage had accomplished many things during his eight-year rule on the Isle of Sare, but *that* turn of events had been a stroke of genius. Over the past year, Athaya Trelane had emerged as the undisputed leader of the Lorngeld on mainland Caithe, beseeching them to defy the laws forbidding the practice of magic and to turn their backs on the Church-sanctioned rite of absolution. But since she proved unwilling to extend her influence into backing a rebellion against Caithe's king—professing that it was only the laws she wanted to eliminate and not the king himself—the Sage of Sare sought to discredit her among her own people. Granted, the spell he placed upon Nicolas had failed—Durek had not taken a single sip of the poison the prince had offered him—but the damage was done just the same. Athaya had been blamed, thus paving the way for the Sage to replace her in the hearts of Caithe's disaffected masses when the time came.

If he doesn't destroy himself before he gets here. The unwanted thought slithered into Couric's mind and lingered there as he remembered his master's condition on the day he sailed for Caithe. The Sage had assured his people that he had studied the dangers of the sealing spell quite thoroughly and that a certain amount of sickness—and yes, insanity—was to be expected. But if Couric was any judge, Brandegarth was suffering the imprisonment of his magic far more than he ever intended, and the spell could very well kill him before the prearranged date for his release. Whatever additional spells his master sought to obtain by the ordeal, Couric seriously doubted they were worth such awful risk.

"Yes, I've heard of the princess' escapades," Couric replied evenly, careful not to betray any of his own misgivings. "But in truth, I've never laid eyes on Athaya Trelane in my life. I obey another master—a wizard of far greater power and loftier vision than your renegade princess." Couric shifted his gaze to Rob. "He can do great things for you—for all of us—if you and others like you will help him."

"Help him how? My family's farm . . . it's all I know."

Just as Couric started to answer, the barmaid was at his side, bending low to refill his cup—and to provide a generous view of her breasts. Couric jumped when she spoke; he hadn't realized she was so close.

"Anything else I can get for you?" she asked, her eyes silently informing him that far more was available for his purchase than simple food and wine. This time, however, Couric sensed that she was looking for something more—that she was probing him for an answer to some unspoken question. Though feigning the same breezy wantonness, her manner had an edge of coolness to it . . . and an imperceptible measure of fear.

"No, not just yet, thank you."

She shrugged and sauntered away without further argument, her gaze brushing lightly over Dickon and Rob. As she left, two of the men involved in the fistfight, now busily wrestling on the floor, rolled into her and sent her spiraling into an empty table. Mouthing a curse, she tipped the dregs from her flagon onto their heads.

"As I was saying," Couric continued, "my master means to

rule in Caithe and we need to gather an army to take it. He is coming, friends. Soon. Those who support him in his task will be richly rewarded; those who do not will perish."

"A-are you asking me to turn against the king?" Rob asked, mouthing the words rather than daring even to whisper them.

"The king and his laws will kill you for being a wizard," Couric replied matter-of-factly. "Is that the sort of man you owe allegiance to? Stay loyal to him and the best you'll get out of it is a hasty absolution service."

Fear flared anew in Rob's eyes, and Couric quickly used it to his advantage. "Is that what you want? Your friends and family gathered in church to watch you drink a cup of poison, the lot of you convinced that it's some sort of sacrament? Yes, I know, I've heard the whole speech—your priests say that our powers come from the Devil and that we can't defeat him except by giving our lives back to God." Couric snorted indelicately. "Your priests also say that a man can't lead a pious life unless he keeps his breeches on day and night, and I've never seen the sense in that, either.

"Athaya Trelane promises what? Life—a thing you have already! My master promises wealth and power and the homage owed to us as stewards of this world." As one of the Sage's most trusted servants, Couric's eyes gleamed with the knowledge that his share in this glorious future would not be small. "And if you want to turn your back on absolution and accept what you are, why should you join Athaya? Her people almost starved to death this past winter, and I doubt they're much better off now. And since they refuse to fight for what they want, they're all but asking the Tribunal to come and slaughter them! But the Sage can offer you food and money and a warm bed to sleep in—not a tent in the woods and a ball of pemmican for your dinner."

Couric knew Rob was interested, judging by how silent and attentive he'd become. Lofty concepts were all well and good, but it was the simple things like food and shelter that would win the masses to the Sage's side.

"The Sage's people won't sit back and do nothing," he went on, luring Rob into a web of glory. "Our army will take what we deserve. The Sage has hundreds of well-trained wizards at his command—wizards who have been working their spells since before Athaya Trelane was ever born! Our powers make us special, Rob—not cursed. We're better than other men and our place is to rule over them. It is God's will. It is the reason our magic was given to us."

Dickon made a rumbling sound in the back of his throat. "Now wait just one minute—"

"Perhaps 'better' isn't the right term," Couric added quickly, aware that he had waxed a bit too poetic in the presence of an unblessed man. And he had no wish to lose Rob by casting indirect aspersions upon his brother. "But we *are* different. The Lorngeld are graced with a special gift—a gift that is also found among the saints and angels ... and to a far greater extent, in the good Lord Himself. Princess Athaya may be a wizard, but she refuses to believe in the sanctity of her own people. She is not worthy to lead us, Rob. The Sage *is*."

Couric ended his sermon then, aware that Rob would need time to chew on everything he'd been told. Beside him, Dickon scowled in profound confusion. Princess Athaya had preached the sanctity of magic all along, but Couric suspected that Dickon was having trouble putting theory into practice. Believing that magic comes from God is one thing, but seeing his younger brother as some sort of heavenly incarnation was something else again.

Rob opened his mouth to ask something when Couric realized that the tavern had fallen eerily silent; so silent that he heard the rumble of a man's stomach from the opposite side of the room. The bloodied brawlers halted their fistfight in midblow, and even the woodsmoke stopped swirling in the air above their heads. Warily, Couric glanced over his shoulder. Each man and woman in the common room had gone rigid as a stone gargoyle, as if it were the king and his full entourage rather than a slender priest and two armed bodyguards that stood silhouetted in the doorway in silent tableau. One of the guards licked his lips hungrily, as if he were planning to devour his prey rather than merely arrest it.

The priest's eyes scanned the room, scraping an unforgiving gaze over it like a dull razor. The black surcoat emblazoned with the blood-red chalice of absolution clearly marked him as a Justice of the Tribunal. Spotting Couric and his two companions, he slowly inched his way toward them, stepping cautiously over globs of wax, puddles of spilled beer, and chunks of moldy food. The others mouthed prayers of relief as this angel of death passed by, and after an encompassing glare from the priest that bade them all attend to their own business, they went nervously back to their drinks and games, though in a far more subdued fashion than before.

Couric didn't have to ask who was responsible for the Justice's unexpected appearance; the barmaid was taking great pains to appear innocent—an expression Couric doubted she had ever worn sincerely in her life. Of the dozens of folk gathered in the tavern, only she did not appear shocked by the priest's arrival.

"Now you've gone and done it," Dickon snapped under his breath, giving Couric a nasty kick in the ankle.

"Shut up and calm down," Couric replied with an unmistakable touch of command. "I'll handle this. Just don't look so damned guilty—they'll smell it on you." Then, in a fluid and well-practiced motion, he dipped his finger into the small leather pouch at his belt and lifted it to his nose; one sniff, and the brown powder vanished up his nostrils.

Gaunt as a corpse, the priest was as hungry looking as his bodyguards; he was, Couric thought, the kind of man who could gorge himself daily and yet never be sated—much like the heinous Tribunal for which he labored. He inspected the trio beneath the stairs as if they were nothing more than cuts of meat for sale in the city shambles, absently stroking his pointed chin and trying to determine which of them would provide the tastiest centerpiece for his dinner table.

"You there. Sarian."

Couric scowled his displeasure. Apparently the barmaid knew Sarian silver from Caithan after all. "Is that a problem? The Isle of Sare is still a Caithan protectorate. I'm allowed to cross our borders at will."

"That may be, but we've had reports of Sarians combing the western shires and stirring up trouble. Trying to raise an army against the king." The priest paused, patiently waiting for his imposing presence to elicit his victim's horrified confession.

Couric did not oblige him, passing the time with a relaxed sip of his Evarshot. The wine, combined with the growing effect of the pastle seed, made him feel quite invincible.

The priest's eyes narrowed to a pair of cream-colored slits. "Come with us. All of you."

Rob swallowed hard, and Dickon began to tremble as a fine trickle of sweat snaked down his cheek. Few who departed with the men of the Tribunal ever came back whole and healthy. More often than not, they never came back at all.

"I believe you have the wrong man," Couric said, with the cool grace of a prince.

"Oh, we do, do we?"

With theatrical flair, the priest reached inside his robe and brandished an acorn-sized corbal crystal suspended on a leather thong. He dangled it before Couric's eyes and waited.

On the brink of his *mekahn*, Rob would feel nothing from the purple gem; clearly, however, the priest expected Couric to drop to the floor in writhing agony and beg for mercy. Holding back a triumphant cackle of laughter was one of the most difficult things Couric had ever done. Ah, but how could this silly priest know any better? Not a single wizard in Caithe—not even her notorious princess—knew that for many of the Sage's folk, such trinkets held no terror. They would find out one day, of course . . . but by then it would be too late.

Couric released an indifferent sigh, as if bored by the antics of an ill-trained acrobat. "Father, please—you waste your time. I told you I was not a wizard, and even your holy crystal proves I speak the truth."

The priest glared at the crystal, impatiently scouring its surface for flaws and chips. The bodyguards shifted their weight uneasily, betraying their surprise.

"You may not have the power yourself," the priest snapped, refusing to admit he might have been wrong, "but you can still be a traitor. Many have flocked to Athaya's side who have no magic, if only because they know someone who does."

Couric hesitated imperceptibly before replying; though bolstered by the pastle seed, the better part of his mind was engaged with the crystal and he had little concentration left for the Justice. "Yes, I'm sure they have. But please, I'd advise you to put that jewel of yours away. The patrons of this tavern aren't well-off or overly intelligent, and one of them might just be drunk enough to slit your throat for that expensive little bauble."

Although Couric knew such a thing was wildly improbable—judging from their reaction to his arrival, no one in the tavern would dare breathe the same air as the Justice, much less try to pick his pockets—the priest himself was not so certain. His jaw worked silently, on the verge of declaring the audacity of such a crime, but he scanned the array of dirty, drunken men slouched on beer-soaked gaming tables around him and hastily reconsidered. Men had done more foolish things for far less wealth, and a corbal this size would bring enough to feed and clothe everyone in the tavern for months. The priest dropped the gem into a small velvet bag and stuffed it deep inside his robes.

Couric blinked several times in rapid succession as if to dispel a sudden wave of vertigo. "Now, my friend, let me assure you once again that I am no friend of Athaya Trelane. I've never set eyes on her in my life, and I certainly don't wish this senseless crusade of hers to succeed."

The Justice eyed him skeptically. "So you say . . ."

Damn, but these priests were persistent! Before he spoke again, Couric relaxed his muscles and steadied himself with a cleansing breath, reaching inward for those delicate threads of persuasion that would soon wind their way around the Justice's narrow mind.

"I would not dare lie to a man in God's service," he went on. Had there been other trained wizards nearby, they would have easily detected the subtle shift in the rhythm of Couric's voice. But Princess Athaya's hold was not so strong in the capital city of Delfarham, and few Lorngeld dared to venture into public places here.

"In fact, I think you would do well to look to the young lady who summoned you here," he suggested. "Turning in an innocent man to hide one's own crime is a common enough ploy. Especially if she thinks to earn a rich reward for a false accusation."

The priest's brows furrowed inward like angry stormclouds building on the horizon. "There are severe penalties for deliberately interfering with the Tribunal's justice."

Couric cocked his head toward the barmaid, now seated on a husky man's lap and pressed tight against him, brazenly offering her wares. She stole a glance at the priest and, sensing the deadly shift in his thoughts, started to wriggle from the man's grasp. But her customer was beguiled by the goods she had for sale and roughly hauled her back.

"See how she glances this way too often?" Couric said, pulling the strands of his persuasion ever tighter. "She has a bit too much interest in our conversation . . ."

"As if she wanted to make sure we arrested you," the priest murmured, obediently completing the thought.

"Exactly."

The priest turned to his men and gestured sharply. "Bring her."

Like a rabbit flushed from its thicket, the barmaid bolted for the safety of the kitchens, but stumbled over a tin cup left on the floor after the earlier brawl and went sprawling across an empty table. She grabbed the rim of the table as if it were the edge of a cliff, but the guardsmen quickly descended upon her and roughly pulled her away, sending dozens of piercing splinters deep into her palms. She kicked and shrieked in savage futility as they secured her wrists with iron shackles and dragged her away for questioning. Despite her wretched screams, no one moved to help her. Few risked even a glance of pity; to do either was to invite the same fate.

Couric sniffed and turned his back to the door. What would happen to the wench he neither knew nor cared—it served her right for meddling in a wizard's affairs. And the priest? His mind had been pitifully easy to bend. Fanatics the world over were all alike—quick to embrace invented devils when they fail to find the ones they seek.

Still cowering beneath the stairs, Rob and Dickon gaped their astonishment not only at the fact that they were still alive, but at how easily the Sarian had turned the Justice aside. "B-but you . . . the crystal!" Rob stammered. "How did you—"

"Magic can be an effective weapon," Couric explained, with an enigmatic tilt of his brow. "Yours can be, too, if you'll but let the Sage shape it for you. And when the Sage takes power in Caithe, men such as that will never trouble you again."

Rob shook his head in disbelief. "I'll admit . . . you've got my interest now, if you didn't before."

His brother turned on him, scandalized. "Rob!"

"What am I supposed to do, Dickon? I don't want to be absolved, so the only thing left is treason. All I can do is pick which kind of treason I want. And he's right—whoever this Sage is, he's offering more than Princess Athaya ever did. We're not a rich family, Dickon . . . think of what some extra money could mean to Mother, now that Father's gone."

"But if you're caught—"

"You didn't turn him over to that Justice, Dickon," Couric observed. "That makes you just as guilty if he's caught. Better for you—and your family—if Rob joins us and wins you all a rich reward one day.

"Here," he said, dropping a few pieces of silver into Rob's palm. It was as much as the poor boy would earn in a year and the shock in his eyes revealed as much. "Come to Eriston, in the far northwest. Join us and there will be far more than that to line your purse. The Sage is a rich man, Rob. His people pay generous tribute to him, and in turn he protects them from harm and guides them with his divine wisdom."

Couric rested a hand on Rob's shoulder. "Those coins are a mere token. When our people rule Caithe, we shall divide its riches amongst ourselves, taking our rightful due as God's stewards. I'm hoping for a dukedom myself," he added enticingly. "Perhaps if you prove a loyal and worthy servant to the Sage, he shall reward you with a post in his court—or even more." Couric carefully omitted any mention of Dickon's reward, and for good reason. Unless Dickon developed the power himself, whatever came to him would be solely from the benevolence and charity of the Lorngeld.

"There can be no doubt of the outcome of this battle," Couric concluded. "Caithe cannot hope to stand against an army of wizards—especially if her only weapons are corbal crystals. You can stand with the victors within the space of a year, Rob. The whole of Caithe will be ours for the taking; no landless mercenary hired to sack a wealthy city has ever been promised so much reward for so little effort."

Rob thought for a moment, pensively rubbing a coin between his thumb and forefinger. Then, his decision made, he folded his hand over the small circle of silver and gripped it tight. "When do you move?"

Ignoring Dickon's dazed look of dismay, Couric smiled in sweet victory. "When the Sage arrives to lead us," he replied, adding an inward prayer that the Sage would survive his ordeal under the sealing spell and arrive in Caithe whole and strong . . . and reasonably sane. Couric pushed back his stool and settled his cloak about his shoulders. "But don't worry—it will be soon, my friend. Very soon."

Bidding his new ally good night, Couric slipped out of the tavern and melted into the shadows. He walked at a rapid pace through the winding streets of Delfarham, hoping to reach the sanctuary of his bed before the invigorating effects of the pastle seed wore off and left him weary.

He would see Rob again; he was confident of that. With a self-satisfied grin, Couric thought of the great number of men and women he had approached over the past few weeks whom he expected to see again. The Sage had been right all along: Caithe was ripe for full-scale rebellion, and those who had lost faith in Athaya Trelane had shown little reluctance to follow another—especially one who promised far more than the outlawed princess of Caithe had ever done.

Couric whistled softly as he strolled across the cobbled square in front of Saint Adriel's Cathedral. *The place will need rechristening*, he mused, skimming his gaze along the length of the church's massive spires. Once he ascended to power in this land, the Sage would not tolerate any house of God to bear the name of Adriel, the man responsible for instigating the so-called sacrament of absolution: the bane of the Lorngeld—and the death of them—ever since the Time of Madness.

Then Couric turned his eyes to north, where the lamplit towers of Delfar Castle rose serenely into the clement night. *Enjoy these times of peace, your Majesty*, he thought, as a baleful smile spread slowly across his face. *Before the cold winds blow again, Caithe will have a new king—a wizard king.* He let his gaze drift off to the west, toward the distant Isle of Sare. *And every corbal crystal in your treasury will not keep him from your shores.*

CHAPTER 2

※❁※

"HOW LONG IS MASTER HEDRIC GOING TO BE *IN* there?" Athaya asked impatiently, pacing back and forth across a spartanly furnished chamber in the south tower of Belmarre Castle. Nervous fingers picked at the fraying sleeve of her homespun kirtle, and she glanced to the stairwell with rhythmic regularity, as if waiting for news of an imminent birth and expecting a physician to appear at any moment and declare the new arrival a boy or a girl.

Seated at a walnut table cluttered with books and scrolls and leather tubes, Jaren looked up from the fragile slip of parchment he was reading. "Hedric's only been in with him for half an hour," he said, content to temper his own concerns in the absorbing pursuit of knowledge. "Give it time."

"Time is one thing Nicolas may not have," Athaya replied, snapping a loose thread from her sleeve. "And it's been so long already."

Forcing herself to stop pacing for a while, Athaya leaned against the windowsill and gazed out at the lush, rose-scented expanse of late spring surrounding the steward's tower. It had been a cold and snowy night in February when she had delivered her brother Nicolas into Adam Graylen's care; now it was a hot and languid June. The world had undergone a thorough transformation, but sadly, Prince Nicolas had not.

More than four months had passed since the Sage of Sare ensorcelled her brother, coercing the Caithan prince to murder his elder brother and king, Durek. He was confident that the atrocity would be blamed on Athaya—which it had been, she thought with a scowl—thus neatly destroying the reputations, if not the very lives, of nearly every legitimate claimant to the Caithan throne. But even the Sage proved vulnerable to error. Under his sway, Nicolas went so far as to offer the tainted wine to Durek, but his inner self rebelled against the crime he was about to commit, and he was able to resist the spell long enough to break the brunt of its force—and slap the cup from Durek's lips before he took the fatal sip. But the defiance cost Nicolas has sanity, leaving him little more than a child, in need of constant care and with few memories of the prince he had been, or the king—and kingdom—he had almost destroyed.

Athaya whispered a private prayer as she turned her back on the verdant swells of earth before her. Only Master Hedric and his decades of mystic learning could save her brother now.

After a grueling hour of waiting, during which Athaya had yanked an entire handful of loose threads from her sleeve and scattered them like rushes on the floor, she heard a fragile sigh and saw Master Hedric emerge from the stairwell leading to the bedchamber above. Slate-colored robes hung listlessly from his frame like curtains in stagnant air and he leaned heavily on his gnarled cherrywood staff.

Athaya let the last strand of wool fall from her grasp. "How is he?"

"Resting quietly." Reading the agitation on her face, he added, "Just let me sit a moment before we talk. I've done what I can for the moment, but I'm a bit tired."

Athaya nodded, stamping down her impatience. She had waited months already; she could wait a few minutes more. Moreover, she should be grateful that Master Hedric was here at all. When Jaren had returned to his Reykan homeland to find out what he could about the spell of compulsion—a spell long forbidden by the Circle of Masters because of its inherent unscrupulousness—Athaya assumed that Hedric would simply share what knowledge he possessed and send his instructions back with Jaren. She was stunned by Hedric's unexpected arrival three days ago; at seventy-one, travel was a burden to him, and his decision to return with Jaren made Athaya all the more fearful. Nicolas' situation was dire indeed if Hedric thought it required his own personal attention.

"I'm sorry if I'm rushing you," she said by way of apology. "I never should have insisted that we leave for Belmarre the very day that you arrived from Reyka. You must be exhausted by now, after close to a month on the road."

"Oh, I'll manage," Hedric replied, summoning a crooked smile as he rubbed the fatigue from his eyes. "I'm not as old as all that, you know."

Once, Athaya would have chuckled her agreement and thought no more upon it, but now she bit her lip and remained silent. Master Hedric had aged noticeably since she last saw him in October. His movements were slower and more studied, his eyes in need of brighter light by which to peruse his myriad books and scrolls, and Athaya soon discovered that she needed to speak a shade louder if she didn't wish to repeat herself. Although far from a young man when he began to instruct her in the ways of magic two years ago, Athaya never thought of the Master as old before—his keen wit and vitality had always neatly distracted her from the fact. But now that vitality was ebbing, and it was a weight upon her heart to realize that his star would not burn forever.

Athaya's eyes flickered briefly toward the spiral stair. "May I see him?"

"You can look in on him, but try not to wake him. Our first session was somewhat . . . difficult. He needs rest."

"With respect, Master Hedric," Jaren observed, "I think you both do."

While Jaren set about making his former teacher a cup of chamomile tea, Athaya ascended to her brother's bedchamber. The weathered door creaked only slightly as she entered and gave a wordless greeting to Adam Graylen. Despite carrying almost as many years as Hedric, he was neatly tucked in the windowseat like a boy, paging through a book of rudimentary magic that Hedric had loaned to him so that he could better understand the nature of the prince's illness. Adam was the longtime steward of the earl of Belmarre—one of Caithe's few lords who, while reluctant to support Athaya openly, could be trusted not to betray her or Nicolas' temporary presence in his domain. Athaya smiled wistfully as she passed by the older man, seeing as she ever did the image of his long-dead son Tyler, beloved to them both, in the depths of those tranquil green eyes.

She curled up on an oak chest at the foot of Nicolas' bed and gazed at him, his skin delicately pale against the deep blue coverlet. Light brown curls were combed neatly back from the smooth cheekbones, and he slumbered peaceful as a babe, breathing slow and deep. That alone was a striking change for the better. Nicolas no longer tossed fitfully, tormented by the seductive voice of a Sarian wizard whispering murder in his mind.

The voice was still there, but it was silent for now.

Assured that he was at peace, Athaya slid off the chest and went to his side, laying a gentle kiss atop his forehead. She jumped when Nicolas' eyes fluttered open in response; he had not been sleeping so soundly after all.

Nicolas was not startled by her presence; her kiss had convinced him she was a friend. A friend ... but nothing more; her brother's eyes were devoid of recognition. "Is he coming back?" Nicolas murmured drowsily, his voice sandy from disuse.

"Who?"

"The old man that was here."

"Yes," Athaya said, forcing a smile. "Yes, he'll be back."

Nicolas nodded contentedly. "My other friend hasn't come yet. He's a wizard, too. He laughs a lot and tells stories. Mostly dirty ones."

Athaya tried valiantly not to betray any glimmer of despair. "I'm sure he'll come as soon as he can." *If he's still alive*, she added privately. Ranulf had fallen captive to the Sage on the same day as Nicolas and had not been seen or heard from since. The onetime mercenary was Sarian-born, so Athaya doubted the Sage would kill him outright, but who could say whether he would ever leave the island again?

"Do you live here, too?" Nicolas asked through a yawn.

Athaya pursed her lips tightly to keep them from trembling. Hedric had eased Nicolas' suffering, but Nicolas himself was still astray, lost in the dark mists of his memory. "No. I'm just visiting. I'm a friend of the old man, too."

"Oh." Satisfied with her explanation, Nicolas rolled over and promptly drifted back to sleep.

Athaya blinked back a tear as she retreated from the bedside. At least he wasn't in pain, she reminded herself. At least the Sage hadn't destroyed him fully.

"Good night, Nicolas," she whispered.

When Athaya returned to the lower chamber, Master Hedric was visibly refreshed by both his tea and his moment of rest. The deep worry-lines on his face had smoothed back into mere wrinkles, and his eyes had regained some of their sparkle.

"That's as peaceful as I've seen him since it happened." She poured herself a cup of tea and joined Hedric and Jaren at the table, passing her eyes over the staggering array of books and scrolls that they had brought with them from Reyka. "It looks as if you brought your entire library."

"Not exactly," Hedric replied. "Some of these are from my own collection, but most came from the archives at Wizard's College in Tenosce. I told Overlord Basil what I was looking for and he set a small army of students to the task. Basil has only a small circle of intimate friends," Hedric felt obliged to explain, knowing how rare it was for the normally irascible wizard to do anything so magnanimous, "but he counts Prince Nicolas among them."

Hedric picked up one of the older scrolls and smiled. "Confidentially, I suspect that our bounty is partially due to Basil's 'volunteers' being too terrified to come up empty-handed. In addition to the spell of compulsion, Basil's contingent of scholars turned up some references to the Sarian cult—specifically the prophecy that spawned them—and a bit about the Rite of Challenge by which they choose a new leader. Basil brought the lot of it to Ath Luaine scarcely a fortnight later and even offered to fill in for me at Osfonin's court while I'm gone."

Jaren grinned broadly. "I suspect Lord Basil is happier about that arrangement than his Majesty. Osfonin respects his rank as Overlord of the Circle, but thinks Basil is rather ... well, stuffy."

Hedric emitted a dry chuckle. "Osfonin has always been a shrewd judge of character. Oh, that reminds me," he went on, turning to Athaya, "Prince Felgin sends his fervent hopes for Nicolas' recovery. He wanted to pay a personal visit, but Osfonin is quite serious about keeping his eldest son close at heel until he's safely married. And Queen Cecile is endearing herself to Osfonin—if not as much to Felgin—by spending her days in exile helping the prince make his choice of bride."

Athaya's smile was bittersweet, glad that the Caithan queen was making the best of her unfortunate situation. Cecile and her two children had fled to the sanctuary of the Reykan capital once it was no longer safe for them in Caithe. Not only would the Sage be a threat to young Prince Mailen—if he was willing to murder Durek, why not Durek's heir?—but Cecile's well-known friendship with Athaya had spurred the Tribunal to suspect her involvement with the attempt on Durek's life. Rather than offer explanations that the king and his Justices were in no humor to hear, Cecile chose to flee. In Reyka, at least, she could teach her son and daughter not to despise the Lorngeld for what they were. Under Durek's guidance, they would learn nothing so charitable.

"Will she be happy there? It might be a long time before it's safe for her to come home again."

"She is content. The Reykan court has always proved a hospitable shelter to runaway Trelanes," Hedric remarked, the twinkle in his eye reminding Athaya of her own exile there less than two years ago. "If she has one regret, it is the fate of Lord Gessinger. She yearns for word that he is alive and well."

Athaya nodded in empathy; she would like to receive the same news herself. After acting as a decoy to ease Cecile's escape, Mosel Gessinger had been imprisoned in Delfar Castle and, like Ranulf, not heard from since.

"But Cecile is not as eager to return as you might think," Hedric added. "Before Jaren and I left, she sent a letter to Durek, telling him in rather pointed terms that she would not have her children raised in a land defiled by the Tribunal's brand of justice, and that if he continued to abuse the Lorngeld and not let them live in peace, then she and the children would return to Caithe only upon news of his death."

"I'd hate to think that his death is the only solution to this problem," Athaya said solemnly. Over the years, she had argued with Durek, cursed him, struck him, and been thoroughly infuriated by him, but she had never wished him dead, no matter what he, his Tribunal, or even the Sage would have the Caithan people believe.

Athaya pushed Durek to the back shelf of her mind; Nicolas was in far greater danger of death than his Majesty was at the moment. "Now that you've seen Nicolas for yourself, what can you tell me about the spell of compulsion?"

"Not much you'll want to hear, I'm afraid." Hedric looked away, tapping his fingertips together as he carefully phrased his explanation. "The spell acts like a net around Nicolas' mind, constraining its actions. The Sage's thoughts are psychically grafted onto Nicolas' own. If this spell is any indication of his talent, then the Sage is a master indeed. That he is an adept is indisputable. It's almost impossible to tell where Nicolas' own thoughts leave off and the Sage's begin."

"But if you can distinguish between the two, doesn't that mean you can remove the Sage's?" Jaren asked.

"That's not as simple a thing as it sounds. If I try to eliminate the Sage's thoughts, I might very likely snip out many of

Nicolas' as well. Such dabbling can be very dangerous. Despite all we know of it, the human mind is still an abyss of mysteries. I could inadvertently do far worse damage than the Sage did."

"Worse?" Athaya exclaimed, appalled by such a prospect. "I hardly think that's possible."

"No? Think, Athaya. What if I mistakenly plucked out that part of Nicolas' memory that tells him not to wrap his hand around a hot iron, or the deeper part that reminds him to keep breathing at night?" Hedric paused, allowing her to absorb the unpleasant implications. "It is these types of errors that disturb me . . . and they are shockingly easy to make."

Athaya stared absently into her teacup; the fragrant liquid was still reasonably warm, but she had suddenly lost her appetite for it. "Then nothing can be done?"

Hedric shook his head in regret. "Nothing permanent. I think the wisest course of action would be for me to help him live with his affliction. I can loosen the threads of the compulsion, but I think it would be extremely foolish to try to unweave them entirely. No, the spell must be removed by the Sage himself. Or removed indirectly, by his death."

"Or by Nicolas giving in to the compulsion and doing what the Sage wants him to," Athaya said, noting the last gruesome—and least desirable—possibility.

"Yes," Hedric granted, "but I sincerely doubt that will happen—not at this late stage. The brunt of the spell's force was broken at Nicolas' initial refusal to obey. The spell is still there, obviously, and much of Nicolas' mental energies are occupied with resisting its pull—thus his childlike state and loss of memory. But by loosening the Sage's grip, I think I can keep Nicolas comfortable and lucid and perhaps restore his memory somewhat. It will be an ongoing task, like having to dust once a week to keep the shelves clean."

It was a solution, but not the one Athaya had been praying for. And one unpleasant question remained to be asked. "The spell is compelling him to kill Durek . . . but what happens if Durek dies some other way and Nicolas has nothing to do with it?"

Hedric's expression was grave. "Then he would remain in his current state until his death—unless the Sage dies first—since he would have no way of ever completing his task."

The room was silent for a long time—so silent, that Athaya

could hear Adam turning the brittle pages of his magic book in the chamber above.

"You spoke of caring for him yourself," Athaya said at last, "but shouldn't I do that? He's my brother and I feel responsible for him. And the sealing spell made my powers even stronger than they were before . . ."

Her eyes drifted back to the window, and the bar of late afternoon sun that slated into the chamber and burnished it with gold. She looked forward to the coming summer; last spring, with her powers imprisoned by a sealing spell, she had declined into lunacy and lost three months of her life. Athaya shivered at what few memories of those days remained to her; memories of helplessness and rage and pain . . . God, such pain. With no outlet, the pressures of her caged magic began to build to a lethal level, bringing her closer to death with each passing day. But in the end, as was true with most of her life's calamities, the ordeal had made her stronger; now it would be worth every day of hell she had endured if she could use her new level of skill to help Nicolas. Compared to that, her abilities to cast spells effortlessly, to traverse the whole of Caithe in the blink of an eye, and even to detect the dormant seeds of magic before they bloomed inside a wizard's mind—a thing no wizard in history had ever dreamed possible—paled to insignificance.

Hedric's telltale smile broke her out of her reverie and she groped to remember what she had been saying. "I didn't mean to insult you. It's just that—"

"I am not offended—you mean well, I know. I will gladly concede that you are more powerful than I am now; perhaps you were even before the seal . . . my magic has been gradually fading over the years. But in this case, raw power is no advantage. Helping Nicolas is going to take a great deal of delicacy and skill. Only the Sage has both, I fear. Oh, I know what to do in theory," he explained, "but it will be slow going in practice. My lesser level of power will be to Nicolas' benefit—it will give me the gentler touch required for this sort of work. Adam has kindly invited me to stay at Belmarre as long as I like, and I think it would be best for Nicolas if I did."

"But what about your duties at court?" Jaren asked. "Osfonin will start climbing the castle walls if Basil stays on more than a few weeks."

Hedric chuckled in secret amusement, but the humor soon faded into something more indistinct and melancholy. "Everything has been arranged, Jaren," he murmured. Only the slightest edge in his tone warned Jaren not to press the subject. "Adam and I will find plenty to talk about—he may not be a wizard, but magic fascinates him and he wants to learn as much about it as he can. And when I'm not attending to Nicolas or trying to teach magic to someone who doesn't have a drop of it," he went on, turning an anticipatory smile on Athaya, "I can use my free hours to read your accounts of your work."

Baffled, she gave him a blank stare. "Accounts?"

"Your journals and notes . . . that sort of thing."

"My—?" Athaya shot Jaren a desperate look of inquiry. Had she forgotten something, or was Master Hedric growing absentminded as well as frail?

Hedric gaped at her, openly scandalized. "You mean you haven't been writing any of this *down*? Haven't been recording anything you've done since you started this crusade?"

Athaya decided it would be an excellent time to warm her tea. "Well," she mumbled, backing away from the table, "I've been busy."

Hedric threw up his hands in exaggerated despair, like a long-suffering father whose daughter has refused yet another in a long string of suitors. "You must learn to see yourself in a larger context, my dear. Future historians and wizards will not only be curious about your crusade, but interested in your unique physical talents. Little is known about translocation and even less about the long-term effects of the sealing spell. And as for this ability to detect the seed of power long before the *mekahn*—to know who is and is not a wizard before their power starts to develop . . ." Hedric was rendered temporarily speechless at the wonder of it. "Athaya, that's never been done before; it's never been considered *possible* before! If you don't teach us, the knowledge could be lost forever."

Suitably admonished, Athaya refreshed her tea with hot water and ventured back to the table. "I never thought of it that way," she confessed, vaguely embarrassed by Hedric's high praise. "But you know how much I dislike writing—it makes my fingers stiffen up. Besides, you've seen my penmanship," she reminded him. "You called it appalling yourself."

Without arguing the point, Hedric circled back to the central issue. "Then tell Jaren what you want to say and have him write it down for you. He was my secretary for five years—I can vouch for his handwriting. Of course, I do have a more selfish motive in all this," he conceded, the corners of his mouth curling up into a smile. "I'd like to think that generations of future wizards will read about your work in a new volume of the *Book of Sages* and marvel at what an extraordinary teacher you must have had. That can't happen unless you tell posterity what you've been up to."

Athaya held up her hands in surrender. "All right, you've convinced me. I promise to start some sort of a journal the instant I get back to the camp." As she browsed through the books and scrolls scattered across the table, she was forced to admit how grateful she was that their long-dead authors had recorded their thoughts and theories for her—and Nicolas'—present benefit. It proved Hedric's point as nothing else could. "Maybe the work will help keep me from worrying about Nicolas. Damn them," she said suddenly, as some of her former agitation bubbled back to the surface, "what sort of wizards would stoop to using spells like that, anyway?"

"Ones who think that if a spell exists, it should therefore be used." Hedric paused and his face went taut with old rage. "Rhodri's disastrous experiments with the rite of assumption demonstrated the flaw in *that* argument long ago." He snorted his opinion of his former pupil's arrogance, but there was a glimmer of true regret behind his eyes—regret that such vast potential had been turned to such reckless and unethical pursuits.

Athaya exchanged a sober glance with Jaren, history flashing vividly between them. In the year prior to her birth, the wizard Rhodri had befriended her father and persuaded him to assume the mantle of magic—powers that he was not born with, but that Rhodri promised could still be his by simply accepting them from a willing wizard. How could it be circumventing God's will, he argued, if a spell to transfer power from one person to another existed in the world? It only took a clever wizard to set things right. Because of the king's well-known interest in the Lorngeld and his wish to free them from the bonds of absolution, Rhodri knew he would not be able to resist such an offer. But in his conceit, too proud to admit that he might not know as much about magic as he imagined, Rhodri never revealed the dangers of the transference spell—dangers that had caused it to be forbidden among all ethical wizards for decades. Thus it was that years later Kelwyn's false powers began to decay, and he rapidly plunged into madness—madness that ultimately led to his death, leaving a host of hopes and dreams unfulfilled.

Hedric saw the troubled shadows in her eyes and swiftly reverted to his original subject. "From what I've read, Sarians rarely cast compulsion spells on other wizards—only on 'the unblessed,' as they rudely term the rest of humanity. Only in extreme circumstances would a Sarian inflict compulsion on another wizard. Fear of retribution, probably," Hedric explained with a shrug. "I find it hard to believe that ethics are a priority with them."

Jaren concurred with a scowl. "Any group that picks its new leader by killing off the old one doesn't have a whole lot going for it."

"It makes perfect sense to them, though," Athaya added sullenly. "They think God intended magicians to rule the earth, and if that's true, then the strongest magician is logically the most capable ruler since God obviously gave them more magic."

Master Hedric held up a crooked finger. "Basil's army uncovered a bit of information about that. The Rite of Challenge." Hedric rummaged among the scrolls and plucked one out of the pile. "Almost a century ago, a Reykan wizard found himself on Sare and wrote about his travels in a journal." Hedric paused just long enough to toss a meaningful glance to Athaya. "This is only a partial copy, but it might shed some light on the subject. It says here that 'once the witnesses have been assembled and the blood-wards have been cast,' then any and all magic between the combatants is legal. In short, the rules are that there *are* no rules. The wizard to emerge from the blood-wards alive is the winner."

Athaya crinkled her brow. "Blood-wards . . . what are those?"

"I'm not sure. Some sort of arena, I imagine, in which the competition can take place."

Jaren folded his arms across his chest and glared at the parchment in repugnance. "Whatever it is, Brandegarth doesn't plan on having to use one again. If he becomes king of Caithe, the position of Sage is all but obsolete—and with it, the need for a Challenge."

"It would seem so. His followers interpret the prophecy to mean that he will rise from Sage to king. King of Caithe . . . at least for a start," Hedric added ominously. He handed Athaya another sheet of parchment, this one badly yellowed with age. "That has been in the College archives for decades, but without any sort of context it was meaningless. Nobody knew what it was referring to until now."

Athaya scanned the document, conscious of a queasy feeling spreading through her belly. They were the exact words that the Sage had read to her over four months ago; the words of Dameronne of Crewe, who had founded the island cult and foreseen Athaya's coming nearly two centuries before. " 'Our time will come,' " she read in a whisper, " 'when a woman blessed by both heaven and earth comes forth to lead the Lorngeld into glory. She will live among the high and the low and will wield powers unseen since the days of the ancients. She will obtain aid in her endeavor from an unexpected quarter, and in so doing will usher in a golden age of a great wizard king, and thus restore our people to glory. Until her coming, we wait in peace for our joyous return from exile.' "

Athaya looked up, her face wry. "You think I'm the woman in this prophecy, too, don't you?"

"I'm certain of it," Hedric replied without hesitation. "After all, I saw shades of your future myself. It's the reason I sent Jaren to seek you out . . . oh, was it really two years ago? It seems like only yesterday."

Or a lifetime ago, Athaya added inwardly, knowing that she bore little resemblance to the unruly embittered girl that Jaren had encountered. Athaya grinned wryly. Jaren would likely claim that she was no less unruly now, but he had married her anyway, hadn't he?

She inspected the prophecy one last time. " 'Aid from an unexpected quarter' . . . that line isn't very specific. It could refer to anything—the money Jaren's father gave to us, the help Adam's been offering, or even your presence here." Then she laughed mirthlessly. "But aid from *any* quarter would be unexpected at the moment, thanks to the Sage."

Hedric reclaimed the paper and tucked it into a protective leather tube. "Whatever the 'aid' turns out to be, it's one of the last things destined to happen before this 'golden age' commences."

" 'A golden age of a great wizard king,' " she quoted thoughtfully. "That's not very specific either. It could be referring to the Sage, or to Mailen—even to Nicolas. There's still an outside chance it could be Durek, but it's extremely remote. He's thirty now and magic almost never develops that late."

"Or it could refer to someone that doesn't even exist yet. A son of yours and Jaren's, for example," Hedric added, with a hopeful tilt of his brow. "All we really know is that the next wizard to rule Caithe is said to be male, not female. That rules you out."

"Good," Athaya replied emphatically. "I never wanted the job anyway."

She took a swallow of tea and grimaced at finding it had gone cold. "The prophecy may not state it implicitly," she went on, pouring the rest of the offending liquid into a potted vine, "but the Sage is convinced that he is destined to be the wizard king. But if that's true, then where *is* he? The reason I brought Nicolas here rather than take him back to Kaiburn was that I thought the Sage might come after him again. But it's been four months now, and the Sage hasn't even shown his face in Caithe." After such a flagrant bid for power, the Sage's continued absence scraped Athaya's nerves raw. "Maybe something's happened to him," she suggested, knowing it was probably too much to wish for. "Maybe some other wizard has challenged him and has taken his place."

"Or maybe he's just waiting for the right time to make a grand entrance," Jaren added. His expression soured as he recalled his first and only meeting with the Sage; the man had been so cocksure that Athaya would ally with him against Durek that he'd been unpleasantly startled and embarrassed by her refusal. "He seems the type."

Adam Graylen selected that moment to join them in the lower chamber. "Shall we go to supper, friends?" He rested his magic book on the table, his place marked by a strip of red silk. "The earl's table boasts fresh trout tonight."

Athaya shook her head as she rose to her feet. "Jaren and I won't be staying. We're going back to Kaiburn tonight." Despite the earl's generosity in allowing Nicolas to remain in Balmarre, Athaya knew that his Lordship was much more skittish when it came to herself and Jaren.

"Tonight? But it will be dark in just a few hours."

Athaya smiled knowingly at him. "That won't matter. We won't be going home the same way we arrived." Because of Hedric's bulging satchels of books and scrolls, the three of them had chosen to ride to Belmarre rather than translocate there. And much as he would have loved to experience his former pupil's talent, Hedric worried that if any of them were to drop one of his precious bundles during the jolt of passage, it could never be reclaimed from that mysterious and lethal between-realm. Now that the satchels were staying in Belmarre, Athaya and Jaren could travel home by magic, unencumbered.

Adam winked his understanding. "Ah, I keep forgetting. But what of you, Hedric? I pray I can interest you in a meal at the earl's table?"

Hedric placed a bony hand atop his belly, which obediently rumbled its readiness. "You pray correctly."

"Why don't you two go ahead, then?" They had done what they could for Nicolas this day and Athaya was fast growing as weary as Hedric. She leaned down and gave the Master a farewell peck on the cheek. "I'll come back in a few weeks to check up on things."

"Don't worry about us," Hedric told her, easing her fears with a pat on the shoulder and an encouraging smile. "You've got a crusade to run."

"Run," she repeated, rolling her eyes heavenward. "You mean salvage."

"Come now. Things haven't gotten that bad, have they?"

"No, not really," she admitted. "But we've never been able to fully recover from the Sage's blow. We still get new wizards at the camp every week, but not in the same numbers as before. A lot of people don't trust me any more—not that many of them ever did—and more are sitting on fences waiting to see what happens. The Tribunal is coming down even harder on us—did I mention that five more Justices have been assigned to every shire?—and that only gives people more reason to think that I *did* try to bewitch Nicolas into killing Durek." Athaya's shoulders slumped despondently. "And things certainly won't get any better now that Jon Lukin is not only Chief Justice of the Tribunal, but Archbishop of Delfarham as well. Did I tell you that Ventan died in April? Apparently his bouts of indigestion were more serious than anyone realized. Durek nominated Lukin to take his place, and the Curia approved him on the first vote. In short," Athaya finished with a sigh, "Caithe has been close to a stalemate since February—little has changed to push things definitively in one direction or the other."

Hedric frowned deeply. "It won't be a stalemate for long, Athaya. The Sage will make his move eventually. And when he does, you must be ready."

"I just hope he does it soon," she said, exasperated. "All this waiting is driving me out of my mind."

Once Adam and Hedric departed for the Great Hall to claim their supper, Athaya wrapped her arm tight around Jaren's waist in preparation for their journey home. But it was more than love that kept him snug in her embrace; she had seen what it did to a man to slip from her grasp during the hurdle between one place and the next and never cared to witness such horror again. Whatever the between-place was, it was no place for human flesh; were one to stumble off the magic roads, the body was rent apart like carrion, leaving only the spirit behind.

Athaya brushed aside those morbid thoughts and relaxed, conjuring the image of home in her mind. She saw the city of Kaiburn first, then set her vision north through the depths of the Forest of Else until she spied the once-abandoned monastery, now a makeshift magic school. And focusing even further, she saw each detail of her cozy, ramshackle room—the tattered curtains made of discarded cloaks, the table fashioned from an upturned ale barrel, and the straw pallet that served as her and Jaren's marriage bed.

When the image was clear in her mind's eye, Athaya whispered the potent words of translocation. *"Hinc libera me."*

The jolt came instantly—expected, but still jarring despite all her experience, like missing a step at the bottom of the stairs. Next came the eerie sensation of being detached from her body for a fraction of time; a creature of consciousness alone. She sensed Jaren only as a presence at her side, a solid form within the dizzying array of colorful sights and chaotic sounds swirling around her, all of them passing too quickly to be identified.

An instant later, her nostrils were filled with the heady scent of pine and her feet found security on the cool flagstone floor. But just as she cracked open her eyes, a black cloud loomed up before her, obscuring the edges of her sight. Athaya reeled from the aftershock of translocation, dizzy as if from too much wine.

Jaren caught her before she could fall and lowered her slowly onto the pallet. "Athaya? Are you sick?"

She closed her eyes for a moment, opening them only after the last remnants of vertigo were under control and she didn't feel at risk of fainting. "That's strange," she breathed. "It hasn't hit me like that since before my power was sealed."

"You haven't used the spell in a while," Jaren suggested. "Maybe you're just out of practice."

But Jaren's tone betrayed a lack of faith in the easy explanation and Athaya harbored similar misgivings. She recalled something that Hedric had said to her when she first told him how the seal had augmented her power. He had likened the sealing spell to the *mekahn* and theorized that being too close confined with her own magic had recreated the same kind of internal pressure. *But bursts of strength almost always fade after the* mekahn, he had said. *This talent of yours? It might last; it might not.*

Holding her breath, Athaya cupped her hand and attempted to conjure a witchlight. Her power was sluggish to respond; a full minute later, her palm held nothing more substantial than a dim red spark, no larger than an ember plucked from a dying fire.

"Hedric warned me this might happen," she said quietly, trying not to reveal how frightened she truly was. "My magic is starting to fade back to its former level. The effects of the seal were only temporary." Athaya squeezed her eyes shut. She should have expected this, but had grown so accustomed to her increased abilities that the idea of losing them seemed more remote as each day passed. "But why *now*?" she cried, pounding the wall with her fist and then mouthing a curse at the resulting pain. "If the Sage comes—"

"Athaya, don't get ahead of yourself. You were tired when we left—this could be an isolated incident. But even if it isn't, you're still an adept, same as the Sage." Then he leaned over and offered her a kiss of encouragement. "And didn't the Sarians' own prophecy say that you wielded 'powers unseen since the days of the ancients'?" he reminded her, widening his eyes in mock amazement.

His efforts managed to elicit a grudging smile. "All right, I see your point. God knows I have enough to worry about already without making myself crazy over this, too." Athaya propped herself up against a pillow and took a deep breath to steady herself. "Maybe this is just God's way of settling the score. After all, if the Sage and I were both adepts, then having my power extended by the seal might be construed as cheating. This way, the sides are even."

"Even," Jaren echoed soberly, as a shadow passed over his face. "But in readiness for what?"

CHAPTER 3

✳

"**B**UT IT SIMPLY ISN'T POSSIBLE!" DRIANNA EX-claimed, as she hurriedly trailed the Sage's stew-ard up the spiral stair to his Grace's bedchamber. Gossamer skirts of pale blue silk floated on air in her wake and she hastily tucked the last wayward tendrils of auburn hair beneath a beaded chaplet, having barely finished her morning's ablutions when Tullis' urgent summons had arrived.

"I speak the truth, my Lady. He was up at the crack of dawn, calling for his breakfast, demanding parchment to write with, summoning his tailor, his treasurer—and you, of course—not to mention a dozen other things. I've never seen him so energetic. It's all any of us can do to keep up with him." But while it should have been resoundingly good news, the stiffness in his bearing betrayed Tullis' concern that not all was well with the Sage of Sare.

"But you only released him last night!" Drianna persisted, her tender lower lip bearing a crescent-shaped mark where her teeth had bitten down upon it in perplexity. "He's not supposed to recover this quickly. Princess Athaya did, yes, but only after being delirious and near death for three weeks." Drianna began to nibble on the tip of her thumbnail. "I don't like this, Tullis. I don't like it one bit."

Tullis paused at the top of the stair, grasping the wooden railing with a blue-veined hand as if to steady himself. "No, my Lady. Neither do I."

She followed the rest of the way in silence, thinking back to the fateful day when the Sage's trusted servant had laid the sealing spell upon him, imprisoning his awesome powers within the cramped confines of his mind. 'Castration of a sort,' Brand had jokingly called it, 'but not near so final.' He had hidden his fears well, but Drianna knew Brand had harbored them. Still, he wanted more power and this was the only way he knew to obtain it. He refused to be outmatched by a woman half his age and knew that only Athaya Trelane stood between him and the Caithan crown he believed himself destined for.

Drianna pulled her ruddy brows together in a frown. She had never minded his jealousy when she was the object of it, but now it galled her that he would risk his life for an extra measure of magic. Even Tullis had advised him against such folly, though he had been swiftly rebuked for the presumption. Was Brand so uncertain he could win Caithe without extending his already considerable talents? And he was not satisfied to seal his power as long as Athaya had . . . no, he insisted upon remaining sealed for a full week longer to better ensure his superiority.

Tullis halted just out of earshot of the pair of guardsmen posted near the bedchamber door. Their presence was a mere formality, of course; as the most powerful wizard in Sare, Brandegarth of Crewe was fully capable of defending himself if the need arose. And none of the island's wizards would dare attack him without submitting a formal Challenge first. At best, such an omission would be the height of rudeness; at worst, it would be blasphemy—a slap in God's almighty face.

"You should know one other thing before you see him," the steward cautioned her. Drianna's look of alarm prompted him to continue with haste. "His Grace is not ill—not physically," he amended, "but he is not the same man whose magic I sealed four months ago. The changes are not always obvious, but they are there."

Drianna bit down on her lip again, this time drawing blood. "Something's gone wrong, hasn't it? I'm no wizard, but I know this isn't how it's supposed to be." In her erstwhile role as spy at the princess' camp, Drianna had unearthed as many details as she could about Athaya's ordeal, memorizing every word and nuance so she could report it to Brand when she returned to Sare. "Jaren and Master Tonia both said that after her fever broke, Athaya was herself again. She had stronger magic, of course, and a bit of memory loss . . . but her personality hadn't changed at all."

"I know. But I also recall your saying that the princess' powers were released all in a flood, overpowering the two wizards trying to assist her. That was probably the cause of her illness. It took myself and two others to hold the stone back long enough to allow his Grace's sealed power to seep out gradually, but we did not lose control. Still . . ." Tullis bowed his head, sending a thin strand of white hair drooping over his brow. "It disturbs me how completely different his Grace's reaction is to that of the princess. The fact that he wasn't even the slightest bit sick or tired makes me suspect that the poison of his confinement hasn't fully drained. He seems more restless now. Less deliberate in his thoughts and actions. And . . ." His voice trailed off a second time as he labored to find the right words. "He seems—how shall I say it?—drunk on his own existence. Exhilarated, as if he'd sniffed a bit too much pastle seed. Death has Challenged him and lost," Tullis finished, with far less enthusiasm than the remark should have merited, "and his victory makes him giddy."

"Perhaps these changes will fade in time," Drianna suggested hopefully, pushing Tullis' unsettling news to the back of her mind. "A few more days may see him back to normal."

"I hope so, my Lady. Magic requires mental disciplines as well as raw power. If he sacrifices the one to gain more of the other, he'll be no better off—and could end up worse. It could make him careless . . . and that could kill him as easily as any sealing spell."

Drianna nodded solemnly as they progressed to the bedchamber door, passing by her own former lodgings on the way. Until recently, she had occupied the spacious chambers adjoining the Sage's own—a natural arrangement, of course, considering what they were to one another—but as his days under the sealing spell progressed, Brandegarth had grown increasingly volatile and violent; even after securing his master with a binding spell so that he could not leave his rooms, Tullis advised Drianna to move to another wing of the palace so that the Sage's constant shouts, moans, and senseless nocturnal soliloquies would not upset her. It was difficult to leave his side, but not so difficult as listening to him suffer through self-induced pain day after day and knowing she could do nothing to ease it.

This morning, however, the Sage was silent. The storm had

blown over; now all that remained was to see what damage it had done.

"Will you be joining us?" she asked Tullis. "I'm sure that Brand would be glad to share his breakfast with you and thank you for casting and releasing the sealing spell so smoothly."

"No, my Lady. His Grace asked me to deliver the prisoner to him right after I'd fetched you."

Drianna's brows shot up in surprise. "What? Isn't it far too soon for such a confrontation? Ranulf Osgood is no adept, but Brand says he's still a capable wizard. And he's had four whole months to nurse a grudge—he'll try to kill Brand again the moment he sets foot in that chamber." She began to wring her slender hands, increasingly agitated. "And if Brand isn't fully recovered—"

"We've plenty of guardsmen to protect him," Tullis reminded her gently, "and I shall be there, too. One mercenary, however capable, is no match for a palace full of Sarian wizards."

Drianna acquiesced with a half-smile of relief. "No, I suppose not." She bade the steward a brief farewell and for the first time in several weeks stepped gingerly into her lover's chamber.

The day would be unseasonably hot away from the shore, but the sea breezes were kind to the Sage's palace, and the chamber was sweet with salt spray and the lingering scent of cinnamon. Scattered crumbs and a slick of melted butter were the only evidence that the silver tray on the bedstand had ever contained the dozen oatcakes provided for the Sage's breakfast. But despite the seeming calm, the chamber still betrayed signs of the Sage's ordeal; Drianna was certain that the ugly scratch across the sideboard had not been there four months ago, nor the jagged rent in the brocade bedcurtains, now stitched tightly closed like lips vowing never to speak the horror of their abuse.

The Sage of Sare paced to and fro before the open window, ebony hair rippling gently in the breeze, and stroked his freshly shaved chin as if working out a solution to a most intricate problem. He was clad only in simple trews and boots—a sweat-soaked shirt had been tossed into a careless heap on the floor—and wore his customary adornments: a pounded silver torque, a single dagger-shaped earring, and a heavy arm-ring snug upon each bicep. He had grown slightly thinner during his ordeal, and his skin had lost some of its bronze luster, but in all her days, Drianna had never seen him look so handsome or so regal. Truly, the man was a king already . . . what matter that he did not yet have a crown and country to prove it?

"Brand?"

He flicked a glance to her without breaking his rhythmic stride. "What took you so long?"

"I—" Drianna bit back an overwhelming desire to scold him. Was *that* the first thing he would say to her since his awakening? Steadying herself, she made every effort to remember what Tullis had said. Perhaps it was not Brand himself that spoke so, but some shred of the sealing spell that still clung stubbornly to his mind.

"How do you feel?"

Brandegarth stopped in his tracks and flung his arms up to the heavens. "*Why* does everyone in this infernal palace keep *asking* me that? I feel fine. I feel more than fine." He threw his head back and began to laugh, deep from the belly. "In fact, I've never felt so damned fine in all my life!"

With both relief and a shade of apprehension, Drianna moved to embrace him, but he distractedly pushed her aside. "We've no time for that now, Drianna. We have work to do. Here, take this." Ignoring her wounded stare, he snatched a sheet of parchment from his writing table and shoved it into her hand. "Sit over there and write down everything I say. I have tried to do it myself, but my thoughts run far beyond my fingers today, and I end up with naught but pages spotted with inkblots."

Drianna stood paralyzed, gaping at him stupidly and unable to contain her shock at his callous treatment.

"Now!" he scolded, as if she were a novice kitchen maid too slow at serving his dinner. His tone did not invite argument.

Drianna scurried to the enameled desk, her vision swimming from the tears burning in her eyes, while the Sage began spewing out plans for the army of wizards that Couric and his other servants were hiring for him in western Caithe. Names of men, names of cities—most of which she could not spell—numbers, magic spells, and a host of other disjointed information. Unfortunately, Drianna's talents did not include that of scribe, and the Sage did nothing to make her job easier; his thoughts were forever tumbling over themselves, and his sentences came out in bits and pieces, leaving her to divine his meaning.

Drianna sniffled miserably. He remembered all these infernal names and places well enough . . . how could he have forgotten *her*?

Distracted by both her injured heart and her urgency to write down everything he bade her, it took a moment for her to realize that Brandegarth had stopped talking. She glanced up warily to see him staring out of the window, listening to the sea wash upon the shore as if it murmured poetry to him.

Then he turned back to her, his gaze piercing clear through her soul. "I have touched God, Drianna." His voice was hushed, as if he imparted the greatest of secrets. "He has spoken to me . . . through His angels."

Drianna put down her quill. Was this true, or was it only some remnant bit of madness; a side effect of the spell? "W-what did they say?" She wasn't sure whether the Sage was delusional or not, but she thought it best to humor him regardless.

Brand's expression darkened. "They warned me not to encroach upon His secrets." Then, as soon as it had come, the darkness on his face dispersed like woodsmoke in the wind and his eyes glinted with enchantment. "Ah, but perhaps there is one secret that He has imparted to me for my valor, eh, Drianna?"

He favored her with a wickedly sly grin. "You thought I had forgotten, didn't you?" he said, pointing a finger at her in mock accusation. "How could I? It was the chance of obtaining this particular power that drove me to be sealed in the first place."

Drianna's heart fluttered wildly, but to her surprise, she felt a powerful urge to flee his presence. Ever since they had become lovers when she was a mere girl of sixteen, Brand had promised her that if she were to become a wizard, then he would marry her—as Sage, he explained, he could not marry anyone unblessed by God. They waited for the *mekahn* to manifest in her, but they waited in vain. At twenty-four, it was still possible that she carried the potential for magic, but inwardly, Drianna knew that the chance was growing more remote with every passing day. And after eight years of waiting, Drianna realized she would gladly wait another eight years to avoid hearing the wrong thing.

"Are you going to do it now?" she asked, half-expectant, half-terrified.

Brand chuckled lightly. "Let us not get ahead of ourselves. I want to be sure that I have the power first, and then, once I know what to look for, I will test you." He touched a finger to her chin, lifting it up an inch. "I shall not risk error with you, my love."

Then he clasped her face between his palms and kissed her hard; four months of waiting was contained in that single urgent encounter, and it left Drianna dizzy and bruised and breathless with rapture.

With an explosion of energy, Brandegarth strode to the door in three long strides and flung it open, sending it crashing back against the wall. "Come!" he shouted over his shoulder. He dashed off at a gallop and was halfway down the corridor before Drianna could rouse herself to follow.

Hiking up her skirts, she scrambled after him in haste, almost missing a step at the bottom of the great stair leading to the courtyard. He was traversing the yard like a man eager to pass the news of his newborn son, hurrying past the armory and bastle-house, buttery and brewhouse, sending a half-dozen hens, two milkmaids, and a cat scurrying out of his path as he finally disappeared into the palace stables. By the time Drianna caught up with him, wheezing at the effort, he had emerged again and sought a new destination. A stableboy poked his head out of the doorway after him, shaking it in bewilderment.

Drianna trailed the Sage into the kitchens, catching up again just as he lurched across the threshold like a stallion bursting free of his stall. Cooks and scullery maids busily wiped flour and grease from their faces in an attempt to look respectable for their lord, and one young girl hastily swept her worktable clean of onion skins. While everyone in the palace knew by now that the Sage was free of the sealing spell, they had no more expected to see him up and about—much less darting about the castle like a madman—than they would have thought to see a new mother hop on a horse and take a ride around the island within an hour of giving birth.

"Where are the youngest?" he asked them, scanning the puzzled faces before him. "Those less than nineteen. Don't be shy—I won't bite them. Bring them forward!"

One by one, the youngest girls were prodded forward by the older women and placed in a disorderly line, like a squadron of soldiers about to undergo inspection. The girls fidgeted anxiously, rubbing at spots of grime on their aprons or twirling locks of hair around their fingers. Then, one by one, the Sage reached out and brushed against their minds; he placed his hands on their temples and breathed deep, scrying their souls for the sign. If he did not find what he sought after several minutes, he sent them off with a mumbled word of dismissal.

After he had tested seven of the assembled twelve and found nothing, Drianna sensed that his temper was growing thin. He was so desperate to possess the ability, Drianna feared that if he did not, he would seal himself for an even longer time and surely kill himself in his quest for power.

But as he cupped the head of the eighth girl, a sallow-faced drudge smelling of onions, he finally found what he sought. His eyes snapped open, and his face glowed as if he had just been gifted with a visitation by an angel. "Ah! Blessed child!" he cried, kissing the grubby creature full upon the lips. "You carry God's mark! What is your name? How old are you?"

"P-peg, your Grace," she stammered, still reeling from his unprecedented show of affection. "An' I'm almost fifteen." Openmouthed, Peg stared at her lord with a curious mix of delight and terror, but if the girl thought him mad, Drianna mused, she knew better than to say so.

The Sage embraced her warmly, as if she was his long-lost heir. "The seed is within you, Peg. You are one of God's chosen people. In a matter of years, you will come into your magic and will rise up in this world."

Peg's eyes grew round as the onions she had been chopping for the evening's stew. "How do you know?"

The Sage smiled down on her with the benevolence of a saint. "God has given His secrets to me as reward for my devotion," he said. "If you prove yourself worthy one day, Peg, then perhaps He will do the same for you."

He abruptly dismissed the remaining four girls. They crept back to their tasks, some visibly glad for the reprieve and others disappointed that their future would not be told that day. The Sage bestowed a bow of respect upon Peg as he backed dazedly out of the kitchens; the moment he was gone, Drianna saw the other girls cluster around Peg as if she were a new bride, chattering congratulations on her auspicious future.

"I have it," the Sage murmured, as he staggered drunkenly across the courtyard. "I have the power. It is so simple! A shining seed in the darkness . . . one only needs the power to see it and then it is so clear . . . like a pearl on black velvet, or a lantern in the night. Lord of my people, I thank you," he went on, lowering himself to one knee on the graveled walk. "I thank you for allowing me to share your knowledge of who has Your favor and who does not."

He struggled back to his feet, still intoxicated by the grace he had been granted. "Athaya will suffer for this . . . for keeping this power all to herself. When the Caithan people find out—"

"She thought it was wrong to use it," Drianna explained from behind him, though why she felt obliged to do so vexed her. "She couldn't possibly test everyone in the kingdom, so leaving things alone seemed the fairest thing to do. Especially in Caithe, where telling someone they're a wizard is the same as passing a death sentence on them."

"Then more the fool she." But rather than enter into another debate over Athaya Trelane's views on the ethics of magic, Brand motioned Drianna to follow him back to the tower. "Come, Tullis will have brought Ranulf to my chamber by now. After I have dealt with him, we will see what waits in your future."

"Brand, are you sure it's a good idea to see him?" she asked as they reached the foot of the great stair. Her mouth went dry as she spoke; Brand hated it when she questioned him—especially when it had anything do with magic—but if Brand still bore some lingering trace of his ordeal, then Ranulf would be quick to take advantage of it. He was one of Athaya's staunchest allies and knew the threat the Sage posed to her work. "You should be resting, not overexerting yourself so soon after—"

"Bah! I am strong enough for anything." He raised tight fists over his head, flexing the muscles on his bare arms and back. "By God, Drianna, I could Challenge one of God's own angels and win right now!"

Drianna's hand flew to her mouth, expecting lightning to strike him dead that instant. *"Brand!"*

But his blasphemy was forgotten as they returned to the Sage's bedchamber, where Tullis and two guardsmen kept silent watch over Ranulf Osgood. The prisoner was thinner and paler now—and somewhat damp, Drianna realized—but still a powerful man for his forty-odd years. Drianna suspected he could have wrestled almost anyone in the palace to the ground, with possible exception of Brand himself. Ranulf had been kept in reasonably honorable confinement—he was the enemy, but as a wizard, he deserved a certain amount of deference—and had suffered from little more than boredom these past few months.

"Please pardon his appearance, your Grace," Tullis said,

turning a critical eye to Sage's captive. "He has not elected to bathe for months and . . . well, I had to insist that he do so before seeing you."

Brand laughed merrily at the sight of Ranulf's sopping red hair sticking out in all directions; he looked like a wet cat and surely bore the same temperament. "Ah, Ranulf. It is good to see you again."

The mercenary made a hawking sound in the back of his throat. "Sorry I can't say the same."

Drianna could see the hatred in the man's eyes, burning them hollow from within. But Ranulf was not a stupid man, and she saw caution simmering there as well. Ranulf was born and bred on Sare, trained as a soldier in the same mercenary company as Brand, but while Brand had remained on the island, Ranulf had sold his services to the civil war in Caithe. When his magic came upon him soon thereafter, he had ended up in Reyka instead of Sare, and was therefore never properly educated to revere the Sage or his island cult. But he knew of it and knew enough to tread carefully within its leader's abode.

"Him I can understand," Ranulf said to Drianna, flatly ignoring the Sage's presence for the moment. "He always had a cesspool for a soul, even back in the corps. But you! Athaya was kind to you, even though you drove her to distraction with all of yer babbling and fawning. And this is how you repaid her."

Drianna felt her cheeks tingle with heat. Although she had omitted the fact from her report to Brand, she had actually come to like the Caithan princess and enjoyed acting the part of lady's maid to her.

"She did only as I asked her to," Brandegarth pointed out in her defense. "And you must realize that my plans for Caithe were preordained. Little that Drianna told me could have changed them."

The Sage dismissed the two guardsmen with a flick of his wrist, but bade Tullis to remain. Then he paused, silently appraising his captive. "Don't you even want to know why I've sent for you?"

Ranulf sniffled crudely. "You'll get to it. Far be it from me to rush you, your Grace."

"No need to be so suspicious, my friend," Brand replied, overlooking the mercenary's mildly baiting tone. "I sent for you to tell you that you are free to go."

Ranulf studied the Sage without blinking. "Just like that?"

"Almost. You may leave on the condition that you perform one simple task for me."

Ranulf ran stubby fingers through his fresh growth of red beard and snorted. "You lock me up for four months and expect me to do ye a favor? That's rich."

"It is a small thing. When you leave here, I imagine that you will go directly to Athaya Trelane and tell her everything that has transpired here. All I ask is that you add one more thing to your report."

Drianna detected the mercenary's muscles relax slightly; when he had been imprisoned, he knew only that Nicolas was about to be bound by a spell of compulsion. He was clearly relieved to know that the spell had not been crafted to induce the prince to murder his sister, Athaya. But what it *had* induced him to do, he as yet had no idea.

"What did you do to Nicolas?"

Brandegarth waved his hand negligently. "Old news, my friend. Athaya will tell you about it when you see her, I'm sure." He made a clicking sound with his tongue. "A most unfortunate turn of events, I'm sorry to say."

For a man of his bulk, Ranulf was deceptively quick. Rage flared anew in his eyes, burning away all his former caution, and he lunged at the Sage with a growl of untempered fury. "Tell me, damn you!" Shunning weapons of magic, Ranulf was content to tear the flesh from his enemy's body with his bare hands.

With ineffable calm, Brandegarth held up his right hand, palm facing his attacker. *"Salvum fac sub aspide!"*

Drianna had seen the Sage cast a shielding spell many times before, but never to such spectacular effect. She expected a shower of blue sparks to deal a stiff but harmless shock to the prisoner, but this time, the instant Ranulf's flesh touched the invisible shield, the room blazed with sparkling white brilliance like sunlight on the sea, temporarily blinding her. Her ears rang to the point of pain from the loud *pop* that followed.

When her vision cleared, she saw Ranulf sprawled flat on his back, limbs splayed in abandon like a starfish washed up on the sand. His eyes were open and glassy, his body motionless. Beside him, the normally imperturbable Tullis stared in wide-eyed shock, shaken to his soul by the awesome power that had just been unleashed.

The Sage bent down beside Ranulf, slack-jawed with astonishment; clearly, he had not expected his spell to carry such force. His eyes shifted and he stared at his empty palm as if he had never seen its like before.

"Is he dead?" Drianna asked, kneeling beside the fallen man. Black spots danced before her eyes in the spell's aftermath. "Brand, did you—"

Ranulf's groan of misery announced that he was alive, but not particularly glad of it at the moment. "I can't move . . ."

It took several minutes before Ranulf's numbed limbs tingled to life again and he could sit up without toppling over. He cast a furtive glance at the Sage as he swiftly reassessed the odds of winning a fight. Finding them heavily weighted against him, he tossed a scathing glare at Drianna, content to blame her for everything.

Still preoccupied by the stunning bolt of power he had summoned, Brandegarth flexed his fingers and curled them into a fist. "Nicolas is alive," he murmured absently, resuming their conversation. "Or at least he was the last I heard. I've been somewhat out of touch." Then he let his hand fall to his side, bracing it against his thigh like a sword ready to be drawn again at the slightest need. "Now, as to the message I wish you to carry. It is simply this: tell Athaya I have come. By the time you reach her, I shall have touched the shores of Caithe." The Sage graced him with a thoroughly evil smile. "Her people do not trust her as they once did—a pity!—and they need a new leader. I plan to provide them with one . . . one who can offer them far more than your pious little princess."

Before Ranulf's addled brain could think of a suitably acrid retort, the Sage gestured to his steward. "Tullis, escort this man to the front gates. Give him food for the journey and enough coin to hire a ferry to the mainland."

Drianna saw the bitter reply poised on Ranulf's lips. But he swallowed it like sour wine, realizing that the Sage could snuff out his life like a candleflame if he was angered, thus leaving no one to warn Athaya of his plans. Ranulf had not survived all those years as a mercenary soldier without learning the wisdom of retreating from a hopeless battle.

Unnerved by his lord's show of strength, Tullis took the prisoner's arm and hurried him away, almost as glad to be gone from the Sage's presence as Ranulf himself.

"He should reach Athaya's camp in about a fortnight," Drianna observed quietly. "Do you really plan to be on the mainland so soon?" She would have preferred him to remain on Sare and rest for a few weeks to make certain he was fully recovered from the sealing spell. But the faraway glory in his eyes convinced her that he would do nothing of the kind.

"I can wait no longer, Drianna." His smile was enigmatic. "My people need me."

Then he took her hand and led her to the edge of his great feather bed. He patted the fur-lined coverlet beside him, and when she settled at his side, he cupped her face between his palms and kissed her gently. "And now, my love, shall we scry your future?"

Again, Drianna felt torn between wanting to know and wanting to shrink from that omnipotent touch. The moment they had long awaited had come; the moment that would determine the course of their remaining years. She fought down the queasy feeling in her belly and tried to think only hopeful thoughts. The prospect of marriage was entrancing enough, but when he won his prize . . . why, then she would become queen of Caithe! Not a bad accomplishment for the daughter of a poor peasant and sister to a swineherd.

"Look inside of me, my love," she whispered at last. "Look . . . and tell me what you see."

Drianna closed her eyes and waited, her heart hammering wildly in her chest. At first, she felt nothing but the warm flesh of his hands upon her face, but then came the feather-light touch of his presence, brushing the insides of her mind, searching for dormant magic.

One simple test, she thought. And if she passed—and she simply *had* to!—she would belong to him forever.

She remained silent and did not move. Why was it taking so long? It had been much quicker with Peg. Although the chamber was cooled by sea breezes, Drianna began to perspire; droplets of sweat trickled down her back, itching terribly, but she didn't dare to scratch. A minute more and she was close to fainting.

Then he lifted his hands, and Drianna cracked open her eyes. Brand didn't have to say a word; the look on his face as he drew away from her said it all. It was a look not of bleakness or despair, but of . . . nothing. His face bore no emotion at all.

"I see nothing, Drianna."

Suddenly, Drianna was grateful she'd not eaten that morning; sour bile crept up to the back of her throat. "No, look again! You must have done it wrong . . . you must have overlooked something!"

"I am not mistaken." His voice was cold, and there was a hint of warning in it; a warning not to question his abilities again.

"I suspected this," he went on, rising to his feet. "God has seen fit to elevate me, but not to grant you power. You are not worthy to be my wife; He has decreed it, and we must live by His will."

He turned his back to her and went to retrieve a clean shirt from his wardrobe. "You may stay here in the palace, of course. Provided we find some work for you to do. I'll speak to Tullis about it. Perhaps the cook can use another hand."

Drianna blinked disbelievingly. Cook? *Work?* Now she knew he was mad . . .

"But I thought I was coming to Caithe with you."

Brand quashed the notion with a curt shake of his head. "I need trained wizards at my side, Drianna. You would be of no use to me." He tossed the shirt over his head and turned to go.

"No, don't go—not like this!" She sprang from the bed and grabbed hold of his wrist with desperate strength.

"I have more important matters to attend to." His voice remained steady and indifferent. "I have a kingdom to secure. Couric and the others have been heralding my arrival for months. It's time I fulfilled their prophecies."

He peeled her fingers from his wrist as if removing brambles from his shirt and swept out of the chamber.

"Brand, please!" She stumbled to the threshold after him, gripping the doorjamb for balance, the chamber a ship pitching in rough waters. "Come back!"

He didn't even slow his stride as he rounded the corner and vanished.

Drianna staggered backward dizzy with shock; he had been cut from her life like a severed limb, and she was fast bleeding to death.

Alone in the spacious chamber, Drianna crumpled into a miserable heap on the floor. Hot tears scalded her cheeks and left ugly dark spots on her pale blue skirts. Eight years at his side, eight years in his bed, and she was dismissed as perfunctorily as an incompetent scullery maid! With a few spoken words, Brand had plunged her back to the depths from which he had raised her; a fish too small and insignificant to bother saving for one's meal. And someone like Peg—a common drudge!—had the chance to take her place at his side.

In less time than it had taken to choose her dress that morning, her entire world had burned to ashes. She had been summarily rejected—by Brand as well as God, who had refused to gift her with magic—and now there was nothing left. She could never remain on Sare; after such humiliation, she could not bear to face another soul in this palace. And if she could not be mistress of this place, then she would not be anything at all.

The inside of her eyelids felt coated with sand as she wiped away her tears and rushed from the chamber, ignoring the politely unseeing eyes of the guardsmen in the corridor. She was going to Caithe whether the Sage liked it or not.

And if he did not want her at his side, then she would find someone else who did.

CHAPTER 4

✳✳

"**Y**OU'VE ALMOST GOT IT," ATHAYA SAID, KEEPING HER voice low and unobtrusive so as not to break the young man's concentration. She stood directly behind him in the sun-mottled clearing, lightly supporting his elbows with her hands. "Keep the flow of power steady or you might lose control."

Focusing fiercely on his task, Girard struggled to balance the two turbulent jets of green fire streaming from his hands, looking as if he clutched a pair of blazing snakes and was trying to keep them from curling back to bite him. The deadly fire flowed less freely from his left hand—as a permanent reminder of how serious the king's Tribunal was about eradicating wizardry in Caithe. Girard's maimed left limb bore five ugly stumps instead of the once-agile fingers of a carpenter. It took great effort for him to direct more power through his left hand while curbing the flow to his right, and fat beads of sweat formed on his brow as he strove to keep the coils in balance.

"That's good," Athaya whispered, feeling the heat of his efforts against her own skin as well. "Now make the coils do your bidding. Remember that you control them, not the reverse." Silently, she hoped he would heed that counsel better than she once had; fortunately for him, Girard didn't have to contend with the same disruptive memories as those that haunted her own thoughts day after day.

Girard nodded absently and began to weave the twin strands

of fire around the base of a large iron cauldron, gradually channeling more power through each strand until the water in the cauldron began to steam softly, raising a gentle cloud of mist.

"Not too much," she cautioned him when she saw the water begin to bubble at the edges. "There . . . that's it. Now try and hold that level steady for a few minutes."

Still supporting his elbows, Athaya gazed past Girard's shoulder at the fiery dragons he wielded, slipping into a light trance at the hypnotic, circular movement of the coils. Her eyelids half-closed, she felt herself drifting back to another place and time. No longer did she stand in the deep serenity of the Forest of Else, but in the king's sumptuous audience chamber at Delfar Castle; no longer was she a highly trained magician passing on her craft to those newly come to their power, but a terrified girl of nineteen with no more knowledge of magic than she had of astrology or mathematics.

Like a recurring nightmare, the scene came back to her undiminished in clarity after nearly two years. She saw her father, Kelwyn, snared in the deadly ropes of fire that streamed wildly from her hands, the reckless coils burning cloth and flesh as they leeched the very life from Caithe's beloved king. She heard the echo of his voice cry out for mercy as he writhed upon the floor, herself longing to grant it but not knowing how. But clearest of all she remembered his face, its regal features twisted in agony and his eyes desperate to know why she was assaulting him; asking through their growing fog of madness if she truly hated him that much and imploring her with his last shreds of sanity to stop. Begging her . . . *Athaya, no. Please, no!*

She sucked in a startled gasp and swiftly jerked away from Girard, covering her eyes with trembling hands.

"Your Highness?" Girard hastily dispersed the fire coils, the crackling flames retreating into his fingertips like the misty tendrils of a vision sphere. "Did I do something wrong?"

"No. I—" She forced air into her lungs to steady herself and then let her arms fall slack to her sides. The memory had so much power, even now. "That spell killed my father."

Girard paled noticeably. He had known, as all Caithans did, of Athaya's role in King Kelwyn's death, but was clearly unaware of the specifics. "I knew his death was some sort of accident," he said, worriedly adjusting the fit of his spectacles, "but I didn't realize it was the coils. I'm sorry."

Athaya offered him a weak smile of reassurance. "It's not your fault. I . . . don't talk about it much."

Suddenly weary, she sank to her knees in the tall grass cooled by the shade of the ancient bell tower that marked the center of the wizards' camp. It would have been easier to have someone else teach that spell—someone like Master Tonia, who could treat the fire coils like any other hazardous spell without being troubled by past mistakes. But imparting to others the knowledge that she had not gained in time—knowledge that, unfathomable as it was to her, remained illegal under Caithan law—made Athaya feel that she was doing what she could to make up for that horrible blunder. At least no one who came to her camp for training would leave without the ability to control those deadly coils; they would never bear the crushing guilt that gnawed at her own heart like crows on carrion when she paused to think too long upon it.

Absently, Athaya plucked a stalk of grass and worked it between her fingers, quickly tinting the skin of her fingertips bright green. Much as she had loved him, she had been better able to accept Tyler's death, grieve for him, and properly close that chapter of her life. He died to buy her a future, but the final blow came from Durek's hand, not hers—and that made all the difference. When she fled Delfar Castle after her fatal struggle with Kelwyn, Tyler refused to reveal her hiding place to Durek, fully aware of the price he would pay for such loyalty. But Kelwyn had never been granted that choice; his mind already twisted from the borrowed magic souring within it, he had never comprehended why his daughter had attacked him; he never understood that she only sought to defend herself from his magical assault and that the fire coils were simply too strong for an untutored wizard to control.

Burdened by the weight of what she had done, Athaya had vowed to carry on her father's work. She vowed that no other Lorngeld would harm someone they loved because they did not know how to use their powers. She vowed to outlaw absolution as surely as she had been outlawed in Caithe. But despite all that she had done to reach those goals—exhorting budding wizards to refuse absolution, establishing schools of magic, and bringing her homeland to the brink of civil war over the matter—Athaya remained forever haunted by the knowledge that, though his borrowed power would have killed him in time, and possibly in a far more grisly way, hers was the hand by which King Kelwyn ultimately fell. Accident or no, hers was the hand.

She was sure of Tyler's forgiveness. He had inherited the generous heart of his father, who now cared for Prince Nicolas as if his own son had been returned to him.

But did Kelwyn forgive her? Durek certainly never had.

Athaya looked at the grass stains upon her fingertips and imagined the spots turning bright crimson, color that ran too deep to ever be washed away. Did he forgive her?

She would never know.

"Can I get you anything?" Girard asked in quiet apology for bringing painful memories to the surface.

Athaya shook off the last vestiges of melancholy, letting the balmy June breezes carry them off to oblivion. "I wouldn't mind something cool to drink—it's grown warmer since we started. And get something for yourself, too. Weaving the coils is hard work."

While Girard set off for the camp's kitchen, brows folded inward like a worried mother fetching a posset for a sick child, Athaya sprawled indolently in the grass and savored the lazy humidity of the season. The air was thick with the aroma of the camp's dinner being prepared, and her mouth watered at the mingled scents of warm bread, baked apples, and venison. The day was a paradise compared to the brutal winter she and her followers had suffered. Propping herself up on one elbow, Athaya picked a tender sprout from a tangle of wild grape and chewed on the tart, lemon-flavored stalk as if it were the rarest of delicacies.

Girard returned with two frothy mugs of cool beer and a basket overflowing with freshly picked blueberries. "Master Tonia says they're for the feast tonight and for us not to eat more than half," he repeated dutifully.

Athaya's eyes loudly proclaimed "you must be joking" even if her lips did not. "Master Tonia has been in charge of rationing watered beer and pemmican all winter and hasn't quite broken the habit yet," she replied lightly, dropping a handful of berries into her mouth.

With a conspiratorial nod, Girard scooped up two heaping handfuls of fruit. "Are we finished for today?" he asked. The sky was still bright as noon above them, but the hour grew late; on the longest day of the year, sunset would not be upon them for a while yet.

Athaya nodded, unable to offer a verbal reply until she

swallowed. "And tell Jaren to dismiss the others, too," she added, gesturing across the clearing. Jaren was instructing a handful of students on spells of illusion, and throughout the afternoon unlikely pillars of marble and drifts of snow had been popping up in various corners of the camp. "With the luscious smells coming out of that kitchen, nobody is going to be able to concentrate on their magic for much longer anyway."

The feasting began at the first hint of twilight as everyone in the camp set aside the day's lessons and turned to the serious business of celebrating the zenith of summer. The camp had not seen such a festival since Athaya's wedding feast almost a year before, and all were eager to make up for the omission. Rabbit, mutton, pheasant, and venison turned on several outdoor spits, fresh trout sizzled in shallow iron pans over the smaller fires, baskets spilled over with berries and nuts, and ale and wine flowed freely. Not even the shyest souls were allowed to sit out the dancing and when the revelers were in need of rest, there was singing and storytelling to pass the time. With the combined spirits of two hundred folk determined to enjoy themselves—a diversion they well deserved in light of the dangers that lurked just outside the protective wards ringing the camp—it was a merrier evening than any celebration Athaya had ever attended at court.

"I don't remember dancing this much even at our wedding," Jaren said breathlessly, as the two of them relaxed after a particularly vigorous set of reels. He proffered a wooden cup brimming with sweet pear-flavored wine and sat down beside her in the tall grass beneath the bell tower, at a slight distance from the others. Like the queen of summer, Athaya was garbed in the deep green kirtle she had worn for her wedding and wore a ribboned chaplet of roses in her hair like a crown.

"We didn't," she reminded him with a suggestive arch of her brow. "As I recall, you suggested leaving the party early."

"And as I recall," he replied, equally arch, "I didn't have to drag you away kicking and screaming, either."

It was a quiet time between dances, and the fiddles and flutes had been set aside so their players could snatch up a few goblets of wine before the casks ran dry. Near the main campfire, Gilda, one of the camp's most gifted tutors, gently rocked her infant son and began spinning a tale she remembered from her childhood; a tale about an enchanted cradle and the spell cast upon any child rocked to sleep in it to dream visions of the future. If it was a Caithan tale, Athaya mused, then it was an ancient one; a tale from before the Time of Madness, when a wizard's enchantment was not yet a thing to be cursed, but innocent fodder for a storyteller's yarn.

Athaya was not so absorbed by the tale that she failed to hear the subtle rustling noise behind her—if nothing else, outlawry kept her vigilant. She twisted around and peered into the dark depths of the forest. She was ready to dismiss it as a raccoon making its way through the brush until the rustling was followed by a muffled whimper of pain, as if someone had trodden on a sharp stone. "Jaren, did you hear—"

She never finished the question. Just then, a huge man exploded from the shrubbery like a boar flushed from his lair. His ragged tunic and boots were liberally spattered with grime, and a smattering of leaves and sticks were snared in his matted mop of red hair, giving him the air of an untamed forest god out of legend. "And just who up and threw a party without inviting me, I'd like to know?" he roared, every inch the displeased sovereign. "Fine thing this is . . . I go off for a few months, and you all set about drinkin' up all o' my beer."

"Ranulf!" Athaya lurched to her feet and hurled herself into the mercenary's powerful arms. "Thank the . . . I thought you were—" The rest of the sentiment was lost amid a heartfelt kiss, square on his lips.

"Have a care now, Princess," he said, raising a pair of mud-encrusted brows as he glanced covertly past her. "Your husband could walk in on us at any moment."

Athaya drew back a step, belatedly taking in Ranulf's filthy tunic and hose—and his rather pungent aroma; not all of the brownish stains on his garments were caused by harmless mud. "What happened to you?"

"Aw, I thought that mudslick on the trail was one o' my old illusions," he said, jerking a thumb backward into the wood. "Slipped and fell right in . . . and right on top of the leavings of whatever had been there afore me." He drew in a breath and cringed at his own stench. "At least you're shifting the illusions around a bit to keep everyone on their toes."

"Everyone but you, it seems."

By now, Gilda had abandoned her tale and scurried over to greet him, trailed by dozens of others. From Gilda he received a modest kiss, from Kale a quiet handshake, and from Tonia, whose friendship with him was far older than the rest, the expected volley of barbs.

"What's this?" she said, critically eyeing his empty hands.

"You come back from an extended holiday abroad without bringing us any presents?"

"Ha! Shows what you know," he returned with a grin. He retreated a few steps into the forest and emerged with a canvas satchel and a small stoppered jug. "Here," he said, thrusting the jug into Tonia's arms. "The wizards on Sare may be damned full o' themselves, but they know how to make fine whiskey."

But behind the jest, Athaya saw haunted shadows in his face, like a soldier who's seen too much of death. "And it was no holiday, Tonia," he added quietly, letting out an exhausted sigh. "Not by half." He passed a troubled gaze over Athaya, Jaren, and Tonia. "We need to talk," he murmured, tipping his head in the direction of the chapel.

Leaving the others to continue their feast, the four of them retired to the tumbledown chapel on the far side of the clearing. Just as he stepped over the threshold, Ranulf jerked back as if he had suddenly recalled an urgent appointment elsewhere. "Tonia, be a love and fetch me a beer," he said, warming her with a vaguely lewd smile, minus two teeth. "A very large beer, mind. I've a long tale, and I'll need my strength to tell it."

On any other occasion, Tonia would have scolded him for ordering a Master of the Circle about like a common barmaid, but she merely snickered and headed for the casks, warning him not to deliver all of his news before she got back.

Not to fear, she added privately to Athaya, tipping her head imperceptibly toward Ranulf. *I did a quick reading and don't see any signs of tinkering. The Sage seems to have gotten his fill of compulsion spells for a time.*

Athaya swallowed hard, her forearms breaking out in goosebumps. It had never occurred to her that the Sage might have ensorcelled Ranulf as well, commanding him to strike at her—or the entire camp—in retribution for Nicolas' aborted assault on Durek. She felt hot and shaky, as if she had just crossed over a bridge only to be told on the other side that the wood was badly rotted and it was a very lucky thing the structure had not crumbled beneath her feet.

Sobered, Athaya joined Jaren and Ranulf on the cool stone pews near the altar. As they waited for Tonia's return, Athaya told Ranulf all that had happened since he left them to accompany Nicolas to the Isle of Sare. She told him of the prince's sickness, of the king's harrowing brush with death, and of the support she had lost because of her suspected involvement in both calamities.

"Master Hedric is at Belmarre with him now," she concluded as Tonia returned with a suitably monstrous tankard of beer, "but he can only do so much. There's no real cure—not unless the Sage lifts the spell himself. Or does us the favor of dying." Hostility flared behind her eyes; she thought the latter a very pleasing prospect indeed.

"That bastard," Ranulf mumbled into his beer, his cheeks crimson with fury. "That bloody, stinking bastard." He took a long swallow to dampen his rage, wiping the foam from his lips with the back of a meaty hand. "But bad as that is, it doesn't compare to what ol' Brandegarth is up to now. And he let me go just so's I could come and tell you all about it," he added sourly, chafing at the need to do exactly what the Sage wished him to. "Arrogant son of a—"

"We get the point," Tonia broke in. "Stop cursing the man and get on with it."

Ranulf obeyed her grudgingly. "He let me go about three weeks ago. After I crossed over to the mainland, I decided to poke around in Eriston for a day or two, to see if what I'd been hearing was true. Bein' a Sarian myself, it was easy enough to get the Sage's folks to talk—especially if I bought the whiskey. Anyhow, his men are scuttling all over the western shires like cockroaches, hiring recruits. They've even gone as far as Delfarham once or twice."

Athaya folded her brows inward. "Hiring? For what?"

"An army. They've been forming up in the fields west of Eriston. I managed to get a peek at the campsite after a guard let me pass the barricade, thinkin' I belonged there." Ranulf regarded her steadily. "There's over a thousand folks camped under his banner already."

"A thou—" Athaya's tongue went numb. All of the wizards in all of her schools put together probably did not number much more than that. In a matter of weeks, the Sage had gathered as large a following as she had managed to gain in over a year.

"Almost half of them are fully trained wizards, straight from Sare," he went on. "The rest are Caithans they've bought up in the past few months with all their cursed silver."

"I can't believe we haven't gotten wind of this yet," Jaren said, shaking his head in bafflement. "We have people stationed in the west. Mason—"

"Aye, but the Sage's followers are keeping their distance from us, getting as many folks on their side as they can before we get wise to 'em. I stopped in Kilfarnan on the way back to see if Mason's had any trouble at his camp, but the ol' bookworm didn't know what in hell I was talking about.

"Anyhow, these Sarians are tossing silver coins about like birdseed and promising the world to anyone who'll listen. Not just food and shelter—although we're better fixed to offer that now that winter's over—but to the ones as stay loyal, they're offering power, wealth, titles, lands ... summin' it up, the chance to loot the whole damned kingdom and divvy up the goods once they take over. Now, bein' a mercenary myself, I know what a tempting offer that is—and so do plenty o' the poor folk they're targeting. Folk that are sick of being hounded by the king's Tribunal and don't see us doing enough to get rid of it."

Athaya muttered a curse, weary to death of the whole debate. Why had it proved such a struggle to persuade people that outright warfare wasn't going to solve all their problems? Her intent was to win this battle one wizard at a time, not by violence, but by enlightenment—by spreading knowledge about of magic and thus showing the skeptics that the Lorngeld did not have to be feared. If they learned how to channel their power when the *mekahn* came upon them, the Lorngeld were not dangerous; not Devil's Children, but divinely blessed. Many of Caithe's newest wizards—the gentleborn Sutter Dubaye foremost among them—had refused to see the wisdom of her approach, forever wanting to form an army to wage bloody war against the king and his Justices. Sutter was dead now, captured and killed by Lukin's men for failing to deliver Athaya and her people into the Tribunal's hands, but many others still shared his desire to hunt down and kill their oppressors. Now the Sage's men were exploiting that desire to serve their own ends ... and meeting with a disturbing amount of success.

"Did you find out exactly what they're up to?" Jaren asked, shifting to a more comfortable position—if there was such a thing—in the unyielding stone pew. "Are they planning to attack us?"

"They're not planning to attack anything ... at least not yet. Mostly, they were told to get as many recruits as they could and wait for the Sage to show up. But they don't plan to wait long. The day I left Eriston, a few of 'em took over the mayor's house, claiming they needed it for a headquarters of sorts—and that they had to fit it up proper for their fearless leader. Needless to say, the mayor rode straight for Delfarham to ask for men to drive them off, but I can't see what good the king's soldiers are going to be against thousand wizards, even if half of 'em don't know but a handful o' spells yet."

Athaya's face darkened. "If they've readied a house for him, then the Sage must be about to make his move."

Ranulf cast his eyes down, reluctant to pass on the Sage's message. "He told me to say that he'll be in Caithe by the time I reach your camp. And since I did a little spying in Eriston and took a detour through Kilfarnan, I'd guess he's been on the mainland for a few days now."

"There's one way to confirm that." Turning away from the others, Athaya summoned her vision sphere into her palms, willing the misty orb to form between her fingertips, suspended there like a drop of dew on morning grass. She had tried to seek the Sage in her sphere some months past, hoping to learn what had become of Ranulf, but the island palace was thickly veiled by wards to turn aside such wizardly prying and her globe had shown her nothing but smoky darkness. The Sage would have no need to shield himself now that he was in Caithe; not after he had gone to such pains to inform the populace that he was on his way.

Athaya called from her memory the Sage's face—rugged and handsome, but marred by heartless, laughing eyes—and willed it to appear before her. The vision was slow to come, but shortly she began to glimpse colored pieces of a picture, like bits of broken stained glass slowly swirling back into a whole. The fragments gradually formed into an image of a bustling port at twilight, each ship's mast, church spire, and townhouse window reflecting the dying orange light. The Sage of Sare stood on the jutting balcony of a large and luxurious residence—the mayor of Eriston's house, no doubt—elegantly clad in a soft gray mantle adorned with a collar of sun-limned silver links. He spoke to the people gathered in the street below, and though Athaya could not discern his words, his eyes blazed with holy rapture at the glory of them. Townsfolk waved their arms in reply, cheering with varying degrees of willingness, and from time to time the Sage would reward their adulation with some showy bit of magic—a reddish witchlight or a diverting illusion of a dove—much to the delight of the children in the throng. But Athaya could not hold the vision for more than a few moments, and the sphere quickly clouded over, revealing nothing but grayish roils of mist.

Athaya dispersed the globe and wiped the sticky residue on her kirtle. "I couldn't get much, but I saw enough to know that he's in Eriston . . . and making a spectacle of himself already." She let her breath out slowly. "It's a relief in a sense. If the only reason he put off his arrival this long was to stretch my nerves to the limit, then it worked remarkably well."

"That wasn't the reason." Ranulf brooded into his tankard, absently swirling his beer until it slopped over one side and sopped his breeches. "Brandegarth's been trying to catch up to you, Athaya. He's been under a sealing spell all this time." The silence that his words provoked was deafening, a strange counterpoint to the blissful strains of a flute and drum in the clearing. "An' if the shielding spell he used on me is any indication, his magic is a hell of a lot stronger than it was before. And much as I hate to say it," Ranulf finished, casting a remorseful glance to Athaya, "he's even stronger than you are now."

Athaya, Jaren, and Tonia stared at him in wordless unison, temporarily bereft of speech. It was the obvious answer, but one that had never occurred to any of them. The sealing spell was extremely risky and had killed enough curious wizards in years past to incite the Circle to forbid its use to anyone but those to whom they gave permission. Granted, the Sage and his cult held nothing but contempt for the Circle's strictures, but what wizard would willingly put his life at such terrible risk?

Only one as greedy for power as Rhodri had ever been, Athaya answered herself, and one who had recently uncovered a way of obtaining more of it. Until Athaya had inadvertently discovered them, no one had known of the power-extending qualities of the seal. And now, she fervently wished that the discovery, however extraordinary, had never been made.

"I should have known," she said after a time, rising to her feet to pace anxiously around the chapel. "The timing . . . it makes perfect sense. But—"

She and Jaren realized the disastrous implications at the same instant and exchanged a look of muted dread. Ranulf's news was worse than he knew.

"The effects of the seal are only temporary, Ranulf. Since you've been gone, my level of power has completely faded back to what it was over a year ago." Briefly, Athaya told him of the dizziness and loss of strength she had suffered after her last attempt at translocation. Then she sighed heavily and leaned her weight against the back of the spartanly adorned alter. "At least we know *his* powers will fade, too. Eventually."

The rest was left unspoken, but all of their faces reflected her next thought back to her. *But it took almost a year for my powers to fade . . . and Caithe doesn't have that kind of time.*

"At least you're no weaker than you were before the seal," Jaren pointed out, trying to salvage a measure of hope from the situation. "And being an adept is nothing to be ashamed of."

"No. But it's clear that the Sage has the advantage of me now."

Ranulf swallowed the last of his beer in one gulp. "More n' you know," he said ominously, swiftly drawing the attention of three pairs of eyes. "One other tidbit I picked up during my holiday in Sare was that the Sage isn't affected by corbal crystals. Aw, quit lookin' at me like that—I *saw* it. It was incredible . . . he held the damned thing up right in front of me and didn't bat an eye. Not one eye. And that was before the sealing."

Despite his admonishment, Athaya continued to gape at him stupidly, unable to believe what she had heard. All at once, and at the worst possible time, the rules of the game she had taken so long to master were suddenly changed. A wizard unaffected by a corbal crystal? This was a blow indeed; a weapon she never dreamed the Sage would have at his command. At that moment, she felt like a general whose men had marched into battle armed with spears and slingshots, only to find that the enemy was equipped with cannons and siege engines . . . and vastly outnumbered them in the bargain.

"How is that possible?" Tonia said, the first to regain the use of her tongue.

Ranulf offered Athaya a crooked grin, forcing a bit of levity to lift the oppressive gloom. "Kind of comforting to know that even the Circle of Masters don't know everything, ain't it?"

Tonia snorted indelicately as she jammed a wayward strand of steel-gray hair back inside her peasant scarf. "I never claimed we did. Lord, if we'd had any inkling this was possible, why on earth would we have let Athaya learn about the sealing spell in the first place? It's caused nothing but trouble since, but it was the only way we knew that she could shield herself from the corbal's pain."

"Looks as if the Sage knows another way—and so do a few

of his followers. I'm not sure how they do it. On the night Nicolas and I were taken, I remember the Sage saying something about the crystal simply tricking me into feeling pain—try telling my guts that it was only a trick!—and that all you need to do is learn the trick and it doesn't hurt anymore. Nicolas figured out that the Sage couldn't work magic at the same time . . . or at least I think that's what he said—I wasn't feeling too well at the time. Damn it to hell," he spat out, violently yanking a twig from his hair, "if it wasn't for that crystal, I might have been able to get Nicolas away from him before—"

"Don't berate yourself, Ranulf," Athaya said, knowing how deeply he must blame himself for her brother's fate. "How were you supposed to know about the corbals, if even the Circle of Masters didn't?" Like her ability to see the seeds of power—if indeed she could still do such a thing—withstanding the pain of a corbal crystal was a thing never conceived before . . . at least not by those of Reykan training.

Athaya indulged in an admittedly childish scowl. It had been much more pleasant when it was she who was forever coming up with unexpected talents; now that her enemy was doing the same thing, she found it annoying in the extreme.

"I suppose he's gained the ability to translocate, too?" she asked dryly, unsure that she really wanted an answer.

Ranulf's eyes bulged at the notion and he swept his gaze across the chapel as if expecting the Sage to drop in on them at any moment. "I don't know. He may have. He never said." Ranulf set his empty tankard aside. "But there is one more thing . . ."

"Not *more* bad news?" Suddenly, Athaya wanted nothing more than to flee to her room in the dormitory and crawl under several thick blankets. How many more unpleasant revelations could she take in one night?

"No. Well, maybe. Depends on how you look at it."

To her surprise, he got up and sauntered out of the chapel, motioning the rest of them to wait. He returned a few minutes later with a slender figure draped in a hooded cloak. Like a gown ornamented with seed pearls, the hem of the embroidered cloak was richly studded with brambles and delicate hands bore a wide selection of nasty scratches, fingertips dotted with tiny beads of blood like those of an incompetent needlewoman.

"Come on in now, she ain't gonna eat ye," he said, tugging

his reluctant companion over the threshold. "I promised, didn't I?"

The figure inched closer, then lifted apprehensive hands to turn back her hood. A river of auburn hair spilled out across her shoulders as Drianna glanced timidly from one wizard to the other, imagining what horrible spells they might unleash on her in a unified fit of vengeance.

"We met up in the port on Sare," Ranulf explained, absently picking a bramble from Drianna's hood. "She had her bag all packed and was beggin' to come back here with me. I wasn't going to let her, but . . . aw, damn it all, she started to cry. I did a quick truth test on her and it proved she wasn't faking." Ranulf glanced to Drianna with a touch of resentment, reluctant to concede that his soldier's heart had given way to a spate of female tears. "It was her as told me all about the sealing spell and where the Sage's army was holed up. I never would have known otherwise."

Unable to bear their guarded stares any longer, Drianna hastened forward and hurled herself to her knees at Athaya's feet. "I know I don't deserve any kindness from you after what I've done, and you can tell me to get out if you want to, but I simply had to come. I didn't know where else to go. I . . . Brand—" She sniffled delicately, and her lower lip quivered in despair. "He's put me aside. He said I wasn't good enough for him anymore. He . . . he told me to go work in the *kitchens*!"

"This ain't another of your stories, is it?" Tonia asked, her gaze purposefully hard and unforgiving. If Drianna wanted to work her way back into their good graces, Tonia was determined that she not do so too easily. "Like the one about your poor brother in Kilfarnan, or the husband you never had, or—"

"No, no . . . it's not a lie—not this time. I know you have no reason to believe me, but I swear it's all true. You can test me if you like," she offered eagerly. "Ranulf did it that one time, and I didn't mind."

"I don't think that'll be necessary," Jaren said quietly, blinking rapidly as if he'd just been roused from a nap. He shifted his gaze to Athaya. "She's telling the truth. The truth as she believes it to be, anyway."

Athaya took a seat in the first pew and motioned Drianna to get up from the floor and sit beside her. Against reason,

Athaya could not help feeling sorry for her. "Tell me, why did the Sage put you aside?"

Drianna curled her hands into tiny fists to keep from crying again. "H-he . . . searched my mind and said I wasn't ever going to be a wizard. He told me that because of it, I wasn't worthy to be his wife . . . that he could never marry beneath him like that."

Athaya gripped her firmly by the shoulder; her shock at seeing Drianna again had just been rudely eclipsed. Drianna did not know it, but she had just delivered worse news in that one brief sentence than Ranulf had conveyed in the past hour. "He said *what*?"

Stammering, Drianna told her about the seed that Brandegarth had discovered in a kitchen girl named Peg; the germ of dormant magic waiting until its proper time to bloom. To Athaya's dismay, Drianna's description of what the Sage had seen was virtually identical to what she had experienced herself.

"At first I wanted to believe he was lying just to get rid of me," Drianna went on, "but deep down I knew it wasn't true. I know him too well." She took a steadying breath and hung her head in abject misery. "I never should have told him. But once, last winter, I overheard you and Jaren talking about being able to tell who was a wizard before the *mekahn*, and since I wanted to know for myself so badly . . . oh, I never should have told him. It's the only reason he wanted to be sealed at all . . ."

Athaya slouched to one side with her head cradled in her hands. Her mind reeled as she pictured the havoc the Sage could wreak in Caithe with this power. An army, even one peppered with men who could somehow resist the painful influences of a corbal crystal, was no threat at all compared to this errant gift, should the Sage choose to employ it. And Athaya had little doubt what his choice would be. Hordes of young people would flock to his side like hungry birds to an open sack of grain, offering their loyalty in exchange for a glimpse into their future.

And has that talent faded from you as well? she asked herself. Not that it truly mattered—after detecting the seed in a village girl named Emma, Athaya had sworn not to seek such knowledge again. In a land where being a wizard invited nothing but persecution and death, the chance to find out one's fate in advance would ignite an upheaval such as

Caithe had not seen in centuries. And, as Tonia had theorized, scrying such a thing in advance would be circumventing God's will—or worse, twisting it to one's own purposes.
For what else was the *mekahn* but His way of calling to His
chosen? It had only been by accident that Athaya discovered
Durek's son, Mailen, carried the seed, and that volatile secret
she had shared with none but Jaren. But if the Sage could
spy the seeds as well, what good would her secrecy be? And
how long would the heir to Caithe be safe from the Sage's
ambitions?

"The people of Caithe have been taught for centuries that
having magic is a death sentence. In their minds, my refusing
to speak their future is like signing that warrant myself."

"And that's exactly what Brand wants to happen," Drianna
said, reluctantly finishing her tale. "He wants to tell everyone
whether they're to have the power or not and persuade them
that you kept your talent a secret so they'd be forced to join
your side after it was too late for them to do anything else. He
thinks he can turn them against you that way . . . the ones that
haven't already left because of—"

She broke off abruptly and averted her eyes in shame. "I'm
truly sorry for what he did to Prince Nicolas, your Highness.
I know that doesn't help, but . . . I had no idea it would turn
out the way it did."

"He's in good hands," Athaya said, rubbing the growing
fatigue from her eyes. Drianna might know something
about the Sage's compulsion spell that the rest of them did
not, but Athaya hadn't the strength to pursue the subject tonight.

"You haven't exactly brought us good news," she observed,
"but you've given us fair warning. At least now we know what
to expect."

"It's hard to know what to expect from Brand anymore,"
Drianna said worriedly. "The sealing spell . . . it has
changed him. Oh, he was always a bit conceited, I'll grant
you that, but now he acts as if he's the only man on earth
that God has ever deigned to speak to. You may be wizards,
too, but you've never claimed to be better than I am because of it. I knew he felt that way all along, but it didn't
bother me so much . . . until I knew for certain that I'd
never be one of you. But I'm here for good this time . . . if
you'll have me." She sniffled once more and wiped the last

bit of moisture from her eyes. "Just tell me what I can do to help stop him."

"Do?" Athaya laughed mirthlessly. "I don't have the faintest idea what any of us can do. No yet, anyway. But thank you," she said, dividing her gaze between Drianna and Ranulf. "I'm not sure what I'm going to do with all of this information yet, but I'm grateful to have it. And it's good to have you back." She gave Drianna's hand a gentle squeeze. "Both of you." True, she had been hurt by Drianna's betrayal, but Athaya had never disliked her. And now that Drianna had gotten a taste of betrayal as well— and been changed by it—Athaya knew that they all had troubles enough without clinging to old grudges.

Ranulf belched his satisfaction. "Now why don't one o' you prove how happy you all are to see me by fetching me another beer."

Grumbling merrily, Tonia snatched up his mug and invited him to follow her to the casks.

"And send Kale to me on your way out," Athaya called after them, appending a suggestion that Drianna get herself something to drink as well. Drianna was reluctant to be seen among the others at first, but thirst quickly won out—as soon as Ranulf promised to physically close the mouth of anyone who objected to her presence back at the camp.

Once they had gone, Athaya caught Jaren studying her dubiously. "What do you need Kale for?" he asked, easing closer to her. "If you're thinking what I *think* you are—"

"I probably am," she confessed with a shrug. "But do you have any better ideas?"

Kale answered her summons as promptly as if the king himself had sent for him. He had been with Athaya from the beginning, having deserted his post in the King's Guard soon after Captain Graylen's death. Though not a wizard himself, the old soldier was unswervingly loyal and had saved her life—and Jaren's—on more than one occasion. Tonight, however, the scarred hands held a delicate handcarved flute instead of a weapon—an item, Athaya thought, much more worthy of his gentle heart than a sword or crossbow could ever be.

"You sent for me, my Lady?"

"Yes, Kale. I need you to do something for me later tonight, once everyone's gone to sleep. Something very important." With the toe of her slipper, she prodded the edge of a loose stone in the chapel floor. Beneath it was buried the most lethal of weapons—a priceless crown of corbals, stolen from the king on the day he had tried to force her recantation before the people of Kaiburn. The boy who had stolen it later died for his effort, but little had Cameron suspected that he had procured the very item that could hold the key to their salvation.

"I want you to dig up the strongbox and take it away from camp—a mile, at the very least. Open it up someplace extremely dark; if enough moonlight hits those crystals, we may feel them even at such a distance. Then I want you to pry a few corbals loose from their settings. Get a variety of sizes and wrap each one up tight. When you're done, come back and bury the strongbox again. Tomorrow morning, bring the loose corbals to me."

Kale's brows arched substantially. "To . . . *you?*"

"Yes, Kale," she said, knowing it sounded as odd as a prisoner requesting that another rat be placed in his cell. She offered him a crooked smile. "I haven't had a headache in a while and thought I was about due."

Jaren crossed his arms over his chest, visibly displeased, but also aware that they were rather short of options at the moment. "I knew it."

"If we can learn how to stand up to these crystals, too, then we've got a chance to surprise him." Athaya curled into a tight little ball in the pew, hugging her knees to her chest. "I remember the first night that Rhodri came to me in the dungeon—the night I accused him of trying to torture you to death with that corbal crystal. He told me—how did he phrase it?—that it was all a trick, just like Ranulf said. That the corbal doesn't *cause* pain, but deludes a wizard's mind into thinking the pain is there. He said you could have stayed in agony forever, until you either went crazy, or killed yourself to escape a pain that didn't really exist."

Jaren stiffened a bit; the memory of that raking pain, however false, was powerful still. "But to start off cold, without any idea of what to do—"

"We may not know, but I'll wager Drianna does—at least in theory. And if she's sincere about joining us, she'll be glad to tell us anything she knows about how the Sage wields his power." Athaya's eyes blazed with dark intensity as she listened to the singing and laughter of her campmates, as yet ignorant of the peril rising in the west. "Maybe my power isn't as strong as it was, but I'm going to figure out how the Sage resists those crystals. At this point, it may be our only chance at stopping him."

CHAPTER 5

※※

THE MORNING AFTER THE MIDSUMMER FEAST, ATHAYA, Jaren, Kale, and Drianna packed a basket of food, a flagon of watered wine, and a menacing collection of tightly wrapped corbal crystals and set out from the camp. Their destination was a small clearing roughly a mile north of the monastery grounds; at that distance, Athaya's experiments with the crystals should not disturb the others.

She was, on the contrary, expecting to get the headache of her life.

"If you're so certain of making yourself ill, then wouldn't it be best to stay closer to home?" Kale ventured, increasingly unsettled at the growing distance their footsteps took them from the sanctuary of the forest camp. He cast furtive glances over his shoulder every so often, as if suspicious that the seemingly tranquil expanse of pines and brambles and snowy white trilliums around them cloaked the presence of the Tribunal's agents—or the Sage's. "Can't you just do your . . . 'experiments' inside a set of wards?"

"I wish it were that simple." Athaya smiled resignedly at him, grateful for his concern but powerless to alter the reason for it. "Wards may act as a barrier against magic, but they don't work against corbal crystals. Remember the day we found Cordry and that priest—Father Greste, it was—surprised us with a corbal-studded candlestick? Ranulf had conjured wards to keep Cordry's spells from harming anyone, but the

69

crystal's influences passed right through them. Luckily for Cordry, he was early enough in his *mekahn* that the crystal couldn't hurt him much. No," Athaya went on, somewhat pensive, "whatever power a corbal has, it doesn't work quite the same way spells do. I'm afraid we don't know everything about corbals yet," she conceded with a shrug, "but thanks to Drianna, we're about to find out a little bit more."

"Have you told Master Hedric about any of this yet?" Jaren asked her, drawing back a snarled curtain of ivy and grape vines from the trail to let Athaya pass.

"I opened a panel to him earlier this morning," she replied. "He was as surprised as the rest of us to learn that there's some way other than a sealing spell to avoid being hurt by a corbal. And as you might expect," she added with an obligatory air, "he told me to be careful."

"I just don't see how this talent can be commonplace on Sare—and has been for centuries, apparently—and yet not even our Great Masters know a thing about it, much less how it's done. There's not even the slightest reference to such a thing in the *Book of Sages*."

"It was probably something the Sarians stumbled across by accident. I can't imagine they set out to conquer the corbals on purpose." She tossed a wry grin over one shoulder. "After all, how often did it occur to *you* to sit in a room with some corbal crystals and see how long it would take to make them stop hurting? That's like pressing your hand against a hot cauldron and trying to make your flesh stop burning—not something any sane person would do to enliven an otherwise dull evening."

Drianna, having fallen a few yards behind to pick a handful of rose hips for the evening's tea, stuffed the tender treasures into her basket and hurried to catch up. "Bran— the Sage," she hastily corrected with a sneer, determined never to use the endearment again, "told me that it was Dameronne himself who first discovered how to do it—and it wasn't any accident." She snagged her sleeve on a protruding sumac branch and paused for a moment while Kale stepped up to free it. "After King Faltil killed most of the wizards in Caithe two centuries ago, the handful that escaped to Sare knew they needed to find a way to withstand the crystals. Before Faltil's scourge, the crystals had never been used as a weapon on such a large scale. No one truly realized the damage they could do."

"I can believe that," Jaren observed. "In Reyka, everyone

knows what corbals can do, but nobody worries much about it. The crystals are all but nonexistent, and there hasn't been a single instance in our history when they've been used for a massive assault like Faltil's. So why would anyone bother to suffer through a great deal of pain to learn how to defend against a weapon they'll probably never face?"

"But the Sarian wizards expected to face it," Drianna pointed out solemnly. "Dameronne's prophecy convinced them that they were destined to return to Caithe and rule one day—and they knew they would be confronting the crystals then. In order for the Lorngeld to rule Caithe permanently, Dameronne knew they had to find a way around this weakness. They took some of Faltil's corbal-studded weapons back to Sare to use for practice, and then, once the technique was finally discovered, each wizard to become Sage passed the knowledge on. Brandegarth learned how to resist corbals from the man who was Sage before him. That is," she added sourly, "before he Challenged him and took his place."

"But where did Dameronne begin?" Athaya asked, overwhelmed by the immensity of such a task, as if someone had just handed her a pickax, gestured to a vast limestone quarry, and told her to build a castle by sunset. "How did he even know where to start?"

Drianna lowered her thick lashes, shamed by this fragment of her Sarian heritage. "He started with drugs," she murmured, her voice as soft as the summer breeze stirring the pines. "Pastle seed, specifically; the plant is native to Sare. Inhaling the powdered seeds sharpens your thinking and makes physical sensations more acute—that is, as long as you don't use too much or grow addicted to it. No small number of Sarians have, and it eventually leaves them unable to cast a simple witchlight, much less anything more difficult. I've heard it said that Dameronne used pastle seed from time to time—some believe it's the only way he could have foreseen your crusade so far in advance—so it's logical to believe he would have used it to try and defeat the corbals, too."

"Just the reverse of looca-smoke," Jaren said thoughtfully, pondering Drianna's story with a scholar's studied detachment. "Looca-smoke numbs the mind so the corbal's pain isn't as intense, but at the same time, it leaves you too addled to use your magic. Pastle seed does exactly the opposite."

Athaya felt a sickly flutter in her belly. Surely there was some other way of mastering the power of a corbal crystal!

Even if the pastle plant could be obtained, she staunchly refused to scramble her brains by experimenting with its dangerous seeds. After enduring both her *mekahn* and the sealing spell in the span of a single year, the thought of forsaking complete control over her wits was abhorrent to her. "But Ranulf didn't say anything about the Sage using a drug . . ."

"No. Pastle seed is only a stepping stone. Once you know the secret of the corbal's power, you can gradually wean yourself from the drug. Theoretically, anyway. Most wizards still need it as a crutch to defy all but the smallest crystals. But the Sage never had to use pastle seed at all—not even when he engaged more than one crystal at a time. His adept abilities gave him the skill he required without it."

Athaya let out a thin sigh of relief; if Brandegarth had learned to battle the corbals without the drug, then she should be able to do the same. "The drug explains how the trick was discovered, but what exactly *is* the trick itself? What did the pastle seed allow Dameronne and the others to learn about the crystals?" Athaya stepped over the rotting remains of a fallen birch and then turned back to Drianna. "You've seen the Sage work with corbals before . . . did he ever tell you exactly how he does it?"

Drianna bobbed her head, eager to be of use to her new allies in any way she could. "He liked to talk to me about his magic, though I didn't always understand everything he said. Once, he told me that all a wizard has to do is learn to tell the corbal is *doesn't* hurt as strongly as the corbal is telling you it *does*. I can't imagine a piece of rock actually 'saying' anything," she added with a baffled frown, "but I know that's what he said. If you push back hard enough, you can suspend the crystal's power over you."

Athaya's first impulse was to dismiss the explanation as too simplistic to be useful, but then she stopped abruptly on the narrow trail and shifted a meaningful gaze to Jaren. "Just like Nicolas and the spell of compulsion."

Yes, Hedric had described her brother's inner struggle in strikingly similar terms. *Much of his mental energies are involved with combating the spell.* As strongly as the Sage's compulsion bade Nicolas to do his brother harm, Nicolas in turn rebelled against it, but the price of the constant effort left him simple-minded. The Sage's technique was much the same, the only difference being that applying his mental energies to the corbal's covert persuasions left his spells out of reach, but not his elemental self.

"The Sage once told me that it was rather like battling another wizard during a Challenge," Drianna added. "The corbal uses its power to make him feel pain, and he uses his own abilities to resist the compulsion and turn the pain aside."

Athaya furrowed her brows; it sounded simple enough in theory, but she doubted very much that it would prove so easy in practice. "To push back against a corbal without giving in to the pain must take a great deal of focused concentration."

Drianna lifted the hem of her skirt and hopped over a patch of mud in her path. "The Sage spoke quite often about the need for a disciplined mind. Before he practiced with his crystals, he would recite things to clear his mind of distractions— children's rhymes, bits of poetry ... and Dameronne's prophecy," she added with a subtle scowl. "He used to recite them aloud, but as he got better he just repeated the litany in his head. Then, once he faced the crystal itself, he used those same disciplines to overpower it. He likened it to defending against mind-magic—a traditional weapon of the Challenge. You must take control of your thoughts so they can't be manipulated so easily by your enemy."

The longer Athaya thought on it, the more credible the Sage's strategy became. Master Hedric had long since taught her that the key to perfecting wizardry of any kind was to be found in mental discipline; clearly, much as they would chafe in unison at being likened to their Reykan brethren and their more prudent approach to magic, the Sarian wizards used that same philosophy to avoid falling victim to the crystal's seductions. Regardless of the tradition, be it Reykan or Sarian, Athaya had learned the wisdom of discipline first-hand. The rote memorization that Master Hedric forced on her was intended to sharpen her mind and it was that expertly honed control that helped her fend off the devastating effects of the sealing spell as long as she had. Her last memory of the previous summer was reciting the Succession of Circles time and time again to keep her mind from splitting apart at the agonizing pressure of captive power wailing to be free. *Credony, lord of the first Circle, twenty-six years; Sidra, lord of the second ...*

Without the familiar sanctuary of that mindless chant, she would never have lived long enough be rescued.

"This could explain why only the Sage can overpower the

larger corbals without resorting to pastle seed," Jaren mused. "Only adepts have the level of concentration required. After all, they're trained to higher levels of mental discipline out of sheer necessity—they need that degree of control to master their more potent level of power. Curious . . . the stronger a wizard you are, the more intensely you feel a corbal's pain. Now it looks as if that weakness is also a hidden strength."

Athaya plucked a maple leaf from an overhanging branch and shredded it worriedly between her fingers; hidden strength or no, she foresaw one vital drawback to this talent. "I gather, then, that the Sage has to reach this state of concentration *before* someone confronts him with a corbal crystal—I mean, if someone takes him by surprise, he wouldn't be able to focus his thoughts enough to fight it, what with his paths crossing this way and that."

Drianna nodded reluctantly. "Several years ago, he asked me to sneak up on him with a crystal without telling him when or where, just to see whether he could drive the pain back once it already had him in its grip. He tried, but he simply couldn't do it. It made him terribly cross," she added, eyes flashing with belated vengeance.

Frowning deeply, Athaya tossed the skeletal remains of the maple leaf aside. "All this talk about corbals makes me wonder . . . If the crystals make us think we're in pain, then why don't they inflict pain on everyone? Why just wizards? Our paths—and our magic, of course—are the only thing wizards have that other people don't. There's got to be a link somewhere. I can't believe it's just a coincidence."

Jaren offered his hand to help her over a fallen log in their path. "Coincidence or not, the last thing you need right now is another riddle to distract you," he advised. He tilted his head in the direction of Drianna's willow basket. "You've got an appointment with some corbal crystals."

Obligingly, Athaya abandoned the mystery to focus on the task at hand. "So what we know is this: a corbal makes it impossible to work our spells because our paths cross—or we're deceived into thinking they do—making it impossible to locate our spells. And even if we could find the right spell, the pain, real or not, robs us of the concentration we need to cast it. So the secret is to mentally steel ourselves in advance and then block the pain by sending out thoughts of defiance. We can't work any magic while we're doing it, but at least we can think straight—that is, unless we stop pushing back and let the crystal overpower us."

"That about sums it up," Jaren remarked with an approving nod. "Just don't forget to write all of that down in your journal for posterity. The one you promised Master Hedric you'd start the moment you got back to camp, remember?"

Athaya looked away evasively; as Jaren suspected, she had completely forgotten her pledge. "Oh, that."

By this time, they had reached the clearing they sought. Kale spread a pair of wool blankets in a sunny patch of grass near a winding creek, while Drianna unpacked the basket, careful to leave the corbals undisturbed for the moment, and doled out four equal portions of molasses bread, green cheese, and blueberries.

Jaren gathered up his ration in a scrap of cloth and turned to go. "I'll see you in a few hours," he said, offering Athaya a quick kiss on the cheek. "Have a very pleasant headache."

"Sure you don't want to stay?" she asked playfully, swishing away a bee that had grown overly interested in her meal.

Jaren shook his head in adamant refusal. "You'll be in a sour enough mood when you get back. If we both go home with splitting skulls, we'll be sniping at each other all night. And besides, if the Sage's best magicians can't overpower a corbal crystal without resorting to pastle seed, then nobody on our side has much chance of mastering them besides you. I'll go back and help Marya with her wards for a while, and then I'm due in the kitchens." He expelled a shallow sigh of resignation. "I'm not sure what I did to deserve it, but Master Tonia volunteered me to help bake the rest of those blueberries into pies this afternoon."

Athaya teased him with a grin. "Really, Jaren. You ought to find yourself a dutiful wife to do things like that for you."

"I'll keep my eyes open," he replied with a smirk, and then sauntered along the banks of the creek, munching on a slab of bread and quickly winking out of sight behind the massive trunk of an oak tree.

Once they had all finished eating, Athaya brushed a flurry of soft breadcrumbs from her skirt and settled into a comfortable cross-legged position on the blanket. "Start with the smallest crystal you have," she said, motioning to the small leather pouch poised in Kale's hands. "And make sure to hold it away from the shade so that the sunlight can hit it directly."

Athaya expelled a bubble of dry laughter at the instructions she had just given. *A bit like telling the executioner exactly how to hold the ax.*

"I'm not going to try and resist the pain at first, so don't worry if I grimace a bit in the beginning. I've never taken a very close look at a corbal before—not since my magic came, anyway—so I want to study it for a while. Get . . . 'acquainted' with it," she added, conscious of how absurd that must sound to the others. *Not only telling him how to hold the ax,* she mused, *but politely inquiring as to the blade's construction and history of use.*

"That is wise," Kale observed, surprisingly accepting of her strategy. "Knowing the true nature of your enemy is often the key to defeating him, not physical strength alone."

The feathery hairs at the nape of her neck bristled as Athaya lifted her finger and bade Kale to produce the first crystal. Her flesh prickled with sweat as she braced for the expected barrage of pain. With morbid fascination, she watched Kale slowly unwrap the crystal—a tiny one, no larger than an apple seed.

She made no effort to repel the corbal's small measure of power, allowing it to trickle over her freely. The gem was tiny enough to cause only mild discomfort even in daylight. The pain was an irritant, but not overly distracting—like the gentle ache of a tired muscle or the fading itch of a mosquito bite.

Letting the rest of the world fade around her, Athaya reached out and embraced the corbal with her senses. Her touch was wary, like running a tentative finger across a blade to test its sharpness without cutting flesh. Despite its threat of pain, the crystal was quite beautiful. Sunlight danced across its myriad facets, dazzling her eyes with indigo beauty. Some of its edges were flat and shiny, like new glass, others were ridged and murky, like a chunk of ice clouded with dirt and leaf mold. Its purple shade shifted from light to dark with the crystal's grain—sometimes sheer, other times opaque. It was as if Kale held a tiny mountain in his palm, she thought, with slopes and peaks and hidden caves, ripe for exploration.

Just beneath the surface of her awareness, Athaya heard the restless murmur of the corbal's voice like a babbling stream, endlessly bidding her to feel pain and to flee its menacing presence. But though she called it a 'voice,' the crystal did not commune with words, but spoke to her in the deeper, more inaccessible language of emotion and sensation.

Athaya sucked in a breath and held it. *Just like magic.*

When her power was newly born, Jaren had guided her through her inner paths—that labyrinthine chain of caverns whose hidden alcoves were home to all her spells—instructing her to discover her spells by sensation, like groping in the dark for a flintbox with which to light a lamp. Each spell was marked by runes etched on the canvas of her mind; runes that spoke in wordless whispers to the farthest recesses of her mind, telling her the nature of the magic they invoked. When she opened herself to the runes of a witchlight, they warmed her with the gentle heat of a candle's flame; when she touched upon the spell of translocation, she was enveloped by feelings of security and flight.

Likewise, the corbal flooded her with thoughts of pain and warned her away from its presence.

Athaya expelled her breath slowly. If the corbal was, in essence, casting a spell of deception at her, then where was its magic coming from?

She thought again of her paths, and then of the source that was the locus of all those twisting corridors—the inner spring from which all her magic flowed.

Was it possible?

Intrigued, and not a little unnerved, Athaya allowed her senses to drift deeper, determined to seek the treasures of this cavern without regard to the beasts that might be guarding it. But when her senses brushed against the center of the gem, she felt a sudden upsurge in its strength; the pain, slight as it was, came back to gnaw at her more diligently. The crystal's voice grew louder, compelling her to surrender.

Retreating slightly from the crystal's core, Athaya stared in muted awe at the little gem. She saw her own face reflected in her enemy's glittering slopes and realized that their natures were not so different as she first supposed. Just as the locus of her paths was the source of her magic, so was the core of the crystal's facets the root of its own.

Athaya chewed on her lip thoughtfully. A corbal crystal was not a living thing—not in any sense she knew of life—but it was still a thing of power. Was it so odd, then, to think that its power had a source as well?

And what better way to block the crystal's pain, she reasoned, than to dam it at its source?

The crystal's grip on her was weak—too weak to foul her concentration for the task that lay ahead. Breathing deep,

Athaya focused both eyes and thoughts on the crystal's heart. *I feel nothing from you,* she told it, scouring it with her gaze. Her voice was nonthreatening but resolute, as if disciplining a beloved but unruly child. *You cannot harm me now. I know your secrets and you have no power over me . . .*

Athaya repeated the litany over and over until it came unthinkingly, bubbling up from the depths of memory. To sharpen her focus, she pictured each word as her mind gave it silent voice, fixating on the shape of each letter, the sound of each syllable. Soon, she no longer felt the warmth of the sun on her hair, or the tickle of ants as they scurried across her ankles. All she knew were the words, pressed against the crystal's heart like a blade.

I feel nothing from you. You cannot harm me now. I know your secrets and you have no power over me . . .

Not long after, the crystal's power was engulfed and the voice was all but silent. A heady rush of triumph washed over her, but Athaya persisted in her efforts despite the powerful temptation to cry out. She couldn't afford to let her victory distract her. A misstep might not matter with a tiny gem like this, but it would matter a great deal later on, when she met with larger stones.

I feel nothing from you . . .

The corbal's pain was gone, negated by sheer force of will.

Now she faced the second part of her task: to ease out of her intensely focused state enough to reenter the world around her. She had to divide her attentions in two, sustaining her battle with the crystal while she went back to the business of living, exerting conscious control over her own thoughts, words, and actions. Again, the similarities between this task and her first lessons with magic surprised her; dividing her attentions was remarkably like the dual sight she experienced when learning to cast spells within her paths. Until it became instinctive, her mind's eye view of her paths was superimposed over her eyes' view of the world—until the spell was cast and the image flickered away.

Her reflexes were slow but controlled as she tore her eyes from the crystal, floating upward as if from the bottom of a pool. She discerned the details of her surroundings as clearly as before, but the creek seemed to flow more sluggishly, as if the water was thickened with honey, and the wind curled languidly through the pines, like an endless sigh.

"I can do it," she said. She articulated each word with infinite care, but they still came out slightly slurred. She lifted her hand—clumsily so, as if she had never used the limb before—and gestured to the leather pouch. "Try another crystal, Kale. One that's slightly larger."

She felt her control waver when she spoke, and the crystal's tiny voice tugged on her mind, growing louder and more insistent. But its urgings were abruptly silenced as Kale wrapped it in wool and tucked it deep inside the pouch.

Athaya did not move except to breathe, wishing to do nothing to shatter her precarious trancelike state. She braced herself for the next crystal, one whose voice would be louder and more demanding, and sent out continual streams of defiant thoughts, ready to aim them at the crystal's heart.

Kale unwrapped the second stone, but its power was quickly blunted against her psychic shield. Blunted, but not dispelled. It took mere seconds to realize that this would not be so easy a struggle; the crystal assaulted her with more strength than she expected, trying to shatter the walls of her resistance like her sealed magic had once tried to tear its way out of its prison.

Soon, Athaya felt in danger of being swept away in the current of the corbal's demands. *Pain, pain, pain!* it said in its language without words. *Flee from the danger!* Her brain tingled in response, on the verge of unconscious surrender. The corbal's influences teemed over her like rainwater, working their way inside the tiny cracks in her resistance and tainting her concentration. She was a scant step away from caving in to its compulsion before her mind seized once more upon its task.

I feel nothing from you. You cannot harm me now. I know your secrets and you have no power over me.

Pain, pain, pain! Flee from the danger!

She focused her glassy gaze on the crystal in Kale's hand—confronting her enemy face-to-face, staring it down in a contest of wills. *I feel nothing from you . . .*

The pain retreated from her onslaught, but Athaya felt her strength ebbing; she doubted she could sustain the battle much longer. Fat beads of sweat dribbled from her forehead, and she grew light-headed from both the heat and effort.

"I've got it . . . I don't feel—*ow!*" She flinched at the sharp pinch of pain, as if someone had just driven a thorn between her eyes. She had barely drawn her next breath before Kale stuffed the crystal back into the safety of its dark pouch and laced it tightly closed.

"Are you all right?" Drianna asked, arms poised to catch Athaya should she topple over from exhaustion.

"I think so," Athaya glared at the pouch holding the crystal, thinking it pathetic that it took such labor to overcome such a tiny enemy. "I just lost my focus there at the end."

Once confident that she would not faint, Athaya staggered unsteadily to the creek and splashed a handful of cold water on her face to restore herself. Her limbs quivered with fatigue; the struggle had cost her more than she realized at the time.

But the battle could be won, she reminded herself. And that was all that mattered.

It was a success, but an admittedly small step in an arduous journey. The Sage had been perfecting this skill for over twenty years and she for roughly twenty minutes. And by Drianna's own admission, the Sage could resist more than one crystal at a time—crystals undoubtedly larger than the little fragment she had just engaged in battle.

You always said I was a quick learner, Master Hedric, she thought, as she scooped up another handful of water and slapped it on her cheeks. *I hope you were right . . . for all our sakes.*

"Give me a minute to catch my breath, Kale," she said over her shoulder, her determination refreshed as well as her body by the water dripping from her face and hair. She was *not* going to be bested by a tiny chip of purple rock. "And then let's try again."

CHAPTER 6

❋

DUREK TRELANE, KING OF CAITHE AND LORD OF THE ISLE of Sare—though most residents of that island would take great amusement at the latter claim—returned the ivory comb and pair of peach-colored ribbons to their place in the queen's favorite willow basket and fixed an angry glare upon the bruised and battered guardsman standing before him. The interruption itself was bad enough; the reason for it considerably worse.

Durek had ventured to her Majesty's solar earlier that morning to find his son's favorite playthings—Cecile had written that Mailen missed the cloth puppets and would his Majesty kindly send them?—and had somehow lingered until midday, brooding in solitude as he poked through Cecile's abandoned ribbons and beads and scraps of half-finished needlework. He savored the fading scent of rosewater that clung to the queen's possessions—as it had to the lady herself—like a delicate mist. The south-facing chamber was shrouded in gloom due to a soaking summer rain, making Durek peevish enough without the further aggravation of his captain's news.

When the mayor of Eriston had arrived a fortnight before, spinning a wild and disjointed tale of a house seized by wizards and begging for men to expunge them, Durek presumed the man either drunk or a lunatic. Parr's report, however, confirmed that the mayor was neither.

"Are you trying to tell me," Durek said, his eyes narrowing

a fraction more with every syllable, "that of the full squadron of well-armed and well-trained men I sent to expel those foul wizards from that man's foul house, only *three* came back alive?" He slammed his palm down on the enameled surface of the queen's table so hard that a ball of yellow twine toppled from the willow basket, rapidly unraveling as it rolled across the carpeted floor. "What sort of men are you training, Captain, that find it so difficult to lift a corbal crystal to the sun and watch these magicians fall prostrate to the ground?"

Captain Parr shifted his injured arm in its sling and tried to suppress his anger, but could not hide the crimson flush that crept from the base of his neck to the tips of his ears. "The mayor is waiting in the corridor, sire, if you wish to confirm my report. And it wasn't my men's fault," he added, with as much overt indignation as he dared display. "As I said, their crystals were all but useless." The captain's harshly sculpted features settled into a mystified frown—an expression he rarely had cause to exhibit.

Beside him, the newly invested Archbishop of Delfarham was likewise mystified. He knew the captain bore bad news when he met him at the gates and accompanied him to the solar, but *this*? Jon Lukin was not a man to allow himself to be surprised by anything—and would never admit it even if he were—but Parr's news clearly troubled him. His normally scornful eyes betrayed a rare measure of uncertainty, and he pulled absently at the collar of his cassock as if it had suddenly grown too stiff and chafed his throat.

"The six Justices that accompanied your men—they had corbal crystals as well. Gems ritually blessed and sanctified for such work."

"Useless as well, your Grace. And the men just as dead."

Lukin blinked rapidly—as blatant a sign of shock as he permitted himself to reveal. To his own surprise, as well as that of his king, he could think of nothing at all to say.

Durek fixed an unblinking stare upon his captain. "Tell me."

Parr's owl-like eyes went dark with shame as he recounted the unpleasantly one-sided battle. "We thought to eliminate the wizards' leader first, so we surrounded the mayor's house early one morning and began to move in. But we didn't surprise anyone," he added bitterly. "They knew we were coming. Somehow."

"No doubt they were spying on you with those cursed

globes of theirs," Lukin supplied, his upper lip curling with disdain.

The captain agreed with an eager nod, quick to accept the explanation. But even knowing the fight had been unfair, his face burned with humiliation at how thoroughly his men had been defeated. "They jumped us from behind, sire. I held up my dagger to one of them—it had a corbal in the hilt. There was plenty of light, but ... the man just laughed at me. He *laughed*!" Parr winced, still mortified at the memory.

"It was the same with all of us," he went on. He labored to swallow, as if trying to force a poorly chewed piece of meat down his throat. "The wizards took advantage of our surprise to rob us of our weapons and then routed us with magic. They set traps for us, trying to force us all into one room—blocking one hall and then another with images of fire and demons and dogs with foaming mouths. I didn't realize it was all a trick at first, but then I remembered how real those angels were in Kaiburn that day—the ones Father Aldus created to frighten us so that he could rescue Princess Athaya. I tried to get my men to follow me through the illusions, but most of them were too afraid. In the end, only three of us made it to safety. A few of the wizards chased us for a while ... they could have killed us, but seemed content enough with this." The captain's eyes skimmed over his fractured arm, the soiled bandage wrapped tight about one thigh, and the vicious burns striping his throat and hands. Burns, Durek reflected, much like those that had scarred his father's body after Athaya's sorcerous assault. "They probably let us escape so we could tell you what had happened."

Durek studied his captain intensely. Parr had a mature grittiness about him that far exceeded his twenty-four years, and his injuries only added to the aura. He had learned much since inheriting the captaincy from Tyler Graylen, but he still hadn't mastered the art of hiding his emotions; Durek could tell that he was deeply shaken by the attack.

The king's continued silence prompted the captain to continue. "Once the wizards stopped chasing us, I circled around the gardens in back of the house and watched the rest through a small window." Parr shook his head, still reeling from what he had witnessed days before. "The leader didn't even touch the men he had captured. He just told them that their heartbeats were slowing and at the count of ten would stop completely. The men all looked bewitched, sire—as if in a waking sleep. And when he reached the count of ten, the men clutched their chests and fell. Dead. It was like he told them it would happen and because they believed it . . . it did."

Deeply disturbed, Durek tightened his jaw and glanced to his archbishop, silently requesting his counsel.

"It seems your sister has gone beyond simple heresy," Lukin observed, less disturbed by the loss of the king's men than by the loss of Eriston itself. "After denying it for years, she now reveals her true desire—to take Caithe for herself, and in time, your place on the throne."

"The wizards who attacked us claimed not to be among her followers, sire," Parr pointed out. Disbelief was clear upon his face, but it was his sworn duty to report all that he had seen and heard. "One cannot trust the words of a wizard, of course, but these men called the princess a traitor to their kind."

"A—?" The king's brows shot up as he flirted with laughter. "At least we share an opinion on that, if nothing else," he replied. Curtly, he motioned his captain toward the door. "Fetch in this wretched mayor of yours . . . what's his name again?"

"Lafert, sire. Joseph Lafert."

At the captain's summons, a harried-looking old man scurried into the solar. White hair sprouted from his skull in bewildered clumps and his nose twitched like a squirrel who has just spied a hoard of acorns. He favored his king with a low and wholly ungraceful bow. "Thank you for allowing me into your presence once again, your Majesty," the mayor of Eriston said, feverishly wringing a pair of blue-veined hands. "These are dire days indeed, and it is heartening to know that your Majesty takes such an active interest in the troubles of his—"

"What's all this about corbal crystals not working?" Durek replied, squelching the man's flow of flattery before it curdled his mood even further. He patently believed Parr's tale, but wished to hear the mayor's version of it nonetheless.

The old man's nose twitched again. "Y-yes, sire. The captain has the right of it. These eyes may not see what they used to, but I saw *that* well enough. Not even God's holy gems could stand against them, your Grace. They're the Devil's own brood, that much is sure."

At Durek's bidding, Lafert recounted how the wizards had appropriated his house several weeks before, and how, despite the best efforts of both the town's militia and the soldiers summoned from the neighboring shire of Nadiera, nothing would dislodge them.

"How many of these wizards are there in Eriston?" Durek asked his captain.

"I saw roughly a dozen at the house itself," Parr replied grudgingly, furious that his squadron had been bested by so few, "but there are rumors of over a thousand men camped in the fields to the east. I passed near the area on my way out of Eriston, but saw nothing."

Durek's face turned as bleak as the rainclouds hanging low in the sky above them. "None of us has ever seen one of Athaya's camps, either, but we all know they exist. Her people hide themselves with spells and trickery." He flicked a hasty glance of dismissal to the mayor. "If there's nothing else, then you may go."

Lafert cleared his throat, politely informing his sovereign that there was indeed something else, and the wringing of his hands became even more frenzied. "Actually, sire, if I could . . . I was hoping that . . ."

"Yes, yes," Durek growled impatiently, whirling his hand in a circular motion to speed along the man's request. "Spit it out."

"I beg you to send more men, sire. My home must be liberated from these sorcerers!"

"More men?" The king arched his brows. "After losing nine of my best soldiers already? I doubt your town house is worth such a price, sir."

"But the citizens of Eriston are terrified, sire . . . the ones that haven't already been seduced to the enemy's side. And the Sage's men are everywhere—"

"Wait—the who?" Durek felt his stomach sink a little; he had heard the name before, some months ago, but had dismissed it as yet another of his sister's colorful fabrications.

"The Sage, sire," Lafert repeated, eyes darting about the solar as if fearing the words alone were enough to summon the man himself. "The Sage of Sare."

Durek sank back into his chair and scratched at his scrubby beard with one of Cecile's combs. "Again I hear this name." Then he folded his brows into a grim frown and dropped his voice to a whisper. "Maybe she wasn't lying after all." He fired an exasperated glare at his captain, pointing the ivory comb at him as if it were a dagger. "Why didn't you mention that before?"

Rarely admonished by his king, Captain Parr was temporarily flustered. "I . . . that is—"

"One wizard is much like any other," Lukin remarked, rescuing the captain from his discomfort. "It hardly matters what title their leader bestows upon himself."

"I wonder." Durek's gaze returned to the beleaguered mayor of Eriston. "Tell me . . . this 'Sage' and his followers. Are they in league with my sister?"

"I-it's hard to say, sire." Lafert stopped wringing his hands long enough to turn the palms up in a gesture of ignorance. "Myself, I doubt it. The Sage's men do not speak well of her at all."

Durek snorted dryly as he drummed his fingertips noisily on the table. "Few people do."

"They say she cheats the Lorngeld by not telling them their true destiny. They believe that their magic is a gift from God—of all the absurd notions!—and that they deserve to rule Caithe by right of it."

"To rule—" A ghostly chill rippled down Durek's spine. Yes, Athaya had warned him of that, too.

He opened his mouth to draw breath, readying a string of curses that, curiously, never came. It was too puzzling by half, the idea that Athaya had actually been forthright with him. He wasn't about to trust her—that would be going too far—but perhaps he had misjudged her by some small amount. Unless, he mused, her honesty was all part of a ploy designed to make him place false trust in her. But when had his troublesome sister ever been so shrewd?

"Did you hear this as well?" he asked his captain.

"These traitors say that you are not our rightful king and that it was their duty to provide the chosen one. They seem to think it's this leader of theirs." Parr sniffed his contempt for the man, reclaiming a bit of lost dignity. "He seems an arrogant boor." But behind the insult, flung from a safe distance, was the knowledge that the Sage could have killed him without half an effort; the ugly burns striping his flesh were proof enough of that, and they had been dealt by an underling, not the Sage himself. "He styles himself a king already; fine clothes, jewels—even a silver coronet."

"Upstart," Durek huffed, although there was profound concern behind the snub. He waved his hand as if to clear the room of an unpleasant variety of incense. "Leave us now," he said to the mayor and his captain. "I wish to discuss this matter privately with Archbishop Lukin."

Although Lafert yearned to ask whether more men would be

sent to reclaim his house, he dutifully let Captain Parr usher him from the room. The solar was quiet for a long time once the king and his archbishop were alone, utterly still but for the steady sheeting of the rain against the windowpanes. To his dismay, Durek found the gloom even more oppressive than it had been an hour before.

"Jon?" He asked the clergyman's views with that single word, but did not immediately receive a reply. Durek arched a brow; never had he seen the zealous clergymen—or any priest for that matter—at a loss for words.

"Troubling news indeed, sire. These wizards clearly know some sort of spell that protects them from the gems. But how could it be *so*?" he added, addressing the dim recesses of the ceiling as if asking the question more of God than of Durek. "If the Lorngeld know of such a trick, then why did they not use it to save themselves during Faltil's scourge two centuries ago?"

"Perhaps they thought mass-slaughter was their destiny at the time," Durek replied sarcastically. He tossed the ivory comb back amid the ribbons and beads in Cecile's basket. "Or perhaps they have only recently figured out how to do it. Whichever it is, we have a problem."

"Surely Faltil's crown would stop them," Lukin pronounced, nodding approvingly at the idea. "I know precisely where it is. One of your sister's people told me. Right before he died."

Durek leveled him with a glare. "That's just fine, Jon. If you can think of a way to steal that damned thing back from the heart of Athaya's camp, then go do it."

Lukin muffled his ire as best he could, thinking it prudent to change the subject. "The mayor blames the loss of his home on this mysterious wizard from Sare, but I would wager every coin in the treasury that your sister is behind it all. This 'Sage of Sare' is nothing but a soldier in her pay—a mercenary hired to do the foul deeds she does not wish the Caithan people to know she commits."

Durek was only half listening to the archbishop's speech, distracted by how well Athaya's story fit together with recent events. "If Athaya was working with this Sage to undermine me, then why didn't she give me the chance? She came to my bedchamber shortly after Nicolas was arrested and never laid a hand on me—she certainly could have done away with me if she'd wanted to. And for all her damnable preaching," he added reluctantly, "she never *has* tried to steal my throne."

Lukin whirled to face him, utterly scandalized. "Majesty, do not let her trap you in her net of spells as well! Remember the fate of Prince Nicolas. And what she might have done to Mailen . . ." The archbishop did not elaborate, but merely shook his head solemnly and allowed the king's imagination to provide the suitably lurid details.

Durek looked away, picking absently at the frayed ends of one of Cecile's hair ribbons. Yes, he was outraged at his son's abduction; how dare Athaya steal him from his home as if he were nothing more than a string of beads from the queen's sewing basket. And although Durek would have preferred to keep Nicolas under close scrutiny—he *did* try to kill his sovereign, after all—it upset him far less than the loss of his beloved son and heir. But worst of all was Cecile's letter; God, did she really fear him so? He had crumpled the letter up in fury with every intention of burning it to ash, but each time he moved to do so, he smoothed the creamy parchment out again, reading yet again his wife's declaration that she would never return to Caithe as long as he was bent on systematically murdering his subjects.

"Athaya didn't harm the boy," Durek replied grudgingly, after a time. "Cecile said as much in her letter. She also told me that it was her idea to have him abducted, although I suspect she was only saying that to protect Athaya."

"Most certainly," Lukin agreed swiftly. "She has long been deceived by your sister's machinations. But how can we be certain that the boy is unharmed? You'll recall that Prince Nicolas did not try to murder you the very moment he arrived in Delfarham. Your sister could have put a spell upon the boy to murder you twenty years from now."

Durek shifted uncomfortably in his chair. He tried not to think of Mailen; it pained him far too much. And even *he* did not think Athaya would dare endanger the boy; not when she could have taken his life with ease months ago, rather than merely spiriting him away. "These wizards—no matter who is leading them—will aggravate an already unpleasant situation, Jon. The people grow hateful toward me. Though most still accept that the Lorngeld must be controlled, they grow weary of the Tribunal and what its existence has spawned. My councillors report far more violence and outlawry in their shires now, and—"

"Sire, surely you are not reconsidering your decision? You are God's anointed servant doing His divine will; you must not falter now! To betray any misgivings at such a delicate time could be disastrous to your young reign."

Durek glowered; he disliked being interrupted and disliked even more being accused of weakness. It pricked him where he was most tender, reminding him that, despite his best efforts, he was not the brilliant leader Kelwyn was.

"Take care, Jon. You may be Archbishop of Delfarham now, but I am still your king, and it is not your place to scold me like a pageboy. I would advise you to remember that."

Lukin's features shifted imperceptibly, eyes simmering with resentment. "Of course, Majesty."

"I wished to suggest the very real danger that some of these malcontents may join the Sage in his bid for power as a way of taking revenge on me for foisting this Tribunal upon them."

Durek raked his eyes over his archbishop's attire; the man seemed as much a Devil's Child as any wizard in those coal-black robes with their blood-colored chalice device. At that moment, he began to suspect he'd made an error in judgment—not about the Tribunal exactly, though he had always harbored doubts about it—but about nominating Jon Lukin to the Curia as successor to the recently vacated archbishopric. Daniel Ventan had been tiresome, but at least he could be bullied. He would not have proposed something as drastic as a Tribunal, nor dared make his king feel less capable for not sharing his opinion in all things.

"What will you do?" Lukin inquired. His tone was civil but unmistakably cool.

Durek steepled his fingers, hardly able to believe what he was about to propose. "I could appeal to Reyka . . ."

"With respect," Lukin began, careful to keep his distress properly reined, "I believe that Osfonin would bring down the walls of his palace with laughter at the mere thought of aiding us. Not after you were so violently against Athaya marrying his son two years ago. Caithe has had no formal relations with Reyka in close to two centuries, and they've already shown an appalling lack of respect for you by opening their borders to any wizards desiring to flee a proper and lawful absolution."

"He'd help soon enough if Athaya asked him," Durek muttered. "Oh, but why ask for trouble? There are too many cursed wizards in Caithe already." He spat out the words by force of habit, but there was little genuine bitterness behind them.

Durek rubbed his eyes with his fists like an exhausted child.

It was barely noon and already he felt as if he had been awake for days. Nothing in his reign—or his life—had prepared him for this and there was no one he could turn to for advice.

Why now? he groaned inwardly. No king of Caithe had ever faced such a crisis—an army of wizards out to rob him of his kingdom and the inexplicable failure of corbals to repel them. Caithe had known war before, of course, but never like this; never so seemingly one-sided and indefensible. He sighed deep from the soul, suddenly feeling ill-equipped to handle such a conflict so early in his reign. Briefly, he wondered what he could possibly have done to deserve it.

Solemnly, Durek looked to the ruby signet ring on the first finger of his right hand; the ring of kingship, inherited from his father.

What would Kelwyn do?

Durek scowled, curling the hand into a fist. He knew perfectly well what his beloved father would do. He would let these foul wizards go about their business of sending Caithe to the Devil as long as they didn't try to steal his throne.

But they have *tried,* Durek reflected. *And it is only a matter of time before they do so again.*

And they might not have tried to steal it at all, came another voice from even deeper down, *if I had allowed them some measure of mercy in the first place.*

Durek's scowl shifted to a frown of bafflement. Despite his father's radical idea of bringing the Lorngeld back into the fold of humanity, the people *loved* him. That simply made no sense at all.

"Perhaps this is God's way of testing our faith," Lukin suggested, concerned by his king's moody silence. "If we can defeat even wizards such as these, then we will have won a victory greater than any other in Caithe's history."

Durek threw up his hands in exasperation. "Defeat them *how*?"

"I do not know. I shall pray diligently for guidance. Fear not, sire. God is sure to send us a solution."

Durek slouched even further into the cushioned chair, reaching past the sewing basket to run his fingers across Cecile's prized chessboard—a wedding gift from Kelwyn. The black and white courtiers had grown dusty at their posts; Cecile had not touched the board since she last played with Athaya, almost a lifetime ago. Absently, Durek plucked up the white queen and studied it. The features were cold and unmoving, the eyes without love or life.

"Leave me now, Jon. I need to think on this alone."

Lukin's robes brushed gently against the carpet as he approached. "Sire, might I suggest that you do your thinking elsewhere?" Somehow, the archbishop's voice managed to be courteous and condemning at the same time. "It ill becomes you to sit about her Majesty's solar brooding like a rejected suitor over her absence. Not when suspicion still remains that she could have conspired with Athaya to—"

"That will be enough, Jon," Durek snapped back, setting the chesspiece down with enough force to make its companions tremble. "Again you scold me like a child, though you disguise it as wise counsel. Cecile has been gone from me for near two years and I cannot help but think on her at times; she is the mother of my children and I—" He balked, changing his choice of words at the last minute. "I regret her absence." He glanced disparagingly at Lukin's clerical garb. "I hardly expect you to understand."

Lukin bristled at the backhanded insult, but was not so careless as to argue with the king in his sulking state. Only the slight flare of a nostril and the subtle tightening of his jaw revealed his displeasure.

"Tell Captain Parr to send two squadrons back to Eriston with Lafert," Durek went on. "But not our best men, mind—have Parr recruit them from Gorah. Country soldiers will be better with longbows and I think it wise that they attack these wizards from a distance. It may be sneaky and dishonorable, but an unexpected arrow in the back may be the only thing that works against these wizards."

Lukin nodded his blessings on the plan, thinking nothing dishonorable about an arrow in the back when dealing with creatures of the Enemy. "And if they fail?" he asked, keenly aware that such was the likely outcome.

"If they fail," Durek echoed sharply, baring teeth like a cornered hound, "then you'd better damned well hope that God has answered your prayers, because I'll be fresh out of options."

Lukin inclined his head wordlessly, confident that the Almighty would cooperate in a timely manner once He knew which of His servants was calling, and stalked imperiously from the chamber.

Blessedly alone, the king of Caithe moved to his window,

looking out upon the bustle of high summer in Delfarham. Carts laden with foodstuffs rumbled over silvery, rain-slick cobbles as merchants extolled the virtues of their wares, criers called out the day's news, the bells of Saint Adriel's placidly chimed the hour. The city went about its collective business, ignorant of the storm brewing to the west. But even if his people knew of it, they would trust in their king to keep them safe. Durek had vowed to do just that at his coronation, in traditional exchange for his subjects' fealty.

For the first time, he realized it might not be such an easy vow to keep.

It was frightening to consider, Durek thought suddenly, but was it possible that Athaya wasn't the worst of his enemies after all?

He poured himself a glass of wine to steady his nerves, but at the first swallow, the liquid soured in his stomach and he promptly coughed it up into a handkerchief. The red wine looked like blood against the snowy white linen and Durek hastily flung the cloth aside in fear and disgust. God, he was more worried than he'd let himself believe.

He turned to leave the solar, gathering up the collection of cloth puppets that Cecile had requested; he would send a courier to Reyka with the dolls this afternoon. As he reached the door, his gaze swept across the fabric faces of his son's precious toys and the true peril of his situation hit him like a blow to the belly, unsettling his innards more than the soured wine had done. Corbals were his kingdom's defense . . . it's *only* defense. And without it, the Lorngeld, whether they were of Caithe or Sare, could rob him of his kingdom with less effort than it took to snatch a puppet from a child's tiny hand.

CHAPTER 7

✺✺

"H IDE IT—QUICKLY!" ATHAYA CRIED OUT, PRESSING
her palms against her temples as if to keep her
head from splitting open and spilling her brains
into her lap. The corbal crystal had won the battle handily, and
Athaya buckled beneath its greater power as quickly as she
would have lost an arm-wrestling match with Ranulf. "God's
blood," she groaned, eyes squeezed tightly closed against the
pain, "I feel as if someone's hacking at my skull with a white-
hot cleaver."

Kale slipped the acorn-sized corbal back into its leather
pouch, his soldier's face incongruously lined with sympathy.
"You're moving to the larger stones too quickly, my Lady.
Shouldn't you stop for the day?"

"If I had any sense I would," Athaya grumbled miserably. "But there may not be much time; I *have* to master this."

Athaya reclined in a patch of cool clover—a welcome shelter from the heat of early July—and allowed the relaxing murmur of the creek and the silvery shimmer of jewelweed just
beneath the surface to lull her into a healing half sleep. Each
day for the past week, she and Kale had returned to the small
clearing north of the camp, and each day she insisted upon facing a larger crystal than the day before. The grueling routine
was beginning to wear on her; today she had been bested by
a crystal she had successfully defied two days before.

Later—in her aching mental haze, Athaya wasn't certain

how long—footsteps sounded on the trail behind them, and she cracked open her eyes to see Jaren set a willow basket at her feet. "You forgot this when you left this morning. I brought it quite a while ago, but I had to wait until Kale put that crystal away before I could come any closer. Get away," he snapped suddenly, swiping at a trio of bees hovering near the lip of the basket. "They seem to be everywhere this summer." He offered Athaya a much-too-cheerful smile. "So how's it going?"

Athaya rolled onto her back and glared up at him like a drunkard roused too early in the morning by an annoyingly sober friend. "What the devil are you so happy about?"

Jaren took a step back and raised his arms to forfeit the fight before the first blow could be struck. "Maybe I'll just share my lunch with the bees," he suggested. "They're better company."

"Oh, don't mind me," she replied, sighing deep as she closed her fingers around a fistful of clover. "It's these crystals. The larger they get, the less control I have over them. If the Sage's compulsion spell is this powerful," she added resignedly, "then no wonder Nicolas has lost so much of himself trying to fight it."

"She's making herself ill," Kale said, turning his eyes imploringly to Jaren. "Please tell her to stop—she doesn't listen to me."

Jaren let out a trickle of dry laughter. "And you think she'll listen to *me*? I may be her husband, but you've known her far longer than I have—long enough to know how stubborn she can be about this sort of thing."

Ignoring Athaya's baleful stare, Jaren sat down beside her and unpacked the contents of his basket. A boiled egg, two chicken legs, and a wedge of blueberry pie did wonders for her temper, and Athaya felt almost human again after the meal was done.

Athaya?

She started at the urgent voice that sounded close to her ear, like words half heard in a dream that jerked the sleeper rudely out of oblivion. Her first thought was that the corbal crystal had somehow come back to haunt her with its yammerings of pain, but then she recalled that it was safely silenced within Kale's leather pouch.

Athaya? the voice called again, louder this time. It was Ranulf, summoning her through his vision sphere. *Can you hear me?*

Athaya winced, hands going instinctively to her temples. "Do you have to shout?" she admonished him, scowling at the empty air above her in lieu of Ranulf himself. "My head hurts bad enough as it is."

Sorry, Ranulf sent back. The voice was softer now, but the urgency in it still remained. *Mason's opened a panel to us from Kilfarnan—I'm in the chapel with him now. And judging from the puckered look on his face, I'll wager all the whiskey in Sare that none of us is going to like what he's got to say.*

Athaya thought she heard a more distant voice muttering something under its breath—probably Mason voicing his opinion of looking 'puckered'—as she wiped the last vestige of blueberry juice from her chin and scrambled to her feet. Mason's news must be important indeed for Ranulf to summon her home from her corbal work rather than wait another few hours for her to return of her own accord.

"We'll be right there."

They reached the forest chapel in less than a quarter hour, finding Ranulf slouched pensively into the first pew like a man sitting vigil on the eve of battle. An open panel was positioned to one side of the altar—a shimmering window to another part of the world—and framed within it like a living portrait was the gray-robed figure of Dom Mason DePere, sole regent of Athaya's offshoot magic school in Kilfarnan. Somehow, the dom had been able to maintain his cultured and academic air despite a year's estrangement from the comforts of his native Reyka; the folds of his robes were freshly pressed and a wealth of dark hair was shorn to a precise curl at his shoulders. But clues to his distress were evident, though subtle; Mason's hands smoothed down nonexistent wrinkles in his robe in silent agitation and the normally flawless fingernails had been recently bitten to the quick.

"It's good to see you again, Mason," Athaya said, receiving a courtly bow of greeting in return. She dispensed with further pleasantries; Ranulf's summons was proof enough that this was far more than one of the dom's routine status calls. "Ranulf tells me your news isn't good."

Mason shook his head solemnly; the dom had skirmished with the Tribunal before, and the strain he exhibited today convinced Athaya that his current troubles sprang from a far different source. And that, she knew, could only mean one thing.

"After Ranulf stopped in Kilfarnan last month and told me about the Sage of Sare, I sent a few people north to scout the

Sage's camps. Apparently the Sage isn't satisfied at taking over a small port town like Eriston." The dom paused, searching for an easy way to impart his news and ultimately realizing there was none. "Now he claims the whole of Nadiera."

"Nadiera," Athaya echoed, lowering herself into the pew beside Ranulf. "Lord Gessinger's lands . . . and one of the largest shires in Caithe." Athaya was certain that the shire's size and wealth were not the only reasons the Sage had targeted Nadiera. Lord Gessinger was a known ally of hers, and as such the Sage would consider him an enemy, his lands forfeit.

"The Sage and his men seized the manor house last week. The king sent men to repel him, but word has it that he's slaughtered close to three squadrons already—one from Delfarham last month and two more from Gorah. I just heard about it this morning, so I doubt the news has reached Delfarham yet."

Athaya felt the throbbing in her skull return—an ache that had nothing whatsoever to do with corbal crystals. The Sage's threat had grown too serious to delay acting any longer . . . but what form should that action take?

"And there's one more thing," Mason added, dipping his head apologetically.

Athaya squeezed her eyes shut and nodded; she might as well hear all of it.

"I'm picking up some troubling rumors about you from the Sarians—I don't put any credence in them, of course, but you should be forewarned. Many of the Sage's adherents say that you have the power to tell who is a wizard and who is not before the *mekahn*. They also say that you refuse to use this power, in order to force the people of Caithe to come to you for help instead of giving them enough warning so they can flee the country if they so choose. It's absurd, I know," he appended graciously. "It's common knowledge that no one can discern such a thing before—"

"Mason." The besieged tone of her voice stopped him cold, and his eyes slowly widened as he began to realize why she had cut him off. "Some of what they're saying is true. The sealing spell *did* give me the ability to see people's future in that sense, but Tonia and I discussed it and decided that it wasn't right for me to have that kind of knowledge. I've kept the talent a secret—or at least I've tried to," she added dryly, "and resolved not to use it again. But we can't let the Sage's version of things take root. Make sure your people know my side of the story; I'll do the same here. It may be moot at this point, though—I'm not sure I have the talent anymore. Most of the heightened power that the sealing spell gave me has faded away."

Mason took a moment to digest this new information. "So after a while," he deduced, "the Sage won't be able to do it either?"

"Probably not. Unfortunately, we don't have time to wait him out." Athaya shifted uneasily in the pew, trying not to think about what Drianna had confided to her the week before. According to the Sage's steward Tullis, he and two assistants had released the Sage from his seal in a far more controlled manner than Tonia and Jaren had freed Athaya from her own. With the little that was known about sealing spells, Athaya was forced to face the possibility that his power might fade more slowly than hers had. Or worst of all, it might not fade at all. Even if they had the time to wait him out, it wasn't a risk she—or Caithe—could possibly take.

"Is there anything I can do from here?" Mason asked, again smoothing invisible wrinkles from his sleeves.

"No, not yet. I think the next move should be mine." Athaya let out a burdensome sigh, shoulders slumping under the weight of the task that lay ahead. "Just be careful. The Sage is closer to your people than mine." *For now, anyway*, she added sullenly. "And he'll likely consider all of us just as much his enemies as Durek or the Tribunal."

The dom nodded grimly and then touched his fingertips to the rim of his panel. The window clouded over with smoky darkness, and after Ranulf held a ward key to the panel's frame it ebbed out of sight like a mirage.

Athaya slumped deeper into the pew with a muttered curse, while Jaren gazed down on her knowingly. "Is this 'next move' you mentioned what I think it is?" he asked.

"I have to go talk to him, Jaren. It's probably futile, I know, but if there's even the slightest chance of convincing the Sage to stop this invasion and go back to Sare, I've got to take it."

Ranulf jerked upright, horrified at her suggestion. "What, are ye daft? I spent four months tryin' to think up a way to escape that self-deluded demigod and you're just going to dance right into his outstretched arms? Trust me, my girl—I've been his prisoner and I can promise that you won't much care for it. I wasn't mistreated o' course, being a wizard and all, but the stench of arrogance was enough to choke on."

"Ranulf is right," Jaren agreed with a nod. "The Sage is at war with us already whether he's formally declared one or not. If you walk right into his stronghold, he'll likely see to it that you're his first prisoner. What better way to dash your people's hopes than to see their leader be taken?"

"I know it's risky, but . . . I can't quite explain why, but I have a feeling that the Sage won't consider me much of a menace anymore in light of his heightened powers. And if he harmed or captured me, he'd be little better than Durek or the Tribunal. That certainly wouldn't help rally support from the multitudes of people still sitting fences and waiting to choose sides in this conflict—not if he's setting himself up as the Lorngeld's messiah. And I still have the spell of translocation," she reminded them. "As far as I know, the Sage can't stop me from using it.

"And besides," she added, averting her eyes, "I want to ask him to release Nicolas from his compulsion. I don't want to wait for the Sage's death to see my brother whole again, and if the man is as swollen with himself as Drianna says he is, he may just grant my request to prove how trifling a threat the rest of us are to him now."

Ranulf was ready to launch into another round of reasoning when Jaren waved him off, knowing full well that Athaya would go to the Sage whether they advised her against it or not. "Maybe you should hold off until you have more practice turning aside the corbals," he suggested, hoping that if he could not prevent this confrontation he might at least stall it for a while. "The Sage is obviously a master at it and might use the crystals against you."

His hopes were painfully short-lived. "I don't have time for that," Athaya said, steadfast. "None of us do. The Sage's adherents or mine . . . we're all one and the same to Durek and the Tribunal. We have to try and stop the Sage's incursions before Durek and Lukin start taking their vengeance for this invasion out on *us*."

The first thing Athaya sensed when the dizziness passed was the crisp scent of saltwater laced with the stench of rotting fish. From farther away came the calming rush of waves lazily rolling onto the beach just outside the cove's mouth.

Jaren squatted in the dry sand at her side and scried her eyes for signs of illness. "How do you feel?"

Athaya glanced up at him wryly. "A whole lot better than the last time I was here."

Shifting to a comfortable position on the sand, Athaya brushed her gaze over the tiny grotto near the convent of Saint Gillian's, spying telltale signs of her last sojourn here. It had been close to a year ago when Tonia and Jaren had released her from the bonds of the sealing spell, but vestiges of those anguished weeks remained. To her left, the cavern walls bore blackened scars etched by a wayward fire-spell, and to her right were piles of rubble and ash that had been fist-sized stones before her spells had blown them into powder.

"Can you walk?"

"I think so," she said, wobbling a little as she rose to her feet, "but I won't be casting any spells for a while." If she suspected it before, the woolly feeling in her head now proved it for a fact: the extra measure of magic she had obtained from the sealing spell was completely gone. She was returned to what she had been in the beginning; a powerful adept, but nothing more.

Once Jaren was sure she could walk without stumbling, he led her out of the cove and into the blinding glare of a cloudless morning. "How far is the manor from here?"

"At a guess, I'd say twenty miles. Once we get into the shire itself, things should start looking familiar. My family often spent the summers in Nadiera after Father and Dagara were married. We can make it most of the way today and plan to arrive at the manor tomorrow morning."

Athaya wasn't delighted with the thought of such a long trek, but she and Jaren had both agreed that it was their safest course of action. They could hardly pop into view on the manor grounds themselves without being noticed, and Jaren was adamant that they scout the surrounding area in advance— and give Athaya the chance to recover from the strain of the spell—before making their presence known. And other than the manor itself, the cove was one of the few places in northwest Caithe that Athaya could envision accurately enough for translocation.

At least, she mused, *a day's delay will give me some time to think what on earth I'm going to say to the man when I see him.*

The day was fine for walking—this close to the sea, the oppressive heat of July was blown to the south by strong breezes—and instead of seeking an inn, Athaya and Jaren camped that night in a grove of oaks, the bulk of their journey behind them. Late the next morning, they came upon the village of Coakley, less than two miles from the manor itself.

Rather than avoiding the village, Athaya and Jaren decided to pass through it, learning what they could about the Sage's grip on the shire before confronting him directly. In their drab and threadbare peasant clothes, she and Jaren looked like any other villagers going about the day's errands; if they were careful, no one would give them a second look.

It had been several years since Athaya had been to Coakley, but the change in the sleepy hamlet was obvious. Coakley was now an occupied town and temporary home to many members of the Sage's advancing army. Armed men in silver-edged black livery dotted the dusty streets, and villagers went about their business giving them a wide and wary berth. Magic was displayed openly here—even flaunted, as witchlights burned like lanterns in every window despite the glare of the sun. Near the river, a squad of soldiers drilled their battle spells with one another, one row casting out in unison with white-hot arcs of fire while the other methodically turned the flames aside with an unbroken line of shielding spells.

"Look there," Jaren murmured. "What's that up ahead?"

In the center of the village green, beside an unused set of stocks, a fair-haired man was trapped inside a cell; a cell with walls of shimmering air, like living glass. Athaya had not seen its like before, but guessed it to be a type of binding spell. The sheer walls of the man's prison pulsed in time with his rapid heartbeat and when he dared to touch it the rhythm grew erratic and sparks shot out to sear his flesh. Outside of the boundary, a crowd of children harried the prisoner, shouting insults and tossing overripe tomatoes, delighted that their missiles could pierce the boundary while the man inside could not. A handful of adults joined in as well, although with less fervor, as if they needed to torment the prisoner for fear of reprisal by the Sage's men and not because they thought he deserved such treatment. One woman, however, cursed him louder than any of the children, her plump face crimson with rage.

"You would have rather seen me dead!" she was shrieking, her face framed by dirty blonde curls. "I finally have the chance to get out of this foul little village and you want me to throw it all away!" She threw a clod of dirt at him, not bothering to pick the dung out of it first, and as he instinctively raised his arm to shield himself, his elbow caught the edge of the boundary. He yelped in pain as a shower of sparks lashed out at his flesh, leaving a series of ugly red welts. The village children squealed with delight at his misfortune.

"These people are lying to you, Hilda," he said, though his words were countered by a loud chorus of jeers from the adult onlookers. "True, they might actually give you some of the money and lands they promise, but what good is that if you lose your soul to them as well? If you have to use your magic, then why not go to one of the princess's camps? At least they've never tried to overthrow the king."

"And that's the damned problem! What good does her royal Highness do us, might I ask? Oh, she'll show us our spells well enough, but can she stop the Justices from slitting our throats right after? We deserve better and *she* won't get it for us. Think, Ben! We could have ten times the land we do now. And money, too . . . and decent food and clothes—"

"Only by stealing it all from someone else," the prisoner argued back. "Where's the justice in that?"

Hilda sniffed at the irrelevance of the remark. "Where's the justice in absolution?"

Drawn by the dispute, one of the Sage's soldiers strolled lazily toward the prisoner. "If you keep spouting that sort of talk, friend, then the Sage will use that head of yours to decorate the gates of his new manor."

"What difference would it make?" the man said, staring despondently at the toes of his leather boots. He stole a quick glance at his wife. "He's taken everything else."

As the crowd taunted the man with mewling wails of mock pity, Athaya's ears picked up the underscore of hoofbeats rumbling behind them—and coming closer. A half-dozen men galloped into the green a minute later, a thick cloud of dust rising from the road in their wake. One man she recognized instantly; he could not have been overlooked in a crowd of thousands. With seeming idleness, Athaya let her hood fall across her face; this was neither the time or place for their meeting. The people of Coakley had likely been fed the tales that Mason warned her about, and if they were to discover their princess among them, they might assault her—or worse—for not using her power to tell their futures and say who among them was Lorngeld and who was not.

The Sage of Sare eased his ruddy stallion through the crowd of villagers, the archetypal image of a conquering king. Enemy or no, Athaya conceded that he was a glorious sight to behold;

gold glittered at his ears and throat, and he was elegantly clad in emerald-colored silk, his black hair and cape flowing freely behind him. He reined in beside the prisoner, glancing down in mild curiosity.

"What's the trouble here, Dorrit?"

The soldier stepped forward and offered his lord a sharp salute. "This man was arrested earlier this morning, your Grace. His wife is one of us—you scried her seed last week, if you'll recall. He was caught trying to persuade her not to join you."

The Sage grinned at his captive as if amused by the tangled prattle of a child just learning to speak. "He misunderstands me, then, for no one who truly knows my mission could say it is not the will of God."

Like a tickle in the back of her head, Athaya sensed the thread of power in the Sage's words—a single strand of silver in a tapestry of black. Like the subtle pressures a wizard employed to entice a man to sleep, the Sage twined a bit of mind-magic into his speech, adding a touch of arcane power to his already persuasive words. "It is time to absolve Caithe of her sins, my friends," he proclaimed, extending his arms to embrace the whole kingdom. "We shall take back what is rightfully ours—those lands and goods stolen by the Church and her adherents—and then we will take our proper place . . . first in Caithe and then in the world!"

Procuring the expected cheers, the Sage bowed graciously to his audience, gold adornments catching the sunlight and dazzling the eyes of all. Then he approached the prisoner, stepping through the glasslike boundary with ease. The man backed away, but was soon dangerously close to the shimmering walls of his cell with nowhere else to run. The Sage cupped the prisoner's head in his palms. The man flinched once as the wizard's gaze bored into him, but then quickly went limp in the Sage's grasp and slumped to his knees in the dirt.

After a moment of quiet study, the Sage straightened and slowly backed out of the cell, leaving the now-slumbering man alone in his ensorcelled square of earth. "Your husband does not have the power," he said to Hilda. "He will never be what you are." The Sage shook his head in a show of grief as if informing her that the man was dead and not simply barren of magic.

"Tell me, young lady," he continued, placing one finger underneath the village woman's chin. "Have you been anointed?"

Hilda blushed crimson at his touch. "No, your Grace. Not yet."

The Sage smiled broadly in response. "Well, then, this seems a fine day for it. I shall do the honors myself."

"Y-you, your Grace?" The woman's mouth opened and closed several times in succession like a beached fish starving for the sea. "Such an honor . . ."

"All my people are worthy of honor, child. Come," he said, taking her trembling hand in his, "leave your husband to his miseries. I would have you serve me by learning to use the gifts you have been given. But first you need a proper welcome. Attend us!" he shouted to the onlookers, raising his other arm high. "Summon everyone to the village church!"

After a hasty glance back at her husband, Hilda tossed her curls with a dash of insolence and strode out of the green on the Sage's arm. Like an impromptu parade, they were quickly trailed by dozens of villagers and soldiers, all following the winding dirt road to the squat little church on the outskirts of the village proper.

Jaren tugged on Athaya's arm. "Let's go see what this 'anointing' is all about."

Even as she trailed after him, Athaya craned her neck back to the imprisoned man. He had been quickly forgotten, displaced in the attentions of the villagers by whatever ritual the Sage was about to perform. "I wish I knew how to release him, but I've never seen that spell before."

"His heartbeat is linked to the binding somehow," Jaren returned quietly. "Breaking him free would probably kill him. Remember what Master Hedric said about trying to unweave the threads of Nicolas' compulsion?" Resignedly, Jaren urged her forward. "Come. I know you'd like to, but you can't save everyone in Caithe single-handedly."

By the time they arrived at the village church, the pews were filled to overflowing with curious and excited spectators. The Sage's wizards had the privilege of the forward pews, while those without magic were guided to the rear. To avoid being seen among the congregation, Athaya and Jaren concealed themselves with cloaking spells, content to watch the ceremony from the safety of a narrow arched window.

The village woman stood alone before a crudely cut stone altar hastily adorned with sprays of summer flowers and greenery. She picked at her grubby skirt with restless fingers, suddenly shy at the array of attentive eyes upon her. As candidate and congregation both waited restlessly for the rite to begin, Athaya realized that this was the ideal opportunity to discover if her ability to scry the seeds of power was truly gone. Her ethical stance made little difference at this point—Hilda's future had already been revealed. The outcome of the inquiry would change nothing, but at least Athaya would know in her heart that she did not lie when professing the power had faded from her.

Though physical contact would make the reading clearer, Athaya dared not enter the church; even a cloaking spell was risky in a room full of wizards, one of whom might catch her reflection in a random scrap of glass or curve of silver. Instead, from her place at the window, Athaya cast out probing tendrils of thought, searching the woman's mind for a pinprick of radiance. If Hilda felt the gentle touch, Athaya hoped that she would merely think it some aspect of the upcoming rite and say nothing.

Through the murky haze of Hilda's anxiety, Athaya could sense her banked exhilaration, but she also harbored hidden pangs of regret; she knew her husband for a stubborn man and was sure that he would never bow down to the Sage and join his wife in her new future. But aside from these immediate emotions, the rest of Hilda's mind held only darkened swirls of memory and thought, unbroken by the coruscant seed of unborn magic that the Sage had claimed was there.

Unless the Sage had been lying—and Athaya had no reason to suspect that he was—her talent was gone.

After allowing sufficient time for his audience to hone their anticipation, the Sage of Sare solemnly emerged from the priest's closet behind the altar. He had exchanged his riding cloak for a silky white stole, making him look half king, half priest. The church quieted instantly at his advent.

"Beloved of God," he began, raising his palms aloft, "we come together today to welcome another into our brotherhood and rejoice. She who stands before us has been called by God, as have we in our own time before her. It is our charge to instruct her in the use of her gifts and teach her the true and profound worth of the blessings she has been given."

The Sage grasped the woman's hands in his, patting them softly to ease her nerves. "Hilda, do you here in the presence of God and His children acknowledge and take joy in the gifts that He has granted you?"

Hilda looks up to him as if to God Himself, her eyes shining with rapture. "I do."

"Will you use these gifts to His honor, for the betterment of His people and His world?"

"I will."

"And do you promise to obey God in all things and therefore to obey those to whom He has granted greater gifts as a sign of His greater grace?"

"I do."

The Sage released her hands. He stepped up to the baptismal font and picked up a gleaming pewter bowl filled with water. As he turned back and lifted the bowl to the sky, he scanned the congregation; for one uneasy instant, Athaya imagined he was looking directly between her eyes. Even knowing she was cloaked by magic, she shrank down instinctively.

When she dared peer back inside, the Sage had dipped his hands in the holy water and was sprinkling it like raindrops over Hilda's face and hair. Then he set the bowl aside and laid his palms upon the woman's brow. Her flesh gleamed golden where it met the Sage's own, bathing the woman's head in light like an angel's corona.

"I hereby anoint you as one of God's children and charge you be worthy of His gifts."

The Sage offered the woman a ritual kiss of welcome on each cheek; Hilda reeled slightly, on the edge of fainting.

Grasping her shoulders, he turned her to face the others. "Rejoice, friends, for another of our brethren has been found. I commend to your love and care this woman, whom I as God's first servant among you acknowledge as one of us. Do all in your power to increase her knowledge and skill so that her divine gifts can be used to the credit of us all."

While the others sat silent, ignorant of the proper responses, the wizards in the congregation rose to speak in unison. "We recognize and welcome you, Hilda of Coakley, and hereby renew the vows made at our anointment, to uphold God's law with our prayers and our gifts."

"Now go in peace," the Sage concluded, "and rejoice in His power, which He has deigned to share with us. May His blessings come upon us and remain with us, and grant us the grace to rule wisely. Amen."

"Amen."

With the formal part of the ceremony over, Hilda's fellow

wizards slowly formed a line in the aisle, each waiting to offer her a chaste kiss of welcome as the Sage had done. As the rest of the crowd dispersed, Athaya and Jaren slipped out of the village, remaining cloaked for safety. Not long afterward, the Sage and his escort thundered past them, heading for the manor.

"Do you still think we can change his mind?" Jaren asked dubiously, coughing up a mouthful of dust stirred to life by the escort's horses. "After what we just witnessed back there, I think we'd do better to go straight back to Kaiburn."

Athaya sighed, despairing but not yet ready to concede the battle. "I have to try. People will die if we go to war; I owe it to everyone who's believed in me over the years to try and stop that if I can. And I owe it to Nicolas," she added, kicking absently at a pebble in the road. "Maybe I can still convince the Sage to let him go."

Shortly after midday, Athaya and Jaren arrived at the ducal manor of Nadiera, erstwhile home of Lord Mosel Gessinger, late of the king's council and now a prisoner in his Majesty's dungeons. The bulk of the Sage's army encircled the duke's stately mansion, their tents pitched outside graceful iron gates that were never intended to deter such a force. Athaya felt every muscle in her body harden with tension as she scraped her gaze across the landscape. All that she saw seemed to mock her; a sinister parody of her own camp in Kaiburn. In the fields to the north, hundreds of men and women drilled one another in battle magic, producing a constant flurry of explosions, fires, and illusory winged things, while those new to the Sage's forces, some barely out of their own *mekahn*, learned the simpler spells of survival and stealth. This was more than a motley collection of students come to save themselves; this was an army on the march—wizards who sought not only to save their own lives, but to take the lives of their enemies. Suddenly, Athaya felt exposed and vulnerable; the Sage was the unquestioned sovereign here, and she his most formidable opponent. Were he to order her death, who among his followers would hesitate to carry out the sentence?

But it was too late to turn back even had she wished to; she and Jaren had reached the gatehouse and a bored-looking man in silvershot black livery stepped out to block their path. "If you've come to be tested, his Grace only does so for an hour a day, just afore supper," he said rotely. He jerked a thumb to his left. "Wait with the others if you want."

Athaya's eyes followed the man's thumb toward the ragtag host of peasants huddled outside the manor's southern gate. Dozens of people had flocked to the Sage's side hoping to learn whether they bore the seed of magic. Most were near the age of *mekahn* and many had small children in tow, desperate to know if persecution and absolution were the only future they had.

"We're not here to be tested," Jaren explained. "We'd like to speak to the Sage."

The guardsman snorted as he tucked his thumbs in his belt. "You and a thousand other people. You'll need an appointment."

Athaya took a step forward. "I think he'll see me. Tell him—"

"The Sage is a busy man, missy," he cut in, dismissing her as just another demanding villager. "Half the folks in this shire want him to tell their future and if he did it for every pretty wench who strolled up to the gates and asked, he'd have no time for nothin' else. Go on—off with you now."

Athaya drew herself up and leveled him with her finest regal glare. Her tone was cold with command. "Sir, would you kindly tell his Grace that Athaya Trelane wishes to see him at his earliest convenience. Perhaps he will overlook my lack of an appointment."

The man's eyes widened at first, then narrowed in suspicion as he sent subtle threads of inquiry to brush against her mind. His eyes widened again once his truth test was done and he knew her to be who she claimed. Turning on his heel, he retreated into the gatehouse and whispered urgently to one of his companions. "Fetch Sir Couric—and be quick about it!"

A short time later, a sleek young man in a costly blue tunic arrived at the gatehouse. He appraised the newcomers with unhurried care, quietly bemused, as if unable to decide whether Athaya's sudden appearance at the Sage's stronghold was a stroke of tactical genius or shocking stupidity.

"If you will come with me," he said at last.

Couric led them across the graveled courtyard, through an arched doorway, and into a well-tended garden. He guided them to a shaded gazebo and bade them wait while he went to fetch his lord. The look of calm bemusement never left his watchful face.

Athaya sat down on a marble bench near a bush of white roses. Even after many summers at the manor, she had never

been in this garden before, but had only caught glimpses of it
through locked gates. It was Lord Gessinger's private domain;
until now, no one had ever been permitted inside but the duke
himself. Looking about her, Athaya knew why. The garden
boasted nothing but roses ... roses of every shape and size
and color. Mosel must have planted the bushes in memory of
his first love—a woman named Rose, absolved long ago. If
she could not live, Athaya mused, thinking back on the duke's
sad tale, then at least Mosel saw to it that these blossoms
would do so in her stead.

"I've been expecting you."

Athaya whirled around at the unexpected voice, pricking her
finger on a thorn. The Sage stood directly in front of her, grinning with delight that his cloaking spell had shielded his approach so well. He still wore his emerald-green tunic, but with
one sinister addition—for her benefit, she was sure. Athaya
balled her hand into a fist and blood welled up from where the
thorn had pierced her. Around his waist was a scarf of
runecloth—the very scarf she had given to Nicolas when he
had departed for Sare last autumn. The red runes were stark
against the black wool, as if painted in fresh blood. It was a
cheap tactic meant to unsettle her, and she refused to betray
how effectively it had worked.

Athaya rose slowly to her feet. Here, with barely a yard between them, it was difficult not to strike him for what he had
done to Nicolas. But she had to tread carefully; Brandegarth of
Crewe was the more powerful wizard now, and the arrogant
glint in his sea-green eyes told her that he knew that as well
as she did.

"I wasn't certain when," he continued, gazing languidly at
the white clouds drifting by overhead as if considering altering
their placement in the sky to something a bit more pleasing,
"but I knew you would come. Sooner or later."

His words hung heavy with pride, but Athaya would not be
baited. "You remember my husband, Jaren."

The Sage flicked him the briefest of glances. "I do."

Circling behind Athaya, the Sage picked a rose and began
pulling its petals off one by one. Surprising as it seemed,
Athaya got the distinct impression that his full attention was
not on this meeting, but he was instead looking beyond it to a
far more important event.

"You could have saved yourself the walk and spoken to me
in Coakley today," he observed. His mouth curled up at her si-

lent blink of surprise. "I saw you at the window of the church. Your husband's cloaking spell isn't very good," he confided with mock covertness. "The air around him was shimmering. I lifted the pewter bowl to catch his reflection and saw you standing beside him. Your spell is near perfect. But then, you are an adept like myself, so this is not surprising."

"Your Grace—"

The Sage tossed the now-naked stem aside. "I imagine that in addition to the rite of anointment, you also saw me foretell that man's future—the one imprisoned in the green." His gaze became a challenge. "You are not the only one to whom God has granted His gift of foresight; not the only one with whom He shares the secret of who His children are."

"It is wrong for us to know such things. Just because we *can* do it doesn't mean we *should*." But even as she spoke the words, Athaya knew they would fall like seeds upon dry ground. Rhodri had never heeded such advice; why should the Sage, whose ambitions were far more grand?

The Sage snorted indelicately. "I expected you would say something like that. It has the oppressive ring of Reykan philosophy to it."

Athaya fixed a hard gaze on him. "You will not have the power forever." She had long debated whether to reveal that knowledge, but had eventually concluded that it would be better for herself—as well as Caithe—to plant the seed of doubt in the Sage's mind, hoping to convince him to back away from using the gift so publicly rather than keep her loss a secret and have it forever misconstrued as a deliberate refusal to aid her people. "That power has faded from me . . . as it will from you, in time. What the sealing spell has given you is only temporary."

I can only hope, she added privately.

The Sage tucked in his chin condescendingly. "I should have known you would have a ready excuse. It is a most convenient explanation for why you refuse to share your gift with your fellow Caithans. But even if what you're saying is true," he went on, patronizing her with every syllable, "then do not blame me because God has decided that you are no longer worthy of His gift. You did not use it to its proper purpose and so He took it from you."

Athaya felt her cheeks grow hot, appalled at the ease with which the Sage twisted the facts to suit his pleasure. "But you're only using the gift to further your own ends!"

"Yes," the Sage agreed, "I am. But my ends are God's and that makes all the difference."

Athaya squeezed her eyes closed in outraged exasperation. She never would have believed it possible, but talking to the Sage was even more infuriating than having a conversation with Archbishop Lukin.

"But let us get to the point," the Sage continued, growing bored with their dispute. "I gather you have come to Nadiera to bargain with me? To offer me something so that I will take my army and return to Sare?"

"I offer nothing but reason, your Grace."

The Sage smiled thinly. "Then you offer nothing that I do not already have, your Highness."

Then, without awaiting her reply, the Sage spun on his heel and stalked away from her, bellowing for refreshment. With startling speed—the kind borne of fear rather than devotion—an old woman appeared in the garden with a tray of cakes and three pewter cups. She set the tray on the marble bench, not daring to meet her lord's eyes, and scuttled nervously away.

The Sage took a cup from the tray on the edge of the bench. "Will you take some cherry wine? I find it rather sweet, but it suits a summer afternoon far better than whiskey."

Athaya gazed at the remaining two cups of dark liquid, remembering Durek's treacherous brush with death six months ago. "Thank you, no," she heard herself saying, bristling noticeably. "I fear you might have compelled someone to poison it."

Athaya sensed Jaren go rigid beside her, bracing for a backlash, but the Sage merely arched his brows in unison, amused by her impertinence rather than insulted. Idly, he glanced into the bowl of his cup. "Not this time," he remarked.

"What you did to Nicolas was inexcusable!" she cried, even knowing that the Sage would never feel inclined to offer up excuses for anything he did.

The Sage drank half his wine in one gulp, rolling it around his tongue before swallowing. "What you're doing to your own people is no less unconscionable, your Highness. You rob them of their God-given rights. I had to get your attention somehow."

Athaya scowled at him. "And so you did. But you needn't torment him any longer. Please," she said, close to choking on the entreaty, "free my brother from your compulsion spell. He is no threat to you."

"No," the Sage granted with a shrug. "He never was. But he was spying on me, Princess, and for that he must be punished. Prince Nicolas shall stay as he is until I rule here—or until I die. And I assure you that I have no intention of dying until I have served as Caithe's king for many fruitful years." The Sage plucked a pastry from the tray. "You seem to forget that I *did* give you a chance to save him," he pointed out, absently flaking off a bit of burned batter from his cake. "Had you joined me when I asked you to, your precious brother would be at your side right now."

"But for how long?" Jaren challenged, increasingly nettled by the Sage's offhanded manner. "To get what you want, you'll have to murder her entire family eventually."

"Not necessarily. As God's chosen servant, it is my duty to be merciful when I can." His gaze drifted back to Athaya. "You do have certain charms, Princess," he remarked, with what Athaya deemed a distasteful degree of intimacy. "You might be able to persuade me to simply exile the royal family under the condition that they neither attempt to return nor gather an army to make war on me."

"Exile me if you like, your Grace, but I will never leave Caithe."

The Sage drained off the rest of his wine and exchanged his empty cup for the one Athaya had spurned. "*You* wouldn't have to. As Dameronne said in his prophecy, you are doubly blessed—the carrier of royal blood and divine power. You would have the most exalted of places at my court." His eyes grew shrewd and vaguely unkind. "Accepted and admired, as, I gather, you never were under your father's rule. And still are not, under your brother's."

The truth stung deep, as he knew it would. In the face of all her accomplishments, the old hurts of her youth still thrived beneath the surface of her soul—the lingering shame of being an unworthy member of her family. As a girl, her shame had been refreshed each day by Dagara's shrewish words, Durek's cool detachment, and Kelwyn's soul-deep disappointment, blaming her for her mother's death and betrayed when she did not grow up to be like his beloved Chandice in every way to somehow replace what she had stolen in the fatal act of being born.

"You cannot buy me, your Grace." Athaya had to force the words out, but they came, and her voice did not break.

"I do not wish to," the Sage replied simply. "What you fail to understand, your Highness, is that I am only acting in accordance with the divine order of things."

To illustrate his words, he stepped back and swept his right hand out in a wide arc, conjuring an illusion of a man astride a horse. Not just any man, however, but Brandegarth himself, clad as he was today but wearing a golden crown. Athaya hated to admit how masterful the apparition was; each stitch of the ghost's raiment matched the living Sage's own and the ruddy stallion swished its tail to chase off flies as insubstantial as the beast itself.

"God made mankind lord over the beasts, did He not?"

Without awaiting her reply, he turned his wrist again; the image shifted and became that of a man and woman. It was the Sage and herself, Athaya realized as the image took shape, though he had done the courtesy of garbing her in a rather low-cut gown of indigo silk rather than the faded brown kirtle she wore today. Athaya was repulsed, however, to see that her insubstantial twin was dutifully kneeling at the Sage's feet.

"And he made man lord over woman, did He not?"

Athaya looked away indifferently. "Man likes to think so," she said, her voice laden with sarcasm.

The Sage favored Jaren with a distant smile. "You have married quite a firebrand, sir." He dispelled the second illusion as well and then created his most masterful yet; a likeness of himself seated on a golden throne, garbed in stately purple robes and surrounded by dozens of—no, Athaya couldn't possibly call them subjects. They were worshipers, eyes gleaming with rapture at the dazzling sight of their lord.

"And lastly, God made the Lorngeld lord over all, to govern for Him on earth as He does in heaven."

The Sage studied his creation with unabashed approval, admiring both its craftsmanship as well as its symbolism. Then, after paying silent homage to his majestic reflection, he and his phantom both turned to face Athaya, all four of the sea-green eyes brimming with visions of apocalypse.

"This has gone far beyond you and your paltry crusade, Athaya Trelane," the living Sage told her. "Your coming was merely the precursor to mine. A new order is being established that will change the course of history. You were the spark to that transformation, Princess of Caithe, but I . . ." He glanced to his twin, smiling indistinctly as both Sages nodded their respect to one another, and then turned back. "I am the flame."

Athaya took a step back from that sane yet lunatic gaze. Drianna was right—the sealing spell had altered him markedly. It had not only given him great power, but bestowed on him an even greater opinion of his role and worth. Not two years ago, Rhodri's ambition had nearly killed herself and Jaren both, as well as being the sole cause of her father's spiral into madness. Were the Sage to succeed in his own aspirations, he could make that tragedy seem trifling by comparison—a minor footnote in the glittering history of the Lorngeld's rise to power.

"Believe what you will, your Grace," Athaya said at last, weaving together the threads of her composure before they could unravel any further, "but I implore you to do so in your own land. Please, leave Caithe to unfold her own future."

The Sage closed his eyes in quiet exasperation, dismayed that she was so completely blind to the visions he painted so colorfully before her. He banished the illusion with a peevish wave of his hand. "We have had that argument before and I am weary of it. Caithe *is* my land. And would be still, had not King Faltil driven my ancestors from it. But I have no more time to debate history and theology with you—do that with your Reykan friends. Now is the time for action. To reclaim what was once ours. And I am having such a great deal of success doing that so far," he pointed out, almost flippantly, "that I see absolutely no reason to stop."

"There will be nothing left of Caithe for the victor of such a war."

"If you persist in defying me that may well occur. As I see it, there is only one solution to such an unpleasant outcome. The Lorngeld shall rule Caithe. You can be a part of that, your Highness—your due, as a wizard and a Trelane. Or you can fight me until you are defeated and earn nothing more than a scant reference in a history book as one who tried and failed."

Athaya scried deep into the Sage's unyielding eyes. There was no compromise in this man; what had ever possessed her to think she could reason with him? Why had she believed she could turn him from his course? Better to walk to the river and command the waters to reverse their flow, for all the good it would do.

"Come, Athaya," Jaren whispered in her ear. "We can't do anything more here."

Without protest from the Sage, Jaren took her arm and led Athaya toward the garden gate where Couric waited to escort them out of the manor. Jaren stole one backward glance; the Sage had made no move to follow them.

"But be advised, Athaya Trelane," the Sage added ominously as she and Jaren reached the wrought-iron gate, "the next time we meet, I may not let you go so easily."

An icy chill snaked down her back and made her shudder. He meant it; Athaya was certain of that.

Couric escorted them back to the gatehouse, murmured a few courtly words of farewell, and sent them on their way. Athaya was surprised at being allowed to walk away from the manor unhindered, but it was only further proof that the Sage did not regard her as a threat—not here, in his stolen domain. Absurd as it was, the snub galled her. Nonetheless, she and Jaren did not stop to rest until they were several miles east of the manor, assured that their easy departure wasn't instead a carefully crafted trap.

"There are so many of them, Jaren," she said later, retreating into the generous shade of a willow tree at the side of the road. She sank down in the grass rubbing at her eyes; the day's stress had given her a vicious headache and each heartbeat pumped a stream of fresh pain throughout her skull. "Ranulf was right. The Sage's people don't simply outnumber us; they're better trained *and* better organized. My people are scattered all over Caithe, and most of them are novices—the most experienced wizards we have only came into their power a year or so ago. We may have supporters," she finished sullenly, "but it's not the same thing as an army."

Jaren rummaged in his satchel for some cheese with which they could console themselves and divided a small round between them. "Then we'll have to turn it into an army. Frankly, it looks like the only option we've got."

Athaya chewed thoughtfully on her cheese. She couldn't believe she was actually considering the idea that had winged its way into her brain and nested there, but the more she pondered it, the more it seemed to be the only viable solution.

Most startling of all, she thought it just might work.

"No. There *is* one other option left . . . although I never dreamed I'd have to choose it."

Jaren eyed her critically. "I don't like the sound of that."

Suddenly, Athaya's headache was all but forgotten amidst

her growing excitement. "If you need to fight an enemy and don't have an army of your own, what do you do?"

"Hire one, I suppose," Jaren replied dubiously. "But we don't have the money for—"

"Or what else?" she prodded, eyes glittering.

He paused, gradually beginning to see where she was leading him. "Or . . . you form an alliance with somebody who's already got one."

"Exactly!"

Jaren leaned against the massive willow trunk, dispirited. "Not so fast, Athaya. Osfonin may be willing to shelter runaway Trelanes on occasion, but I don't think he'll be so quick to offer Reykan troops. Not even to you. He can't abide Durek, and—"

"I wasn't thinking of Osfonin."

Suddenly bursting with energy, Athaya jumped to her feet and brushed the dusty grass from her skirt. "We'll need to hire a coach tomorrow," she said, rapidly counting the number of coins in her purse. Then she looked to the east, eyes blazing with purpose. "Where we're going next, it will serve us to arrive in style."

CHAPTER 8

✳

THE COACH LURCHED TO THE RIGHT AS IT ROLLED OVER A dip in the cobbled road that led through the center of Delfarham to the gates of the royal palace. After traveling by translocation to the nearby village of Feckham, Athaya and Jaren had walked to the city's outskirts and hired the coach to carry them into the heart of Caithe's capital. The driver studied them cynically at first, doubtful that a pair of ragged commoners—probably laborers in the nearby salt mines—would have the coin it took to hire him, and gruffly demanded payment in advance. The silver coins that Athaya folded into his palm had appeased him readily enough, as had her promise to add an extra coin if he got them to the castle by noon. On a fine day such as this, she knew that Durek might well finish his business early and spend the afternoon sailing the bay on his pleasure barge.

Beside her, Jaren tapped his feet on the floorboards in erratic rhythm. He peeked through the window curtains with uneasy regularity, as if afraid they were being followed.

"You're nervous," Athaya remarked, feeling far from calm herself.

"I have a right to be," he murmured, letting the curtains fall back into place. "This is your home, Athaya. You grew up here. I've only been to Delfar Castle three times in my life, and on two of those occasions I got myself tossed into the dun-

116

geons. Forgive me if I'm a bit skeptical of getting a warm welcome."

Athaya took his hand and squeezed it; his palm was as moist as hers. "Ah, but back then you weren't a member of the family."

Jaren arched a blond eyebrow at her. "And that's supposed to make me feel better?"

The coach rolled to a stop a few yards from the portcullis at the castle's south gate. A few heartbeats later, Athaya heard the approaching crunch of guardsman's boots on gravel.

"Do you really think this will work?" Jaren whispered.

"It has to," she replied with a shake of her head, unwilling to consider any other possibility. "Durek may be stubborn and narrow-minded about a lot of things, but he's not stupid. If he refuses me, then neither one of us has much chance of defeating the Sage." She regarded Jaren wryly. "And don't you think it's a bit late to be asking?"

Athaya swallowed her own misgivings—did she truly know what she was doing?—and drew back the curtains to reveal herself to the gatehouse guard. She recognized the uniformed man that stepped up to question them: it was Lieutenant Berns, Captain Parr's first-in-command.

"State your busi—"

His routine query trailed off into stunned silence.

"Good morning, Lieutenant," Athaya replied cordially, as if her unannounced visit was the most natural thing in the world. "I've come to see the king."

Lieutenant Berns backed away slowly, staring at her as if she were King Kelwyn come back from the dead. His face paled, white as a full moon above his crimson surcoat. "C-captain?" he called out unsteadily, his voice little more than a squeak. "Captain Parr!"

His disgruntled superior stepped out of the cool shelter of the gatehouse and squinted against the midday sun. "What the devil is—"

Like his lieutenant before him, Captain Parr never finished his sentence. "Stand back!" he shouted suddenly, pushing Berns back toward the gatehouse. "Don't let her touch you. This has to be some sort of trick . . . ."

As he began to fumble with the scabbard at his belt, Athaya withdrew into herself, rapidly lapsing into the quiescent preparedness required to fend off the unwelcome advances of a corbal crystal. She gripped Jaren's arm, silently warning him to brace himself as best he could; perhaps if the crystal was not too large—and few guardsmen could afford weapons with any but the smallest stones embedded in them—he would suffer through only a little pain until they were admitted inside.

Though impatience made his fingers awkward, Captain Parr was soon able to strip the leather casing from his sword hilt and hold the corbal-studded pommel up to the brilliant midday sun.

Clearly, he expected something to happen. He gulped very hard when it did not. Though her mind was filled with the hum of the crystal's voice and the denying murmurs of her own, Athaya still managed to smile at him as if indulging the vagaries of an eccentric relative. She touched a finger to the pommel and gently pushed the weapon to one side. "We are in somewhat of a hurry, Captain."

Blanching, Parr let the sword fall useless at his side. "Not you, too," he whispered. Athaya detected a rare tremor of fear in his voice as she continued to speak defiance to the corbal's heart. *I feel nothing from you. You cannot harm me now. I know your secrets and you have no power over me . . .*

The coach shifted as Jaren slid closer to the doorway. He smiled at the captain as if he were one of his dearest friends and not the man who had killed his trusted manservant and very nearly caused his own death as well. "If you'd be so good as to tell his Majesty we're here?" he said, gracefully cool under Parr's heated glare.

Even Athaya flashed him a look of surprise, and it took a moment before she realized what he'd done. To avoid letting his enemy know he could not protect himself as Athaya did, Jaren had placed himself under a sealing spell, trusting that she would release him once they had successfully bluffed their way past the danger.

By this time, several other guardsmen and curious servants had gathered around the coach, all keeping a safe distance as they murmured to one another in agitated whispers. Athaya was known to everyone here. In the courtyard beyond the gatehouse, an elderly laundress caught sight of her and promptly dropped her basket of clean bedding in the dust. Even the driver turned to gape at her in dread, suddenly envisioning the unpleasant fate that might befall him simply for daring to bring her here.

"Is his Majesty expecting you?" Parr asked sarcastically, struggling to regain a few shards of his shattered composure.

"I doubt it," Athaya replied, unable to contain a vagrant smile. "I doubt it very much." She tapped on the roof of the coach with her knuckles. "Driver, take us across the yard to that set of double doors."

The guardsmen let the coach proceed through the gate, doubtful that they could stop Athaya from going wherever she cared to whether they permitted it or no, but Captain Parr followed at a close distance, determined not to let the pair of wizards out of his sight.

The driver gave a sigh of profound relief as Athaya and Jaren alighted from the coach, visibly glad to be rid of such notorious passengers. Before the guardsmen could think of a reason to retain him, he snapped the reins and rumbled out of the courtyard, not bothering to claim the extra piece of silver that Athaya had promised him earlier.

"You needn't escort me to the king if you don't care to," Athaya remarked to the captain. "I know my way about."

"I'll take you," he growled back in reply. Behind his mask of scorn, Athaya knew that Captain Parr was frantically trying to figure out what she was up to and what to do about it. "The king is in council right now. Follow me."

In truth, it was he who followed her, not wishing to turn his back to her for an instant. Athaya kept one eye on the sword in his hand—the corbal was back beneath its leather casing now, so at least she would be able to conjure a shielding spell if he dared to use the blade. Somehow, though, she sensed that the captain was intrigued enough by her presence here not to harm her unless the king gave his permission—something she sincerely hoped he would not do once he heard her out.

The unlikely trio entered the castle proper, skirting the Great Hall on their way to the council chamber. Servants and courtiers alike recognized her, gaping disbelief, but many of Caithe's nobility stared blankly past her as if she were invisible, not bothering to look beyond her homespun kirtle and peasant cloak.

The antechamber to the council hall was occupied by two guards, both of whom snapped to attention at the sight of their superior, then abandoned the posture just as rapidly when they realized who was with him. Through the double doors behind them, Athaya could hear the strident voices of wrathful men.

Captain Parr stepped past the guards and strode into the hall without knocking. Instantly, Athaya heard her brother's voice soundly berating him for the interruption. Then came the low murmur of the captain's voice, and afterward, an eerie spell of silence.

"WHO?"

Athaya grinned in spite of herself, suspecting that Durek's cry had been heard at the opposite end of the city.

She selected that moment to move into the arched doorway, unhindered by the guardsmen. As she gazed upon the array of goggle-eyed gentlemen seated at the enameled table, each of them transfixed by her presence, it was all she could do not to break into self-indulgent laughter.

Congratulations, Athaya, she told herself with a touch of pride. *That was without doubt the most dramatic entrance of your life.*

"Good morning, Durek," she said cordially, inclining her head to her brother. "My lords of the council." Her gaze darkened as it came to rest on the black-robed man standing at the king's right hand. "Archbishop Lukin."

Durek rose slowly to his feet, not daring to take his eyes from her, but as he began to step toward her, Lukin rushed to block his way. "Stand back, sire!" he cried dramatically, reaching for a leather pouch at his waist that undoubtedly contained a corbal crystal. "I shall protect you from—"

"Don't bother," Captain Parr remarked, his upper lip crimping sourly. "I already tried it. Seems she knows the same trick those Sarian wizards in Eriston do."

Ignoring the fitful mutterings of the council, Athaya looked past the now-horrified archbishop and focused her attention on Durek as if the two of them were in the room alone. Curiously, now that he was past his initial shock, Durek seemed of all his councillors the least surprised at her appearance. It was as if, like the Sage before him, he had expected her to come eventually, though knowing neither the time nor place.

Durek, however, clearly welcomed the fulfillment of his prophecy far less than had the Sage.

"Your Majesty, may I speak with you in private?" Athaya asked him formally, careful to do nothing to offend. She made no attempt to approach him, aware that her slightest move would be interpreted as a threat. "It's about the Sage of Sare."

"I've no doubt that it is," Lukin snarled in response, placing a protective hand on the king's shoulder. "Don't listen to her, sire. The Sage is simply another of her many agents. Her appearance here is merely a ruse designed to—"

Durek closed his eyes and sighed irritably. "Jon, be silent."

He flicked the archbishop's hand from his shoulder as if it were a speck of dirt. "And do move out of my way."

Lukin's jaw dropped as if weighted down by lead.

"Archbishop, you will conduct the council in my absence," Durek instructed him curtly. "I will speak to Athaya in my private audience chamber."

"Sire, I cannot allow you to—"

Durek wheeled on him in cold fury. "It is not your place to allow *me* anything," he snapped. Behind him, Athaya's eyes opened a fraction wider; she rarely heard that amount of venom in her brother's voice . . . unless, of course, he happened to be talking to *her*.

Durek stalked out of the council hall leaving both archbishop and council speechless in his wake. His footsteps halted abruptly the moment he reached the antechamber and saw that Athaya had not come alone. "What's *he* doing here?" he demanded, jerking his thumb rudely in Jaren's direction.

Jaren offered the king a courteous nod—as courteous a one as he could provide to a man who had twice sought his death—and murmured a brief greeting that Durek flatly ignored. The king turned a flustered gaze upon Athaya and began to sputter, more upset by Jaren's presence than he had been at her own. "Cecile wrote me about your . . . I can't believe you—"

"We would have invited you to the wedding," Athaya cut in, "but frankly, we didn't think you'd come."

Durek made a rumbling noise in the back of his throat and marched off in the direction of his audience chamber, brusquely motioning his captain and his unexpected guests to follow.

"You stay here," he ordered Jaren once they had reached the small waiting room outside the audience chamber. He pointed toward an array of wooden benches on which were perched other petitioners awaiting the king's pleasure, none of whom seemed overly pleased at sharing their place with a known wizard.

"Captain, I want you to keep an eye on him. But don't kill him," Durek added, aware that Parr would do just that if not specifically instructed otherwise. After a moment's pause, the king clarified his orders even further. "And see to it that no one else does, either."

The last trace of hope faded from the captain's eyes.

Just before she left him, Athaya touched Jaren's arm as if in farewell. *"Aperi potentiam,"* she whispered, releasing his self-imposed sealing spell. She could not trust Captain Parr to obey the king's command—even the most well-trained hound would strain to resist a juicy mutton joint tossed at his feet despite his master's order to leave it be—and Jaren might have need of his protective spells.

Athaya followed her brother into the sun-drenched chamber and closed the door firmly behind her. While Durek poured himself a steadying glass of wine, Athaya surveyed the familiar chamber, acutely aware of the volatile history contained within its wainscoted walls. It was in this room that she had endured countless reprimands from her father, in this room that she had inadvertently caused his death, and to this room she had been brought after her last arrest so that Durek could demand that she cease her treasonous crusade.

Her brother looked far less sure of himself today than he had then, perhaps already aware, as she was, of the peril his kingdom faced. Belatedly, he offered her a cup of wine as well. Once she would have hesitated, suspecting him of seeking retribution for what Nicolas had done; now she accepted it graciously.

"I don't think I have to ask why you're here," he said, slouching wearily into a cushioned chair near the window. Odd, but he did not seem to fear her. He was gruff with her, of course, but Athaya sensed that he acted thus mostly out of habit and not out of any existing feelings of resentment. More than anything else, she reflected, he looked resigned. Weary. And maybe a little desperate.

"This has something to do with that Sarian wizard running rampant in my western shires, doesn't it?" he went on, swirling his wine absently around its pewter cup.

Athaya sat down on an ornately carved walnut bench across from him, setting her shabby skirts to one side. "I went to see him in Nadiera yesterday. I tried to convince him to return to Sare, but he refused. He is quite resolute."

"Wizards are a stubborn lot." Durek paused, waiting for a rejoinder that did not come. "The council and I were discussing what to do about him when you made your appearance." He did not say whether they had come to any conclusions, but judging from the angry voices she had heard coming from the council hall before Parr announced her, she doubted that they had.

"As I told you once before, the Sage is totally convinced

that he is destined to rule Caithe. The core of his cult's belief is that wizards were meant to rule mankind by right of their magic. And as their leader, the Sage is regarded as some sort of messiah."

"I thought that was your job."

Again he waited for a rejoinder and again he waited in vain. Athaya had not come to quarrel this time. "Durek, can we try to have a rational conversation just once in our lives?"

Durek sipped at his wine. A begrudging mumble of assent echoed benignly in the bowl of his cup.

"I already know he's taken over Eriston and Nadiera," she went on, "but we both know he won't be satisfied with that for long. Not at the rate he's gaining support."

"No." Durek shifted uncomfortably in his chair. "My men have tried to assassinate him twice, but I imagine you've already heard what a dismal failure both ventures were. Eriston was bad enough, but Nadiera! The Sarians crushed my forces before they could get close enough to even *try* using their corbals. And what good was having the damned crystals anyway? His followers—and you, apparently," Durek added with a troubled frown, "know how to resist them. And that's the only weapon my men have."

"It is," she agreed. "At the moment."

He rolled his eyes, irritated by her cryptic reply. "So what can you possibly want from me? I haven't any magic spells to use against him. Or have you simply come to offer terms for my surrender?"

"I've come to offer my help. You want the Sage out of Caithe. So do I." She leaned forward, seizing his gaze with her own. "I'm proposing that we join forces and do it together."

Durek blinked slowly, like a barn owl. "I can't possibly be hearing this. You want an *alliance*?"

"If we join forces, then the Sage can no longer exploit a divided kingdom, but will be forced to face a united one. Caithe would no longer be split into three factions, but two—and you and I would have by far the larger one. If we keep fighting amongst ourselves, Durek, it will only advance the Sage's cause."

Durek gazed at her intensely, searching for signs of a trick—as she was a wizard, he fully expected her to have a few deceptions tucked away for safekeeping. "What exactly are you proposing?"

"You have an army. The men are organized and they're

well-trained fighters. I have followers, but they're scattered and in hiding, without any central control. But if we combine the two—if we distribute *my* magicians throughout *your* army—we might just have a chance of defeating the Sage."

Durek snorted. "My men would never work with wizards." He gestured indistinctly toward the antechamber. "It's all Captain Parr can do not to kill that husband of yours where he stands."

"They'd have no choice about joining forces if you ordered them to. Durek, listen. The Sage already has one of the largest shires in Caithe under his control and he got it with very little effort. He's recruiting more people every day—people who are angry at what's been taken from them and want it back. I can't defeat him if I have to spend most of my time watching my back for the Tribunal, and you can't win a war against wizards without the kind of help I'm offering."

"Blackmailing me into this alliance, are you?"

"You can think so, but you know that isn't true. Frankly, it isn't *my* crown he's after."

Durek chewed on his lip thoughtfully, trying to find a flaw in her plan. "But what about the corbals? If the Sarians know how to withstand them, the Sage will simply use them against us. Then what good will all of your proffered magicians be? I'd be right back where I am now."

"Most of his people can't resist them," she replied. "In fact, I'll wager that the men you sent against him in Eriston were carefully manipulated so that they encountered the only wizards in the Sage's army who can. But you had no way of knowing that, and it's in the Sage's best interest to make you believe he has a greater advantage than he does. I can resist the corbals, it's true, but only because I have a great deal of power."

Durek pointed quizzically at the antechamber doors. "But he—"

"Jaren used a different sort of trick, I'm afraid," she confessed, sensing that Durek would not take advantage of the knowledge. But as for others . . . "Although I'd rather you not pass that information along to your captain just yet."

Athaya lifted her yet-untouched goblet and swallowed some of the fine Evarshot wine to soothe her dry throat; though she felt her words were having some effect on him, she remained anxious in his presence. Too much was at stake this time.

"This business about resisting corbals isn't as imposing as it sounds," she continued, hoping to allay his fears. "Just because I know how to stop a corbal crystal from hurting doesn't mean I always can. I have to be ready for it." Seeing Durek's puzzled stare, she added, "It's like a shield—the steel won't help me if it's resting at my side when the enemy strikes a blow. I can't cast spells while I'm doing it. No wizard can. It takes too much concentration. If you ask Captain Parr, I suspect he'll tell you that his corbal weapon was taken away before he and his men were pelted with magic."

Vital as that fact was, Durek merely acknowledged it with a nod, his mind busily working on some other concern. "Why wouldn't you want the Sage to win?" he asked abruptly. "He's practically offering you the crown."

"Not practically," she corrected, "he already has. But for the price of Caithe's enslavement." Athaya met his pointed gaze. "I've rebelled against you in one thing only: the treatment of my people. I've never wanted your crown, no matter what Lukin and those like him have tried to make you believe."

After pondering her words for a moment, Durek set his cup aside and walked quietly to the bay window overlooking the sea. For several minutes he let the breezes tousle his thinning hair, staring at the waves as if reading something in their motion that would tell him what to do. Once, he whirled on her suddenly, on the verge of ordering her from his sight, and then, trapped by his internal struggles, he turned his back to her again. He did not want her help, she knew that perfectly well, but he desperately needed it and the conflict was a torture to him.

When he next spoke, each word seemed forced out from the deepest part of him. "I assume you have . . . conditions?"

Athaya smothered the flare of triumph that blazed up inside her. Now was the time to tread carefully. Everything she wanted was within her grasp, but it could all slip away if she snatched at it too quickly. Durek was a proud man and needed to feel this was his doing as much as hers.

"First of all, I'd ask you to disband the Tribunal. I know you've never been entirely comfortable with their tactics, and if we're to work together it makes no sense to allow them to continue persecuting my people."

Durek nodded vaguely, neither granting nor denying her request. "And?"

Athaya swallowed, her throat parched as sand despite the wine she'd drunk. "And I want the Church to stop enforcing the rite of absolution. I can't stop Archbishop Lukin and his priests from preaching against us if they want to, nor stop anyone from being absolved if they truly believe it's the right thing to do. But I won't have absolution forced upon anyone against their will. Besides," she added, "until this campaign is over, we'll need all the wizards we can get."

Again, Durek nodded noncommittally. "And?"

"And I want it to be legal to teach magic in Caithe again. There would be no sense in freeing the Lorngeld from absolution if laws still exist forbidding them from being trained."

Durek's sidelong glance was darkly wry. "So basically, you want the same things you've always wanted."

"Compared to what the Sage wants," she replied, "my demands are rather benign. If we are successful, the Lorngeld gain their freedom and you get to keep your throne . . . not to mention your life. The Sage tried to take it once before," she reminded him. "He'll surely try again."

Durek leaned against the windowsill and studied her in silence for a long time. She felt as if they had been separated since birth and he was searching her face for signs of a family resemblance. He was not seeing the wayward little sister of his youth, but a grown woman who, despite her peasant garb, was just as passionate about the future of her homeland and its citizens as he was. They simply possessed vastly different notions of what that future should be.

"Durek, I know we've never been close. But we have to work together in this. We'll both lose everything if we don't."

With that, the breath went out of him. He had no choice but to accept her offer, and they both knew it. Nevertheless, he wasn't desperate enough to give her everything she asked for so easily. "We'll have to discuss your conditions in detail, of course. I can tolerate them on a temporary basis, but anything more than that will have to wait until your people have proven themselves trustworthy allies. We can renegotiate our agreement once this campaign is done. Assuming we're both still around to do it," he finished solemnly.

Athaya appraised him, looking for hidden meanings behind his words. He hadn't promised not to betray her later once he had used her people to fight off the Sage, but at least he hadn't refused to cooperate outright. It was as much as she could hope to get from him at this point in their precarious alliance, and she had to be content for now.

Durek steepled his fingers and tapped them together restlessly. "And I have a few conditions of my own. I don't know where you've hidden him, but I want you to bring Nicolas back here where I can keep an eye on him. I won't harm him, but he did try to kill me, intentionally or not, and he should be placed in my custody so I can have him watched."

Athaya considered that for a moment. Nicolas couldn't possibly remain in Adam's care forever, and Master Hedric had already assured her that there was little chance of his attacking Durek again now that the brunt of the Sage's compulsion had been broken. Besides, Delfarham was his home. And deep inside, she believed that Durek would not punish him.

"I can send Jaren to fetch him this very afternoon," she offered. "But if I do, will you release Lord Gessinger? He is an old and frail man and can no longer threaten you. And it would please Cecile so."

Durek stared blankly at her for a moment; he had utterly forgotten the old councillor. "Very well." Then his eyes grew distant. "I suppose I could send him to Reyka to keep her company . . . and to deliver a few of Mailen's playthings that she has asked for. I meant to send them days ago, but I wished to enclose a letter . . ."

He didn't finish, but he didn't have to. Athaya knew what he was thinking. *And I didn't know what to say to her.*

As long as he was granting boons, Athaya decided it couldn't hurt to ask something for herself. "And technically, I'm still an outlaw. If we're to work together, then it seems only proper to—"

"Yes, yes, I suppose you're right," he said gathering in his truant attentions. "It won't take but a few minutes to draft a pardon. A temporary one," he noted.

"And I'd also appreciate it if you could reinstate Kale Eavon to his post in your guard—if he wants it back."

Durek wrinkled his brows at her; he wasn't vexed yet, but he was growing so. "Just how many other demands do you have?"

Athaya backed off a bit, aware that she might be asking for too much too soon. "It was only a request. If we're to be on the same side of this conflict, we may as well start with a clean slate."

Durek laughed mirthlessly. "I suppose next you'll be wanting Archbishop Lukin to lift your excommunication?"

"No," she replied, perhaps more firmly than she intended.

"I'll be a part of his church when they will accept me for what I am. Not before."

Durek snorted something unintelligible, but did not offer further comment. In the silence that followed, Athaya bowed her head in a gesture of humility. "Is there anything else you would ask of me?"

"Only that you make it clear to your people that they are under *my* command in this, not yours."

"I'll tell them."

He stuck a finger in her face and his ruby signet ring sparkled with sunlight. "That includes you as well."

"I understand."

"And . . ." He winced and turned his back to her. This was clearly a request he did not wish to make of her, but tugged on him more strongly than did his pride. "Cecile . . ." he began, absently twisting his signet ring as if it had suddenly grown too snug. "She does not answer my letters. But I think she would come home . . . if *you* asked her to."

Athaya ventured a step forward. "Perhaps. But we're at war now, Durek, whether the Sage has formally declared one on us or not. I think that Cecile and the children will be safer where they are—especially Mailen."

Durek sighed heavily as he stared out across the sea; the sea that led to Reyka and the city where his family had fled. "I suppose so. I just thought . . . but never mind." His eyes were burdened with regret. He was too proud to admit it, but he missed his wife and children a great deal. "My daughter . . . she would be over a year old now."

Athaya recalled the only time she had seen the child, during a secret visit to Cecile last autumn. "Lillian is a happy child, Durek. And beautiful. She looks much like her mother."

Durek nodded, seemingly pleased.

"I'd best go tell the council about this," he said abruptly, shaking off his cloak of melancholy. He drained the rest of his wine in one bracing gulp. "God's blood, they'll be furious. I won't be surprised if the word 'abdicate' doesn't come up at least once."

"With respect, Durek, some of my people will be just as appalled at what I've done. I haven't actually consulted them about this," she admitted. "I simply saw no other way."

"The council will say you bewitched me," Durek said as he reached the door. It sounded like an accusation; a challenge that he defied her to meet.

Athaya shrugged. "Or they might say we're finally setting aside our differences to do the best thing for Caithe."

Durek grunted his disbelief. "Why should they believe that when I wouldn't have an hour ago?"

Athaya followed him to the door but bade him wait before he opened it. "Always remember that I will aid and advise you, but it is your army to command. You are the king of Caithe, and I have no wish to alter that. I never have."

He glanced at her curiously, puzzled how she could say such a thing to him, knowing he had sought her downfall, if not her death, for almost two years. But he believed her now—Athaya saw it in his eyes—and she sensed that he was vaguely ashamed of himself for never having done so before.

"Come. The council will be waiting."

He closed his hand around the door handle. "Just remember, Athaya," he cautioned her, his gaze suddenly cloaked with shadows. "We may be allies in this, but we are far from being friends."

Despite the warning, Athaya followed her brother out of the audience chamber feeling that she had won two victories that day. Not only did Caithe now have a fighting chance to survive the Sage's onslaught, but she felt closer to Durek than she ever had before. That did not say a great deal—they had never much liked one another—but maybe after all this time, each was finally coming to understand the other better.

But if we don't act quickly, she realized, *then all the understanding in the world isn't going to save us.*

Under the pink and orange skies of twilight, the Sage of Sare sat cross-legged on the crest of a hill a short distance away from the gates of his Nadieran manor. He was an island in a sea of wide-eyed suppliants, all of them gazing on him like children engrossed in a well-told tale.

A six-year-old girl knelt motionless on the grass before him. Her mother hovered close behind as, eyes closed, the Sage burrowed gently in the child's mind. His hands cupped the girl's head, almost obscuring the tiny orb in their fleshy mass, and his thumbs pressed down lightly on her thick-lashed eyes, making her slightly dizzy.

"I am sorry, child," he said at last, drawing his hands away. "The token of God is not with you."

Crestfallen, the girl's lower lip began to tremble. Her mother murmured a few words of thanks to the Sage and then led her daughter away; the girl departed bravely, valiantly trying not to cry. In contrast, her mother breathed an indebted sigh to the heavens, unable to comprehend a world in which magic was not the most abhorrent of fates and where her daughter would not grow up to be hunted and absolved.

"Your Grace?"

Couric was picking his way swiftly through the crowd to his master's side, his creamy yellow tunic standing out like a beacon amid the expanse of tattered brown wool. "A word with you, your Grace?" he asked, with a shade more apprehension than was his habit. "In private?"

A chorus of dissent rose up from the people gathered on the hill. "No, don't go!" one man begged, reaching out to touch the Sage's sleeve. "I've been waiting for three days to see you!"

"Yes, please stay!" a dozen others cried.

"I have already stayed longer than I ought," the Sage replied amiably, rising to sandaled feet and shaking the grass from his wine-colored cloak. "But do not fear, I shall return tomorrow."

The summer air was lightly scented with roses as he and Couric strolled back to the manor. Behind them, the crowd reluctantly dispersed, downcast peasants returning to their makeshift tents.

"Well?" the Sage asked, cocking an ebony brow. "What is so important that you must tear me away from my devoted subjects?" His tone was limned with mockery.

"News from the capital, your Grace." Couric cleared his throat and fixed his gaze on a prickled weed at the side of the path, loath to deliver his unpleasant message. "It appears . . . that is, it—"

"Bad news, indeed, to foul *your* slippery tongue."

Couric drank deep of the sweet-scented air, steadying himself as if with wine. "King Durek and Princess Athaya have formed an alliance."

The Sage reeled backward as if he had stumbled into the confines of a binding spell. He glared at his companion with distaste. "If this is your idea of a joke," he said, his voice a low and threatening growl, "then it's a damned poor one."

"No, your Grace. A trusted agent in Delfarham heard the news from the king's own criers this very afternoon and relayed it to me directly. The princess and her brother have made peace with one another."

The Sage's cheeks flushed crimson with rage, matching the

color of his cloak. "But that's impossible! They *hate* each
other! It's—" Then he broke off, staring into pastel-colored
space.

Couric ventured a step closer. "Your Grace?"

"No. It can't be . . ."

The Sage clutched the trunk of a nearby dogwood tree as if
his world had suddenly tilted sideways. His eyes took on a
pained and glazed expression.

"Your Grace? Are you ill? Shall I fetch—"

"Dameronne's prophecy . . ."

Slowly, the Sage paced a circle around the tree, speaking
with a flat and faraway voice. "Our time will come when a
woman blessed by both heaven and earth comes forth to lead
the Lorngeld into glory. She will live among the high and the
low and will wield powers unseen since the days of the ancients. She will obtain aid in her endeavor from an unexpected
quarter, and in so doing will usher in a golden age of a great
wizard king . . ."

The Sage did not finish his recitation. "Aid from an unexpected quarter," he repeated, staring blindly into the dying sun.
"Aid from an *unexpected quarter*! Dameronne foresaw this . . .
but I did not." He struck a blow at the dogwood tree, harming
his fist far more, and then, rage spent, his eyes clouded over
with disgrace. "God's greatest servant should not make mistakes such as this."

"Your Grace, that line of the prophecy was not at all specific. Do not take it—"

"Enough, Couric."

The Sage squared his shoulders, as if regaining dignity lost
by a clumsy fall, and proceeded toward the manor. "This alliance complicates matters," he conceded. "Still, it cannot stop
us. A wizard king is destined to rule this land, and that dis-
counts both the princess and her oldest brother. But our future
conquests will not come to us as easily as Eriston or Nadiera."
He shook back his mane of hair, whisking the last cobwebs of
shock from his brain. "Prophecy or no, it would have served
us better to keep those two quarreling with one another."

"If the princess would rather be the king's ally than yours,
then it is proof that she will never join us."

The Sage paused a moment before replying. "Not willingly,
no."

They passed through the manor gates barely acknowledging
the crisp salutes from the guardsmen on duty.

"Your orders?" Couric asked.

The Sage halted in the center of the courtyard, surveying the area as he had upon first arriving as the manor's new lord. "I have been in Nadiera long enough, I think. Tomorrow you will appoint someone to hold this manor for me in my absence. It will be yours, as I have promised," he reminded his trusted friend, "but until I am the undisputed ruler of this land, I want your clever head with me."

Then he glared up at the limestone towers of the manor, showing little pride in his possession of them. "Perhaps it is time we turned our attentions to the south. I understand that the princess has a large following in the city of Kilfarnan. If we move quickly, we could be there in a matter of days. And if the wizards of that city do not join us," he went on, shifting his gaze to Couric, "then at least we can keep them from going to the princess' aid. Or the king's."

Couric nodded, pleased with his lord's decision. "Yes, your Grace."

The Sage drew his cloak closer about him; the sun had slouched below the horizon and the air grew chill in its absence. "Inform my officers that we will depart in the morning. And don't spread this about any more than you have to," he added, setting off toward his private room in the north wing. "Best to strike at Athaya's allies before they can prepare for our coming."

CHAPTER 9

✳✳

"**I** REFUSE TO LISTEN TO THE ADVICE OF A . . . A *WIZARD*,"
the earl of Tusel cried in frustration, pointing his finger at Athaya like one child accusing another of tat-
tling. "It's unnatural!" He wiped a sodden handkerchief
miserably across his brow, his once-cheerful disposition curdling rapidly in the stifling heat of mid-July. The temperature
in the council hall had risen steadily since the king's advisers
convened that morning, and the topic of discussion only worsened already cranky tempers.

Durek's glare was incongruously icy. "You will listen, sir, or
you will be dismissed from this council. Permanently."

Defiance evaporated from the earl's youthful face and he
promptly sank into moody silence.

Athaya tucked a sticky lock of hair back inside her beaded
chaplet and tried not to explode. She had been an unwelcome
fixture in the council hall for ten days now, and the strain of
the council's obstinacy was mounting. Even Durek's demands
for their cooperation helped little, as most of his advisers were
of the unspoken opinion that it was far riskier to deal with wizards than to resist their king's commands—commands they
suspected he issued simply because his sister bewitched him
to. She fervently wished that Mosel Gessinger was here and
not halfway to Ath Luaine; he was the sole member of Durek's
council who knew firsthand of the Sage's threat and might
have been able to sway them where she could not.

Unlike the great lords of Caithe, Athaya's following in
Kaiburn proved cautiously willing to embrace this newfound
alliance. Not that the wizards were quick to trust their king—
Ranulf had expectorated his skepticism quite clearly when
Athaya had made the announcement—but a practical assess-
ment of their plight forced them to realize that they could not
defeat the Sage without assistance. And even if Durek re-
scinded the temporary concessions he had granted, it was generally accepted among the residents of the camp that the
Lorngeld of Caithe couldn't possibly be worse off than they
were now.

"As I was saying," Athaya went on, giving her brother a
subtle nod of thanks for his intercession with Tusel, "the Sage
has likely heard of our alliance by now and will be making his
next move quickly. We've already received scattered reports of
armed men moving across the shires southeast of Nadiera. We
can't sit around this table any longer and debate the best way
to proceed; we have to *do* something even if it turns out to be
wrong." She jabbed a finger at the gilt-edged map unfurled
across the table. "Again, I propose that we concentrate no
fewer than seven hundred magicians throughout the central
shires to block the Sage's progress eastward."

"I don't want all those spells going off in *my* shire," one of
the older lords grumbled—one whose lands rested in the lush
countryside of central Caithe—then retreated back into silence
at Durek's potent glare of warning.

"Using wizards to defend ourselves will only make things
worse," complained the man to his left. "Country soldiers
would just as soon kill our wizards as the Sage's. They won't
see the difference. Assuming there is one," he added, barely
audible.

"The lords of the land will never stand for any of this,"
Lukin declared. He stood apart from the others, keeping near
the window to reinforce his profound disapproval of Athaya's
presence among them. Not a drop of sweat shone on his brow,
and Athaya speculated that the archbishop was simply too
stubborn to perspire and thus admit he was just as human as
the rest of them.

"They'll damn well stand for it if I tell them to," Durek
pointed out sharply. "If they refuse, they are freely declaring
themselves enemies of the Crown, and I can revoke their titles
and lands in reprisal."

Athaya noticed a few of Durek's advisers shifting in their

seats, suddenly recalculating the risks involved in resisting their king's wishes. Earning his anger was one thing; suffering tangible retribution was quite another.

"Many of Caithe's lords are more willing to help us than you might think," Athaya pointed out. She addressed the archbishop directly but he refused to look at her, unwilling to acknowledge that she was present, much less that she existed at all. "I spoke with several of them over the past year and most only refused to aid me out of loyalty to Durek—and fear of the Tribunal." That earned her a quick and venomous glare. "But now that those two obstacles are gone, albeit temporarily," she added for Durek's benefit, "they should assist us gladly."

"And betray their God at the same time," Lukin muttered. He turned on Durek in a blur of black wool. "I cannot sanction any of this! As spiritual lord of this land, it is my sworn duty to shield your subjects from sorcery."

"As it is mine to see to their survival."

"Is that more important than their *souls*?"

Durek's gaze frosted over with austerity. "Jon, do not defy me in this—"

"Shall I then defy God? It is *His* judgment that will be the harsher." Despairingly, he closed his fist around the silver Saint Adriel's medal he wore around his neck. "I am glad that our sainted Bishop Adriel is not alive to witness this travesty."

"Damn it all, Jon—"

Before the quarrel could escalate further, a crimson-clad sentry knocked softly and slipped into the council hall. "Sire? You asked to be informed the moment Prince Nicolas arrived. He and his escort are waiting in the Great Hall."

"Good," Durek breathed, grateful for the interruption. "Bring them here at once." The king rose to his feet. "We'll continue this later," he announced, dismissing his council with the timbre of his voice. As the men filed out of the hall— rather eagerly, Athaya noted—Lukin drifted to the king's side and lingered there like an unpleasant odor.

"Sire, I do not think it wise to have the prince within the walls of this castle." He flicked his eyes meaningfully toward Athaya. "After what he did—"

"*Tried* to do, Jon," Durek replied without looking at him. "And you've already made your opinion on the matter more than clear . . . and with great frequency."

Lukin's expression of bitter defeat was not lost on Athaya. She doubted that her brother had ever defied his archbishop as staunchly as he had these past few days, and the suspicion that he was not as influential as he liked to think must be eating at the cleric's innards like maggots on spoiled meat. Athaya felt Lukin's acerbic eye upon her as they waited for Prince Nicolas' arrival, convinced that she was behind the whole of the king's stubbornness. He never dared to consider that perhaps Durek was simply showing a bit more of Kelwyn's spirited blood than he had in the past and was gradually growing more comfortable with kingship after a somewhat precarious start.

Jaren and Nicolas entered the room first, closely trailed by the ever-watchful Captain Parr. Jaren's eyes went right to Athaya, warming with surprise as he surveyed her attire. Having reclaimed her old wardrobe, Athaya had forsaken her tattered peasant's kirtle for a simple but elegant gown of pale blue silk trimmed with silver thread. The infant alliance with Durek was shaky enough at it was, and she did not want to appear to be baiting his Majesty's council by dressing in rags when better garments were available to her.

I haven't seen you look so beautiful in a long time, he sent.

Thank you, Athaya returned, frowning good-naturedly at the backward compliment. *I think.* She flicked a studious glance at her brother. *How is he?*

Her query was answered instead by the entrance of Master Hedric. He greeted her only fleetingly, keeping his attention fixed upon the prince to ensure that he remained well under control of his compulsion in Durek's presence. Waiting in the doorway behind Hedric was the unexpected figure of the earl of Belmarre. Durek gave the earl an ambiguous nod, aware that he should remember him from one court function or another but unable to match a name to the face. As for Hedric, the king glanced to him without a wisp of recognition.

"I am Hedric MacAlliard," Master Hedric supplied graciously, stepping forward and offering Durek a shallow bow. "High Wizard to King Osfonin of Reyka."

Durek concealed his surprise well; only a slight twitch of the lip betrayed him. He knew of the title and of the man who held it—this was the wizard who had first told Athaya of her destiny, the wizard who had trained her to her fullest level of magical potential, the wizard whom, were Durek in a more petulant and vengeful mood, he could blame for all that had befallen his kingdom of late. He appraised the old man with regal impunity, studying the wizened eyes, the cut of his robes, and the gnarled cherrywood staff, and finding him a far more benign sight than expected. Archbishop Lukin, standing near Captain Parr in the corner, glared at the old wizard with a unique form of abhorrence normally reserved for the beggars that forever polluted the steps of Saint Adriel's Cathedral. If he, as prelate of Delfarham, was God's favored servant, then Master Hedric, the most accomplished of magicians, was surely the Devil's.

"I am sorry our arrival was delayed," Hedric said, propping his staff against the council table. "We should have been here days ago, but we had to take a slower pace so as not to upset the prince. Travel seems to worsen his condition. I am the prince's caretaker, you see," he explained, trying to banish some of the confusion clouding the king's face. "With the Sage's spell still threaded in his thoughts, he needs constant care to avoid lapsing back into madness."

"Threaded in his . . . what?"

"I shall explain at your leisure. But now," he said, prodding Nicolas forward like a child, "I think his Highness has something he wishes to say to you?"

Nicolas crept forward reluctantly, his head slightly bowed like a pup fearful of being kicked. He glanced first to Durek, then to Athaya, and then frowned deeply. He seemed to remember that his brother and sister disliked one another— though he was not entirely sure why that was so—and sensed that their being in the same room together, much less being on reasonably good terms, was quite extraordinary.

Athaya scrutinized him closely. Signs of his hidden self were there, but they remained nothing but enticing glimpses, peeking out from behind the Sage's spell like a random thread of sunlight on an overcast afternoon. Thanks to Hedric's tireless attentions, much of Nicolas' childlike manner had been successfully subdued, but he was yet a boy dressed up in prince's clothes, stilted and nervous as a new squire on the first day at his duties, terrified unto death of bungling before his lord.

"Master Hedric told me what I did and I am truly sorry," he began, eyes averted. The words sounded rehearsed, as Athaya knew they must be, but they also rang sincere. "I will gladly accept any punishment you think I deserve."

Durek's face was pinched with bewildered pity as he listened to his brother's brief speech of submission, perhaps grasping the true scope of Nicolas' affliction for the first time.

Perhaps realizing what atrocities his Sarian enemies were capable of, and that if Nicolas could succumb to them so easily,
then so could he.

"I think the spell that binds you is punishment enough,"
Durek murmured uneasily. The archbishop made a disapprov-
ing grunting noise, but his Majesty chose to ignore it. "And it
wasn't exactly your fault if magic forced you to it. However,
while you're here," he added more stiffly, as if to make
amends for the uncharacteristic show of mercy, "you are to
stay confined to your rooms unless I give my express permission. Do you understand?"

Nicolas offered an obedient nod, then waited to hear the remainder of his sentence. Blue eyes gradually widened as he
realized that Durek wasn't going to say anything else. No
doubt Master Hedric had prepared him for the worst, warning
him that imprisonment could be a likely outcome.

"That's all of it," Durek told him, a slight edge of chagrin
to his tone. Then, with a resigned sigh, he added, "I know I've
got every reason to lock you up in a dark room somewhere,
but I have every reason to lock Athaya up, too, and . . . well,
as you can see, I'm letting her run roughshod all over my palace." Durek snorted quietly and looked away, as if to dispel
any notion that he had anything whatsoever to do with their
newfound alliance and sustain the facade that he was simply an
innocent man caught up in events far beyond his meager control

Having dispensed with Nicolas, Durek turned his attention
to the earl. "And you, sir? You look familiar to me, but . . . ?"

"The earl of Belmarre, sire," the gentleman replied with a
bow. "It has been many years since I've been at court." The
earl framed his next words cautiously. "The prince has been at
my estate these last months, in the care of my steward. I hope
you will forgive my role in keeping him hidden from you."

"I have Athaya to thank for that, not you," Durek replied
dryly. He glanced toward the antechamber. "Is your steward
with you? He deserves my thanks for his service, unsolicited as
it was."

The earl shifted his weight from one booted foot to the
other. "No, sire. His . . . duties kept him at Belmarre." A quick
glance to Athaya proved that this was only a fraction of the
truth. More likely, Adam did not wish to see his king at all,
fearful that he would fail to keep a civil tongue in the presence
of the man who had signed his son's death warrant.

"I have come to offer whatever help I can," the earl went on. "My companions have told me of the Sage of Sare and of the threat he poses to us all. Trust that Belmarre will stand with you against him."

Durek's smile was unexpectedly sincere. "I'm glad to hear it. My council is reluctant to believe Athaya's claim that the lords of Caithe will lend their aid now, when they would not do so before."

"Doing so before would have been treason," the earl pointed out. "Now we can serve you both and betray no one."

Lukin turned his back to them in subdued disgust and glided toward the window like a retreating fog. "And may God help us all."

Instead of ignoring the archbishop's invective as the rest of them did, Master Hedric approached the black-clad clergyman, unwilling to let the remark go unchallenged. "You do not wish our assistance? You wish to fight the Sarian wizards alone?"

Lukin whirled on him in a fit of frustrated rage, as maddened by the words as by the very existence of the man who asked them. "I wish that the *lot* of you would go back to hell where you came from!"

"Jon!" Durek barked, resorting to the same tone he employed when scolding young Mailen for touching something he ought not. "Think what you will, but this man is a guest here—"

"Oh, it's all right," Hedric said, lifting a blue-veined hand dismissively. "I've run into this sort of thing before." He turned back to Lukin with a benign half smile and his calm grace made the archbishop look even more vindictive than usual by comparison. "You despise me already," Hedric observed, "and yet we have never even met."

"I despise the taint that you carry and the fact that you take so much pride in it."

Hedric's half smile vanished. "Hatred is itself a taint, your Excellency. A worse one than simple magic could ever be." He spread out his hands, palms up. "We are both God's servants, each in our own way."

The archbishop's nostrils flared like a heated stallion's and his cheeks assumed the striking plum-colored hue that had graced them so often of late. "How *dare* you imply such a thing! I have nothing at all in common with you!"

Hedric studied him in silence, looking past the priest's unforgiving eyes and gritted teeth, deep into the well of his soul.

"No," he said at last, his voice carrying the finality of a funeral bell. "I don't suppose you do."

The air was electric as Athaya hastily moved to Hedric's side. "Why don't I show you to Nicolas' room?" she suggested, pressing the cherrywood staff back into his hand. She was quite certain that a theological debate between the Archbishop of Delfarham and the High Wizard of Reyka would be most unproductive.

"And I shall have my steward find you suitable quarters as well, sir," Durek said to the earl, equally desirous of averting a quarrel. "This way."

They had barely reached the threshold when a uniformed guardsman hastened into the chamber and wiped a ragged salute across his forehead. "Preceptor Mobarec has just arrived at the south gate, your Majesty. He begs immediate audience."

"Mobarec?" Durek's brows furrowed worriedly at Archbishop Lukin; the news must be dire indeed to bring the leader of Caithe's most militant priesthood to his doorstep unannounced. "What brings him here from Kilfarnan?"

The guardsman swallowed audibly. "Sire," he broke in, his voice wavering slightly, "Kilfarnan is taken."

Preceptor Mobarec, spiritual head of the Order of Saint Adriel, was hunched over a mug of cool ale in the Great Hall, looking far older than his sixty-five years in the wake of his breakneck flight from the western city of Kilfarnan. His once-fine traveling cloak was mud-spattered and frayed, and knotted hands shook wildly, splashing drops of ale on the front of his robe whenever he tried to quench his thirst. Athaya knew little about the man other than he had educated Jon Lukin years before, but that told her as much about Mobarec and his sentiments toward the Lorngeld as she ever cared to know.

With Hedric and Nicolas secure in the prince's chambers and the earl of Belmarre safely in the care of his Majesty's steward, Durek, Archbishop Lukin, Athaya, and Jaren gathered around the preceptor to hear his tale. Captain Parr lurked in one corner like a spy, unwilling to let either Athaya or Jaren venture too far from his hawkish gaze. Athaya could not fail to notice how the preceptor avoided looking at her and Jaren as he spoke, as uncomfortable with this new alliance as Lukin was, if not as willing to voice his opinion of it. He slid to the farthest edge of the bench, keeping himself as far from the royal family's most nefarious member as propriety would allow.

"It was as if all the powers of hell had been unleashed upon us," he declared, eyes glazed with memory. "Fire rained from the sky in great, orange sheets; gaping pits opened in the earth to swallow us up; winged creatures swooped down on us, belching smoke and snapping huge rows of teeth . . ." Mobarec shook his head in awesome dismay. "These wizards must truly be the Devil's Children to have command of such things."

"Most of what you saw was probably illusion," Athaya said, although she doubted such a fact would ease the preceptor's mind. "Or more likely, the Sage was using a careful mixture of illusion and reality to keep you constantly guessing if what you were seeing was real or not."

"It hardly matters now, does it?" Lukin said acidly, barely deigning to look at her. "The city is lost."

"And our chapterhouse with it," Mobarec added sadly, expelling a lingering sigh. "There was little anyone could do to fight them. Hundreds of God's faithful flocked to the cathedral for succor only to be caged like hapless pigeons, forced to join the Sage's men or die. Those that refused to join were killed . . . right there in the sight of God Himself! And the invaders were most brutal to the Adrielites—especially those that had served as Justices of the Tribunal. I . . . cannot even speak of what was done to them." Mobarec squeezed his eyes closed, choking back a flood of rage and grief. "Had the mayor not surrendered the city, these Sarian wizards surely would have razed it."

"Don't you have people there?" Durek asked Athaya, his voice carrying more than a hint of accusation. "Why didn't they do anything to stop this?"

"They were probably taken by surprise as much as anyone else. And besides, Mason DePere may be a fine magician but he's no battlefield commander—neither am I, for that matter. My people are students, Durek, not warriors."

Durek threw up his hands in exasperation. "Why on earth didn't you teach them how to *fight*?"

"I taught them to defend themselves, not to go out and kill people," she shot back. "If I *had* trained them for combat, then *you* would have accused me of trying to steal your throne!"

"Arguing about it isn't going to help," Jaren said, well aware that a quarrel between the two of them could go on all afternoon if not checked quickly—an unneeded threat to their too-fragile alliance. "We have to find out what's happening in Kilfarnan. Maybe we can send help."

The preceptor assessed Jaren silently for a moment, surprised that a wizard would suggest anything so sensible. Still, the suggestion was in vain. "I fled the city nearly a week ago. I imagine it's far too late for that now."

"Why don't you just spy on them all with that cursed little globe of yours?" Lukin said caustically. "Isn't that how you people find out everything you want to know?"

Athaya pretended not to notice the archbishop's baiting tone. "A fine idea," she replied, deftly turning the gibe against him by taking the advice. "But perhaps I'll open a panel instead; that way we'll all be able to see." She got up from the table and positioned herself at the foot of the dais. "I'll try to reach Mason. His camp is tightly shielded—it might have escaped the attack."

She opened the small purse tied to her girdle and fished out the proper ward key; a slice of blue agate flecked with silver runes. Extending her arms to the side, she murmured the words of invocation. White mist flowed quickly from her fingertips at her urgent command, forming a rectangular window to another part of the world.

Mobarec gasped in horror and jerked back, narrowly avoiding spilling the dregs of his ale into his Majesty's lap. "Sire, are you going to *allow* this?"

"Do you have a better idea?" Durek looked only slightly less uneasy than the preceptor—not since Rhodri's day had there been such a blatant display of sorcery within these walls—but he also knew that magic was the fastest way of learning what was happening in his western shires. Discovering the plight of his people was his first concern; he could ill afford to argue over methods.

"Mason?" Athaya called into the swirling mists as if seeking a lost child that had strayed too far from her side. "Mason, are you there?" She waited impatiently, hearing nothing but resonant silence. "Is anyone there? Anyone at all?"

Athaya waited for what seemed an eternity, gazing into the impassive haze. She tried not to think about what the lack of response might mean—that there was no one alive to answer her call—but then the window flashed with blinding whiteness as the link was forged, her summons answered.

And when the afterglow of black spots faded from her sight, Athaya once again found herself facing the Sage of Sare.

Brandegarth was resplendent in white silk, the shimmering fabric all but glowing against deeply tanned skin. Gold winked at his ears and throat, and a thin emerald-studded coronet circled his brow. He sat on a wealth of cushions inside a well-appointed tent, absently perusing a tray of tarts and cheeses resting at his feet. Athaya almost did not recognize the woman who had set it there before moving out of the panel's range; it was Hilda of Coakley, bathed and scented and draped in costly silks, lifted out of impoverished anonymity as an example of what the Sage promised to do for all those who followed him.

"Good evening, Princess. How kind of you to call upon me again so soon." His smiled stank of arrogance. "But then, it wasn't me you were expecting to reach, was it?"

Athaya's limbs began to tremble against her will and she tried to still them so as not to betray her shock. "What have you done with Dom DePere?" she demanded. "Where is he?"

The Sage glanced to one side, considering. "I really don't know. Alive, I imagine. I haven't heard otherwise . . . yet." He leaned forward, resting his forearms on broad thighs. "His people put up a decent fight, though—for relatively untrained wizards. Unfortunately, I've had to contain most of them. They are mulishly loyal to you and interfere with my purposes here."

He plucked a pastry from the tray and absently popped it into his mouth, taking time to lick the sweet icing from his fingers. "You will be glad to know that your alliance with the king surprised me to no small extent," he went on, inclining his head to her in tribute. "Not that it will affect the eventual outcome, of course, but at least you can take comfort in knowing that you were able to surprise me. Few people ever do."

Athaya heard the shuffle of footsteps behind her as the others moved within view of the panel. Durek and Jaren ventured closest, while Lukin, Mobarec, and Parr hung back at a watchful distance, fearful of being tainted by too close a communion with sorcery.

"What do you want of us?" Durek demanded, injecting every scrap of royal indignation he could muster into his words. It was the first time he had ever seen his enemy face to face, and while Athaya knew he was rattled, he managed to hide it fairly well behind a familiar mask of bluster.

The Sage studied him with polite contempt. "I want my country back," he said simply. "And I want its government in the hands of those God has deemed worthy of it."

Durek flinched; the words stung more fiercely than perhaps

the Sage would ever know. But he let the blow glance off him
as best he could, and when he spoke again his tone was men-
acingly formal. "As king of Caithe, I command you to return
to Sare at once. You are committing treasonous acts."

The Sage lifted his brows and smiled broadly, balanced on
the brink of laughter. "Of course I am. It is my destiny to do
so."

Durek's stony facade cracked in the face of his enemy's glib
reply. "Of all the—"

"Now if you will excuse me, I have pressing business to attend to." He waved the back of his hand at Durek as if to dismiss a bothersome servant. "I have had difficulty persuading
the brothers of Saint Adriel that God is *not* going to answer
their fervent prayers for deliverance and see me driven out of
Caithe. I am sorry to report that the order has far fewer members than it did seven days ago." The Sage clicked his tongue.
"A stubbornly persistent collection of priests."

"God shall smite you from the earth for this outrage against
His anointed servants!" Lukin bellowed from the rear, swollen
near to bursting with righteous wrath. His plum-colored cheeks
had flushed to the shade of grapes.

The Sage glared at him coldly, raking his eyes over the
archbishop's clerical garb with unveiled contempt. Durek was
merely an inconvenient obstacle; Lukin was the true enemy of
his people. His eyes narrowed further when he recognized the
Saint Adriel's medal resting against Lukin's chest. "I could say
the same," he replied evenly. "This is war . . . a holy war. People die. And you needn't be so livid about it," the Sage added,
the slightest hint of a smile crimping his upper lip. "I am, after
all, only doing God's will."

Lukin recoiled sharply, as if someone had just dashed a cup
of wine into his face. Hearing the Sage mouth the very words
that he might have chosen to defend his own beliefs reduced
the archbishop to flabbergasted silence.

"And now, Princess, I must go. Though it is ever a delight
to speak with you, there is nothing further to discuss at the moment . . . unless," he appended, shifting a vaguely mischievous
gaze to Durek, "his Majesty cares to abdicate now and save his
people from my further incursions?"

"Never!" Durek shouted back.

Brandegarth shook his head in mock pity, and his coronet
glittered in the tent's lamplight. "No, I didn't think you had
quite that much sense." He glanced to Athaya, flashing her a

smile of admiration through his disdain. "You Trelanes are a stubborn lot."

The Sage leaned deeper into his cushions, absently brushing a pastry crumb from his sleeve. "Should you wish to contact me again—to bargain, perhaps?—then you know where to find me. Until I decide to move on, of course. I wonder where I shall go next?" he asked, tapping his chin like a dandy unable to choose which feathered cap to wear to dinner. "There are so many unsuspecting shires to choose from . . ."

With a taunting chuckle, the Sage touched the rim of the panel and abruptly severed the contact. As if entranced, Athaya stood before the empty window for a full minute before banishing the mists. The Sage had not only taken over Kilfarnan itself, but the camp where hundreds of her followers had made their home. Where were they now? Or more importantly, were there any left?

"That boorish, egotistical, ill-bred son of a—" Durek wheeled around in disgust, abandoning his stream of abuse. "How can he sweep across my shires so quickly?"

"His people have had a long time to prepare for this, Durek," Athaya reminded him. "They've been planning to reclaim Caithe ever since King Faltil drove their ancestors out two hundred years ago."

"And the timing of the assault is nothing short of masterful," Jaren added somberly. "The Caithan people are in just the right state of mind to be receptive to the Sage's magic-laced speeches. They're confused by new ideas about magic—"

"Your wife's to blame for *that*," Lukin snarled, turning a spiteful glare to Athaya.

"—and they're tired of being persecuted and browbeaten by the Tribunal, willing to join any cause that promises to make it stop and perhaps make them richer in the bargain," Jaren finished pointedly, settling the rest of the blame squarely on the archbishop's mantled shoulders.

Durek paced in a tight circle, worriedly scrubbing his sparse beard. "Eriston was a small port town, and Nadiera mostly undefended farmland. But Kilfarnan is a major city . . . it should never have fallen to an enemy so easily."

Archbishop Lukin fixed a critical glare on the foot of the dais where Athaya's erstwhile panel had rested. "The man is as dangerous as he is proud. He must be stopped."

Athaya arched a brow at him. "At last, your Excellency, it seems we can agree on something." She stepped past him and

moved to her brother's side. "It might be a good time to recon-
vene the council," she advised him. "Perhaps now they will realize that the danger is real—and closer than they think."

Archbishop Lukin watched with profound disapproval as his
Majesty departed, Princess Athaya and her sorcerous husband
trailing him a short distance behind.

"Fool," Lukin said bluntly. He folded his arms tight across
his chest, eclipsing the gleaming silver orb of his Saint Adriel's
medal. "The king has become as much the Devil's puppet as
his brother." Belatedly, his gaze swept across the Hall. He was
alone with Mobarec and Parr in the cavernous chamber, but
that in itself gave the archbishop scant comfort; with wizards
in the palace, one was never sure one's words could be spoken
in privacy.

The preceptor scratched at his chin with artful negligence.
"His Majesty appears much committed to this alliance." The
remark was benign enough, but Lukin knew that his former
mentor shared in his censure of the Lorngeld. He also knew
that the preceptor was a master at soliciting other mens' opinions on delicate matters without ever fully betraying his own;
it gave the man an enigmatic aura—and made him difficult to
trap when charges of treachery began to fly about.

Lukin, however, was not so discreet as his elder. "Too committed, I think. I fear for his soul."

"And I for his life," Captain Parr inserted, his right hand absently curling itself around the leather-cased pommel of his
sword. "Can he truly believe that his sister will let him live
once she gets what she wants? The king is helping her get rid
of the only genuine obstacle between herself and the throne,
and he doesn't even realize it!"

Lukin nodded in grave agreement. "Yes, he no longer sees
her for the scheming witch she is. She murdered Kelwyn in
cold blood—God rest his soul; why should he believe Athaya
will spare *him*? No, the moment the Sage is dead, she will be
grasping for the crown like an infant for a shiny bauble—we
can be certain of it. Something *must* be done to save his Majesty from the disastrous course he has set himself upon before
it is too late . . . for all of us."

"Save him," Mobarec echoed. "But how?"

Lukin's eyes darkened as he shifted his gaze to the doorway
through which the king and his companions had recently
passed. "By removing the one who exploits him."

Mobarec scratched at his chin again, this time more deliberately. The Hall had fallen eerily silent, and each time his nails scraped across the stubble on his face, it sounded like rats skittering amongst the rushes on the floor.

"Removing her could be dangerous." Lukin noted that the preceptor did not say it was a bad idea, only a risky one. "Best to let her rid us of this Sage first. Like it or no, Jon, she may be the only one who can."

"Perhaps. Or perhaps that is simply what the Devil would have us believe. But think on this," he went on, leaning in close to the preceptor. The dim light turned his eyes to tiny black beads, like a fox's. "Should she succeed in crushing the Sage, the people will be in her debt and this loathsome alliance between the Lorngeld and his Majesty will strengthen. If that happens, we may never be able to cut this canker from our midst . . . or risk far more than we do now if we attempt it."

Mobarec mutely weighed the archbishop's argument. "And the Sage?"

"God will send us a solution. We must all have faith."

Mobarec scowled slightly, less willing than his protégé to trust in divine intervention. "And the king . . . what of him?"

"What of him?" Lukin echoed, as if that were the least of their present concerns.

Parr eyed the archbishop with bright conspiracy, speaking what the preceptor would not. "You mean to defy him."

"I obey God before any mortal man, Captain," Lukin replied, with a piousness that did not suit him. "If that means I must defy my king, then so be it. But let us all remember that the king himself has, in his more rational past, condemned his sister from his own mouth: once to death at Rhodri's hand and once to a life's confinement in a convent. Were we to remove the princess permanently, we would not be going entirely against his will, but would instead be doing his will as it existed before her sorcery deluded him into changing it."

The captain's eyes glowed with subtle appreciation of Lukin's truthful—if twisted—logic. "I would gladly be of service, if you have need of it."

"Such service could place you at grave risk, my friend. I have sworn higher vows—you have not. But," he added, tapping a finger to his cheek, "I may impose on you to . . . say, leave a gate or two unlocked of a night . . . ?"

The captain tipped his head.

"The princess," Mobarec murmured. "You have a plan, then?"

"Not yet," the archbishop replied, "but it should not take long. The means of her demise needn't be neat or complex . . . just permanent. But allow me to handle this, Preceptor. I will not have you involve yourself in this if you yet harbor doubts. Still," he added, lacing his fingers together in an attitude of entreaty, "it would please me to have your private support, if not your public sanction."

Lukin did not have to ask the man's leave—as Archbishop of Delfarham he outranked the preceptor by no small extent—but he knew the solicitation would appease him. Moreover, it would serve him well to have the man speak the damning words before a witness such as Parr, so that he would be more certain to avoid betrayal. Mobarec might have been a mentor to him, but it did not do to let sentiment muddle one's thinking where treason was concerned.

"Do as you must, my friend," the preceptor said at last. If he had any further objections to Lukin's chosen course, he was too wretched and travel-weary to bother raising them. "I will say nothing of it."

The old man struggled to his feet with Lukin's swiftly proffered aid. "When . . . ?"

"Soon," the archbishop replied. "Soon. We have no time to lose. And do not fear that you have done wrong to offer me your blessing," he added, laying a comforting palm upon the shorter man's shoulder. His eyes were again filled with shadows. "The Devil has sunk his claws deep into our king, in the guise of Athaya Trelane. It is my solemn duty—to God and to our sovereign both—to extricate him."

CHAPTER 10

✻

ATHAYA PUSHED BACK THE EMBROIDERED COUNTERPANE and cracked open one eye, squinting against the shaft of sunlight that flowed through a gap in the bedcurtains. Jaren was already up and dressed—apparently for quite some time now—and sat peacefully in the windowseat, sea breezes gently tousling his hair as he picked through a tray of cherries and fresh-baked bread.

She paused for a moment before speaking, thinking it pleasantly strange to have him here in the room of her youth, its elegant furnishings scarred and pitted from countless childhood tantrums that took place years before she knew of his existence. How slight those childhood tribulations seemed now in the light of present-day problems: being forbidden to go riding with her brothers because she'd torn her dress tussling in the dirt with Nicolas, or being sent to her room without supper for blurting out to a lady of the court that she smelled too strongly of lavender. Suddenly, all of the unhappy days she had spent in this chamber sulking over one perceived injustice or another seemed a fair price for the contentment she now enjoyed.

"I didn't hear you get up," she said, drawing back the brocade bedcurtain.

Jaren looked up at the sibilant rustle of cloth. "I was trying not to wake you. You spent a lot of time with those corbal crystals before you came to bed last night and I thought you could use the rest."

149

Blinking away the last vestiges of sleep, Athaya noticed that Jaren had left off his peasant garb for a dark green doublet over butter-colored shirt and hose; he looked much as he had on the morning of her first magic lessons with Master Hedric—so very long ago, it seemed!—when she had first seen him dress befitting the nobleman he was. Her heart fluttered a bit even now, as if she were a young girl still being courted and not his wife these nine months past.

"I haven't seen you look so handsome in a long time," she remarked, playfully echoing his backward compliment from the day before.

Jaren smirked at her. "It belongs to Nicolas. A bit snug in the shoulders," he added, tugging at one sleeve, "but it'll do. Hedric let me borrow a few things from the prince's wardrobe so I wouldn't look so conspicuous. People around here stare at me enough as it is, as if they expect me to sprout horns in my head the minute they turn away. Here," he went on, bringing her the tray of bread and berries. Athaya ate a cherry eagerly and Jaren deftly kissed away the sticky red juice that trickled down her chin.

"And I've brought you something else." Jaren fetched a leather satchel from beneath the bedstand and produced a sheaf of creamy parchment and an inkwell. "For your journal. The one Master Hedric says he's certain you've started by now."

Athaya groaned and pulled the counterpane back over her head. "I knew he wasn't going to forget about that."

"Well, you can't very well leave your fate in the hands of minstrels and storytellers," Jaren cautioned her. "As a rule, they're terrible historians. You know how they are—they'll get the facts wrong, embellish the truth out of existence, and make you sound twice as heroic as you really were."

Athaya poked her head out from beneath the quilt like a turtle and offered him a good-natured glare.

"You don't even have to pick up a quill, Athaya. Just give me the gist of what you want to say and I'll do the rest. So," he said, extracting a quill from the satchel and settling beside her on the bed, "what do you want the people of Caithe to know about you a hundred years from now?"

Athaya propped herself up against the feather pillows and munched on another cherry, rolling the tiny pit thoughtfully around her tongue as she mused upon the question.

What do I want them to know?

Absently, Athaya began to weave her hair into a braid, temporarily at a loss for an answer. How could she ever impart on a few sheets of paper the changes that had come upon both herself and her homeland these past two years? Once, she'd had no other future than to be wife to whatever foreign prince her father chose, and her reluctance to blindly accept that future—though never able to say exactly why—was the scandal of the court for years. But now, in the wake of her *mekahn*, her entire world had been irrevocably transformed; at times, she felt as if she had drawn her first breath only after her magic had been born, and that everything prior to that was an illusion, a fragment of memory from some other life, or a glimpse into another woman's mind.

Two years ago, absolution was the inevitable consequence of power; no one questioned the notion that wizards must sacrifice their mortal lives to save their immortal souls. Kelwyn had been the first monarch in two centuries to gently prod for change, but had not lived to see his desires fulfilled. Today his subjects had a choice over their destiny—a choice his youngest child had fought diligently to provide. Every citizen of Caithe had been touched as a result—forced to rethink their assumptions about magic and its practitioners whether they wanted to or not. Some had been grateful for the upheaval, others had condemned Athaya as the Devil's agent and deserving of nothing more than a public execution, but it was the rare Caithan indeed who did not have a fairly strong opinion on their princess one way or another.

Athaya indulged in a smile of wry pride. *Better to inspire love or hate, I suppose, than absolutely nothing at all . . .*

"Maybe that was a rather broad question to start with," Jaren remarked, when her interval of silence showed no signs of breaking. "How about just starting from the beginning?"

Athaya placed the cherry pit back on the edge of the tray and took up a chunk of bread. "Well, it all really began with King Faltil, when he exterminated most of the trained Lorngeld in Caithe and left the others to lapse into madness and die. But my part started when my power came. No, even before that . . . it started with my father, I think."

In truth, she had built her crusade upon a foundation laid well before her birth: Kelwyn's design for the Lorngeld's future, his assumption of magic at Rhodri's behest, Rhodri's obsession with ascending to the Circle. When her own power came, it was yet another link in an existing chain. She had not conceived this grand plan for the Lorngeld; she had only

vowed to continue what Kelwyn had already started. But for
his vision, she may well have been absolved herself; at the
very least, she would have fled to Reyka in self-imposed exile
while her homeland remained as it had always been, devoid of
magic in all but its most frightening and destructive forms, its
native wizards trapped in the vicious cycle of killing those they
loved with untrained magic before being put to death themselves.

Or, she considered, was history inevitably destined to unfold
as it had, even unto her father's demise? Master Hedric—and
even Dameronne of Crewe—had foreseen her coming, as well
as the great task committed to her hands. Athaya shifted uneasily at the idea of forces far more powerful and unfathomable
than her own fallible spells working around and through her,
slowly molding the fates of nations.

She and Jaren worked on the journal for several hours, and
in time, Athaya lost her resistance and began to enjoy herself.
But while her recollections made her realize how far she'd
come since her first spell was cast, she could not shake a powerful sensation that her return to Delfarham signified more than
mere symmetry. Her power had almost been stolen from her,
her life almost taken as well, friends and lovers had been lost
and found, and after all of that, here she was at home again,
back where she'd begun, poised at yet another crossroads. But
this was nothing so simple as her own decision to take the path
of power rather than absolution; now she—and all of Caithe—
faced the Sage's forces with a chance for her lifework's complete success . . . or its complete destruction.

Athaya burrowed deep into the pillows. Jaren's first question
still haunted her. *What do I want them to know about me a
hundred years from now?*

Absent fingers kneaded the bedsheets. *That I wasn't the
scheming harridan some people said I was. That I made mistakes, but was only trying to do what I thought was right.*

Her fingers stopped their motion. *That I never meant to hurt
Kelwyn.*

Athaya looked toward the window, speaking more to
herself—or to posterity—than to Jaren. "I just want them to
know that I was never any kind of saint. I'm nothing more or
less than they are . . . or could be. I didn't have the vision my
father did—not at first. He wanted to understand the Lorngeld;
by adopting the powers of magic, he hoped to make himself as
good a king to them as he yearned to be to rest of his subjects.

As for myself . . . well, unflattering as it sounds, I probably wouldn't have given the Lorngeld's plight a second thought if I hadn't developed the power myself." In retrospect, it was almost comical how viciously she had raged against her destiny, only to make it the focus of her life and the foundation of her very existence. "Magic matures you that way . . . or it can, given the chance. Any gift can, I suppose. If you don't shrink from it or fight it, but accept whatever gift God has given you in all its aspects—the whole length and breadth and depth of it—then that's when you've got real power."

Jaren's quill scratched feverishly for a while and then stopped. He stared at her in hushed respect. "That's a sentiment worthy of the *Book of Sages*."

"Oh, it's not as profound as all that," she replied with a self-conscious shrug. "Just simple logic."

Jaren set quill and parchment aside and was massaging the stiffness from his hand when the distant bells of Saint Adriel's chimed the noon hour. "Hmm, it's about time I got dressed," Athaya said. She crossed to her wardrobe and rummaged through the colorful selection of silks; the fabric felt delicious against her skin after countless months in coarse homespun. "I doubt the council would approve of my attending this afternoon's session in my dressing gown."

Jaren laughed lightly. "Considering the scandals that typically surround you, Athaya, they probably wouldn't notice."

Athaya threw a pillow at him, sending up a light spray of feathers from a small hole in one end. Then, before the first sally could develop into a full-fledged battle, Drianna hurried into the chamber and dumped a basket of freshly laundered bedding in one corner. She had begged to come to Delfarham with them, happily resuming the role of lady's maid that she had abandoned the previous winter. "Someone's here to see you," she said, breathless from taking the tower stairs so swiftly. "He's waiting in the king's audience chamber—a wizard from Kilfarnan. He says he's the leader of your school there."

Athaya whirled around, her arms full of pale green silk. "Mason?" She threw the gown clumsily over her head, Drianna lending nimble fingers to the laces while Athaya stuffed her hair ungracefully into a jeweled caul.

She and Jaren arrived in the audience chamber to find Durek alone with Dom Mason DePere, erstwhile instructor of illusion at Wizard's College in Reyka. Slouched miserably in a chair near the bay window, the dom barely resembled the gentle scholar that Athaya had spoken to but a few weeks before; his once-fine cloak was torn and soiled, his left arm was snugly wrapped in blood-caked linen, and his throat and cheeks were swollen from a too-close brush with flame. His delicately arching eyebrows had been neatly singed off.

Athaya took a seat on the cushioned bench across from him. "Thank God you're alive," she said, reaching out to his uninjured right arm. "When news came about Kilfarnan . . ." She shook her head, abandoning the dreadful thought. "I tried to contact you yesterday but I got the Sage instead. He led me to believe you'd been captured."

"He was just taunting you. He's rather good at that." The dom's gaze turned even more grim. "So you've already heard what happened?"

Athaya nodded. "Preceptor Mobarec arrived only yesterday. Odd as it sounds, he's as much a refugee here as you are."

"Odd bedfellows, indeed," Mason remarked, arching the naked fold of skin that had once sported a brow. "I managed to avoid getting captured by the Sage's men, but it wasn't easy. My magic school was one of their first targets—little surprise in that. But talented as the Sarians are, I'm not half bad at magic myself." A glimmer of pride flickered in his tired eyes. "All those years of teaching illusion paid off handsomely. I got away by simply casting an image of myself. A simple decoy. It's not at all difficult," he added, lapsing briefly into his scholar's regard for detail, "a drop of essence and a small mirror is all it takes. And a decoy is easier to sustain than an illusion . . . a good thing if you're being chased by people who'd like very much to kill you." Mason managed a rasping chuckle. "Not even a first-year student at Wizard's College would have fallen for such an old trick, but apparently the Sarians didn't expect me to try anything so obvious. They took the bait, and I slipped away."

He ran tentative fingers over the swollen flesh at the base of his throat. "Of course, they managed to get a few blows in before I came up with the idea. I almost went up like a torch for mistaking a pillar of fire for an illusion. It gave off no heat . . ." He clicked his tongue in self-reproach. "Careless."

The rest of his tale was disturbingly like the one Preceptor Mobarec had told the night before: the tale of a city in panic, attacked by arcane forces it could barely understand, much less repel. "We were taken completely by surprise," Mason admitted, "and were badly outnumbered. Those of us that escaped the attack on the school tried to fan out across Kilfarnan to defend it, but . . . oh, Athaya, my wizards are mostly novices and few of them know anything about battle magic. And these Sarians knew exactly what they were doing. They summoned darkness in midday; they terrorized people with illusion; they even cast spells of sickness on their enemies. It's rather difficult to concentrate on your spells when you're busy vomiting and trying to control your bowels. My apologies, Princess," he added, seeing her face wrinkle in revulsion, "but these people fight to win, and they don't much care about their methods."

Durek leaned against his writing desk, shaking his head in desperate confusion. "I just don't understand why out of the hundreds of wizards you apparently had living in your camp, not one of them saw the Sage's army coming—especially when you can all use magic to spy on them. It's damned hard to hide over a thousand men."

"Not when they keep cloaked and warded and travel only at night," Mason informed him. "It's a common enough tactic in Reyka." When the king did not argue the point, Mason turned back to Athaya; his head sagged against his chest, as if it took too much effort to hold it up. "At least the Sage wasn't lying when he said as many wizards as possible would be spared. We may be his enemies, but we share the same gift. Those that refused to join him were not killed outright, but imprisoned in what used to be the Tribunal's jails. And if the Sage determines that one of us is simply too dangerous to keep alive, then he ensures that the death is an easy and honorable one."

"How noble of him," Jaren murmured.

Despite his battered exhaustion, Mason rose to face the king. "I am sorry we were not more help, your Majesty. Truly, we did try to save your city. But please . . . do not fault your subjects for surrendering so quickly. Sheltered from magic as they have been for two centuries, even the simplest spells terrify them—like children frightened of a paper mask. The Sage knew that all too well."

Durek grunted noncommittally, but Athaya thought he was secretly appeased by Mason's words. Had it not been for the efforts of the dom and his following, Kilfarnan would likely have fallen well before it did.

"I think what you need now is a hot meal and a few days of rest," Athaya told him. "You can take the empty chamber next to Nicolas. And I'll have Kale look in on you—we brought him with us from Kaiburn, and he needs someone to watch over besides me and Jaren."

Mason shifted his weight uneasily. "I . . . didn't come alone, Athaya. I brought a good two dozen wizards with me. They're waiting outside the castle gates. We weren't sure we'd all be welcome, so I came to see you alone first."

Durek's jaw dropped open. "Where will they all—"

"There's plenty of room in the barracks," Athaya countered, sensing that it wasn't the number itself, but the fact that each one was a trained magician. "Twenty or thirty people is a smaller entourage than the earl of Tusel totes with him everywhere he goes. And their presence might prove valuable. Now we have a small battalion of wizards to help defend the castle in case the Sage attacks it."

"He wouldn't dare!" Durek exclaimed, but behind the show of indignation was a palpable surge of dread.

"After what I have seen, sire," Mason said softly, meeting the king's gaze, "know that the Sage would dare anything."

Athaya spat out a uniquely vulgar curse learned from Ranulf. "If the council had simply acted on my proposal to station a few hundred wizards in the central shires, we might have been able to call on reinforcements before the entire city fell."

"It's too late to worry about that now," Jaren replied. "The question now is what do we do next?"

Durek made a disgruntled grumbling noise in the back of his throat. "Next? We've barely had the chance to do anything at all yet. It's obviously too late to send a force to Kilfarnan or expect much help from your people there. All we can do now is figure out where the Sage is likely to strike next and prepare for it."

"For what it's worth," Mason offered, "several of my people heard rumors that the Sage's next target was Kaiburn—and the forest camp, of course," he added, stealing a disquieted glance at Athaya. "It's little more than hearsay, but it may be the only lead we've got."

Durek scraped his fingers over his beard as he mulled the dom's news. "It makes sense. He'll probably try to keep your people contained as much as he can. And I think it's more than hearsay," he added, turning to Athaya. "You weren't awake yet when it arrived, but I received a letter from Belmarre's steward this morning. Adam Gray—" He broke off abruptly, realizing only at that moment why Athaya had chosen Belmarre as a hiding place for Nicolas. "Graylen," he finished, swiftly gathering up the scattered scraps of his composure. "He says that several small groups of men have been seen roaming the countryside east of Halsey. He thinks they may be scouting parties."

"And Kaiburn is only two days' journey from Halsey," Athaya murmured in reply. "They could be planning to circle around and attack from the south."

Durek pondered the matter in intense silence for a while, then whirled around with a decisive flip of his cloak. "I shall leave for Kaiburn tomorrow. I will speak to the people and tell them to ready themselves. And I will pledge the bulk of my army to the city's defense . . . Anders!" he shouted at the door, the command instantly producing a crimson-clad sentry. "Summon my messengers. Tell them they are to be ready to leave by sundown. And send for the lord chancellor."

"Shouldn't you stay here?" Athaya asked, once the guardsman had hastened away to carry out his duty. "Going to Kaiburn yourself might be dangerous—"

"No. I must show myself to them . . . assure them that they have my protection. I also think . . ." He balked, glancing to Athaya like a child forced to make an apology to his elders. His hands anxiously worked at the folds of his cloak, alternately rumpling the fabric and then smoothing it out again. "I think I should speak to your people as well and persuade them to do their best to defend the city. Perhaps if they are prepared, as those in Kilfarnan were not, we stand a better chance. I doubt they'll trust me overmuch, but perhaps . . . if you came with me . . .?" He let the query trail off into uneasy silence. Durek desperately needed her presence to sway them to obedience, but it galled him to admit it.

Athaya knew there were other reasons for his discomfort, but was sure he would not speak of them. The last time he addressed the people of Kaiburn, it was to force her into a public recantation and burn Jaren to death as an example of what happens to those who defy the king's law. She caught him glance uneasily to Jaren, debating whether to ask pardon for his past brutality, but pride won out for the moment and he chose to say nothing.

"Yes," she answered him at last, "being seen together will help prove to the people both in the city and the camp that our alliance is real and not some sort of elaborate hoax. But don't call them my people, Durek," she chided gently. "They're your subjects."

Durek's expression was unreadable. True, they were his subjects, but even Athaya knew that the Lorngeld were subjects
that their sovereign had no real power to rule should they not
wish to obey him.

"Shall I go with you?" Mason asked.

"There's no need," Athaya assured him, knowing he needed
nothing so much as a few days of peace. "You can be more
useful to us here; perhaps you and Master Hedric can see to
the castle's defense if there's any trouble from the Sarians."

"It's not a question of 'if' at this point," Mason said, his fatigue making him dismal. He turned his eyes to the window as
if, even now, he could see Delfarham burning. "It's only a
matter of 'when.'"

Athaya did not reach her bed until well after midnight. It
had been no trivial task to persuade the council that his Majesty should travel anywhere at all in his sister's company,
much less to the heart of her wizards' camp. What if the
Sage's army was closer to Kaiburn than anyone knew? they
bleated. What if the bands of men Adam Graylen had seen
were only meant to lure him there, to be killed on sight the
moment he arrived? Only Durek's eventual eruption of ill temper, heavily spiced with curses, had convinced them to grant
the journey their sanction, though Athaya clearly sensed that
more than one of Durek's councillors did not expect to see his
king survive this bit of folly.

Shivering, Athaya woke in the still hours before dawn to
find the brocade bedcurtains slightly pulled back. A tendril of
chill night air snaked through the breach to tingle bare flesh.
The pale glow of an oil lamp drew her eye to the windowseat,
where Jaren sat cloaked in a heavy fur wrap, squinting at a
sheet of parchment by the lamp's wan light.

"Jaren?"

The paper crackled softly in his hands. "Shh, go back to
sleep. I thought I'd read for a while . . . maybe tidy up what
we wrote for the journal this morning."

Athaya frowned. "You haven't gotten a decent night's sleep
since we've been here."

"Can you blame me? In case you haven't noticed, we're not
exactly well-loved in this place. It's like trying to doze off in
a wolf's den."

Athaya extended her hand; the feathery hair on her forearms
bristled in the cool air. "Come back to bed. My feet are cold."

"I know," he said dryly, "that's the other reason I got up."

Athaya dipped her head, allowing a lock of black hair to fall seductively over one shoulder. "Then why not come back and try to warm them for me?"

Jaren's eyes skimmed the curve of her shoulder and the rise of one breast, limned with golden lamplight and peeking out from beneath the coverlets like a crescent moon from a cloudbank. Weighing the relative merits of his options, he soon abandoned the parchment on the windowsill. "Yes, your Highness," he said, smiling as he came to her. He set the oil lamp on the bedstand and slid under the quilted coverlets, out of the brisk night air. Athaya moaned quietly as she sank into the mattress beneath his weight, content as she'd ever been inside these four walls.

Then Jaren pulled away, abruptly breaking off what had promised to be a long and intoxicating kiss. "What was that?"

"Nothing," Athaya murmured dreamily, drawing him back. "Probably just Drianna laying a fire in the other room."

"Isn't it a little early for that?"

She brushed his throat with her lips, slowly working her way to his mouth. "Don't be so suspicious."

"Athaya, there's more than one person in this castle who would like nothing more than to have us murdered in our beds. I can't help but be suspicious." Despite her groan of protest, he rolled out of bed and crept to the doorway, peering into the outer chamber.

Where does the servant's door lead to? he sent urgently, shunning spoken words for the safety of silence.

Athaya stiffened; Jaren was rarely so cautious without good cause. *Past Drianna's room and down to the courtyard at the base of the tower.*

Jaren lurched back from the door, snatching up his fur wrap and throwing her a dressing gown draped across the foot of the bed. *Quick—get up and hide yourself. Someone's coming.*

Drianna?

Jaren snapped his head to one side. *Not unless she's grown a beard since dinnertime.*

In breathless silence, Athaya fought her way into the gown and retreated to the far corner of the chamber. She called her cloaking spell to shield her from sight, and Jaren ducked beneath it as well, tightly clasping her hand when he joined her there seconds later.

Mason used a decoy with some substance to it, he sent, *but as I don't have a mirror, a simple illusion will have to do.* In the space of three heartbeats, Athaya saw an image of herself and Jaren take shape upon the feather bed. The phantoms slept peacefully in one another's arms, intangible legs entwined in blankets and incorporeal faces glowing golden by the light of Jaren's lamp.

The ruse was finished only seconds before the intruder padded cautiously to the bedside, drawing up sharply at an unexpected squeak from one of his boots. The illusion was hastily crafted, but in the dim lamplight it would have taken a keen eye to notice that the features were not quite true; Athaya's cheekbones were a shade too sharp and Jaren's eyes spaced a bit too far apart. And had the intruder looked closely enough, he would have noticed that the slumbering figures' chests did not rise and fall with breathing, nor did their weight make the slightest indentation in the mattress.

The hooded figure crept closer, careful to keep his boots silent. He gave a cautious glance to the lamp, looked to the sleeping wizards, and after a moment's pause, concluded that the feeble light did not disturb their rest, whereas dousing it might do so. He passed by Jaren's phantom presence and circled to the other side of the bed, closer to Athaya. As he rounded the foot of the bed, he came perilously close to his true victims, unseen not an arm's length away; both Athaya and Jaren took care not to make the slightest sound so as not to betray their presence until the time was right.

He's got a corbal with him, Athaya sent, conscious of the irritating itch beginning to form behind her eyes. *More than one, I think. They're covered, but I can sense them.*

Jaren's counsel was composed, yet urgent. *Then get ready to fight them—now, while you have time.* Then, after a moment's thought, he added: *But if he has corbals, why isn't he using them?*

Athaya lifted one shoulder in a shrug. *Maybe he knows I can repel their power. The whole court knows that by now, after what happened at the gates when we arrived. He must have brought the crystals to use as a last resort. They may not hurt me, but they'd keep me from casting spells to defend myself.*

Jaren clutched a fist around impotent air, wishing he had thought to grab a knife as well as his fur wrap. *And they'd keep me from doing anything at all.*

Anything magical, Athaya reminded him. *Here's your chance to find out how well you can fight without the luxury of spells.* She touched a finger to his forehead and soundlessly mouthed the words of the spell; the next instant, Jaren was wrinkling his nose at the stuffed-up sensation that accompanied the seal, his powers corked inside of him like fine Evarshot wine. *Now we'll be prepared no matter what he does.*

In the little time that remained, Athaya steeled herself against the intruder's still-hidden crystals, taking command of her thoughts and shaping them into readiness should the need to fight arise. She called on the Succession of Circles to lull herself into familiar self-control, her mind responding to the regimen like a highly trained gelding to the slightest tug on his master's reins. *Credony, lord of the first Circle, twenty-six years; Sidra, lord of the second, eleven years* ... She envisioned a crystal in her mind's eye, a dazzling miniature landscape of purple plains and peaks, and envisioned as well the corbal's heart—the source of its power, from which the deceitful messages of pain would come.

The hooded man's shadow danced on the wall behind him as he worked the stopper from a slender vial and spattered bloodred liquid over a gleaming silver blade—a peasant's hunting knife, used to murder beasts. Then bending over the princess' phantom form, he swept the blade down and across her undefended throat with one brutal stroke. But where the blade should have sliced through tender flesh, it bit instead deep into the pillow, leaving an ugly, crimson gash in the white casing and sending a thin fountain of feathers gushing upward.

The man gasped and stumbled back, the tip of the knife shaking wildly in his startled grasp. Before he could recover his wits, Athaya eased out of her private mental sanctuary enough to conjure a small witchlight that bathed the room in a dull, reddish glow. The man started at the sudden ball of fire that bloomed above his head and started yet again when Athaya dispersed the cloaking spell that shielded her and Jaren from sight. The illusory figures in the bed faded into nothingness like smoke cleared off by the breeze, and the assassin, realizing the deception, backed away like a cornered dog, baring teeth.

"You should be flattered, Athaya," Jaren remarked steadily. His eyes never left the blade in the intruder's hand, the steel still smeared with poison. "He went for you first."

Malcon, lord of the third Circle, seven years.... With the part of her mind not busily priming itself for battle, Athaya considered that she could simply scream; could simply raise an alarm and call the guard. But the knowledge that someone was daring enough to attempt her murder here, not fifty yards from his Majesty's own apartments, caused her to question whether she would be any safer with Durek's guardsmen at her side. Durek she trusted, but she could not say the same for his many servants; in fact, it was likely one of the guardsmen who had allowed this man access to her apartment. Perhaps her cries for help would only betray to the assassin's allies that he had failed and summon others to finish the job.

Athaya tipped her chin up fearlessly, acutely aware that she did not look particularly imposing in her linen dressing gown. "Who hired you to do this?" If the words sounded garbled in her ears, her speech fouled by the demands of her inner recitations, the assassin was too distracted by his own predicament to notice.

"The Sage of Sare wants you dead," the man said, but his answer came a shade too quickly, a shade too rehearsed.

Athaya's eyes narrowed. *Kyria, lord of the fourth circle, one year* . . . "That wasn't my question."

"If the Sage wanted us killed," Jaren observed, "then he would have taken the pleasure of doing it himself."

Out of the corner of her eye, Athaya saw thin tendrils of smoke beginning to curl up from the ruined pillowcase. "*Kahnil* on the blade," she remarked evenly, even as her belly twisted itself into a fleshy knot. "You wanted to be sure."

Jaren glanced to the knife with newfound caution; the weapon was dangerous enough as it was, but the *kahnil* made it doubly so. "Hardly the sort of weapon the Sage would have selected, is it?"

Silently realizing the prearranged ruse wasn't going to hold, the intruder's eyes flickered covertly to the doorway to the outer chamber. Athaya and Jaren were blocking his route of escape, but his stony expression revealed that escape was not his sole intent; he had not yet forsaken the bloody service he had come to render. In a blur of pale flesh, gleaming silver, and grubby wool, the man's hands darted to the purse at his belt and, not bothering with the laces, sliced it open like the belly of a dove, cupping one palm so that the treasure spilled into it like innards. Grinning now, he dangled his prize just above the oil lamp on the bedstand. It was a delicate lady's necklace worked in silver, bearing one large crystal in the center and two smaller stones on each side—a vaguely familiar design, but one that Athaya had neither the time nor resources to place. The lamplight lent them strength enough, but that gentle glow added to the flare of her witchlight made the crystals inflict twice their power. And now, neither Jaren nor Athaya held the power to snuff the witchlight out.

Sacret, lord of the fifth . . .

"No, no—please! Put it away!"

Jaren's performance was so well acted that for a moment Athaya almost believed it herself; believed that the sealing spell she had set upon him had somehow failed. Crying out in pain and begging his attacker to lay aside the crippling weapon, Jaren collapsed to his knees on the floor, catching his balance on the rack of iron tools near the hearth and sending them spilling onto the floor. Then, as the intruder dared a step closer, his grin inching wider, Jaren sprang to his feet, fully lucid and armed with a sharp iron poker, ready to strike the gems from the man's grasp.

The ruse was over in mere seconds—though to Athaya's deadened perceptions it seemed to take far longer. The assassin was startled at Jaren's unexpected immunity to the crystals, but was well trained in his base art; as Jaren lunged forward, the man's wrist jerked once, sending the *kahnil*-streaked blade flying from his hand to bite the flesh of Jaren's bared shoulder. Jaren let out a low-pitched grunt of pain and stumbled backward, the iron rod clattering uselessly to the flagstones. Hissing in pain—none of it feigned this time—he hurriedly worked out the blade so that its remaining stripes of poison would not leach into his blood.

The shock of the blow was enough to set Athaya's focus badly off balance—had the assassin had another second to perfect his aim, the knife would have gone home in Jaren's heart. She fought to regain control, turning her eyes from the sticky red liquid trickling down Jaren's arm and coldly instructing herself not to be distracted by the wound, aware that her own presence of mind was the best hope for both of them. *Where was I, then?* she thought through gritted teeth. *Yes, yes . . . Kyria, lord of the fourth Circle, one year; Sacret, lord of the fifth . . .* But even in her trancelike state, Athaya could tell that Jaren's pupils were wide and swelling still, proof that what little poison had tainted his blood was already doing its work.

Satisfied that Jaren would be no further hindrance, the assassin turned to his true prey. Athaya ignored the smug look of success on his face and glared at the necklace as if it were a trio of snarling dogs threatening to bite. *I feel nothing from you—any of you!* she declared, masking her fear with the forcefulness of the assertion. *You cannot harm me now. I know your secrets and you have no power over me.*

Light danced across the jewels' myriad facets, beautiful in their deadliness, imbuing them with the power to lure her from her fragile sanctuary of control. The crystals called to her in trio, the center stone's voice the loudest while the smaller two murmured in dreadful consonance. *Pain, pain, pain!* they cried in their wordless language of emotion. *Flee from the danger!* Athaya stood her ground against them, but knew she could not do so for very long. She had never tried to resist so many at a time before, and their clamor was frighteningly powerful. Honing her focus further, she gave full attention to the largest stone and began to scry its center—the source of its magiclike power—but the other two corbals remained to niggle at her brain, distracting her with urgent whispers.

The assassin betrayed no surprise at her own immunity to the gems; someone had clearly warned him what to expect. "Looks as if you don't have any tricks left, wizard," he said, inching closer. He ran a lazy tongue over the few teeth he had, as if debating how good a meal she might make once dead. "You're just like the rest of us now ... and only a woman at that." He looped the necklace over his wrist and produced a short strip of cord from his tunic. "And you're the one I really came for."

Athaya's throat constricted; she tried to cry out, but as if held in the grip of nightmares, nothing emerged. Aside from wrestling in the dirt with Nicolas as a girl, she knew nothing of hand-to-hand combat; chances were good that if she did not run *now*, her attacker would kill her with relative ease; not only did he outweigh her by no small margin, but most of her concentration was focused on repelling the corbals' lure, making her physical reactions as slow as her mental ones ... and slow enough to be fatal.

"Athaya, go!" came Jaren's halting call. His breathing grew labored; the poison was taxing him badly. "Don't stay for me!" He made a painfully useless attempt to shove Athaya from the room, but the assassin merely twisted his lips into a scornful smile and kicked him aside with a well-placed boot to his already injured shoulder.

That done, the man crept closer with a telltale gleam of triumph in his eyes, backing Athaya against the wall. He coiled the slender cord around his hands, ready to snag it around her throat and pull it taut. Just like . . .

She stiffened, remembering; remembering the last night she saw her father alive. In his mad rage, he had tried to strangle her with magic—an invisible rope of thorns and nettles—just as this man wished to do with a twopenny scrap of twine. Then she had called deadly coils of green fire to her rescue, not knowing what she did or how to use them; now she had the mastery of the deadly spell but it resided far beyond her, trapped in paths her divided concentration could not reach.

The man's arms were thick with muscle; the cord would be as tight as Kelwyn's spell had been, draining her of consciousness as quickly as the corbal, did she falter in her guard, would drain her of magic strength. What was she to do? Her mind floundered, torn between two equally urgent tasks. She could not stop fighting the crystals; if she did, she would succumb to their crippling power and be a pathetically easy victim for the man looming before her. Nor could she break away and flee, leaving Jaren vulnerable to further attack. So, not knowing what else to do, Athaya pushed back even harder against the corbals, focusing desperate rage upon them, knowing their power was at least a thing she could control until she thought of something better. Perhaps, she reasoned, if she could quiet their clamor a bit further, it would dispel enough of the sluggishness to allow her mind to slip her a solution . . . preferably in the next few seconds.

"This won't take long," the man said. Briefly, his gaze skimmed the length of her body, barely concealed by the thin gown of white gauze, his eyes reflecting indifferent regret at having to rob the life from it. "And then you'll be back at the Devil's side where you belong."

Swallowing audibly, Athaya turned all of her energies onto the larger center crystal, turning aside the ceaseless but softer murmurs of the other two. She surrounded the crystal with her presence, fiercely smothering its influences with her own. *I feel nothing from you. You cannot harm me now. I know your secrets and you have no power over me.* The words were fueled with dreadful purpose as she pushed beyond the crystal's voice, forcing her way closer and closer to the heart of the gem itself. The voice grew more frantic and insistent the nearer she came, but she shunted it aside with equal earnestness, refusing to heed its false warnings of pain.

She did not know what to expect when she reached her destination, but when she forced her way past the crystal's defenses, past the barricades of deceit it thrust up to block her, and invaded the core with her presence, the din in her ears fell abruptly silent, the corbal's center tranquil as a crypt. The cobwebs fouling her thoughts and actions were suddenly swept aside, like the lifting of a sealing spell to free congested magic. The corbal's voice was gone, and here in its heart, as long as she held the vision steady in her mind, Athaya did not have to push back at all; did not have to shout defiances. The pulse of power still flowed, but it went around and past her, unaware of her existence. It was as if she had slipped past a castle's tight defenses to stand in the king's own chamber, none of the shouting guardsmen in the courtyard thinking to look for the intruder so deep within their midst.

From this place of seeming peace, the world had shifted just *so*; offering her a new perspective, like the first time one sees a city from its highest spire rather than its cobbled streets. The corbal seemed tilted to a new angle, allowing her to glimpse aspects thusfar hidden, though they had been there all along. Now she saw not walls of purple stone, solid and unyielding as ice, but myriad tunnels branching this way and that—a maze of veinlike runnels through which the corbal's power flowed. And without its frenzied voice, Athaya felt nothing from the gem but a curious sensation of communion. Of alignment. Of potential, barely bound.

She had known that the corbal bore a source of power, just as she did. But that was not all.

It had more than simple facets ... it had paths. The corbal had *paths* ...

Deep inside, she felt her own power tingle in response, sensing affinity. Like reached out to like, poised for release to whatever purpose she saw fit and eagerly awaiting her will.

Paths, she echoed, through which power could be sent. *Her* power. She gasped as the last curtain was pulled aside to show a vista of frightening and unlimited potential. *You can do it. It can be done* ...

The realization came none too soon. Her assailant took her sharp intake of breath as a sign of surrender and decided that the moment to strike had come. But in the same instant he sprang for her, the cord pulled tight between his hands, Athaya lifted her hands and cried: *"Ignis confestim sit!"*

At her command, raw magic surged like floodwaters through her paths. Then, at her direction, she aimed her power at the corbal's heart, from which it coursed through the crystal's labyrinthine tunnels like blood pumping through living veins. Its power was magnified a hundredfold by the glittering facets, like a single candle in a room of mirrors, growing with intensity as it surged from the center crystal to the smaller two beside it, flooding their paths as well.

Bright fountains of green-tinted fire leaped from her fingertips, embracing the strip of cord. The rope was consumed in seconds, leaving a living line of fire in the man's fists, glowing green and turning his sallow and astonished face the color of moss. The necklace looped around his wrist began to pulse and glow with milky white light and, stunned by spells he had been told she could not cast in the gems' presence, the intruder flung the necklace to the ground in fright and bolted for freedom. But the fire-coils snaked down his body to snag his ankles, dropping him hard to the floor. Then the single coil became two, then four, then six ... until the man was trapped in a writhing cocoon of fiery ropes, crackling and searing, smelling of smoke and the acrid stench of cooking flesh.

The corbal isn't just a barrier to magic, she thought drunkenly, in the midst of a miracle, *it's a conduit* ...

She felt the spell's power swell and grow as she pumped more magic through the crystals, and then felt a subtle jolt of transference as control shifted to the gems themselves; vaguely, she was aware that she was no longer feeding them power, but that the corbals were taking it on their own. Without her conscious bidding, the coils took on the twisting forms of serpents with angry red eyes and flaming tongues, winding their fiery bodies around the assassin and squeezing the breath from him as he had tried to do to their mistress. Shrieking from both pain and mortal terror, the man jerked and writhed upon the floor, futilely trying to free himself from the net of flaming serpents.

"Athaya, what are you ...?"

Jaren's voice was the merest scrape of a whisper, barely audible, but even through pain his shock was unmistakable. Athaya did not think to answer, so enthralled was she. Paths, Jaren ... can't you *see*? Fatigue began to blacken the edges of her vision but she thought little of it; she was caught in the grip of a force far more powerful than herself—a force she could no more push aside than she could a lover in the heady moments before rhythmic bliss held dominion over her body.

Every spell at her command was open to her and at as many times its original force as there were facets in the stone. Her head spun wildly with the magnitude of what she knew could be done here, of the might that could be raised against her enemies, and for an instant she felt as if she'd been granted the powers of the angels to do with what she would.

"Athaya, stop ... for God's sake, let it go!"

Jaren's labored warning barely registered in her mind. His rasping voice was fearful ... but of what? Couldn't he see what she was doing? Couldn't he *realize*? Through an intoxicated haze, Athaya was awestruck at her work, swept away in the tide of her creation. More than simple fire, she had endowed the coils with a semblance of life. Even as that thought crossed her mind, one of the serpents turned its fiery eyes to her and hissed in alien deference.

Then, like a thick blanket thrown over her head, her power suddenly sputtered and dimmed. Jaren had spent what little strength he had to throw a coverlet over the necklace on the floor, imprisoning the gems in darkness. Without them, the drain on Athaya's power suddenly stopped. The snakelike creatures she had crafted slowly retreated into her palms, the blackened scars striping the assassin's flesh the only testament that they had ever existed at all.

The man crawled to the farthest corner of the room and cowered like an injured dog, rocking on his knees and gibbering in the shadows behind the bedstand.

Blinking dazedly, Athaya turned to see how Jaren fared; how badly the *kahnil* had drained him. Her steps were slow and unsteady as she staggered to his side. Only then did she note that he was gaping at her in wide-eyed wonderment. "Y-you used magic. You couldn't have ... but you did." He reached out to clutch her hand, as if to assure himself that it was still made of flesh and blood, and not something less tangible or mortal. "But then it started to use *you*," he added, "and you didn't even realize—"

Barely listening, Athaya steadied herself against the bedpost, still drunk on what she had done; still feeling the unearthly *thrill* of it. "I just wanted to fight him off ... to bind him up the way he meant to do to me."

And her next thought, as she gathered up the blanket-shrouded necklace and cradled the bundle against her chest, was that she had uncovered a weapon that Sage and his allies did not possess, and more, a power that no Lorngeld in all of history—neither Reykan Master nor Sarian Sage—had ever dared to dream existed.

CHAPTER 11

✖✖

S HE DIDN'T KNOW HOW LONG SHE STOOD THERE, DUMBLY
shifting her gaze between Jaren, the huddled form of the
assassin, and the bundled corbal necklace in her arms,
feeling both lethargic and high-strung at the same time. But
sometime, seconds or minutes later, the bedchamber filled to
overflowing with people all shouting at one another in unison.
In the outskirts of her vision, Athaya caught the crimson blur
of guardsmen's uniforms, the black swirl of an archbishop's
cassock—odd, came the vagrant thought, that Lukin should be
so properly clad at this late hour—the glint of lamplight on
Durek's gold-embroidered dressing gown, and the disheveled
shapes of Master Hedric, Mason, and Drianna, all of them in
rumpled bedclothes and hastily donned slippers.

Even before Durek had finished barking a command for
them to do so, a pair of guardsmen surrounded the quailing intruder, now convulsing with fright, and clapped a set of irons
firmly around his wrists. While Hedric hurried to Athaya's
side, murmuring frantic inquiries, Mason crouched beside
Jaren and peered into his eyes, and then beyond, into what lay
behind them.

"He's . . . still under a sealing spell," Athaya told him haltingly. "And he's got some *kahnil* in his blood." Although still
dazed from what she had done with the crystals now resting so
benignly in her grasp, the cold fact of the assassin's presence
and intention was beginning to sink in, pushing away any pride

170

in her accomplishment to make way for the harsh reality of what she—and Jaren—had come dangerously close to losing. "It was only a few drops, but . . ."

"It doesn't look too serious," Mason assured her. "I can only sense a small measure of disruption." He pressed a palm flat across Jaren's forehead and offered him a thin smile. "You probably won't feel so well for the next few days, but all things considered, I suppose it's better than being dead."

Jaren gave him a fragile nod of agreement, but didn't attempt to get to his feet just yet.

"Drianna, would you go make up some tea?" Mason asked. "He'll get through this faster with lots of fluids to flush out what little poison is in him. And Master Hedric, if you would take care of his other . . . er—'problem?'"

Joints popping, Hedric knelt at Jaren's side and deftly released the seal with a touch and a whisper. Then, returning him to Mason's care, the Master turned back to his other erstwhile pupil. "Your spell woke me like a thunderclap," he said to Athaya quietly, curious eyes begging for an explanation. "The force of it was like nothing I've ever felt before."

Nor I, she thought, but couldn't begin to find the right words to tell him the full scope of what he had heard. She took a deep breath to steady herself, but before she could offer even the vaguest of explanations, one of the crimson-clad guardsmen wheeled around sharply to address his king.

"Sire, this man is dying."

The sickly taste of bile inched up Athaya's throat; even though the man had sought her death, she had not meant to kill him. Justified or no, the cloud of Kelwyn's death still hung over her in the minds of many Caithans and she wanted to do nothing to further worsen her reputation. But a quick glance at the bottle the guardsman dutifully passed to Durek proved that her spell had not been the intruder's downfall; just before the men had reached him, he had apparently swallowed what remained of his *kahnil*. He had clearly ingested far more than the few drops in Jaren's blood; already the man's muscles were twitching uncontrollably as the poison did its work.

"Let me," Hedric said, moving from her side to cup the assassin's head between his palms. "We may yet be able to learn something from him." The guardsmen drew back, suspicious that something unnatural was about to take place. The senior officer cast a worried inquiry to his king, who flatly ignored it.

"Find out who he is," Durek ordered as he stalked forward

to tower over the dying man. "And find out who put him up to this."

"But sire!" Lukin cried. Aghast, he slapped a meaty palm over his heart. "This ... this is *necromancy*! It is wicked and immoral—"

Durek motioned sharply to the slashed pillow casing, now ruined beyond repair by corrosion caused from the acidic *kahnil*. "So was trying to murder my sister in her sleep," he snapped back, thin lips curling back in distaste as he turned his royal scrutiny back to the shackled intruder. "Now be silent and let the man work."

Master Hedric closed his eyes and sank deep into the assassin's dying mind, scrying what remained of his memory. Hedric flinched once during the reading, as if he had brushed against residual traces of fright and pain, and then his frown deepened as the impressions became fewer and harder to discern. He retreated shortly after that, leaving what was left of the man's thoughts and memories to vanish slowly into death.

Hedric rose slowly, aged joints popping like burning logs of pine. "I didn't get much. He was almost gone."

Athaya thought she saw the archbishop's features relax slightly, but the expression of barely contained hostility on Hedric's face revealed that Lukin had no cause to relax just yet. Not even when speaking of his onetime student Rhodri had Master Hedric ever come so close to losing control over his emotions.

"Well?" Durek demanded, dragging splayed fingers through a crop of tousled hair. "What did you see?"

"What I saw," he replied, frosting the chamber with the icy glare he directed at Lukin, "is that your archbishop hired this man to murder her Highness—and her husband—as they slept."

Archbishop Lukin snorted indelicately as he pulled himself up to his full height, overshadowing the old wizard by several inches. "How *dare* you!" he bellowed, injecting every drop of righteous indignation he could muster. "Sire, this ... this *wizard* is quite obviously lying. He would say anything to protect his precious protégé—"

Jaren's retort was hushed but furious. "Master Hedric would *never* lie about—"

"—and you've only got his word for it. How can we ever know what he supposedly saw in that man's mind?"

"You can't," Athaya admitted, leaning heavily against the

bedpost to fight back ever-increasing exhaustion. She could hardly be shocked at the archbishop's hand in the plot and silently cursed herself for having ever thought herself safe within these walls. "But," she added quickly, eager to wipe the smug grimace of satisfaction from Lukin's face, "who else could have so easily obtained Dagara's corbal necklace?" She had known the design was familiar, but it was only after its threat was gone that she was finally able to place it. "Or didn't you think I'd recognize it? She wore it at Durek's wedding, you know ... to keep Rhodri from going." Fighting down a subtle surge of nausea, Athaya handed the bundle to Durek, whispering what it contained but requesting that he not open it in their presence.

"Apparently this man—I believe his name was Noel—was arrested by the Tribunal not long ago," Master Hedric went on, pretending not to notice the archbishop's wrathful glare. "He has a history of theft and other petty crimes—not exactly one of Delfarham's finest citizens. This time, however, I didn't perceive that he'd committed any particular crime; an associate of his held a grudge against him—something about not getting a fair share of some stolen money—and turned him in to the Tribunal, claiming he was sheltering wizards. I didn't sense that Noel had any strong opinions one way or another about the Lorngeld—he was mostly concerned with himself.

"In any case, Archbishop Lukin offered the man his freedom if he would secure Athaya's death and promised that he would have easy access to the princess' apartment. I tried," Hedric added apologetically, "but I couldn't find out which of the guardsmen helped to arrange that. If Noel failed—or implicated his employer in any way—Lukin threatened him with the worst that the Tribunal was capable of. Truly, he would have been better off dead than failing; from what I have heard," Hedric inserted dryly, "the Tribunal's Justices are not generally known for their goodness and mercy. If he succeeded, the archbishop promised him not only his freedom, but a small estate confiscated from some other unfortunate prisoner—lands rich enough to support him comfortably for the rest of his life."

"The Tribunal's activities have been suspended, Chief Justice," Durek said darkly, shifting a narrow gaze to Lukin. "You have no authority to distribute its appropriations as yet."

Lukin's eyes darted from his king to Hedric and back again, reflecting shock, outrage, and, Athaya thought, a measure of very real fear. "You trust the accusations of a wizard over *me*?"

Durek's pause was eloquent. "I think, Archbishop, that I have trusted you far too much of late."

Athaya saw painful indecision on her brother's face. He was reluctant to place more trust in a Reykan wizard he had met only days before than in the long-serving and duly anointed primate of Caithe, but he also knew that Jon Lukin, man of God or no, was not beneath hiring assassins to eliminate an inconvenient member of the royal house. He had no real proof of the crime beyond Master Hedric's word, but was inclined to trust it nonetheless—and that, Athaya knew, rankled her brother more than he cared to admit.

"Wait here, all of you," Durek instructed brusquely. He stalked from the room without another word, leaving Archbishop Lukin, two guardsmen, and four wizards glancing at one another in uneasy silence. When he returned a few minutes later, his eyes no longer betrayed frustrated confusion, but stern resolve.

"It is Dagara's necklace." It was spoken without inflection of any kind, but the words alone were damning enough.

Still, Lukin persisted. "Sire, surely you realize that I am not the only one at court with access to the royal strongroom. And any wizard can pick a lock . . . why, this is nothing but a ruse to deceive you into shunning your closest—"

Durek held up one finger to silence him. Athaya thought her brother might explode with rage—she had been the victim of such outbursts often enough and saw the warning signs in his flushed cheeks and grinding teeth—but instead he remained strikingly composed. Not, she thought, unlike Kelwyn, the depths of whose wrath could often be gauged by how softly and rationally he spoke, rather than the reverse.

"If I could strip you of your title without the Curia's approval, Archbishop, then I would be sorely tempted to do so for this audacity. However, since it is true that I have no proof other than the word of one wizard, I cannot rightfully indulge myself so." Despite the words of acquittal, the king's gaze did not soften. "You will leave this court, Jon. In fact, you will leave this city altogether. I believe you still keep a house in Kaiburn; perhaps you should take yourself there for a time. And since I am leaving for Kaiburn myself, I will be happy to escort you—to make certain you arrive safely." Durek's eyes thinned to menacing slits. "And you will not return until I send for you . . . if I ever do so again."

Lukin's lips worked silently for a moment before any sound came out of them. "But Kaiburn—"

"And if the Sage is indeed bringing his army there," Durek went on, well aware of the reason behind Lukin's hesitation, "then your godly presence will be valuable in giving the people strength to stand against him."

The air crackled with tension for a full minute before a wide-eyed Lukin, without waiting for leave, turned on his heel and swept from the chamber, slamming the outer door none too softly on his way.

Durek's muscles relaxed slightly in the archbishop's absence. Sighing, he fingered the wrappings of the corbal necklace in his hand. "As for Dagara, it's likely that this was taken from the strongroom without her knowledge. It's no secret our stepmother dislikes you, Athaya," Durek remarked, "but she's never come right out and wished you dead."

"No, you're the only one of the family who's done that." Athaya bit her tongue the moment the words were out, realizing that the days of habitually exchanging barbs with her brother were now over—or at least suspended. The statement itself was true, but Athaya fervently wished she had not voiced it. It didn't make Durek angry; instead, he looked vaguely hurt.

"Still," he went on, clearing his throat uneasily, "I think I'll let her know about this necklace in an offhanded way—maybe pretend I've forgotten it's hers and promise to punish the owner if I ever find out who it is—"

Athaya closed her eyes, barely able to hear what her brother was saying. His words were rapidly blending into a nonsensical drone and she was suddenly far too occupied with keeping herself upright.

"Athaya?" Durek asked, steadying her by the elbow. "Are you ill?"

She couldn't find the strength to answer. Only minutes before, she was drunk on the heady rush of power that the corbal had given her; now she felt as if every drop of blood had drained from her body, leaving a hollow husk that the slightest wind could blow into fine powder. She hugged the bedpost even harder, fending off a wave of nausea and then saw the room start to spin beneath her feet.

"Catch me . . ." she choked out, just before the floor came up to meet her.

* * *

Athaya woke several hours later, comfortably tucked between a feather mattress and a goosedown quilt. Master Hedric sat on a wooden stool at her bedside, while Jaren was fast asleep beside her, his flesh radiating unhealthy warmth from a *kahnil*-induced fever. The sour taste in her mouth betrayed that she'd been sick sometime in the night, but now she felt lucid enough—no worse than she ever had after too many tankards of mediocre ale. Mason and Durek were also still present, pacing about the chamber like worried fathers-to-be. Athaya glanced cautiously to the corner; to her relief, Durek's guardsmen had disposed of the assassin's body.

"How is he?" she asked. Her voice cracked from disuse as she reached out to brush a sweat-dampened strand of hair from Jaren's forehead.

"He'll be fine," Hedric assured her. "He drank most of the tea Drianna brought. Now he just needs to sleep."

Once she was certain her head wasn't going to start whirling like a spinning wheel again, Athaya tossed back the coverlets and slid her legs over the edge of the bed. Durek frowned disapprovingly at her, but it was a refreshing frown of concern, not of rebuke. "You shouldn't be getting out of bed yet."

"I have to."

"But you're not—"

"Durek." Athaya glanced meaningfully to the chamber pot in the corner, after which his Majesty reddened and excused himself.

After a moment to herself, Athaya stuffed her feet into a pair of deerskin slippers and shuffled out to join the others in the outer chamber. Drianna had left them another pot of strong tea and a tray of oatcakes; Athaya plucked up a cake and lathered it with honey before curling into a cushioned chair by a low-burning fire.

"I suppose you're all wanting to know what happened," she said dryly, noting the expectant expressions on each of the three faces before her.

"Jaren . . . told us what he saw," Mason said tentatively, as if not altogether sure the vision wasn't a hallucination brought on by the *kahnil* in Jaren's blood. "It would seem that corbal crystals have more than one type of power."

Eager for details, he and Hedric both leaned forward in unison, their scholars' eyes hungry for new knowledge; they gave Athaya all the attention a pair of stray cats would give a man waving a scrap of fish between his fingers. In contrast, Durek's countenance was markedly apprehensive—and with good reason. The implications of the night's events would have a different meaning for him; without the security of corbal crystals, he no longer had a weapon he could use against her, should she not prove as loyal an ally as she pledged. And if she could not only defy that weapon, but turn it against him . . .

Athaya poured herself a shallow cup of tea. "In short, I found out that a corbal does more than simply block our spells. It channels them." She recounted everything she could remember; the intensely sharpened focus that mortal fear had given her, the voices of the crystals, the abrupt silence of the crystal's heart, and the startling glimpse of veinlike tunnels where none had been perceived before. "They have paths and a source just like we do and a special kind of magic that tricks us into feeling pain where none exists. It's . . . almost as if they're alive."

"At least when they're close to light," Mason said, absently studying the fire. "That's the force that kindles their power, whereas simply being alive kindles ours. But they're not alive in the same sense as we are; you said yourself that the corbal's source isn't at all like ours—not a jumble of noise and images, but utter stillness. Logical, when you think of it, since the gem has no 'thoughts' or 'memories' to clutter up the place."

As Mason spoke, Athaya recalled her only direct encounter with the center of her self; she had touched upon her source on the night Rhodri had stolen her power and she sought a way to regain it. It was an experience whose vividness would never fade. Standing in that blinding abyss of light that formed the heart of her being, her life played out before her in colorful and clamorous panorama; everything she was or would be danced around her in a timeless jumble of motion, swirling past too quickly to regard any one moment apart from any other.

"The nature of the crystals is fascinating, of course," Hedric interrupted, "but at the moment I'm far more concerned with why you passed out not long after using them." The Master's bushy white brows were tightly knitted with worry. "Tell me, Athaya . . . when you were channeling your magic through the corbal, did it feel the same as casting your other spells or was it different somehow?"

"Different?" Athaya whistled under her breath. "That doesn't do it justice, Master Hedric. It felt like I had unimaginable resources at my command; there was no limit to what I could do. It was intoxicating—more so than any spellwork I've ever done in my life. I'm not surprised that I passed out," she added with a shrug. "I feel dizzy enough after translocation, and that's the strongest spell I know. But this . . ." She shook her head in awesome reverence, recalling the unspeakable *Power* that had been at her command, if only briefly. "This was far more potent."

Absently, Mason poured a drop of honey into his tea. "You probably would have collapsed a lot sooner if you hadn't just fought off an attempt on your life. Once the shock of the attack wore off, the drain from your spell hit you with full force."

"It was more than just exhaustion, I suspect," Hedric murmured, brows still linked together in a frown. "Jaren said you couldn't counter the spell once you had cast it."

Athaya returned his frown; she'd thought nothing of it at the time, but yes, Jaren *had* said something along those lines, just before covering the corbals with the quilts. *It started to use you,* he had told her. *And you didn't even realize.*

"I'm . . . not sure if I could have stopped it or not," Athaya told him, shivering from a sudden chill. "It didn't occur to me to try. If I was 'trapped' somehow, I wasn't aware of it. I do remember getting awfully tired at one point—as if the crystal was pulling power from me faster than I could give it—but I was too enthralled by my spellwork to care."

Hedric steepled his fingers, tapping them thoughtfully against his lips. "I think we're talking about something more serious than we realize," he said gravely. "It's my guess that you were siphoning power directly from your source . . . 'bleeding' magic, as it were, rather like opening a vein. You see, when casting inborn spells with your paths, there is a finite amount of power available to you; when you've drained it all, you simply can't work any more magic—such as after translocation, when you can't even cast a simple witchlight. The rest of your strength—the force that keeps you alive— isn't affected. But channeling power through the corbal lets you overextend yourself . . . quite possibly to the point of death. It taps into not only your magic power, but your life force as well."

Hedric, Mason, and Athaya exchanged deeply pensive glances, while Durek looked from wizard to wizard, utterly baffled. The discussion had clearly grown too esoteric for his taste.

"It was fortunate that Jaren applied the proper 'tourniquet' by covering those crystals when he did," Hedric continued. "If he hadn't, you might well have bled to death—magically speaking, that is. If, as you said, you were oblivious to the danger you were in, then who knows what might have happened if your spell had gone on much longer or if there had been even more crystals present to drain the power from you? You might not have been able to stop before it was too late. And like bleeding to death, there would have been no pain to warn you—just a gradual fading away into unconsciousness."

Athaya hadn't thought of it quite that way before and her oatcake suddenly turned to sawdust in her mouth.

"That's probably why the corbals induce pain in the first place—and do so only in wizards," Mason offered, setting his teacup aside. "Pain of any kind is a warning—a signal that the body is being endangered somehow. People without magic can't harm themselves with the corbals, so they feel nothing; the pain—the warning—is meant specifically for us. It keeps us from discovering just what the corbal can be used for, and therefore keeps us from harming ourselves. If we ignore the warning and use the crystals to cast spells, we could kill ourselves. The gems may be tools of great power," he concluded, "but the price of using them is dangerously high."

Hedric concurred with a solemn nod. "Like a Circle charm," he murmured. Unfocused eyes stared blindly into the distance as if reliving an unpleasant memory or scrying an equally unpleasant future.

Athaya turned to him quizzically; in all her months of study at his side, he had never mentioned such a thing before. "A what?"

"It's . . . a sort of talisman," he replied, recalling himself to the conversation with a series of rapid blinks. "A weapon of last resort—rarely used. I don't think anyone has used one since . . . oh, my great-grandfather's day. And that was quite a few years back, I assure you," he added, brushing the subject aside with a dismissive chuckle.

Durek shifted forward in his chair and made a decorous coughing noise to remind the others that he was still present. "So, the gist of what you've been saying is that Athaya can use these crystals to work magic, but she can't stop it once she starts?"

"That's the essence of it," Hedric said. "But if your sister remains true to form, she'll soon find a way around such an obstacle. My prize pupil never ceases to amaze me." He regarded her with unabashed pride for a moment, then cracked a wry smile. "I trust, Athaya, that you will find this experience of significant enough import to include in your journal."

Athaya averted her eyes. "I think so, Master Hedric." In truth, it was the journal that had saved her life; if Jaren had not roused himself from fitful sleep to work on it, it was likely that neither of them would have been alerted to the assassin's presence until it was too late.

"Are you well enough to travel?" Durek asked, abruptly getting to his feet. Unable to comprehend much of what they'd been discussing for the past quarter-hour, he was eager to shift the conversation to more mundane matters—ones that he had the power to control. "I hate to delay our journey to Kaiburn, but if you're not up to it yet—"

Athaya drained the rest of her now-lukewarm tea. "I'll be fine—just give me an hour or two to get ready. The Sage's army is moving too quickly; we can't afford to put this off even for a day."

"This could be a more dramatic conflict than the Sage is counting on if you can use corbal crystals against him," Mason observed, plucking another oatcake from the tray and shaking off loose crumbs.

"Only if I can find a way to avoid killing myself in the process," Athaya replied. "I don't want things to get quite *that* dramatic."

Once she had bathed and changed, Athaya made a brief stop at Nicolas' apartments to see how he was faring before leaving for Kaiburn. Someone had arrived before her, however; as she entered the outer sitting chamber, she could hear low voices coming from the adjoining bedroom. That one of the voices was Hedric's did not surprise her—as Nicolas' tutor and caretaker, he rarely left the prince's side—but to her surprise, the other voice belonged to Durek, who was apparently in intimate conversation with him.

"So as High Wizard," Durek was asking, "you advise Osfonin on matters relevant to the Lorngeld's welfare?"

"Exactly."

"Then what purpose does this Circle have? I've heard you mention it before—"

"It is a governing body within the Lorngeld themselves, no matter what their nation of origin," Hedric replied, in the same tireless tone of voice he used with his novice magic students.

"The Circle does not involve itself in the politics of the world, but only in the practice of magic."

Durek paused. "I still don't see why they weren't helping Athaya all along. They obviously support what she's trying to do."

"As I said, that would have been an overtly political act, since magic is not yet legal here. The Circle has some considerable influence in lands where magic is accepted and allowed to flourish, but we do not presume to interfere in those lands where it is not. When magic once again returns to Caithe, be assured that you will feel our presence here."

"When it returns," Durek echoed. His voice was dry but not angry, with only the slightest edge of defensiveness. "You sound rather certain that I'll permit that."

"With respect, your Majesty, I think that you have already decided to do so, whether you know it yet or not."

Athaya braced herself, expecting her brother to lash out at him for such a presumption, but instead of taking offense at the Master's observation, he lapsed into a spell of studied silence. "I . . . you puzzle me, sir. You're nothing like Rhodri was."

Athaya didn't need her eyes to see the clouds that crossed Master Hedric's face just then. "No," she heard him reply. She wondered if he would tell Durek just who had trained Rhodri in his art, but he did not, perhaps deciding that such knowledge would do nothing to further relations between himself and the king of Caithe. "But then, most wizards are not like him. Your sister is not. Athaya is a highly skilled magician—I should know, as I trained her myself." Athaya heard him loose a thoughtful sigh. "She cares deeply for the future of her people, your Majesty . . . more so, perhaps, than she will ever admit to you. And she has never in my presence spoken hatred for you. Resentment, perhaps," he conceded. "Disappointment. But never hatred."

Without a word, Durek crossed the chamber to the window, passing into Athaya's view. She studied her brother's profile carefully. He looked as if he had been given a gift he knew he did not deserve and was fumbling for a suitable response. He felt embarrassed and awkward—definitely in need of someone to rescue him.

"Ah, here you are," she said, striding into the chamber as if she had just arrived. "The coach and escort are ready. It's time we left."

Durek was quick to agree. "Yes. Yes it is. I was just . . . that is, I came to see Nicolas before we left. See how he was doing."

Athaya nodded obligingly, careful not to betray her suspicions that Nicolas was not the real reason he had sought out this chamber. Absently, she wondered if this was not the first time that Durek had spoken privately with Master Hedric, perhaps seeking out his advice where he was too proud to ask for hers. If he was, it would be the best of all possible signs that he was slowly trying to comprehend her people, just as Kelwyn had—if with admittedly more enthusiasm—so many years before.

To her right, Nicolas was tucked up on a stool before his writing desk, clad as befitted a prince but for the pair of fine leather shoes carelessly tossed to one side. The tip of his tongue protruded slightly as he scratched a series of letters onto a sheet of parchment, taking special care not to blot the ink.

"Hello, Athaya," he said, looking up. She was startled that he knew her, but the vacant expression in those upturned eyes told her that the greeting was not so much a result of his true memory coming back as it was that he'd simply been taught to parrot her name.

"Master Hedric is teaching me my letters again," he went on. "I can't believe I ever knew how. It's *hard*."

"You'll get it, Nicky. Hedric is an excellent teacher—of all manner of things." She offered him an encouraging smile as he turned back to his work, trying to smother the dull ache of sadness that came upon her every time she looked at him.

"Has he made much progress?" she asked Hedric. She was far more tempted to ask about his seeming progress with Durek, but restricted her questions to Nicolas.

"Quite a bit, actually. The compulsion spell is interfering with his ability to read and write; I've had to teach him his alphabet again, but he's catching on quickly. I think being back home again is helping him to remember things more easily as well. That reminds me," he said, his face growing troubled, "last night, he remembered taking some books from Rhodri's library and delivering them to one of the Sage's men. Do you know anything about that?"

Athaya started to shake her head, but stopped abruptly. "Wait—Lord Gessinger mentioned something about books when he came to my camp last winter, but I was so worried about Nicolas that I forgot all about it. Delivering the books must have been part of the compulsion." Athaya leaned against the doorjamb, suddenly in need of support. "I don't like the sound of this. The Sage's ideas are dangerous enough without his getting wind of Rhodri's. Still," she added, "the Sage hasn't said anything about the books and doesn't seem to be making any use of them. He obtained them before he was sealed, so maybe he's forgotten about them by now."

Hedric shrugged mildly; it was as good a hope as any. "Is Jaren awake yet?"

"He was, but only for a few minutes. He's not too happy about staying behind, but I think even he realizes that the journey would do him more harm than good. He can barely sit up without feeling queasy, so the thought of three days bumping about in a coach wasn't too enticing."

"We should be back in a little over a week," Durek said to Hedric as he ushered Athaya out of the room. "I've told Captain Parr and the guard that if there's any trouble from the Sage's wizards while we're gone, that they are to defer to your judgment and obey you as they would me."

While Hedric calmly inclined his head in acknowledgment—expertly suppressing astonishment, if indeed he felt any—Athaya almost stumbled over the threshold. "You said *that*?"

"Yes," Durek replied with a grimace, "and you can imagine the look he gave me. If he ever thought I was under one of your spells, he thought so then. But if we're going to have this alliance, then I may as well make use of it. Even my capable captain has to admit he's no match for the Sage; he found *that* out in Eriston. Now come," Durek said, striding swiftly down the hall. "If we can get to Kaiburn before the Sage does, we might just have a chance to save it."

CHAPTER 12

✳✳

BLESSED WITH FINE WEATHER AND DRY ROADS, THE JOUR-
ney to Kaiburn took less than three full days. And good
thing that was, to Athaya's mind, since it was all the
sooner they could part company with the disgraced Archbishop
Lukin, who traveled in a separate coach behind them and was
deposited at his townhouse in the affluent west end of the city
without so much as a parting word from his king.

"He'll bear watching," Athaya murmured, as the last of
Lukin's voluminous black robes swept indignantly through the
townhouse's richly carved front door.

Durek motioned the driver to move on, then reclined into
the cushions shaking his head. "I never dreamed he'd be so
bold." He stole a glance out the curtained window as if to assure himself that Lukin was not trailing them. "I didn't know,"
he added suddenly, turning to Athaya with something akin to
entreaty in his eyes. "I didn't have any idea what he was planning."

An odd feeling of reassurance trickled though Athaya's
veins. "I never thought you did," she replied, as surprised to
speak the words as Durek was to hear them.

News of the king's visit reached the city well before the
king himself, and as the royal coach crossed the western bridge
into the city proper, every window and doorway was clogged
with people hoping to catch a glimpse of him—and, Athaya

suspected, hoping to see the even rarer sight of his Majesty openly tolerating his sister's company.

As the coach approached the cathedral square, however, Athaya began to notice an unusual number of wagons and carriages sharing the cobbled streets, all of them heavily laden with trunks and baskets. These were not merchants with goods to transport, she quickly realized; these were people fleeing the city. Those with a place to go, she added inwardly, noting that most of those taking flight were the wealthier of Kaiburn's citizens, most of whom would have a country house at their disposal. Occasionally, though, she saw someone heading toward the city gates with little more than a few clothes tied into a bundle, only wishing to be where the Sage was not.

"It looks as if they've heard the same rumors Mason did," she observed. "Or gotten wind of the scouting parties Adam Graylen saw near Halsey."

When the coach rolled to a stop in the cathedral square, Lieutenant Berns, second-in-command to Captain Parr, quickly informed Durek what his advance scouts had gleaned of the present situation. "The sheriff reports that roughly four hundred of the Sage's men were seen yesterday near the village of Leaford, just south of here. He said people have been streaming out of the city ever since, afraid for their lives."

"Only four hundred?" Athaya said, turning a quizzical frown to her brother. "I don't mean to flatter myself, but my camp probably has enough wizards to put up a decent fight against that many. If the Sage wanted to destroy us, why not bring his whole army? He must have thousands under his banner by now."

Durek shrugged uneasily. "You always said he was an arrogant sort. Maybe he just underestimated your numbers."

Somehow, Athaya doubted the answer was so simple, but said nothing as Durek alighted from the coach and waved greetings to his subjects. As he reached back to hand her down, Athaya was acutely conscious of the stares and whispers of the crowd, feeling much like an oddity on display at a village fair. But the eyes of the people were warmer than on her last visit; today they looked upon her with admiring curiosity—she was the king's friend and ally now, not a felon to be condemned, and so the populace was content to wave kind greetings to her and not toss rotten fruit and insults as they had done before. Her appearance certainly helped matters; Athaya was not clad in a tattered and ink-spotted kirtle this time, but matched her brother's understated grace in a flowing gown of pale gray silk trimmed with silver. A delicate white veil framed her face, giving her the look of a penitent novice rather than a one-time traitor and excommunicate.

Durek's guardsmen cleared a path for them to the cathedral steps, forcing back the crowd. "Just let me do the talking, all right?" he advised. His tone was surprisingly light; dryly sarcastic, but not angry. "As I recall, the last time you addressed the people of Kaiburn, a riot broke out."

He mounted the steps and turned, the rubies in his coronet sparkling like a thousand tiny fires in the blinding midday sunlight. Two guardsmen stood on each side, each holding one end of a silken canopy to shield the king from the sun's unforgiving glare.

"People of Kaiburn," Durek began, lifting his hands to ask for silence. "I come to you with the gravest of news."

The square grew hushed, as if preparing to be led in prayer, and Durek's words carried effortlessly to the far edges of the square. Athaya didn't hear much of her brother's speech, however; he had already rehearsed it with her in the coach, so she let her attentions wander, scanning the faces before her to gauge their mood. All were anxious for a savior—that much could be seen in their eyes. They desperately needed someone—anyone—to protect them from the advancing army of magicians against which they had little defense. Fortunately, Athaya sensed that they thought well of her presence at Durek's side, more than willing to accept her aid if the king would.

"But Caithe has endured war before," Durek was saying when she turned her attentions back to him, "and will so again. I will protect this city with men and arms and my sister will do so with wizards and magic."

Athaya ascended the steps to join him and, to the delight of the assembly, took his arm.

"With your courageous help," he concluded, "we can drive this intruder back to Sare where he came from—perhaps even destroy him altogether. Athaya and I will defend you even unto our deaths, if need be. This we promise you."

Durek offered his sister a chaste kiss of friendship, pecking each of her cheeks lightly. A murmur of approval rippled through the crowd as Kaiburn accepted the king's gesture as proof that his unlikely alliance with his sister was no farce.

Athaya's hand lingered on her brother's arm as Durek led

her down the cathedral steps and back to the waiting coach. It had not been a long speech, nor was it the most important address his Majesty was to make that day, but the citizens of Kaiburn thought well of it and cheered their acceptance, shouting wishes of long life to their king. A handful of more adventuresome souls passed the same wishes on to Athaya.

The coach rolled slowly out of the city—a far more leisurely departure than that of a year before, when Kaiburn had erupted into a frenzy of burning and looting—and headed northeast, toward the sprawling Forest of Else. Durek was conspicuously silent during the brief journey. His words to the people of Kaiburn had come with relative ease. His next speech, Athaya suspected, would be the most difficult he had ever given.

The king's entourage halted at Athaya's signal, in a tranquil expanse of meadow tucked between a ramshackle sheepfold and the western edge of the wood. Above them was an ocean of cloudless blue sky, broken only by a single hawk circling idly over the fields below. It had grown hotter as the afternoon progressed; Athaya's gown clung stubbornly to sweat-soaked skin, and her veiled hair felt sticky and damp. The cool shelter of the trees would be welcome indeed.

Durek stepped down from the coach and looked uneasily about. "Should we let them know we're here?"

"They already know," Athaya replied. "We post sentries at the edge of the wood—the moment the coach came within sight, word would have been relayed back to the main camp. Besides," she added, "I sent word last night that we were coming. I used my 'cursed globe,' as Lukin calls it."

Durek winced at the name as if the very thought of his once-trusted archbishop gave him pain. He turned toward the forest, peering into its depths but making no move to approach it. As a royal hunting preserve, the Forest of Else was technically his property, but he was profoundly reluctant to enter its bounds, knowing there were those within that would not welcome him as easily as had the people of Kaiburn.

"Very well, then," he said awkwardly after a time, aware that his men were patiently awaiting orders. "Let's go find this camp of yours."

Athaya took him aside, a short distance from the others. "It might be wise to leave your men behind," she suggested softly. "My people are understandably skittish about soldiers and could interpret the presence of guards as a sign you don't trust them. No one will harm you—not as long as you're with me. I ... can't make any promises for what might happen if you wander off on your own," she admitted, "but ..."

"No, you're right," he said, as if he'd never considered any other alternative. "I'll go alone."

As alone as you have ever been, Athaya thought as she watched him pass a hand across his brow to scrape off the sweat, not all of which was caused by simple heat. *And perhaps as courageous a thing as I've ever seen you do.*

Not surprisingly, the king's guardsmen were unanimously appalled at Durek's pronouncement that he would enter the forest alone with Athaya, all of them certain that he would never emerge again. But none would dare to forcibly restrain their king; in the end, they could do little but watch him go, their eyes burning Athaya's back with warning of what would happen if he did not return safely ... and soon.

Glad to be away from the oppressiveness of both Durek's watchdogs and the sun, Athaya led her brother through the blessed shade of the forest, following the rune trail that led to the camp. Thin beams of sunlight snaked their way through the twists of pine and oak branches to spot the forest floor with gold and the majestic silence was only sporadically interrupted by the rustle of leaves as a bird took flight or a rabbit darted from one hiding place to another. As they walked, Athaya felt as if she had crossed into another world—a realm like the between-place of translocation, not bound by the normal passage of time—in which she and Durek were the only human inhabitants. When, she wondered, was the last time she had been alone with Durek and they had not been quarreling? When had he ever trusted her enough to put his very life into her hands? When had she trusted him?

Athaya snapped a leaf from a low-hanging maple branch. When, exactly, had they stopped being friends?

It was long before her magic was born, that much was sure. Her power—and most importantly, her decision to accept it and not submit meekly to absolution—was only the catalyst that had driven them even further apart than they had been before. Perhaps she had always been envious of the attention he merited as the eldest, destined to rule after Kelwyn, while she and Nicolas were relegated to the gallery—herself farthest of all, worth only what she could bring to Caithe as a royal bride. And perhaps, she mused, Durek had envied her, too, in his way; wishing, despite his protestations of duty, that he could set his responsibilities aside at times and go exploring in shadowy coves for a pirate's long-forgotten treasure, as his younger siblings had often done.

God's breath, there were so many things she should be saying to him! But Athaya's tongue was strangely still, fearful of unraveling the delicate tapestry of friendship that had been woven these past few weeks. She gazed at her brother imploringly, wishing he would speak instead, but when he met her eyes, sensing the train of her thoughts, he awkwardly looked away.

Durek made to circle around a tangle of brambles in his path, but Athaya caught his arm with a grin and guided him through the thorny mess. An illusion—and one of Ranulf's best.

"How ... do you know the way?" he asked wide-eyed, peering back at the illusory brush, and then ahead at the maze of green and brown before them.

"Marks. On the trees."

Durek frowned. "But I don't—"

"Only wizards can see them."

He nodded. "Ah."

And for the remainder of the hour they talked of trivial things; admiring the abundance of the trilliums, remarking upon the heady scent of pine, and estimating the number of deer that made their home in this royal wood.

Before long, the trail opened into a clearing dotted with canvas tents, haphazard shelters of branches and pine boughs, and an assemblage of crumbling stone buildings. The king's arrival was indeed expected, and as in Kaiburn, curious faces filled every doorway and window. The mood was not as accepting here as in the city—little wonder, Athaya reflected, as Durek and his clergy had been trying to exterminate the citizens of Kaiburn for almost two years—but while no one raised a cheer to their king, none spoke openly against his presence, following Athaya's lead in offering him trust and friendship until he proved himself unworthy of it.

Durek instinctively stepped back as a huge red-haired man, knife brazenly hanging from his belt, strode up to greet them. "Welcome back m'dear," Ranulf said, sweeping Athaya up into a hearty bear hug of a welcome. He set her down and touched a meaty finger to her pearled chaplet and gossamer veil. "Haven't seen you look so fine in a damned long time."

Athaya offered him a lopsided smile. "Why does everyone keep saying that?"

"And you're welcome, too, o' course," Ranulf added to Durek, though with an unmistakably vigilant glint in his eye.

"Er, thank you," Durek replied, equally vigilant.

"Pass the word that his Majesty and I are going to rest for a few minutes before he speaks to them," she instructed Ranulf. "And could you have someone bring us each a mug of something cool to drink? We've had a long walk and I'm parched."

Ranulf gave a jaunty salute of obedience and then Athaya led Durek around the edge of the clearing toward the chapel where he could prepare his next address. He had known what to say to the people of Kaiburn all along, but to her following of wizards, Athaya suspected that, as yet, he had little idea of what words to offer.

"This is where you've been living?" he murmured as they walked, sneaking glances at the compound and inwardly appalled that a Trelane would ever have to live in such reduced circumstances. Before she replied, Athaya quickly bade him duck before entangling himself in a line of freshly washed clothing strung across two trees.

"It used to be a monastic retreat before King Faltil's troops slaughtered all the wizards here." She hoped her answer didn't sound accusatory; it was simply a statement of historical fact. She took him inside the empty chapel, murmuring a brief apology for the debris littering the floor. No matter how often it was swept, leaves and twigs found their way inside daily, and Durek's boots crunched on them like gravel as he walked up the narrow aisle to the altar. His fingers touched upon the various objects placed there—the bowl of a broken chalice, the curl of a silver brooch, an ancient, worm-eaten copy of the *Book of Sages*—all relics of the brotherhood that once lived and worshiped peacefully in this place.

Durek sighed heavily as he lifted a fragment of colored glass to the sunlight; the gesture sent a bright red line slanting across the floor like a trickle of blood running from the altar. He was uneasy here; this sanctuary offered him no comfort. Perhaps, Athaya reflected, he feared that he had inherited far more from his ancestor Faltil than he had from Kelwyn, feeling himself a partner in the slaughter as he and his Tribunal carried on what the long-dead Faltil had started. For the first time, those deaths seemed to disturb him, as if he could sense the multitude of ghosts in this place, rebuking him for his callousness and naming him unfit to be king.

"Lukin told me that King Faltil's crown is buried here," he remarked, not turning around. He held up another scrap of glass to the sunlight, this time striping the floor with blue.

Athaya felt her muscles tense as her eyes flickered to the flagstone beneath which the crown was buried, not ten yards from where Durek stood. The dried mud sealing it in place was slightly darker than the rest; someone who knew what to look for would have little trouble picking out the right stone.

"One of his prisoners told him where it was," Durek continued with seeming idleness. "Or confessed it under torture, more like. A friend of the boy who stole it."

"I won't return it, Durek," Athaya said guardedly. "I can't. Not yet."

Durek let out a brittle wisp of laughter. "I didn't think you would." He did not mention the crown again.

In the silence that followed, Gilda slipped into the quiet chapel with two mugs of frothy beer; leaving them, she departed with a courteous, if uneasy, curtsy to her king. Athaya brought Durek his mug and then settled into the first pew. Although the day's heat was subsiding as evening approached, the stone still felt cool and refreshing against her back. Durek did not join her, but lingered at the altar, strangely unwilling to leave it.

"What am I going to tell them?' he asked, sipping absently at his mug. For a moment, Athaya wasn't certain if he were referring to the people in the clearing or the myriad ghosts of long-dead wizards, waiting to judge him when he finally came to answer for his deeds.

Athaya wasn't sure if he meant to ask the question aloud, but she ventured a reply. "Just tell them the truth, Durek. Tell them what's in your heart. They can't ask any more of you than that."

"They can ask for my head on a platter and you damned well know it!" he snapped, his composure splintering under the onerous weight of the task before him. He drained half of his beer in a single, frenzied gulp. "You're probably enjoying every minute of this, too. Seeing me here, without defenses, and about to make an utter fool of myself."

Once, such a remark might have instigated a vicious quarrel, but here in this place, Athaya knew it was only fear that made him speak so and let the insult pass. "Durek, you're not being foolish at all. It took great courage for you to come here today. In fact, I can't think of a time when I've respected you more than I do right now. And that's God's own truth, Durek. I swear it."

His mouth jerked open, ready to accuse her of not knowing the first thing about God's own truth or any other kind, but then it snapped closed just as quickly. He gave her a peculiar look just then, knowing she had to be lying but at the same time certain that she wasn't. He set his mug down, grunted something unintelligible, and then stepped away from the altar. Outside, the bright glare of day was slowly fading into the muted colors of twilight and the hum of voices was growing louder as the Lorngeld gathered to hear their king. He could delay no longer.

"I may as well get this over with."

Nodding silently, Athaya led him to the campfire near the derelict bell tower; there was no need to ring it, as every single member of her following was already assembled. She hopped up onto a tree stump so that everyone could see her, then offered a few words of greeting, professing her happiness at being 'home' again. Then, stepping down, she offered the platform to Durek, apologizing that they could offer nothing more dignified.

"Dignity is the least of my problems right now," he mumbled, awkwardly shifting cloak, sleeves, and other regal trappings aside as he clambered onto the stump. Despite his jitters, he almost laughed at the picture he presented—a bejeweled king balancing himself on a rotted tree stump in the middle of the woods—and vagrant smiles of empathy appeared on the faces of many in attendance.

Even before he began, Athaya could tell how difficult this was for him. Like a wizard facing the Tribunal, Durek stood before the victims of his policies with only words to aid him. And devoid of magic in a place where nearly all possessed it, he would be powerless to save himself should his words not have the hoped-for effect. He was afraid, but only those who knew him intimately could discern it. His fingers curled and uncurled in steady rhythm, the ruby signet ring catching the firelight with each anxious movement.

"I thank you for permitting me to come here," Durek began, sweeping his gaze over every face before him. "It shows greater charity than perhaps I would have offered, given reverse circumstances."

His audience was silent. Waiting. Listening. Judging him. Unlike the Tribunal, their verdict was not preordained. "My father devoted his life to uniting a long-divided kingdom. He brought together disparate provinces plagued by civil war for centuries." As Durek briefly summarized the brilliant series of campaigns that led to Kelwyn's victory, Athaya noted that he never broached the subject of their father's adopted magic, hoping to avoid adding that volatile agent to the mix of his speech. It would not serve his purpose here to be led into confessing how adamantly opposed to such an act he had been, even as a young boy of eight.

"Caithe has been thus united for only a short time and now the Sage of Sare has come to divide us again. I say that we should not let this happen, but should do everything in our power to repel him; to stand as one against him."

He reminded them of the Sage's frighteningly rapid sweep from Eriston to Kilfarnan, of the ruin and death brought down upon all those who refused to join him, and of the reports that hundreds of the Sage's men were even now gathering near Kaiburn, readying an attack. "My soldiers can fight those in the Sage's army who have no magic—he has swayed many to his side, either by telling them they will develop the power later or by reminding them that they will share in the future rewards of a Lorngeld brother, sister, husband, or wife. But my soldiers can do little against wizards—especially those among the Sage's men who can turn aside the influences of a corbal crystal. But you have the ability to fight them!" he said, jitters all but forgotten in the passion of his speech. "And it is in you that Caithe's only hope rests."

Ranulf got to his feet and regarded Durek coolly. "So now you need our help, and suddenly we're not the Devil's Children anymore, is that it?" Several heads bobbed behind him at the question, wishing they'd had the gumption to ask it.

"I won't lie to you and say I've completely changed my mind," Durek admitted. "I was taught certain things about the purpose and origin of the powers that you possess, and I simply can't dismiss those beliefs overnight. But there are wizards at my court who are eager to explain their views to me and perhaps one day I can resolve my feelings on the subject. But none of us have time to wait for that day," he urged, sweeping his gaze from Ranulf to the others gathered in the clearing. "In the same way Athaya and I have set aside our differences for the greater good, I ask that you do the same. Only together can we drive this intruder from our land. After that danger is past, we can try to resolve our disputes to everyone's satisfaction."

After a moment's thought, Ranulf sat back down on his blanket, seemingly appeased.

"I won't order you to help me," Durek concluded. "But I beseech you all to lend your unique talents to the defense of this city—and to Caithe itself—for the good of us all."

In the ensuing silence, Athaya gazed up at him with a pride that she had not felt since she was a child, easily awed by all the wondrous things that an older brother could do. She looked upon his face—the meager beard, the thinning hair, the slouching eyes—and for the first time, noticed how he was growing to resemble Kelwyn as the years wore on. And, slowly, growing to be like him in other ways. At last.

The clearing was unusually quiet as Durek clumsily climbed down from the tree stump. Before he could shrink away, Athaya enclosed him in a warm embrace. He drew back, visibly puzzled. This was no ritual kiss of friendship done to please their audience, but affection straight from her heart.

"I don't think Father himself ever made a finer speech," she whispered, so quiet that no one else could hear.

Somehow, coming from her, he knew it for the deep compliment it was; embarrassed, he simply cleared his throat and said nothing, his hands worrying at a sudden wrinkle in his surcoat.

As the Lorngeld in the clearing began to whisper among themselves and disperse to their tents, Master Tonia came forward and offered Durek a cup of crimson-colored wine.

"We'd be honored if you would stay and share our supper with us, your Majesty. It's simple fare, but we're not such bad cooks as all that."

Durek balked as he took the cup, flustered by the woman's sincerity. His first instinct was to decline, yet Athaya watched him struggle with himself, unable to voice the words.

"Why not?" Athaya whispered in his ear. "We're far better company than your guardsmen—especially if Ranulf gets drunk and starts singing."

Tonia winced and rolled her eyes in mock-anguish. "Lord help us."

Despite lingering feelings of awkwardness, the thought of staying for a meal was oddly appealing. Durek offered a slight bow to Tonia. "The honor would be mine."

Honored or no, Durek stayed close to Athaya's side as they waited for the rabbits to finish roasting—and a pair of deer,

though his Majesty made no comment on poaching game from
the king's forest. Guardedly at first, he accepted the greetings
of those who ventured forward to address him. Among them,
Gilda brought her son to meet the king—a boy, Athaya quietly
remarked to Durek, that would never have been born had Gilda
been absolved. Girard offered cautious respects as well, not
bothering to hide the hand whose fingers had been severed by
a Justice's blade or the story behind his injury. Durek accepted
the tales with growing solemnity, each an added weight upon
a conscience already disturbed by the forest chapel and the
ghosts he knew still tarried there.

"Do you think they believed me?" he asked Athaya later, as
they went to the spits to claim their share of meat. "What
some of them have been through . . . it's a wonder they let me
come here at all."

Athaya didn't argue the point. She didn't tell him so, but she
was almost as surprised as Durek that her people had shown
such benevolence "Well, they're not all as mulish as I am."
Then, more seriously, she added, "You're their king, Durek.
And you were honest with them—no false promises or professed changes of heart. Frankly, I think it's more than they expected. They may surprise you with their loyalty."

Durek was able to relax even further as the evening wore
on; he reclined near the bell tower with a second helping of
venison, enjoying the informal supper in spite of himself. As
Athaya prophesied, Ranulf had indeed begun to sing, and she
even caught Durek's lips moving along silently in time to a
bawdy drinking song she had no idea he knew.

It was an hour before midnight when Tonia came up behind
them with a grave expression on her face. "Jaren's opened a
panel to you in the chapel," she whispered to Athaya, not
wishing to disturb the others' revels. "I'd think you'd better
come quickly. Both of you."

Durek followed at her heels as Athaya made her way across
the clearing, deftly dodging tent stakes and strings of laundry.
The silvery panel stood just before the altar, framing Jaren
neatly within it like a life-sized portrait. Instantly, she knew the
pallor on his face was not the result of his recent fever. He was
calling from the king's council hall, and behind him, almost
out of the panel's range, Athaya glimpsed Master Hedric and
Captain Parr engaged in openly hostile conversation. Hedric
pointed urgently toward the panel; Parr, refusing to look,
sniffed with disdain and stalked away.

A handful of other men huddled in the rear of the chamber, all of them sharing the same deeply troubled expression. Athaya fumbled at her purse, cursing as she frantically searched for the proper ward key. It was extremely rare for the council to still be in session so late; the news must be grave indeed.

Finally, she found the proper key and applied it to the panel's frame to complete the link, opening her side with a lightning-flash of white. "I'm here, Jaren. What's the matter?"

At the sound of her voice, the king's councillors turned toward the panel in unison, eyes wide and pleading like a flock of frightened children. "Majesty, we are undone!" one cried, seeing Durek's image in the panel just behind Athaya. "This is terrible. Terrible!"

"You've got to leave Kaiburn now," Jaren told her, ignoring the clucking councillors behind him.

Athaya felt her supper churn unpleasantly inside her belly. "Why? Is the Sage ready to attack?"

"No, Athaya. He already has. Kaiburn was just a ruse; the Sage's entire army just launched a massive assault on Delfarham. They haven't reached the castle yet, but we can see the fires from here."

Durek tensed beside her. "But hundreds of his men were seen near here just yesterday," he protested, "at Leaforth. The sheriff saw them . . ."

"Did he?" Jaren countered. "Or did he only see an illusion? A decoy? Mason himself proved how easy it is—he used the same trick to get out of Kilfarnan. And remember what he said about using mirrors? Chances are good that the 'hundreds' of men your sheriff saw were only a dozen wizards casting decoys. Mason is furious with himself for not seeing through the ploy—"

"It's not his fault," Athaya said quickly. "Hell, none of us saw through it either."

Jaren nodded wearily, rubbing at his eyes with the heel of his hand; he looked exhausted already and the battle was barely under way. "None of that matters now. We need your help, Athaya—and the help of every wizard you can bring with you, if it's not already too late. The council and the Guard are in an uproar—orders or no, Parr refuses to do what Hedric tells him, much less listen to a word I say. Mason and his contingent are out in the city doing what they can, but their efforts will only slow the Sarians down. At this rate, it won't be long before the Sage reaches the castle itself."

Durek slammed a fist against the back of a pew in frustration, heedless of the pain. "Even if we rode without stopping, it would take almost two full days to get back to Delfarham!"

"Not for all of us," Athaya replied, a knowing glimmer in her eyes. "I can't very well bring an entire army with me," she resumed into the panel, "but I can come back right now and do what I can. Maybe . . ." Her words trailed off for a moment as she pieced together a plan. "Find out where Kale is keeping that pouch," she said vaguely, careful not to mention the corbals specifically. Not only was it best that only a very few people know of her newfound ability to channel power through the corbals, but she seriously doubted the extent of the council's loyalty to her. If one of them were taken during the assault, they might blurt out her most valued secret in an effort to buy back their freedom. Even worse, the inconstant Captain Parr might decide for himself that this heretofore-unknown ability made her a worse enemy than the Sage could ever be and, ally or no, deliberately betray her. The last thing any of them needed was for the Sage to learn of her only trump card and discover a way to counter it.

"Bring the pouch to the council hall. Maybe I can use it to whip up a spell the Sage hasn't seen before—or any of us, for that matter. It might surprise him into retreating long enough for reinforcements to arrive from the camp."

Jaren didn't bother to hide his opinion of the plan. "Athaya, that's damned dangerous and you know it. Hedric said it could kill you."

"Only if no one's there to cover them up if I can't stop my spells. That'll be your job. Now, are we going to stand here arguing about it or do we give it a try? I haven't got any better ideas and you said yourself that we don't have much time."

Jaren's mouth formed a firm line of disapproval, but he didn't debate the matter for long. "All right. Just hurry. And send as many wizards as you can."

He closed the panel abruptly, leaving behind only a doorway of smoky mist. When Athaya touched on her ward key to shut down her side as well, the silvery oblong vanished. Then she took Durek's arm and hustled him down the leaf-strewn aisle. "I'm sorry I have to desert you like this, but I'll have someone guide you back to your men—"

"No," he said, wresting his arm away and rooting his feet to the flagstones. "I'm going back with you." Durek didn't even pause to consider what he was asking: to travel by ways that few wizards ever see, much less other men. He only knew that he had to get home.

Athaya stared at him, aghast. "Don't be a fool—the Sage would like nothing more than to capture you and parade you through the city in chains as his prisoner. Like it or not, this camp is probably the safest place for you. And besides, we need magicians for this battle, Durek. You can't help."

"Damned if I can't! You heard what he said." Durek jabbed a finger at the spot where Jaren's panel had stood. "The guard and council won't listen to wizards—we both need to be there to hold this alliance together. And I have to let the people know I haven't deserted them!" He cut off her next word with a sharp gesture. "Athaya, I have the greatest obligation of anyone to be in Delfarham right now. I won't launch into another speech about family duty . . . but don't you see?" He set both hands upon her shoulders, holding her firm. "I'm not speaking to you as your brother, but as your king. I command you to take me back to Delfarham. Now."

Athaya almost refused. But it only took an instant to realize that her refusal would be an irreparable betrayal of trust; a betrayal that would shatter the fragile trust upon which their alliance was built. She had sworn to obey him, and obey him she must.

Durek waited for her answer, likewise aware that her answer would prove her commitment—or lack of it. He let out a thin sigh of relief when she offered him a reluctant nod. "Then come along," she said, "there's no time to lose."

They had only gotten as far as the threshold when Athaya skidded to a stop and clutched her forehead; yet another complication had reared its ugly head. "Wait—what are your guardsmen going to think when you vanish from here without a trace?"

"Damn! I'd better warn them. They'll attack this place if I don't come back—assuming they can find it," he added dryly. "Have you ink and parchment?"

"In my old room . . . but wait! Why don't we send them all back together?"

Athaya rapidly detailed her plan and then summoned Ranulf and Tonia to meet them in the dormitory. While Durek scribbled orders for his men, Athaya told the others of the surprise attack on Delfarham. "Ranulf, I want you to be in charge of finding as many wizards as you can to join up with Durek's men—they're waiting for him right now near the sheepfold. You're all to return to Delfarham together."

Ranulf grinned roguishly. "Well, won't that be an amiable journey?" he remarked, arching a bushy red brow. "I'll wager the fighting will start long afore we reach the enemy."

"See that it doesn't," Durek said sharply, handing over a folded sheet of parchment. "You'll outnumber my men easily, so they shouldn't trouble you unless you goad them to it. At least I hope you'll outnumber them," he added, biting his lip in concern. "I suppose I'm about to find out just how effective my speech was."

"Once you get there," Athaya continued, "do anything you can to help free the city. I don't know how yet . . . try to contact one of us when you arrive. Maybe we'll have a plan in place by then. As for you, Tonia, I need you to stay here—at least for now."

Tonia expelled a shallow sigh of resignation. "Aw, I figured you'd say that."

"I know, but someone has to look after the newcomers whose spells aren't under control yet. And if the Sage does send a force here, I need someone with your skill to defend it. Gilda's good, but she's not a Master."

Once everything was settled, Ranulf and Tonia set off to patch together an army, while Athaya quickly told Durek about the spell of translocation and what he should expect from his journey back to the capital.

"You might be frightened by the place we pass through; even the Overlord of the Circle was rattled when I took him through it. Just don't let go of me, whatever you do." Without going into grisly detail, she told him what would happen were he to release her during the spell. Durek paled a bit, but his resolve to go was not shaken.

"Just don't expect me to be of much use right away," she warned him, as she motioned him to the center of the tiny room. "This spell takes almost all of my power."

"But I thought . . . I mean, when you came to see Nicolas the night he got sick, you said that it didn't anymore—"

"That was before the sealing spell started wearing off. It's all a bit complicated to explain right now. Just know that I'll need at least an hour's rest before I can work any real magic."

Durek nodded mutely.

"Ready?"

Durek swallowed, wiping slick palms across his surcoat. "What do I do?"

"Just hang on tight. And remember—don't let go."

Athaya reached out to fold him into a tight embrace; the first time, she realized, that she had embraced him so snugly since offering congratulations at his wedding to Cecile five years ago. Relaxing as much as she could, Athaya rested against Durek's chest and conjured a vision of the council hall in her mind, focusing on every detail: the leaded glass windows, the enameled table, the cushioned throne. And then, just before whispering the words that would send them hurtling through that between-place, she added one more piece of advice.

"And pray, Durek. Just pray."

CHAPTER 13

✵✵

L IKE CRICKETS SILENCED BY AN APPROACHING STORM, THE
din of frantic voices was abruptly extinguished when
Athaya and Durek winked into existence before the
crimson-cushioned throne in the council chamber at Delfar
Castle. Durek reeled for an instant, shaken and speechless at
the manner of arrival, and braced himself on the arm of his
throne to keep from toppling ungracefully to the floor. With
Jaren's prompt assistance, Athaya staggered to a chair at the
council table and rested her head atop folded arms, woozy and
drained by the effort.

In striking contrast to the peacefully merry evening she and
Durek had left behind in the forest camp, the council chamber
at Delfarham was fraught with dread at the advancing battle.
The great lords of Caithe whickered like restless horses preparing to bolt from a burning barn, sensing impending doom. Outside, the night sky flickered angrily with distant lightning
while thunder rolled continuously, as if a legion of children
were rolling empty barrels up and down the city's cobbled
streets. Fat drops of rain pelted the latticed windows, eerily in-
effective against the arcane fires dotting the cityscape. The
briefest of probes was enough to tell Athaya that this was no
natural storm, but one of the Sage's making.

She gave Durek a sluggish nod to assure him she was light-
headed but otherwise fine, and then the king got down to the
serious business of saving his capital city.

"What's our situation?" he asked of Master Hedric. Across the room, Captain Parr bristled at not being asked to report first, but the danger of losing everything was all too real and Durek was unwilling to waste precious time keeping his servants' feathers smoothed.

"All but five squadrons of your guard have been sent out to the city to help put out fires, force back the attackers, and try to keep the populace from panicking worse than they already are. The rest are here manning the battlements. I asked the captain to hold another squadron or two in reserve should the Sage reach our walls sooner than we expect," he added, his irritation revealed only by the slight angle of his brows, "but he felt that securing the castle accomplished little if the entire city fell around it."

Durek shot his captain a scathing look for refusing to heed Hedric's counsel, but refrained from giving the man a tongue-lashing . . . at least for the time being.

"Jaren and I have taken the liberty of warding the castle," Hedric continued, moving toward the window. The hem of his forest-green robe stroked the flagstones as he walked, picking up a whisper of dust. "That won't keep anyone out physically, but it should keep them from spying on us with spheres."

Athaya tilted her head up just enough to see the misty-white ward curtain shrouding the castle environs, suspended in the air as if some giant spider had cocooned the fortress in cobwebs. Hedric's wards were strong, and if Jaren had reinforced them it should keep them all safe enough from the Sage's prying eyes.

"Our best guess is that the Sage's men slipped inside the city walls before dark," Jaren ventured. "Most likely under cloaking spells. Then, at some prearranged signal, they attacked several different quarters of the city in unison."

Durek muttered a curse under his breath. "Damned bad luck that this happened when neither Athaya nor I was here."

"Luck?" Jaren shook his head dubiously. "It was planned that way. Without the two of you, this alliance was fraying badly at the edges." He cast a quick glance to Captain Parr and the members of Durek's council, but diplomatically opted to say nothing. "The Sage might have suspected Athaya could return to the capital in time to lend a hand, but I seriously doubt he expected both of you."

Athaya sat back in her chair with excruciating care, but the walls around her still seemed to tilt crazily to one side. "Have any of the Sage's wizards reached the castle yet?"

"Not that we know of," Hedric told her, "but it won't be long."

"Mason and the others have stationed themselves around the city and are trying to counter the Sage's spells," Jaren added, "but they're barely holding their own. About the only thing the Sarians aren't doing is attacking us by sea, but the storms they've conjured make escape by boat all but impossible anyway." The remark was punctuated by another flash of lightning, this with a sickly tint of green that lit up the chamber like daylight.

"Escape?" Durek asked, his royal pride bruised by Jaren's suggestion. "What are you talking about?"

"We can't afford to deceive ourselves, your Majesty. The reinforcements from Kaiburn will be close to three days in coming. We simply can't hold out that long . . . not unless Athaya's idea works." He studied her worriedly, questioning her ability to stand without assistance, much less channel her power through a corbal crystal. "We'll need you as soon as possible," he urged quietly.

Athaya nodded weakly, but made no move to get up from the table.

Slowly, as if uncertain he truly wished to see what awaited him below, Durek walked to the bay window and looked out upon his city—the crown jewel of Caithe was now a city under siege, trapped in the grip of peril more dire than had befallen it in centuries. The streets were clogged with terrified citizens fleeing their homes, streaming into the castle courtyard with fragile hopes of sanctuary; fires both real and illusory painted the skies a hellish orange; the air was ripped by the drum of rain and thunder, and cut by wails from both human and inhuman mouths; and last, glowing dragonlike creatures swooped rabidly about the spires of Saint Adriel's Cathedral like living gargoyles, mocking those who thought to find comfort within God's walls. The chaos was all at a distance for the moment, but inching steadily closer. And like the swelling tide, Durek knew he did not have the power to turn it back.

"My God," he breathed, surveying the growing ruin of his capital, "it must have been just like this during the Time of Madness."

Master Hedric moved to stand beside him, his head slightly bowed. "Except this magic is very much under control," he said solemnly. "These are not untrained novices setting off spells by accident because their teachers had all been slain; these are highly trained magicians casting practiced sorcery. Granted, much of it is harmless show," Hedric added with a critical shrug, "but Caithe is unaccustomed to magic. Even the most benign illusion can spark a panic here, making it all the harder for our scant collection of wizards to fight back."

Durek laid his palms flat against the windowsill, steadying himself. "Thank God that Cecile and the children aren't here to see this," he murmured under his breath. He dropped his gaze to the ruby signet ring adorning his right hand. "My son," he added, so quiet that only Master Hedric could hear, "look what has become of your inheritance."

A crimson-clad sentry slipped into the chamber just then, begging the king's pardon with a bow. "Sire, a priest has come from the cathedral with news and two of the guard have returned to report and then see to their wounds. Will you see them?"

"Yes, yes . . . but not here," Durek said, turning away from the turmoil in the streets below. "Send them to the Great Hall. At least from there I will not have to watch my city burn to ash before my eyes. Come, all of you," he bade the others. He paused to touch his sister's shoulder in genuine concern. "Athaya?"

Athaya leaned back, eyes closed. "I'll be along in a few minutes; I just need to rest for a little while longer."

And Jaren, she sent privately, cracking open one eye, *have that pouch of corbals ready. I don't know what spell I'll try to channel through them yet, but I'll think of something.*

Frowning concern at her weakened state, Jaren reluctantly followed Master Hedric, Durek, Captain Parr, and the rest of the king's council down to the Great Hall.

Left alone with only the distant sounds of bloodshed and havoc in the city below, Athaya put her head down again; the worst of the dizziness was receding, but she still felt weighted by bone-deep fatigue. *Not that I wouldn't be exhausted anyway,* she grumbled to herself, knowing it was fast approaching midnight. It hardly seemed possible that she and Durek had stood before the people of Kaiburn that same afternoon; had she known she would be battling the Sage that night, she would have stolen some sleep during her brief stay at the camp.

A subtle rush of air brushed against her cheek, air carrying the faint scent of leather and smoke. Suddenly, Athaya knew that she was not alone—nor had she ever been. The door had not opened, she was sure of it. No, something had remained when the king and council quit the chamber; from somewhere very close came the sound of breathing and the delicate chime of an earring ...

Her experience with Lukin's assassin made her wary and she jerked her head up—far too quickly, for it brought the dizziness back. But her vision did not blur so much that she failed to recognize her companion. There, standing near the bay window against a backdrop of destruction, was the Sage of Sare himself, a playful smile glowing white upon his face. He struck her as a pirate dressed for plunder, clad entirely in black leather but for the single gold earring gleaming at his jaw. Shoulder-long hair was tied back in a queue and a sheathed sword hung unused at his hip. Reflections of fire danced in his eyes, rendering him a demon.

Athaya scrambled to her feet, fighting back the vertigo, and opened her mouth to scream—

"Do not cry out," the Sage suggested calmly. "It will be Prince Nicolas' life if you do. One of my men hovers near him even now, waiting for my word." The glowing smile broadened, delighted that he had taken her so completely by surprise and bent her to his will so quickly. "Do not doubt my capacity for murder, Princess. Nicolas is not important to me. I have scried his future and found no seed in him; he will never be one of us. However, he proves himself quite useful in making you tractable."

Although shaking with the urge to strike him, Athaya knew the price of defiance was far too high. Whether he lied or no, it was too great a risk to take, and so she kept her silence, knowing the Sage would have no qualms about killing one brother when he had already tried to use him as a tool to murder the other.

Only then did she fully digest the rest of what the Sage had said—*he will never be one of us*. Athaya felt a sharp pang of regret that she would never share the miracles of power with Nicolas, with whom she had shared nearly every other joy in her life. She did not think the Sage was lying; had Nicolas carried the seed, he would most certainly be dead by now, no longer a rival for the prophesied role of the wizard king.

"How did you—"

"Get here?" he finished for her, strolling casually to her side as if taking a turn around the garden. "Actually, I've been here for quite some time. Since long before you arrived, in fact. I've been listening to the Caithan council argue amongst themselves like fishwives." He rolled his eyes skyward. "They're really quite pathetic."

Athaya didn't bother to reply; in this, the Sage was sadly correct.

"So you have a plan, do you?" he went on, clasping his hands behind his back. "Some clever little ploy that you think will frighten me away?" He didn't bother to ask what it was; it did not matter, so certain was he of victory. He shook his head and emitted a quiet rumble of laughter. "I assure you, Princess, it is far too late for that now."

Athaya was infinitely grateful that she had avoided all mention of the corbals in front of the council and prayed that her relief did not show on her face.

Passing behind her—too close for Athaya's taste—the Sage sank into the throne at the head of the council hall as if he already held rights to it, knowing himself king in fact if not yet in name. He slouched down, crossing his booted legs at the ankles, and steepled his fingers before him.

"I anticipated you would return, although I thought it would be alone. I did not expect your brother to accompany you; the notion of his stooping to magic . . ." The Sage sighed resignedly and then fixed a studied gaze upon her. "Again you have surprised me. That isn't easy to do once, much less a second time."

He waited for her reply, as if expecting mumbled words of thanks for his compliment, but Athaya offered him none. "Why are you here?" she asked coldly, perfectly aware of how absurdly obvious the answer was. But it was time she needed; time to get her strength back. If the only way to buy that time was to lure him into recounting in loving detail the brilliance of his plan, then she would do so.

"You were expecting me somewhere else?" he replied glibly. "Kaiburn, perhaps?" He looked away dreamily, as if thinking back upon pleasant memories of his youth. "I considered taking Kaiburn next. In fact, Couric urged me to it strongly. He said it was far better to wipe out both of your largest nests than to leave one full of hornets to sting me later. But if Kilfarnan was any indication, your wizards have little sting to them—they are young and relatively untutored. It would have been crude of me to hand you two such defeats in short succession, and I thought that my time would be better spent elsewhere. And I also realized that you would be expecting me to target Kaiburn next," he added, favoring her with a courtly smile, "and I very much dislike being predictable."

"And that's why you deceived us into thinking you were close to Kaiburn already. Those soldiers we saw were only decoys . . ."

"Diversion is one of the first rules of war, Princess, whether one is using magic or not. I shouldn't expect you to know the intricacies of battle," he added, with an intentionally patronizing edge to his tone, "but I rather thought someone at this court might. In any event, it made my task here all the easier; and, one might argue, will save more lives in the long run than otherwise. If I'd taken Kaiburn first, you surely would have realized that I would target Delfarham next. It would have been the only logical choice. And thus, the casualties would have been far worse."

"You are magnanimous," Athaya replied dryly, without dropping her gaze.

The Sage inclined his head slightly, pretending that she had meant it as a compliment. "I know you've sent to Kaiburn for help, but they will be vastly outnumbered and able to do little more than hurl shadow spells at me. This city will be mine by dawn. Enemy wizards will be imprisoned in the castle dungeons and those without the gift will swear obedience to me or die. We are their betters, you and I," the Sage reminded her, grasping the arms of Durek's throne, "and they must be made to see that."

"Then as their venerated leader, why are you not out riding in the streets with your sword aloft and showing the people who rules them?"

"All in good time, Athaya," he replied, enchanted by the image she had conjured, albeit sarcastically. "But I think it wise to deal with you first."

Athaya felt her innards recoil as the Sage rose from the throne and approached her. "Deal with me?" she echoed. Time . . . she needed more time! Her dizziness was gone, but her magic would still be weakened to near uselessness; it was unlikely she could defend herself for long against the Sage's newly enhanced spells.

"You needn't fear me, Athaya. I simply want you out of the way until my dominion in Caithe is undisputed. The enemy always sags when it sees its banner go down, and you, my dear, are that banner. You would lend considerable strength to this conflict, and I do not wish to deal with the added inconvenience. Although," he added wryly, "you are not particularly imposing at the moment."

Athaya tilted her chin up a bit, but knew the gesture of defiance was futile. He had seen her condition upon arriving in the council chamber; it was no use trying to deceive him into thinking her spells were at full potency. At least he didn't know about the corbals; a corbal, she knew, would likely be her only chance of escape.

If, of course, she had one.

The Sage drifted to her side and extended one hand, as if in silent invitation to a dance. "Without you," he said softly, "this alliance will crumble and Delfarham will quickly fall to me. And without Delfarham, Caithe itself will do likewise."

He placed one arm around her, waiting only for the music to begin, and reached out with the other. She tried to send up a shielding spell in one last gesture of defiance, but his hand passed through the feeble spell with ease, leaving only a few trace puffs of blue to mark his passage.

"Now, sleep, Athaya," he whispered, pressing his fingers to her forehead. "Sleep until I bid you wake."

Athaya had expected his magic to be strong, but she was not prepared for the *force* behind his command; this was no blanket wrapped gently around her thoughts, lulling her to rest, but a pillow pressed hard against her face, smothering her will into unconsciousness. She never even had time to struggle; her resistance was brushed aside like tendrils of smoke from a snuffed-out candle. And as she fell limply into his arms, unable to pull away, she heard the soft roll of triumphant laughter and felt the hot touch of his lips upon her cheek.

Durek slumped broodingly in a high-backed chair on the dais, weighted down by the dire reports pouring in from all corners of his city. He sipped absently at a cup of lukewarm tea as he listened to the latest, delivered by an elderly priest from Saint Adriel's who had barely escaped the city's landmark cathedral with his life.

"The Sage's men are using the choir loft as a court," he explained. "Their captives are forced to swear fealty to the Sage or be cut down right before God's own eyes! The priests and Justices weren't even given a chance to swear fealty; they were killed outright. And the brutality of it! Beasts are slaughtered more mercifully. Oh, sire," he wailed, sinking to his knees in the rushes, "we are undone! God punishes us dreadfully . . . but for what sin?"

Durek scowled in self-reproach as the image of Athaya's forest chapel came to mind; he had a fairly good idea why his Lord might be upset with him and his Tribunal, but he wasn't of a mood to voice it.

Drianna glided behind the king and added hot water to his tea to warm it. "I never knew he could be so cruel," she said softly, as distressed by the flood of bad news as anyone in the Hall. "I used to believe that he would make a good king; now I can't think of a worse fate for Caithe."

Durek looked up to her, a small spark of hope in his eyes. "You knew the Sage . . . rather well," he said carefully, glossing over the extent of that relationship. "Do you know anything about his tactics . . . anything that might help us to stop him?"

"I only know what he chose to tell me about his magic, sire," she replied, shaking her auburn curls regretfully. "And not being a wizard myself, I didn't understand most of it. Mostly, he told me what it would be like once he ruled here; he never spoke much of how he planned to go about it . . . at least, not to me."

Durek grunted his dismay as Drianna silently withdrew to the kitchens to help prepare a small meal for the king and his council, all of whom would be awake throughout the night.

Lieutenant Berns approached the dais next. "Sire, the courtyard is almost full, and there isn't an inch of space left in the barracks or the keep; we simply can't leave the gates open any longer."

"But we can't leave them to the Sage!" Kale argued, who stood by his onetime comrade to argue the opposite case before the king. After two years in the company of Athaya and her destitute following, he was acutely concerned with the plight of Delfarham's swelling number of refugees. The irony of the situation was not lost on Durek. This time it was not the Lorngeld fleeing the Tribunal, but the ungifted of Caithe fleeing the Sage. And he was now playing Athaya's role as deliverer, sheltering Caithe's refugees from slaughter.

Reluctantly, Durek nodded to his lieutenant. "Close the portcullis, then. There's no help for it," he added to Kale, sincerely moved by the look of despair on the older man's face.

Although Kale had once deserted the guard to serve Athaya, Durek felt surprisingly forgiving toward him—even liked him. Too few of his soldiers had such soul-deep integrity. "We can't house the entire city. The rest will have to find safety elsewhere."

Secretly, however, Durek doubted that the citizens of Delfarham would be any safer within the castle walls than without; at his present rate of success, the Sage would reach the king's fortress before the night was out.

As Kale dourly retreated from the dais, Captain Parr marched up to take his place. "Sire, thirty-two more of the guard have been brought back dead. And eight of DePere's wizards," he added grudgingly, the sour curl to his lips speaking his opinion that counting the number of dead rats in the city would be a far more worthwhile pursuit. "We've lost nearly an entire regiment of men in less than two hours. I suggest we call for reinforcements from Gorah; the Sage's army already controls over half of the city."

Durek scanned the Hall with knitted brows before replying. "Where is Lord Garson? Martrave is a half-day closer than Gorah; we can summon a regiment from there."

The council lords traded uneasy glances at the suggestion, none of them eager to answer the king's inquiry. "Lord Chancellor?" Durek said, fixing his gaze on a silver-haired man with the ill luck to be standing closest to the dais. "Where is the duke of Martrave?"

"Er . . . Lord Garson is not here, sir. He . . . er—"

"Just say it, Counley!" a younger, less timid man cried, jostling his way forward. "Garson's turned traitor! He ran off to swear fealty to the Sage in exchange for keeping his lands and title." The councillor spat his disgust into the rushes.

Instead of erupting with rage at the betrayal, Durek merely squeezed his eyes together and expelled an aggravated sigh. "Never mind Martrave . . . or Gorah," Durek replied sullenly. "More soldiers aren't going to do us a damned bit of good anyway." Privately, he wished he had possessed enough foresight to remain on speaking terms with Osfonin of Reyka—at least some of *his* soldiers were highly trained magicians. Durek had already recalled the troops dispatched two days ago for Kaiburn, but knew they would make little difference in a war waged almost entirely by magic.

"We're expecting help from Athaya's people in Kaiburn," he told his still-waiting captain, "but not for at least two days.

Just do anything you can to hold the Sage's men at bay as long as possible. Damn it all, where *is* Athaya?" he shouted to no one in particular. It was, he realized, the first time in recent memory that he would have far rather had his wayward sister at his side than otherwise.

In desperate need of a moment's respite from the chaos battering him at all sides, Durek withdrew to his private audience chamber accompanied only by Jaren and Master Hedric. Hedric he had beckoned inside specifically; Jaren he tolerated simply because he knew Hedric would wish him to. And Athaya, too, he supposed.

"We can't wait any longer," Durek said, pacing to and fro before his writing desk. "You heard what Captain Parr said— half of the city is lost already. We need her now," he said accusingly to Jaren, as if it were somehow his fault that Athaya was not properly in tow.

Jaren touched his hand to the pouch of corbals tied to his belt, waiting for Athaya's unique brand of magic to bring them to life and, with luck, surprise the Sage's men into retreat long enough for the much-needed help from Kaiburn to arrive. "I'll take a quick look and see if she's on her way."

He retreated to the bay window, turning his back on the storm-wracked waters of the Sea of Wedane, and put the rain and winds far from his mind as he called his vision sphere into his palms. He sat hunched over the glowing orb rather longer than Durek thought necessary, and when Jaren finally banished the sphere and raised his head, Durek knew something was very wrong. Jaren's face was waxen—as pale as the mists into which he had just gazed.

"I can't see her."

Master Hedric clasped his hands tight around his cherrywood staff, threatening to crack it. He tried to hide the extent of his concern from the king, but Jaren knew him well enough to know how desperately alarmed he was.

"What does that mean?" Durek demanded. Fear made the words come out more harshly then he intended.

"It means," Jaren explained, "that either she's left Delfarham for some reason—and gone fairly far away—or she's warded from my sight, or . . ." His pallor grew even more pronounced. He scrambled out of the bay window, eyes warily scanning the chamber as he moved to the king's side. "Your Majesty, I fear the Sage's wizards are already among us."

Durek's face went white.

"I have to get you out of here while I still can," Jaren continued softly. "Before they realize we know they're here."

"You mean Athaya's been captured?" Durek asked disjointedly, unable to believe that he had been robbed of his last, best hope.

"I'm not sure. But I can't think of any other reason why someone within these walls shouldn't appear in my sphere readily enough."

"B-but how? How could they have gotten inside?"

"Cloaking spells, perhaps. Or maybe the Sage came through by translocation somehow—if he can do it. I'll wager they've been here since before the attack on the city began . . . probably long before the wards went up."

Durek clutched his head between his hands as if to shut out the clamor of his world crashing down around his ears. "But I can't leave now. I—"

"You have no choice, sire," Hedric urged him, quiet but firm. "If Athaya is missing, then it is almost certain that the castle walls have been breached. You must flee while you still can. If you fall to the Sage, Caithe will lose what hope it has left."

It grated him to do so, but Durek surrendered with a nod. Hedric was right in this, as he seemed to be in so many things. "What about the others? The council? The servants? The refugees in the courtyard?"

"I shall pass the word for everyone to leave as quietly and unobtrusively as possible. It won't take the Sage's men long to realize we're on to them, if indeed they are here among us, but at least some may be able to flee to safety. Those poor folk in the courtyard would have been better off staying in the streets," he added sadly. "They are caged like rabbits here."

As if the gravity of the situation had finally reached him, Durek suddenly went into action, hastily collecting items of importance that he didn't wish to see fall into the Sage's hands. The royal seal was an obvious choice, but though they said nothing, Jaren and Hedric silently marked what else the king chose to take: a toy horse crudely fashioned out of clay—a gift from Mailen, he had said—and the last letter he had received from Cecile.

"If I must go, then I've got to take Nicolas with me," Durek added, tucking the precious articles into his surcoat. "I can't leave him here; the Sage has done enough to him already."

Jaren hastened him toward the door. "I'll go with you."

"No, no," Durek said, visibly unsettled. "You needn't bother. I can manage—"

"Your Majesty, it's no secret that given the choice, we'd both rather be in someone else's company," Jaren said bluntly, perfectly aware of the reason behind Durek's reluctance, "but I can't leave you unprotected . . . not now. Athaya would never forgive me, and your guardsmen won't do much good against the likes of the Sage. Besides, it'll be safer for us to move about under cloaking spells from now on and you'll need a wizard for that. I could go spread the word to evacuate instead of Master Hedric, but frankly, your court and servants are more likely to take his advice over mine."

"I'll try to find out what's happened to Athaya while I'm at it," Hedric said, as he hustled them both to the door. "Now hurry—you must get out of this castle as soon as possible." *And I suggest,* he added to Jaren, keeping the thought safe from any as-yet-unseen Sarian wizards, *that you take the king directly to the forest camp. When the Sage discovers that most of its wizards are on their way here—as I'm sure he will sooner or later—he'll likely consider the camp not worth attacking. His Majesty will be safe there.*

They split up with a mutual wish for good luck, and while Hedric hurried back to the Hall to sound the alarm as inconspicuously as possible, Durek led Jaren up a little-used staircase leading to the prince's apartments. When they reached the upper hallway, Jaren angled a polished piece of brass down the corridor to catch a glimpse of any cloaked wizards skulking about—much like they were doing, he mused. Seeing no immediate threat, they reached the prince's rooms in a matter of moments. The rooms were not guarded; per Captain Parr's orders, all but the most meager contingent had been sent into the city to repel the Sage's forces.

Once safely inside, Jaren followed Durek to the inner chamber, casting about with his mirror of brass and grateful to see no unexpected reflections there. He sloughed off the cloaking spell and approached Nicolas's bedside—asleep through all of this!—but soon realized that the prince's sleep was far from peaceful; Nicolas tossed fitfully and his forehead was slick with cold sweat.

Worriedly, Durek laid a palm across his brother's forehead. "Hedric didn't tell me he'd fallen ill."

And that could only be, Jaren knew, with a sickly warmth curdling his belly, because this "illness" was very recent . . .

He whipped around, but it was already too late to flee. He and Durek had not been the only ones to slip into the chamber under a guise of magic, but the other had possessed the foresight to simply step behind a tapestry; a sanctuary from which no mirror would betray him.

"Your Majesty," the Sage sang out in greeting. His courtly bow resonated scorn. "How thoughtful of you to pay a visit to your brother before fleeing for your life. You've saved me the trouble of coming to look for you."

Durek lurched back toward the door, but it was already blocked by two uniformed men with swords poised. They did not wear the crimson livery of his own guard—no, thanks to his shortsighted captain, most of them were out in the city dying by the dozens—but the black and silver of Sare; the colors of night.

The Sage swept his gaze from Durek to Nicolas and back again. "Why, if Athaya was here, I would have the whole royal family at my disposal. But," he added with a meaningful arch to his brow, "Athaya will not be joining us. I have seen to that."

"What have you done to her?"

Jaren surged forward, determined to throttle the Sage with his bare hands, but Durek grabbed his arm and roughly wrenched him back. "Don't be a fool! The man could kill us all with a gesture."

"Not to worry," the Sage said, waving indifferently in Jaren's direction. "I've no intention of harming Athaya. Quite the opposite in fact," he added with an insolent smile. "But I cannot say the same for you, so you'd best do as I tell you unless you wish to make a widow of your dear princess at such a tender age."

Jaren glanced to the pair of guardsmen at his back; if they hadn't been wizards, he and Durek might have been able to slip past them with a bit of trickery, but he soon abandoned all thoughts of attack, resigned to the fact that the slightest move against them could well result in the deaths of one or both of Athaya's brothers—not to mention himself. As for Athaya, the Sage seemed to have other plans for her . . . or so he would have them believe.

"I would suggest," the Sage went on, pacing casually around the king like a tailor estimating how much cloth to cut, "that in the future, your gatehouse guards use the mirrors allotted to them. My men and I walked right past them and they didn't even blink. Of course, there were so many refugees clamoring for their attention . . ."

"How many are here with you?" Jaren asked. He didn't expect an answer, but perhaps if the Sage thought victory was assured, he might just get one.

The Sage's smile was thick with malice. "Not as many as there will be shortly."

He spun on a booted heel and strode to the window, throwing open the shutters and stretching out his arms to embrace the sky. Then, with a murmured phrase, a raw blast of power swept outward like a tidal wave, shredding Hedric's potent wards in one brutal blow and leaving them in tatters, like fine silk rent by claws.

No sooner were the wards destroyed than there came another blast, equally raw and powerful. *"Columen flammosum fac!"* the Sage shouted, his magic giving birth to a column of fire that shrieked up from the courtyard and exploded into multicolored fireworks; a flare, Jaren realized, to signal his men to attack the castle in force. His next spell blew out the iron-banded portcullis with the ease of a rock flung through a stained glass window, leaving the gateway open to the Sage's army.

"It won't be long now," the Sage informed them, reluctantly turning away from his handiwork. "Thousands march under my banner. The scattered few you sent against me were but a petty inconvenience. I will rule here by dawn. As for you, my little king . . ."

The Sage raised his palm and hurled shock waves of sickness at Durek. Durek crumpled to the floor like a cloth doll, clutching at the sharp cramps cutting through his belly and unable to resist the impulse to retch. Beside him, Jaren frantically began to weave a counterspell, all the while knowing that his mundane skills were no match against the Sage.

"You are the king!" Brandegarth taunted, smiling down at Durek's pain even as he deftly turned aside Jaren's efforts to relieve it. "Command me to stop—beg me!—and perhaps, just perhaps, I shall obey you."

Just as Durek struggled to voice a scathing refusal, another blast ruptured the air, this one from behind them. In an explosion of wind and blinding light, the guardsmen at the door fell back, blown aside as easily as stalks of wheat in a storm, moaning in anguish as they clutched their heads against sudden pain. The Sage spit out an angry curse of surprise as Master Hedric stepped into the chamber. Far more than a frail old man in a simple green robe, Hedric was electric with power, calling forth every ounce of adept power at his command.

"I cannot allow you to do this," he said calmly, his benign tone in glaring discord with the massive and deadly magic he wielded. He eased himself between the Sage and his captives. "No wizard shall use his power for domination. Such is the law of the Circle."

One gesture to Durek, and the spell of sickness was dissolved. The king struggled to his feet, woozy and pale, but otherwise cured of his affliction.

"Your Circle holds no sway here," the Sage said. All traces of his mocking ways were gone; remaining was the wrathful god. "And even if it did, old man, I would not obey it. You threaten me with no more than the strictures of shortsighted philosophers who have no concept of what our power is for, denying themselves its full extent like priests who swear to celibacy to uphold some misguided sense of propriety."

"You have ruined my wards," Hedric observed mildly, refusing to be baited as his eyes drifted past the Sage to the open window where once-fine wards now hung in tatters. Then, without speaking, he sent a different message to Jaren. *I knew you were in danger when the wards went down. The Sage may be powerful, but his technique leaves much to be desired; his spells are atrociously loud.*

"And you have tightened your bindings upon the prince," he continued to the Sage, "undoing all of my careful work . . ." *The word is spreading through the castle to evacuate, but I fear it is already too late for most.*

Did you find Athaya? Jaren sent back.

Hedric paused. *No, Jaren. If she is here, then she is well warded.*

"Nicolas only lives because his sister wishes it," the Sage said darkly. "He is of no other use to me." Brandegarth lifted his hands to cast another spell, but Master Hedric quickly countered with another potent blast of light, scattershot with silver and stars.

Take the king and go, Hedric sent. *I shall see to Prince Nicolas. You cannot take him with you and hope to escape.*

Jaren heard the growing exhaustion in his Master's voice and grew fearful; Hedric was not a young man and the Sage was at the peak of his power. Hedric needed a weapon that the Sage did not have; something he would never expect . . .

The crystals! Jaren sent urgently, subtly touching a finger to the leather purse at his belt. *Master Hedric, I have them! If Athaya can do it, maybe you—*

No, came the firm reply. *Even if I knew how to use them, I would not do so. We cannot betray what might be Athaya's only hope of defeating the Sage; if he knows such a thing can be done, he may well find a way to do it. He's powerful now, Jaren. Not tightly controlled, but with enough raw force to make up the difference . . .*

"The sealing spell has damaged you," Hedric remarked to the Sage, betraying nothing of his other, private dialogue. "Your spells are potent, but not so refined as ought to be the case with an adept."

Master Hedric, what will you—

I have other means, he replied obscurely. Jaren could hear the vitality ebbing from his voice; whatever Hedric was planning, it would take all the strength that remained to him. *Now go, and take the king to safety.*

The Sage raised his arms aloft as if to invoke God's blessing upon the contest to come. "Then we shall see who among us is the finer wizard. I have won many Challenges over the years against those who fancied themselves my betters." He narrowed his eyes and stepped back, readying a killing blow. "I am a greater wizard than any clucking hen of your Circle. God has granted me gifts that have never before graced this world!"

I can't just leave you—

Jaren, don't argue with me. I haven't the time for it and neither do you. Now go! Get as far away from this room as you can!

Hedric's placid face betrayed none of the frightful urgency of his words. "Despise us if you will," he said to the Sage, one blue-veined hand sliding inside of his robe, "but we of the Circle do know one or two useful tricks."

He extracted a small charm; a charm that Jaren recognized at once, though he had not seen it since the early days of his service to Hedric. It looked like nothing more than a peasant woman's poppet—a harmless scrap of cloth tied with twine—but Jaren's eyes widened with horror as he realized what Master Hedric intended. Empowered by all seven wizards of the Circle, the charm was meant to be used only in the direst of need. Like the brutal, psychic jolt that Rhodri had once dealt

him, its deafening screams echoing within the corridors of his
paths, Hedric's charm was charged by the Circle to do the
same, but on a killing scale. An extremely potent weapon, but
one that discouraged careless use by killing any wizard in the
immediate vicinity when it was discharged . . .

His paralyzing shock was broken by the touch of Durek's
hand on his shoulder. "Don't you see? Hedric is buying time
for us. You can't help now. Neither of us can. Please, Jaren,"
Durek added, as humble as Jaren had ever heard him. "I need
your help to escape."

It was, Jaren realized, the first time that Athaya's brother
had ever called him by name.

And Durek was right; if they did not leave now, Hedric's
sacrifice would be in vain, and he would be dead as well. And
Nicolas would be safe in the end; the charm was only deadly
to wizards and Nicolas had no paths to damage. And with the
Sage dead, his wizard's army would have no Sage to follow,
no king to crown, and thus no more reason to continue their
assault on Caithe.

A promising outcome . . . as long as the charm worked.

With one last look at Master Hedric, committing his face
forever to memory, Jaren grabbed Durek's arm and fled. The
Sage's shielding spell, intended to block their escape, was shattered like fine crystal by the force of Hedric's counterspell—
the last spell he would ever cast before whispering the
keywords, hurling the Circle charm to the ground, and destroying both he and his enemy in one brilliant psychic explosion of
pain.

The last thing Jaren heard as he bounded down the corridor
at Durek's side was the Sage's angry voice, echoing like thunder as he rained down curses upon Master Hedric's head.
"Now, old man, you've made me angry. Do you really think it
will take me long to find them again? You've given yourself
up for nothing. Now you shall see what the true chosen one of
God can do . . ."

As he and Durek hurtled down the spiral stair leading to the
castle's lower level, Jaren heard the deafening roar of a thousand oceans churning in his head; the very stones seemed to
shake beneath his feet, as if a god-child had picked up the fortress and shook it like a toy. Shock waves from the explosion
rippled through him, battering his paths and sending him crashing to his knees with a strangled gasp before Durek hauled him
up and urged him on. He clutched Durek's arm and ran blindly,

sick with grief and pain, wondering what had become of
Athaya, praying that Hedric's charm was potent enough to kill
the Sage, and torn with anguish that if it was, then he would
never see his mentor again.

Athaya unconsciously obeyed the whispers in her mind that
bade her wake only to find herself in the same dungeon cell
where she had been confined the night Rhodri had come to
steal her power. The wall beside the pallet was scarred with the
scratches she had made to mark the time of her confinement
. . . and, she noted with a shudder, spattered with dark stains
never fully scrubbed away—the last earthly traces of Rhodri's
shattered body, unable to contain the stolen power that it bore.
But as Athaya massaged the sleep from her eyes, bringing into
focus the man looming over her pallet, she dearly wished that
it was only Rhodri come to torment her again. She possessed
the power to challenge him now; she could not say the same
for the Sage.

The farther she emerged from her cocoon of magic-induced
sleep, the more aware she became of the sensation inside her
head. Her skull felt solidly stuffed with wool—a feeling that
was dishearteningly familiar. This time, the wool was packed
more tightly, proof that the spell was cast by a more powerful
wizard than the last one who had bound her so.

Damn. She should have expected as much. The Sage had
taken advantage of her weakened state and confined her power
with a sealing spell while she slept. Now she was unable to
use any spell at all, much less channel one through a corbal. *If
I had one,* she added sullenly, realizing that the pouch of gem-
stones was with Jaren. Wherever *he* was.

The Sage bent over her and nodded curtly, satisfied that she
had roused at his command. "Come with me," he said, though
his voice wavered curiously, without its usual arrogant vigor.
"Someone wishes to see you."

Athaya sat up, still drowsy, but it did not take long to realize
that something had happened to her captor since they had last
met. The Sage was badly shaken; his powerful hands trembled
like an old woman's and the normally haughty eyes were
shrouded and disoriented, as if he had been rudely jolted from
an achingly beautiful dream to attend his own execution.

He did not speak at all as he led her to Nicolas' rooms. The
room was not guarded, but Athaya did not fail to notice two
blanket-shrouded bodies lying in the corridor; a scrap of black

cloth laced with silver peeked out from one of the shrouds. Her stomach twisted into a tight knot as the Sage pushed open the familiar set of doors, suddenly terrified that she would enter the room only to see a priest muttering prayers over her brother's body, consigning him to heaven and bidding him fair journey.

The sitting chamber was deserted, but bore telltale signs of magic. An ugly black scar marred the center of the carpet, the air carried the acrid stench of scorched wool, and bits of cloth and twine were scattered across the floor as if a child's puppet had been rent apart. Something else lingered in the room as well, though it was far less definable; vibrations of a sort, just now fading away.

"What happened here?" She bent down to touch a scrap of cloth and the vibrations intensified slightly.

"What happened, Princess," the Sage replied with a respectful tone that she had rarely heard him employ, "was that I very nearly introduced myself to God before I was ready, thanks to your mentor. That should make you proud. But God gave me the power to prevail," he added, lest she draw too much satisfaction from his tale. "He protects His servants well."

He escorted her to the inner chamber. Nicolas was nowhere to be found; instead, Master Hedric lay across the quilts, dangerously close to death.

"Oh God, no . . ."

The change in him was a brutal shock; for the first time, he truly looked old. Thinning locks of white hair hung limply around a sallow face and once-bright eyes were glassy and distant, already set upon their journey home. Only by looking very closely could she detect the shallow rise and fall of his chest to know that he lived at all.

In an unexpected gesture of respect, the Sage retreated to the sitting chamber, allowing them to speak in private.

Athaya crept to the bedside, each step an effort, as if her shoes were weighted with lead. She pulled up a stool and clasped his hand, running her fingers lovingly over the labyrinth of veins that bulged beneath paper-thin skin. Once, these hands had cast spells she could only dream of; now, they were white and bloodless and cold.

"Master Hedric, can you hear me?"

With only those scattered senses not imprisoned by the seal, she brushed against his mind, recoiling in horror at the widespread destruction there. His paths were all but gone, the once-majestic caverns reduced to crumbling bits of rubble from which his magic trickled steadily, hemorrhaging, unable to be stopped.

"God, what has he done to you?"

Hedric's eyes fluttered open. When he spoke, every word was a labor. "He did nothing, Athaya. This was my own doing. Although, I did not expect either of us to survive it. His experience in repelling the corbals must have given him enough strength to turn aside my charm. Sadly, I had no such strength remaining."

Athaya squeezed his hand, as if to give some of her own life-force over to him. "Charm? What charm?"

Hedric's eyes closed again; keeping them open was too taxing. "Ask Jaren later. He took the king to safety. Do not fear for them."

Athaya bowed her head in a quick prayer of thanks.

"The Sage has sealed my power," she whispered. "If you can release me, I can take us both to safety."

Alas, I cannot, he sent, no longer able to rouse the strength to speak aloud. *My power is dead. As will I be . . . very soon.*

Athaya strengthened her grip. "Don't talk like that. Why, you'll begin to sound as dismal as I do and Jaren always chides me for it."

Hedric managed a crooked smile. *I have lived long, my dear. I bear the Lord no grudge for taking me home. I only wish that I could have been with you on your day of victory, rather than having to watch it in Kelwyn's company. And Tyler's, too. They are watching even now, Athaya. Be certain of it.*

A cold shiver snaked down Athaya's back. Somehow, although it unsettled her to think on it, she knew it, too.

Do not grieve for me, he sent, though his voice was becoming as faint as the errant vibrations in the air around them. *I can think of nothing more honorable than to die so that other wizards after me may live. But . . . do ask the Sage if he would let me rest in Reyka. It is my home.*

Athaya bit her lip hard; she would not cry—not yet. "I will ask . . . I will demand it."

You will defeat him, Athaya. Dameronne did not foresee everything . . . I know that now. He struggled for another breath and Athaya felt a trickle of strength flow through his grasp. *The Sage calls himself God's greatest servant,* he told her, *but at this time in history, Athaya, that honor is yours, in part, perhaps, because you would never dare to claim it for yourself.*

Athaya took little pleasure in the accolade; how could she, when the man responsible for setting her on that path was dying? "Master Hedric, please don't leave me—"

But he was already drifting away and she did not think he heard her anymore.

Finish your journal, he admonished her by way of benediction. He opened his eyes, taking in one last glimpse of his beloved protégé, and then, with a contented smile, sank deep into her pillows. Vision swimming in tears, Athaya bent down and kissed his cheek; the flesh dry as parchment against her lips. Just as she drew back, he gasped once, eyes wide with awesome wonder, and then his breath was expelled for the last time and his eyes closed upon the world, even as they opened to another.

The Sage was at her side shortly thereafter. His hands had stopped trembling and a sense of normality was returning to his demeanor. He gripped a glass of wine in one hand, however, and Athaya suspected that it was not his first.

"He wishes to rest in Reyka," she said, too paralyzed with grief to cry just yet.

The Sage nodded, and for once his benevolence was not tainted with insufferable superiority. "He was an honorable foe. I shall grant his request."

Athaya rose to her feet, surprised that she had strength enough to stand. "Where . . . where is Nicolas?" she asked, hoping to distract herself from the sorrow pressing down upon her by busying her mind with other problems.

"Elsewhere in this castle," he told her evasively, "but alive and under my protection. And I shall keep him so, as long as you do not trouble me. Now come." He set the empty glass aside and extended a hand to her. "We must go."

"If I'm to be your prisoner, I'd rather be held in my own rooms. The dungeon is cold and damp."

The Sage shook his head imperceptibly. "You will not be staying in Delfarham. Or in Caithe, for that matter. Holding you here would be risky; there would be a chance, however slight, that one of your allies might find a way to free you. They have shown themselves thus resourceful in the past. Now come."

This time it was not a request, and with Nicolas' life balanced on her response, Athaya knew she had to obey.

She turned to look upon Master Hedric one last time, so peaceful now, all his earthly cares concluded. He had set her to the task of restoring magic to the Lorngeld of Caithe, and now all of her work lay in tatters. As the Sage led her off to some unknown prison, Athaya could not help but think how twisted all of her dreams had become. For the first time in two centuries, wizardry had indeed returned to Caithe, but not at all in the guise that she had intended or foreseen.

CHAPTER 14

THAT SAME NIGHT, FAR FROM THE FIRES AND BLOODSHED IN Delfarham, Archbishop Lukin sat awake in the darkened solar of his Kaiburn townhouse brooding over his reduced fortunes. News of his disgrace had spread like a pestilence, and not even his successor Eldrid, Bishop of Kaiburn, had sent a note to welcome him back to his former see or offer him an honorary place at his supper table. Lukin drummed his nails on the armrest of his chair, glowering passionately. God's breath, had the whole world been set upon its ear? How was it possible that Princess Athaya and her ilk continued to gain ascendancy in the land, while he—prelate of Caithe, no less!—found himself shunted out of court like a troublesome peasant. What was next? If the Devil's Children could gain the king's ear and bend him to their will, then there was no telling what sorts of havoc would reign in Caithe. Would serfs begin to tell their lords which crops to sow and where? Would laymen bless their priests?

"Your Majesty," Lukin murmured, his voice little more than a dry scraping sound in the darkened chamber, "you grow as big a fool as was your father on matters of magic."

A sleepy-eyed servant stumbled into the solar just then, knocking only as an afterthought. He scowled only slightly less earnestly than did his master, none too happy at being roused from his bed in the dead hours between midnight and dawn. "Pardon, Excellency, but you have a visitor."

"What? At this hour?"

"He is a member of the King's Guard. I told him to come back in the morning, but he claims his news is most urgent—"

"Bring him," Lukin's curt reply came. Perhaps the king had realized his error and sent a messenger to summon his archbishop back to court. Perhaps, Lukin considered sourly, but not damned likely. Not as long as wizards like Athaya ruled his every thought and deed.

The servant ushered in a tawny-haired young man in crimson livery and, yawning deeply, returned to his bed. Archbishop Lukin didn't bother to rise to greet his guest, but merely cocked an inquiring brow at him. "And who might you be, disturbing me at such an hour?"

The guardsman's bow was crisp and respectful. "Hugh Middlebrook, Excellency. I am truly sorry for the intrusion, but I bear the gravest of news." He paused, curling his gloved hands into fists. "Delfarham has been attacked by the Sage of Sare."

The news enticed Lukin from his chair quickly enough and he made rapid circular gestures with his hand, silently demanding details.

"When the princess learned of the attack, she and the king immediately returned to the city. Using magic," Hugh added, shifting uneasily. "Every wizard of any skill has left their hidden camp for Delfarham, hoping to liberate the city. My squadron was to return in their company, but . . . I could not. I know it was against orders," he confessed. "I saw them written in the king's own hand—but the thought of associating with those *sorcerers* . . ." He shuddered, as if a rat had just scurried across his boots. "I slipped away as soon as I could. I felt it my duty to tell you of this calamity. Surely you, as God's most favored servant, can find a way to stop this unholy invasion and free Delfarham from sorcery."

Shaken by the news, Lukin poured himself a generous glass of strong wine and swallowed half of it in one gulp. He went to the latticed window and stared blindly at the moonlit spires of Kaiburn Cathedral.

"So Princess Athaya makes her move at last, it seems," he said after a time, aware that Hugh was patiently waiting for his reply. "I have always suspected that this 'Sage' is only her hireling, paid to clear her way to the crown . . ." He turned his gaze northwest and squinted, as if trying to discern the distant turrets of Saint Adriel's, wondering if they still stood.

"Part of me thinks this is as the king deserves," he mumbled to himself, "but that does not mean the rest of us should pay the price as well. As prelate of Caithe, it is my holy obligation to save us all from this madness. God would expect no less of me."

"I will aid you in any way I can," Hugh offered.

Lukin nodded amenably. "Then stay with me for a few days, Hugh; I may have need of you."

"Gladly, your Excellency." Grimly, he added, "There's nothing to be gained by going back to Delfarham now."

Lukin called for his servant to show Hugh to a room, ignoring the man's grumbles at being awakened a second time, then settled back into the shadows of his solar. To his surprise, he was not at all fearful; he had faith that God would guide him to a solution. Perhaps his recent disgrace was only meant to humble him a bit in readiness for his great task.

And humility, he knew, was not something for which the Sage was generally known. Perhaps that, in the end, would be the fatal flaw that led to his undoing.

If it could be properly exploited . . .

"The Devil has his own instruments, just as You do, Lord," he said. He plucked his prayer book from the table and ran his fingers over the gilded cover. "But we shall prove ourselves the stronger. I swear it."

Athaya's heart lurched into her throat as the journey came to an abrupt halt; she was rudely deposited upon a rush-covered floor, and promptly tumbled ungracefully to her knees. Unable to stop shaking, she dared not try to stand just yet, fearing for one unpleasant moment that she might lose whatever still remained in her belly. She took deep, bracing swallows of salt-laced air, trying—without much success—to block out the last minute of her life.

The translocation had been terrifying, and not, she suspected, because she was a mere passenger this time. She had never lingered out of the world quite so long; never brushed that close to the churning chaos of the between-place; that close to the gruesome death that awaited those who strayed from the magic path. The Sage was barely in control of the potent spell—that had been the most terrifying thing of all—and Athaya felt as if she had spent the last few moments riding in a carriage with a loose wheel as it careened along a cliffside road, frantically wondering whether she would reach her destination safely or plummet screaming to her death.

Beside her, Brandegarth of Crewe simply got to his feet and dusted himself off as if nothing had occurred. And perhaps to him, she realized, nothing had. That turbulent passage might have been the best he could do—enough raw power to send them hurtling across the world but not enough mastery to make the passage bearable.

"Here, you look in need of this." Without any sign of dizziness, he strolled to a walnut sideboard and poured her a generous glass of Sarian whiskey. *Sare.* She should have guessed he would bring her here. "You have made such crossings before; you should not look so shaken."

Athaya held back a caustic comment on his proficiency as she clambered to her feet. Let him think her spell just as deficient, her translocations just as turbulent. She accepted the glass of amber liquid with trembling hands, desperately in need of something to steady her after such a hellish ride.

"Breathtaking, is it not?" he said to her. His eyes shone, as if he beheld some invisible glory that she was blinded to. "We should be honored that God allows us to use His realm as a bridge to another part of our own."

Athaya's glass stopped halfway to her lips. "His what?" she asked, even while the truth of it stirred quietly inside her. It was an obvious connection; why had she not thought of it before? That Master Hedric had entertained such notions she did not doubt; Athaya recalled the studied reverence that had settled over him when, months ago, they had talked of translocation and of the mysterious realm through which it led. The spell, it seemed, was an even rarer and more priceless gift than she had realized.

The Sage took great amusement at her ignorance and laughed robustly. "You truly did not suspect?" He shook his head in mock pity. "And I thought Master Hedric said you were bright." Chuckling, he sipped at his whiskey, gleaming like molten gold in the dim lamplight of the chamber.

A bedchamber, she realized, and then swiftly shoved the thought aside.

"Tell me, what does that place most remind you of?" The Sage addressed her in the same conciliatory tone of voice her childhood tutors often employed when they know full well she did not know the answers to their queries. "Your source of power, of course; that place within you where magic dwells.

Did you never think how much alike they are? They're linked, Athaya. Divinely so." He rolled a sip of whiskey around his tongue, then swallowed thoughtfully. "Both are places of sight and sound, confusing to our narrow human senses—places that exist, but yet do not in any earthly sense. Within us—within our source—is all that we are, or were, or will be. That place . . ."

He looked away dreamily, eyes brimming with wonder. "That place is everything, Athaya. Everyone who has ever lived—or will. Everything that has ever happened—or will. It is the ultimate Source. Heaven, if you will. The whole of Creation; the whole of God's plan, unfolding in one timeless Instant. If what we bear within us is only the tiniest fraction of that," he concluded, closing his eyes against the excruciating glory of it, "then can you even begin to imagine what awaits us *there*?"

Somehow, looking at the rapture on his face, Athaya suspected that if the Sage could tarry in that otherworldly between-place instead of whisking through on his way to some other less wondrous destination, then he would pay any price to do so. It would be death to remain there, Athaya knew—though likely the Sage did not. If heavenly realm it was, then it was no place for flesh to venture except in quick passage, like a finger through a candle's flame.

After his lapse into bliss had passed, the Sage drained the rest of his whiskey in a single gulp, disconcerted by his unintended display of emotion. "But enough of that," he said curtly. "If I start exchanging theories of divinity with you, Reykan-trained as you are, then we risk prattling all night . . . or what remains of it."

Then, as if they had only arrived that instant, he stretched out his arms, encompassing the spacious chamber. Athaya's eyes had adjusted to the dim light enough to discern her surroundings; the furnishings were all carved of costly Selvallanese mahogany, the tables and mantel adorned with gleaming silver plate, and the draperies, coverlets, and cushions supplied the room with every conceivable shade of blue.

"This was Drianna's chamber," he told her. Athaya watched him carefully, but he showed no indication that he knew of his past lover's presence in Delfarham. "It shall be your home for a short time. But not too long, I promise you. I do not intend the sealing spell to do you the slightest bit of harm. Nor do I intend," he added more significantly, "to leave it on long enough to enhance that power of yours again."

She frowned at him skeptically. "You don't intend to kill me, then? I find that rather hard to believe."

"Yes, yes . . . I suppose it's time I explained everything to you." He strolled to the fireplace and rested his arm on the mantel, absently toying with a small ivory statue displayed there, carved in the shape of an angel.

"You see, Athaya . . . since the resolution of the civil wars, Caithe has grown accustomed to being governed by your family. With the perennial exception of the Lorngeld, its people have prospered. For me to simply step in and remake the world anew would cause unnecessary strain. But the transition to a dynasty of Lorngeld can be eased greatly—and very simply—in the same manner by which most political difficulties are healed." A smile broke across his face, slow and sure. "By marriage."

Athaya felt all the breath go out of her in a rush, as if a horse had just kicked her in the belly. His knowing gaze left no room for doubt. "You mean me?"

The Sage arched a brow. "I don't feel inclined to marry either of your brothers."

He set down the little statue and folded his arms across his chest, serenely confident. "A wizard king requires a wizard queen, Athaya. And despite your prior protestations, I do not think you would find it at all unpleasant being queen."

His placating tone was infuriating and Athaya focused on her outrage to avoid thinking about the sheer dread of such a dual fate. "Frankly, Brandegarth, if I had wanted to be queen, I could have taken the crown for myself instead of waiting about for you to give it to me."

The sharp reply only managed to encourage him. "I offer you far more than a crown, Princess. Ah, you know what I mean—do not be coy. Even you must realize what a marriage between us could mean. You know the ways of it when wizards mate together," he said, dropping his voice to what he intended to be a seductive whisper. "It is not a mere bond of flesh, but a bond of mind and spirit. And we are the most gifted wizards in the world . . . can you not imagine what the nights would hold for us?"

Athaya found the very idea appalling in the extreme and fought to keep the bile where it belonged. "I hate to intrude upon your fantasy," she replied coolly, "but in case you've forgotten, I'm already married."

She disliked the way his smile changed, transforming into something more malicious. "Are you?" he challenged. "In Reyka, perhaps. But in Caithe? You have been excommunicated for almost two years, and even were you not, your marriage was performed by a Reykan wizard—not even an ordained priest! It is not binding here. No, as far as the law of Caithe is concerned, you remain quite the eligible young lady."

The worst thing about his assertion was that it skirted dangerously close to truth, depending on how one chose to interpret the law. Not that it mattered, of course; in her heart, Athaya knew the ritual performed by Overlord Basil was far more solemn and binding than a liturgy conducted by Archbishop Lukin could ever hope to be. "How dare you even *think* that I—"

"Don't be difficult about this, Athaya. You seem to forget how easy it would be to simply translate you into widowhood and thus satisfy both Caithan and Reykan law."

The cruel words slashed through her fury like a blade cutting to the bone. He would do it, too; the contempt in his eyes whenever he looked at Jaren was unmistakable, unable to fathom how Athaya could settle for a man of such mundane skills when there were adepts like himself available for the asking.

"I know your past makes you unsuitable for some," he went on, "but I care little that you are—how shall I say it?—not unspoiled. I find your willful reputation quite captivating rather than otherwise, and as both of royal blood and magic, you are the only woman in this land worthy of being my consort. Between us, Athaya, we shall found a dynasty of Lorngeld such as the world has never seen."

Instantly, Athaya detected a flaw in his grandiose plan. "Dynasty? Aren't you forgetting something?" Indeed, it was one of the first facts Jaren had ever taught her about magic. "Power isn't hereditary. These children you're talking about—the ones that will never exist," she hastily pointed out, "would not necessarily be Lorngeld."

It seemed he had been waiting for her to make that very point. "Perhaps not," he said, smiling at her with all the benevolence of a demon. "But we can make them so."

The words were like ice against her skin. She had heard such mad notions before . . .

"Over the past few months, I have been perusing the notes left by a Caithan wizard named Rhodri—a gentleman of your acquaintance, I believe," he added, mocking her with his gaze. "He developed some very interesting theories on the nature of magic and its transference."

Hot needles of fear prickled beneath Athaya's skin, tiny points of flame that burned her in a hundred places at once. The books. Nicolas had given him those books . . . the one part of the Sage's spell of compulsion that he had obeyed. But she had been so distracted by her brother's illness that she had paid little attention to what that seemingly trivial act could lead to.

"Theories, nothing more," she asserted, with a boldness she did not feel. "Rhodri's experiment was a failure. He was proved wrong by his own death and the death of my father."

Again, she felt as if she had moved her chesspiece to the very square where Brandegarth wished it to be. "Ah, but what Rhodri did was transfer power *after* it was fully formed—after a wizard's paths had matured and the magic flourished within them. What would happen, I wonder, if a wizard's power was moved—transplanted, if you will—while still in its seedlike state . . . days, weeks, even years before the *mekahn*? In infancy!" The rapture that had gripped him earlier now returned to bloom across his face in full measure. "Paths would develop normally, without the need to construct them artificially, as Rhodri was obliged to do with your father. The wizard who gives up his power would lose nothing and the one who assumes it would have no ill effects. The power would run true, as if it had always been there."

Athaya reached back for a chair and sank dazedly into it. The idea was no less than diabolical, and the simple logic of it—the notion that it just might *work*—frightened her more than Rhodri's scheme ever had.

"How can you, who speaks of doing God's will, *dare* to interfere with His choices about who is granted the gift and who is not?" Her own voice sounded alien in her ears, so horrified was she by what the Sage was planning.

"He has appointed me His First Servant, Athaya," the Sage replied, unperturbed by what she, the Circle, or any wizard of Reykan traditions would consider an unconscionable act. "He gave me the ability to see seeds for a reason—and this *is* that reason. So that I may establish His kingdom in Caithe, and from there, the world."

Athaya turned her back on him in disgust. "The ability will

fade," she reminded him. "You will not see the seeds
forever—"

He grunted impassively. "So you wish me to believe. But
even if it did, I know how to regain it."

"And when others learn it isn't God's grace, but only the ill
effects of a sealing spell that gives you such foreknowledge?
Would that not spoil the stature of your 'gift'?"

The Sage shook his head in defiance, fast growing irritated
by her ceaseless reproaches. "None could gain what I have.
The ordeal would kill them—as it almost did you—their disciplines too weak to save them. See the future for what it is,
Athaya!" he urged her. "You cannot turn it aside. We are on
the threshold of glory, you and I, and all you need do is step
across—"

"It will never work."

Brandegarth threw back his head and laughed, his merriment echoing up to the vaulted ceiling. "Ah, the eternal cry of
those who lack vision!"

"Fine, then," Athaya snapped, "so you have our futures all
plotted out. What about the rest of them? Durek and Nicolas,
Cecile and the children? Jaren?"

The Sage shrugged indifferently. "I shall allow them to live
if they promise to leave Caithe and never return—assuming, of
course, that you do as I ask and become my queen." He did
not overlook her expression of disdain. "You do not believe
me?"

"What sort of usurper leaves his enemies alive to raise an
army against him later?"

"One quite confident of his ability to hold his crown. And
his wife," he hastened to add, eyes hastily skirting the curves
of her body.

Athaya gripped the armrest so tightly that her fingertips tingled with numbness. She had been so sickened by her own reaction to his proposal that the more disastrous implications
only now began to reach her. Even the most nebulous rumors
of such a marriage could be a death blow to all that she had
built with Durek, not to mention the ruin of all her work in
Caithe. It would be Lukin's prophecy come true; in her enemies' eyes, a crown was the attainment of all her goals, the intended result of all her schemes. Were she to claim that she
took it against her will, only to save the lives of others, her
protestations would be deemed a farce. And those as preju-
diced as Lukin might even go so far as to dismiss her marriage

to Jaren as one more part of an elaborate ruse, intricately complex so as to better dupe the people.

It was patently absurd; anyone who knew her would see that. But her enemies had always proved willing to credit her with far more craftiness and ambition than she could possibly possess in one lifetime. And she had witnessed the Sage weave threads of power into his speeches before, lending credibility to his words. If he wanted the people of Caithe to believe such a thing, then in time, they would.

Having finally managed to stun her into silence, the Sage went to the bedstand and picked up a tiny brass bell. Athaya heard nothing when he shook it, but within moments, an older man stepped into the room and bowed low to his lord; he was clad all in black but for a collar of silver links.

"It grows close to dawn," the Sage observed, "and I must go to Delfarham and see how my army progresses. Tullis will look after you until I return. Until then, I would advise you not to leave this room; the results will be most unpleasant for you, as anyone who has encountered Tullis' binding spells can tell you. But I will return for you soon, right after I am crowned." He lifted one finger, making a mental note. "I must remember to write to your esteemed archbishop and command him to attend me at my coronation—ah, the joy of humbling that pompous cur! Then I will come for you ... and make you my queen."

He extended a hand toward her, as if silently requesting a kiss, but she roughly slapped it away, equal parts fearful and furious.

"Never fear, Athaya," he said with a dry chuckle. "I would not be so crude as to force myself upon you. But once you are my wife, it will be your duty—and a pleasant one, I assure you, if Drianna's contentment was any sign—to fill our nursery with little adepts. We will make them so," he added covertly, "if God does not."

"You reach beyond yourself, Brandegarth of Crewe," she said, too stricken by his mad and lofty aspirations to be angry anymore. "Reach for too much and everything you hold will slip from your grasp."

"Reach for nothing at all," he replied glibly, "and you are still left empty-handed. Why not take the risk?"

Athaya backed away from him, shivering against the crisp night air. "I will never do as you ask."

"Of course you won't," he echoed mockingly. "And Prince

Nicolas would have likewise sworn never to bring me Rhodri's books or to offer *kahnil* to the king. What I am saying," he warned her, all levity gone, "is that your desires can be changed . . . and you would never know the difference."

On that menacing note, he uttered the words of translocation and vanished from the chamber in a shimmer of mist and starlight—an exit Athaya might have found beautifully impressive under any other circumstances.

"Is there anything you wish, my Lady?" Tullis asked, still lingering obediently in the doorway.

Athaya shot him a look of pure loathing. "I wish to get the devil out of here," she snapped. Balling her hands into fists, she glared at the empty spot on the floor where the Sage had stood only seconds before. "But it appears," she added acidly, "that he's already left."

Looking acutely uncomfortable, Tullis departed, murmuring absurd wishes for her pleasant stay in Sare.

Blessedly alone, Athaya went to Drianna's bed and threw herself across the quilts, exhausted and sickened to the point of tears. She wanted nothing more than to drift off to a dreamless sleep and seek refuge where the Sage and his lunatic plans could not reach her. The evening had become a horrible reprise of that night in the dungeon, with Tyler's death warrant suspended in Rhodri's hand. But this time, it was not just one man's fate in the balance; this time it was all of Caithe. Her actions would set the course of history—and again determine whether those she loved would live or die.

Rhodri had wanted her power, but Brandegarth wanted her soul. And unless she could think of something quickly, the chances were all too good that he would get it.

CHAPTER 15

"MAKE YOUR CHOICE," COURIC DRONED, STANDING in silver-edged black livery at the Sage's left hand. The man's tone was flat and dull; everyone in the Hall, including the Sage himself, had lost count of how many times he had delivered the same perfunctory command that afternoon. Within days of the initial assault, the Sage's rule in Delfarham was undisputed, and the last of the enemy's forces had been rounded up and brought to meet his justice.

"And think on your answer more carefully than did he before you," the Sage advised his bedraggled captive. As if already comfortably ensconced as king of Caithe, the Sage reclined upon Durek's throne in the Great Hall, glaring unforgivingly at the prisoner before him, this one clad in the bloody remnants of a crimson guardsman's uniform. "You do not bear the seed of power. I have no need for your life unless you swear it to my service."

The prisoner's eyes darted to his right, where Preceptor Mobarec's half-naked body dangled from the rafters, his face grotesquely twisted with terrible awe at the extent of agony an old man could be made to feel in the final seconds before death. And if the sight of a hanged priest was not gruesome enough, anyone still uncertain whether to swear loyalty to the Sage only had to look upon the preceptor's slashed belly, his innards snaking down to the flagstone floor in grisly parody of an umbilical cord, to know that the Sage delivered on his threats.

Paling noticeably, the prisoner closed his eyes and swallowed. "I . . . all right. I'll swear."

"Damn you to hell, James!" an enraged voice shouted from the antechamber. "You're sworn to the king, not to that bloody usurper!" The Hall echoed with the loud smack of a mailed glove scraping against flesh; the man did not object again.

"Say it all," Couric prompted.

The prisoner was visibly shaken by his comrade's curse, but managed to get the treacherous words out. "I p-pledge to you my life and limb, and promise to use both in your defense and service for all of the rest of my days."

Couric snatched his hand and stabbed his index finger with a needle, then squeezed a fat drop of blood into a thimble of ink. "Sign here," he instructed; he handed the man a fresh quill and shoved him toward an open book at the far end of the trestle table. "Or make a crossmark if you can't write."

Trembling, as if readying to commit his soul to the Devil himself, the prisoner stumbled forward and scratched his name in the Sage's book with the blood-tainted ink. A bluish glow followed his hand as he wrote, fading into the page to bind his oath more securely than ink and words could ever do.

"You are a wiser man than our esteemed preceptor," the Sage remarked mildly, his eyes flicking briefly to the grisly display at his left. "Not that I would have accepted his pledge anyway—though he certainly seemed more than happy to offer it. No, I will not suffer those to live who spend their days hunting wizards in the name of God. But to you," he went on, "I will pledge my steadfast protection for as long as I shall live in governance." The ritual response completed, he curtly signaled his guardsmen to usher the man out. "But do not think to betray me," the Sage added in warning. "Your blooded mark binds your very life to me. Did I wish it, I could make you pray you had opted for death when you had the chance."

Before the next pair of prisoners were brought forward, the Sage called for refreshment to salve his throat. The thick stone walls offered some relief from the sweltering heat of late July, but several wizards were needed to cast gentle windspells and keep the air from growing too stagnant and oppressive. The vaulted ceiling was peppered with witchlights, lighting the chamber without adding heat. Delicate strains of a flute flowed softly from a porcelain jar at the edge of the dais to soothe the attendants—an incongruous touch of delicacy amid the somber proceedings.

A young woman set a glass of wine at his right hand, her slender hand hesitating only slightly before releasing the cup, as if considering whether to dash the contents in his face instead. "Thank you, Drianna dear," he said, ignoring the glowing hatred in her eyes. He had fancied that perhaps the girl had drowned herself in the sea after he cast her aside, heartbroken and despondent. It had angered him to find her thriving among his enemies—he never let her know how much—but it amused him to spare her life, letting her live so that she could spend the rest of her days in servitude to him, drinking deep from the bitter cup of degradation.

"Do wipe that puckered scowl off your pretty face, Drianna," he teased her, gently pinching her cheek. "God's blood, you look as sour as the queen dowager. Take care, or I shall send you off to Saint Gillian's to join her."

"Please do," she replied bitterly. "I'd far rather be shut away with a flock of dreary old nuns than suffer here at your side." Her gaze drifted unbidden to the preceptor's mutilated body and, shuddering, she looked away. "You're a cruel and loathsome man, Brandegarth, and you don't deserve to be Sage at all, much less king of Caithe. I hope Athaya kills you," she added, grieved as well as angered by what he had become, "and I hope she takes her time over it."

"Ah, but Athaya is not here," he observed. His eyes narrowed ever so slightly. "And if you value your mistress' welfare, Drianna, you will not insult me again."

Biting back words of rage, Drianna crept back to the kitchens—flashing a vicious glare at Couric on her way—knowing she had little choice but to endure her abasement.

"Bring forth the next prisoner," Couric called.

The Sage began to indulge himself in a lethargic yawn—the day grew long and the Hall damnably stuffy—but curtailed it as the next pair of captives were brought forth. At last things were getting interesting . . .

"Ah, the elusive Dom DePere," he said, shaking off some of his heat-induced languor. "You evaded me in Kilfarnan, but you were not so fortunate here, I see."

Bloodied, bruised, and shackled by glowing blue cords pulsing at his wrists, Mason nonetheless managed to face the Sage with cool dignity. "What have you done with the king? And where is Princess Athaya?"

"Haven't you heard? His Majesty fled Delfarham days ago with his tail tightly tucked between his legs. An abdication in deed, if not in words. And his sister is well cared for. That is all you need know."

The Sage shifted his gaze to the second man; likewise shackled, he was a mess of soiled bandages, greasy hair, and jagged red scars. "Ranulf, old friend, we meet again. And again you find yourself my captive." His eyes clouded over; for the first time that day he was genuinely angry. "I should kill you right now for what you did to Connor. He was no wizard, but he was a loyal man and served me well."

"He should have known better to turn his back on a man with a crossbow in his hand . . . even if his tunic *was* on fire." Ranulf returned the Sage's menacing gaze with equal fervor. "Just call it revenge for what you did to Prince Nicolas."

"I still hold your precious prince, my friend. Take care, or I will do far worse than tangle his simple mind with spells." He leaned back, studying the two men before him. "You are both worthy opponents and talented wizards; I would rather see you join me than die from stubbornness."

"Of the two alternatives," Mason replied evenly, "only death has any honor in it."

The Sage scowled at him. "Yes, I should have expected to hear such pious drivel from the mouth of a Reykan scholar. But what about you, Ranulf? Mercenaries spend their lives selling their souls for one thing or another; why not hire yourself out to the clear winner of this game? I could use a man like you. Your politics and theology may be wanting of some adjustment, but you do know how to fight."

Ranulf merely snorted at him. "Even mercenaries have standards."

"If you join me, I might be persuaded to spare your friend the dom as well. As it is, his future looks none too promising."

After a swift glare from Mason warning him not to agree, Ranulf shook his head. Sighing resignedly, the Sage motioned his guardsmen to take the captives away. "Think on my offer during your stay in my dungeons," he called after Ranulf. "I will ask you again once I have been crowned king; if you still refuse, only then will I be forced to kill you both. Mind you, it is a far more generous offer than most have received today."

Once they were gone, Couric quickly presented the next pair of prisoners; the day grew long and there were many lives yet remaining to be judged. "Kale Eavon and Avery Parr, your Grace."

The Sage raked his gaze over the two men, searching for signs of worth. "I will not even ask whether you will swear to me," he remarked to Kale, "because I know you will not. Still, I am told that you have done Athaya great service and that she values you for it. Because of that, I will permit you to live so that you may continue to serve her when she returns. I will make of your life a gift to her."

Stone-faced, Kale neither thanked nor denounced him, but the Sage did not neglect to notice the spark of relief that glimmered behind the man's gray eyes; at least Athaya would return.

"And you are his Majesty's Captain of the Guard, eh?" the Sage asked, turning a derisive smile to Parr. The captain was badly out of uniform, his body barely covered by the bloody shreds of a crimson tunic. "So it is you I must thank for allowing me such unimpeded entry into this castle."

The captain spat on the rush-covered floor, promptly earning him a ringing blow to the head courtesy of his jailers. "Devil take you . . . *all* of you! I don't care what you do to me. I'll rot in hell before I'll bow down to one of your kind!"

The Sage mocked him with an indulgent smile, as if listening to the tirade of a child whose favorite toy had been taken away. "Then I shall grant you that which you so fervently desire."

The Sage pointed lazily toward the rafters. Two uniformed men hustled their captive to the left side of the Hall, where another noose had been readied, waiting for the next man who dared defy the Sage's commands. Parr said nothing as the rope was secured around his neck, though he sweated profusely and did everything he could to avoid looking at the dead man suspended beside him.

"On your orders, your Grace," one of the guardsmen said with a bow. The hands of four men clasped the rope tightly, ready to haul the prisoner off his feet.

The Sage did not signal right away. "No. No, wait—"

He paused, staring through and behind Parr's defiant eyes for a full minute. Then he gripped his sides and laughed as if he'd just heard the finest jest of his life. "Our Lord has a sense of humor, I see." He smiled knowingly at his bewildered captive. "You have no idea, do you? Tell me, how old are you?"

Parr stared at him blankly, failing to see what his age had to do with his imminent death. "What? I don't—"

"You do *know*, don't you?" the Sage asked dryly.

"Of course I do. I . . . I'm twenty-four."

The Sage's smile grew broader than ever. "Late. Late, but not unheard of."

Captain Parr's face turned the color of onions as he realized what the Sage was implying. He choked on his next breath, as if already sent aloft by the hangmen.

"Ah, you catch on slowly, but you do catch on. It won't be long, sir—not by the swollen size of your seed. In time, you will be worthy to serve me. This one has the power," he told Couric. "Keep him close confined until his *mekahn* begins. We will then see how badly he wishes to die."

"Liar!" the captain cried, struggling like a hawk in a net as his captors fought to remove the noose from his neck. "Filthy, stinking liar! I don't have the curse, damn you . . . I don't!"

The Sage eyed him steadily. "Then answer me this, Captain: Why is your heart still beating and not lying cold upon the floor like the preceptor's bowels? It is only because God has made us brethren that I suffer you to live. Only His gift has saved you. Tell me," he went on; his voice dropped low, ominous as distant thunder, "when your power comes upon you, fouling your mind with madness, will you give yourself over to the glory of it or beg for absolution like a kitten mewling for milk, covering your cowardice with false valor? Death is the easier choice, my friend; you know what death will bring you. But magic is an enigma—a divine riddle for each gifted man to solve in his own way. It is the ultimate Challenge! Why cannot you Caithans *see* that? Why do you all persist in forfeiting the contest before it has even begun?"

"No, no . . . He would not *do* this to me!" Parr was not listening; he continued to shriek his torment as he was dragged ungracefully from the Hall, as if the Sage had just condemned him to die rather than to live. Behind him, Kale's expression was artfully ambiguous.

The Sage did not signal the next pair of captives to be brought forth just yet. "Have we received a reply from Archbishop Lukin yet?" he murmured to Couric.

"No, your Grace, but I'm certain it will come. He has no choice but to submit to you."

The Sage nodded, languidly waving for the procession to continue. It was one of the more onerous duties of a ruler, but there were many more prisoners to pass judgment on before the day was out and he wished them all to look upon him and know who held true dominion over Caithe.

Jaren and Durek reached the forest camp on the first day of August, exhausted, hungry, and travel-stained, looking nothing remotely like either a duke's son or a king. To make matters worse, it had rained sporadically for most of the day, leaving them damp as well as weary as they collapsed in bedraggled heaps before the campfire near the bell tower.

Tonia and Gilda bustled out to greet them, while a handful of others—wizards too unseasoned to have joined the main force a week ago—squinted curiously from the compound's windows and doorways. "Thank God you're both safe," Tonia said, embracing Jaren snugly. She drew back and wrinkled her nose in distaste; Jaren and Durek were wrapped in ragged peasant cloaks, the lingering smell of hay and dung only slightly obscured by that of sodden wool. "Lord, you're a sight. Fragrant, too."

"We couldn't very well slip inconspicuously through the countryside dressed for court," Jaren said as he sloughed off the cloak and tossed it over a fallen log.

Satisfied that they were safe and well, Tonia's troubled gaze wordlessly asked the fate of those left behind.

"We don't know where Athaya is," Jaren told her, sagging down onto the log. "No one's seen her since the night of the attack. For what his word is worth, the Sage told us he didn't plan to harm her. He must be keeping her captive until he's got a solid hold on Caithe. Athaya is the only legitimate danger to him now, and he knows it."

"He never even bothered to send anyone out after us," Durek said, relieved yet oddly affronted. "Nobody we saw, that is. Jaren kept us—warded, is it?—most of the time, but I suspect the Sage's men know we'd have little choice but to come here. He probably figures he can come after us whenever he gets around to it." Durek peeled off his boots and propped his stockinged feet near the fire to dry. "Has there been any news from the others? The wizards you sent to oppose him?"

Tonia nodded grimly. "Ranulf tried to contact me just before . . . oh, Lord, they never stood a chance," she said, a rare show of tears welling up in her eyes. "Almost half of them were killed the first night they arrived, and the rest were taken prisoner. Maybe a few got away," she added, struggling to salvage a few scraps of hope from the debacle, "but if they did, they wouldn't have made it back to camp yet. We can only hope."

Jaren stared vacantly into the campfire, pained by the remembrance that hope was already lost for one of their number. "Tonia—"

She patted him gently on the shoulder. "I know about Hedric." Jaren cast her a puzzled look of inquiry, but she merely sniffled and turned away, electing not to elaborate on how she had obtained such knowledge.

Durek picked up a scrap of wood and tossed it listlessly into the fire; the wood was damp and the flames hissed angrily at him. "What do I do next?" he asked himself quietly. He hung his head in abject dejection, unable to believe that he was as much an outlaw in his own land as Athaya had ever been. "I can't fight the Sage with soldiers and you can't fight him with wizards. Our only choice is to kill him, but no one can do that except perhaps Athaya, and we have no idea what he's done with her!"

He picked up a birch twig and absently began stripping off the feathery white bark. "It seems I have no choice but to beg Reyka for help."

"You could try," Jaren said cautiously, "but don't be too hopeful of getting it. Caithe and Reyka haven't exactly been friends with one another over the years. And even were Athaya to ask it of him as a personal favor, Osfonin is certain to point out that, ultimately, this conflict is a civil war; Sare is a Caithan protectorate. As a matter of policy, Osfonin is averse to getting involved in somebody else's domestic quarrels."

"Don't take this the wrong way," Durek said sullenly, "but from a purely objective stance, it occurs to me that I might not be having that problem if Athaya had simply married Prince Felgin the way my father wanted her to."

Jaren shrugged, conceding the point. "Maybe not. But personally, I'm rather glad it never worked out."

To add to his Majesty's misery, the rain began to fall again, coming down in fat, soaking drops. Tonia scowled up at the sky and hurried back indoors, leaving a trail of footprints in the thickening mud, while Jaren motioned Durek toward the chapel. "Come, we can talk there."

"The kitchen might be better," Gilda suggested, gathering up Durek's boots and the pair of shabby cloaks. "You both look in need of a hot meal. Besides, there's someone using the chapel at the moment, and I doubt he'd welcome the company.

A cousin of Cameron's came looking for him earlier today," she quietly explained to Jaren. "Didn't have any idea the boy was killed by the Tribunal last year. He took the news awfully hard."

Jaren glanced to the decrepit little church. Maybe I'd better go say something to him," he said, though the slouch in his shoulders indicated that he would far rather avoid such a gloomy errand.

Fortunately, there was no need. "I'd wait until morning," Gilda advised him. "He asked to be left alone for the night. He didn't come right out and say it," she added, "but he's furious with us for what happened to Cameron and doesn't trust himself to be civil for a while." She stole a glance at Durek; the man would be even less civil to the king who had instigated the Tribunal.

"I can't very well blame him." He turned back to Durek. "Let's get something to eat, then, and afterwards I'll see about finding you a room. There should be plenty to choose from now," he added, sadly aware that many of the camp's wizards would never be returning to use them.

"Jaren, wait . . ." Even though the rain was falling harder now, Durek paused to let Gilda get a few yards ahead of them. He shifted his weight from one stockinged foot to another, fidgeting like a child forced into making an apology to his elders. "I . . . just wanted to thank you. Not just for bringing me here—though God knows I couldn't have found the place without you—but for putting up with me these past few days. I . . . wasn't always the most congenial of traveling companions."

Jaren didn't leap to dispute the fact; the most engaging conversation he'd had since fleeing the capital had been with the peasant who sold them the cloaks. Still, Durek's acerbity was easily forgiven in light of the devastation they had left behind them in Delfarham. "You don't have to apologize—"

"Yes. Yes, I do. It's important." Durek frowned deeply, struggling to sort out his tangled skein of thoughts. "I'm finding that a lot of things are important now that never were before . . ." He winced as if he had a dagger lodged in his back, twisting at every uttered word. "Athaya . . . she did well in choosing you, I think. Hedric told me so once, but I didn't want to believe him at the time. Of course, if you ever tell Athaya I said that, I'll deny it," he added, mildly sardonic. He let out a breathy wisp of resigned—almost sad—laughter. "She'd never believe I said it anyway."

"Oh, I don't know," Jaren replied, cracking the very faintest of smiles as he brushed a trickle of rainwater from his face. "Athaya believes a lot of crazy things."

The slightly martyred tilt of his head proved that Durek did not disagree. Then his expression turned solemn. "I'm sorry about Hedric. I barely knew him, but . . . I think I know what you and Athaya have lost. I know that probably doesn't mean much coming from me, but . . ." He let the words trail off, standing in uneasy silence in the rain; barefoot, drenched, smelling like a wet dog, and feeling as less a king as he ever had in his life.

"On the contrary," Jaren replied. Then the steady rain began to fall in sheets and he hurried the king toward the inviting warmth of the kitchens. Like any other fugitive from justice, Durek would be welcome there.

Just as dawn drew a pink smudge across the eastern horizon, Hugh Middlebrook was admitted into Archbishop Lukin's solar to deliver the treasure for which he had been sent. His cloak was still drenched from the night's rain, his borrowed clothes still soiled with mud, but these discomforts could not stop a triumphant smile from breaking across his face.

As Hugh set the strongbox on the table, Lukin's eyes lit up the world. He reached out slowly, only to pause and draw back, as if this were a thing too holy to set his human hands upon.

"You have done well," he murmured, breathing the words more than voicing them, as if whispering seductions into a woman's ear. "I take it everything went smoothly?"

"They never even questioned my story," Hugh replied, somewhat taken aback at the ease of the theft. "I called out to them at the forest's edge as you suggested, and when one of the wizards finally approached me, I said exactly what you told me—that I was Cameron's cousin. The woman led me to the camp—she didn't even notice I was leaving a trail so I could find my way back—and told me he'd been killed by the Tribunal. I blinked up a few tears for her—as simple as thinking of the puppy I had as a boy, run down by a carriage. Then I asked to be left alone in the chapel for a while. It worked like a wizard's charm! The strongbox was right where you said it would be, and there are so few wizards left at the camp that nobody was loitering about to spy on me as I took it. But later . . ." Hugh's feelings of triumph receded for an instant. "I almost choked when I heard the king's own voice in the clearing! He and McLaud arrived at the camp only a few hours after I did. It was a great relief to know that his Majesty escaped the attack on Delfarham, of course, but . . . God only knows what I would have said to him if he had seen me!"

"I'm certain you would have thought of something clever," Lukin responded absently, only half listening as his fingers stroked the strongbox's brass locks as if a woman's cheek, spellbound by his prize. "Thanks to you, we know his Majesty is alive. And you have obtained the instrument of his enemy's destruction."

Then the archbishop snatched up a crumpled piece of parchment and waved it in the guardsman's face. "The audacity of the man, sending me letters commanding that I officiate at his coronation! He thinks to humiliate me. He wishes me, as prelate of Caithe, to humble myself and thus all of Mother Church at his feet. But God's ways are indeed amusing at times," he added, setting the offending letter aside. Chuckling softly, he smoothed out another of its wrinkles; he would keep this letter as a trophy—something to laugh at when his enemy was nothing more than a memory. "The Sage's own command will be the manner of his undoing. The rest is in my hands now."

"But I forget myself," he said abruptly, recalling himself to the present. He pushed a leather pouch of gold across the table to Hugh; it was twice what he had promised, but Caithe's future was well worth it. "Here. Use this in any way that God guides you, for your loyalty to church and crown. You could resign your post and buy a country house somewhere. The Tribunal has confiscated several charming ones . . . perhaps a manor in the south would suit you?"

Hugh gulped audibly as he felt the weight of the purse. "T-thank you, Excellency! I never expected—"

"I only ask one more task of you. Go to the cathedral and hire a courier for me; I am long overdue on my reply to his Grace and must tell him how delighted I will be to attend him upon his coronation."

Hugh bowed crisply and departed, leaving the gold behind to collect after his final task was done. Once he was gone, Archbishop Lukin drew a slender key from his cassock—a key he doubted Durek knew he had—and unlocked the strongbox. Holding his breath in dizzy anticipation, he lifted up the priceless crown—Faltil's crown, encrusted with brilliant purple corbals. How fitting, he mused, that God would provide such an object of beauty with which to rid the earth of His enemies.

He turned the crown from side to side, holding every facet up to the newborn sunlight streaming through the windows, and spat out a curse when he saw that close to a dozen of the costly gems had been pried out from the crown's base. "Grubby little thief," he murmured. "Probably sold them off one by one to fill his belly with beer and sausages." But Lukin's ire did not last for long. Cameron had received his punishment at the end of a hangman's noose; the Tribunal had seen to that.

"Ah, but even so, it still has the power I require," he said, reverently returning the crown to its box. "What the Sage of Sare fancies to be my humiliation will instead be his death— his and any other wizard who attends him. I'm sure Caithe's cunning princess will be there to see her puppet crowned . . ."

Lukin set his hand upon the strongbox and laughed aloud more heartily than he had in weeks. "I shall be happy to crown you king, my Lord," he said, bowing obeisance to an invisible Sage. When he arose, his eyes glittered with malice. "And it will be the first and last ceremony of your very brief reign."

CHAPTER 16

❈❈

ATHAYA KNEW SHE SHOULD BE QUITE ACCUSTOMED TO PRIS-
ons by now—within the past two years, she had endured countless hours in both Delfar's dungeon and the
convent of Saint Gillian's—but her confinement in the Sage's
fortress was proving to be the most punishing of all. The fate
of her homeland was being determined at this very hour, and
not knowing what was happening, not being able to help when
she was needed most, tore away at the delicate cloak of faith
she still struggled to grip about her. By the seventh day of being bound within Drianna's sumptuous chamber, with little else
to do but pick at the food Tullis brought to her, ignore his half-
hearted attempts at conversation, and wish dreadful plagues
upon the wizard who had brought her here, she thought she
would go quite mad.

The day was humid, the air unsettled, and the gray-green
clouds cloaking the island, lingering over a decision on
whether to storm or not, made Athaya even more restless than
usual. Time and time again she paced to the window, hoping
to catch a glimpse of Caithe's northernmost shoreline across
the hazy channel. Even when she knew it unlikely, she imagined that she spied the outline of Saint Gillian's among the distant crags. A year ago, she would have scoffed at the notion
that she might one day wish herself back within those bleak
and clammy walls. From there, at least, she would have a
slight chance of escape; from here, there was none.

Athaya had lost count of the number of times she had gone to that same bay window this past week, toying with absurd plans for scaling down the fortress's rocky face to freedom. But while she could stand before the open window, she could not lean out of it; binding spells had been drawn across the aperture as well as the door—an invisible curtain trapping her securely inside. "Probably afraid I'd jump and kill myself at the thought of marrying him," she had grumbled after first discovering the enchantment.

Then, with aggravating frequency, she would remind herself that even if she could escape the fortress, she was, ultimately, on an island; stranded, with no money to hire a skiff and no spells to call for help.

If there was one aspect of her confinement that she did not look upon with complete misery, it was that the sealing spell's pressures were not so quick to affect her as they had been the summer before. Then, she had lapsed into forgetfulness within a day of her confinement, unable to keep proper track of time; now she was plagued by little more than a woolly head and a tendency to bump into things if she wasn't careful. Why that was she did not know; the Sage's spell was more potent than the one Aldus placed upon her. Although it oftentimes chafed like an ill-fitting boot, Athaya felt Brandegarth's handiwork within her constantly, the seal's fetters tight and unforgiving, as if her spells were bound with irons rather than cord. Perhaps, she reasoned, she had gained some small immunity from her past experience with the seal and would thus be able to combat her present ordeal more easily. Or perhaps, she dared to hope, the Sage's spellcasting grew sloppy, carried off by sheer force rather than technique; a likely surmise, if their hellish translocation to Sare was any indication of his ability.

Tullis brought her supper at the usual time—some variety of fish, by the smell of it—and found her picking through Drianna's extensive and abandoned wardrobe, having finally concluded that she should change into some other dress after a full week in her own. She hated to take anything that the Sage had provided for her, but the sight of her wrinkled silk gown, so lovely on the day of Durek's speech in Kaiburn, was beginning to disgust even herself.

"I've brought you some whitefish tonight," the steward said, passing with aggravating ease through the binding spells upon the door—spells that raked her skull with white-hot claws of agony whenever she drew too close to them. "And I found a bottle of Evarshot wine from the mainland in his Grace's cellars; I thought that might please you."

Athaya scowled fleetingly at him, more out of habit this time than any palpable sense of resentment, and tossed aside a gown of butter-colored silk, certain that the color would look appalling on her. She had been surly with Tullis all week, and at the moment, relaxed by the gentle sheeting of rain that had finally begun to fall, she felt somewhat sorry for it—he was, from what she had seen, a gracious and conscientious man who was simply doing his duty. He reminded her strongly of Kale: mature and steadfast, without a great deal to say, but richer in compassion and integrity than the casual observer might suspect.

Why then was he here, she wondered, servant to a man who so clearly lacked all of those qualities?

Athaya closed the wardrobe doors and leaned against them. "Why do you serve him?" She asked it as a challenge, daring him to provide a reasonable reply.

Tullis looked up as he set her tray down on the table, startled at the question. Not because it was the first complete sentence she had spoken to him in six days, but because he had never encountered anyone who needed to ask.

"He is the Sage. We all serve him."

"Yes, yes, I know. But *why*?"

Thoughtfully, Tullis folded a linen napkin into the shape of a seashell and placed it beside her plate, then filled her goblet with the hearty Caithan wine. "He has been a good lord to us, my Lady. And he wants the same thing you do—a better life for our people."

"Yes, but I never planned to usurp my brother's place to achieve that."

Tullis was not eager to argue the point. He frowned, silently disquieted, and Athaya wondered if it was the first time he had considered that Dameronne's prophecy deftly sidestepped the fact that for the Sage to assume Caithe's crown, someone else would have to lose it.

She sat down in the chair Tullis pulled out for her and sipped absently at the Evarshot. Its smooth, familiar taste should have comforted her, but at the moment, it only made her more frustrated and homesick.

"He thinks to make me his wife," she observed, as Tullis graced her fish with a spoonful of slivered almonds.

The steward nodded, painfully aware of her opinions on that subject. "Yes, he spoke of that . . . after Lady Drianna left."

"Left? More like he cast her off."

Athaya's goblet stopped halfway to her lips; what had she just done? Drianna hadn't told anyone where she was going when she left Sare, and if he had not already discovered her presence in Delfarham, the Sage might make a concerted effort to do so were he to learn she had joined the ranks of his enemies.

Tullis put that particular fear to rest at once. "I knew she would go to you. Where else was left to her?" He let out a heavy sigh, genuinely regretful. "Lady Drianna was a charming and spirited woman. I saw her leave the fortress that day, heading for the port. His Grace did not ask what had become of her, so I suppose it wasn't too deceitful of me not to mention what I'd seen. She was devastated by his rejection." He shook his head sadly. "I miss her a great deal. She brought much laughter to this place. His Grace should not have hurt her so; if he did not wish to marry her, at least he could have broken the news to her more gently."

Athaya lanced a bit of fish with her knife, savoring the tender filet in spite of the lord who provided it. "If he had wanted to marry Drianna as much as he claimed, then why didn't he simply put this lunatic plan of his to the test and give her a seed of power? But no," she went on, biting down angrily on an almond, "he heard about me and decided a trained adept would be a more suitable wife for someone of his godlike stature." She cast the knife at her fish again, fancying that the blade sank deep into the Sage himself. "But if not Drianna, he will try his scheme on someone else, presuming to do what it is not our place to do by granting the gift of power. Not satisfied with God's miracles," she finished scornfully, "he sets about working his own."

Tullis's face was profoundly blank. "What are you . . . I don't—"

"Hasn't he told you yet?"

She knew by the bewilderment in his eyes that the Sage had not. Perhaps Brandegarth had shared his schemes only with her, hoping to lure her from her convictions—and her husband—with the untold glory of founding an unbreakable dynasty of wizards in Caithe. As the Sage's devoted servant, Athaya waited for Tullis to launch into a fervent defense of his lord's plans, confident that anything the Sage did was sanctioned by God. Instead, his gentle face sagged with despair, as if he had long anticipated bad news and was simply saddened that this was the day he received it.

"The books," Tullis murmured, as if she were not there. "He was reading those books . . ."

Then he aimed his gaze at her like a blade, and Athaya felt an ensuing tickling sensation around the inside edges of her skull; feathers of inquiry, silently seeking proof of her claims. When the feeling subsided, Tullis sank down at the table across from her, his eyes hollow and lost.

"You speak the truth. His Grace has indeed told you these things." He drew in a long, melancholy breath, and for a brief moment, his lower lip trembled as if his composure was close to crumbling.

"Tullis, I know this plan of his sounds crazy, but I can't promise you it won't work. It just might, if he ever gets the chance to try it. Don't you realize what that means? Once he starts interfering with the natural order of things, taking magic from those he doesn't think worthy of it and giving it to those he does, the power will consume him. I tried to tell him that the ability to see the seeds will fade in time, but he didn't believe me. And I can't even guarantee that I'm right," she pointed out. "Drianna told me his power was released from its seal under rigid controls—that it took you and two others to contain it—whereas mine flooded out in a rush and made me ill for weeks. Maybe that made a difference—I just don't know. But even if his ability does fade, it won't do so for months yet . . . and think of all the lives he can disrupt in the meantime."

Never mind stealing Mailen's future from him, she added inwardly. As Durek's heir, Mailen's very existence would be a constant threat to the Sage's position; Athaya put no credence in the Sage's claims that he would let the boy live in peace as long as he remained in exile. At the very least, he would seek him out to determine what kind of foe the little prince might grow up to be. And were he to discover the dormant magic within the boy—as Athaya had done months ago, without intending to—the Sage could stop that precious seed from sprouting, robbing Mailen of his gift before he ever realized he possessed it.

Tullis avoided her gaze, fixing his attention on the half-eaten filet on her plate. "His Grace could not . . . he will see his error . . ."

"He won't reconsider," Athaya told him, as sure of that fact as she was that the full moon would inevitably follow the new. "Rhodri never did."

It was too much for Tullis to bear; everything that he had believed in was suddenly disintegrating before his eyes. He scrambled from his chair and hurried away, shaking his head in fervent denial, as if he had just been told of a beloved wife's infidelity. "I must go. I can hear no more of this tonight."

"Tullis, wait—" But he paid no heed to her as he stumbled blindly from the chamber, and Athaya could not pass beyond the binding spells to pursue him.

Tullis did not come to her chamber the next day. Nor did he come on the second day . . . or the third. Her meals were delivered by another of the Sage's staff, this one far more dreary and closemouthed than his predecessor. When she asked whether the steward was ill, she was first ignored, then told it was none of her concern, and finally informed—quite tersely—that an unspecified emergency had called him away from the palace for a time and that she should not inquire about it again.

The steward's continued absence made her uneasy. Their last conversation had clearly unsettled him, and Athaya feared he may have gone to see the Sage, perhaps to gain his lord's assurances that her dark prophecies were simply the ramblings of a desperate woman.

Then, three days later, she was eased awake in the predawn hours by the gentle shake of a knotted hand. She blinked against the nearby radiance of an oil lamp, glimpsing in its dim glow a weathered face framed by white hair, and thought—for only an instant—that it was Master Hedric's phantom come to haunt her.

"Tullis, where—" He placed his finger over his lips and Athaya quickly dropped her voice to a whisper. "Where have you been?"

He offered her a pensive smile. "Out searching my soul."

As Athaya slid out of bed, Tullis gallantly turned his eyes away until she had covered her shift with one of Drianna's embroidered robes. Strange, she thought as she looped the silk belt around her waist, how unusually alert she felt despite being roused at such an hour. Her head was unclouded and she did not feel even slightly off-balance.

She looked at Tullis sharply. The sealing spell was broken. "It was not easy," he remarked, subtly proud. Even in the dim light, Athaya could see the fatigue shading his eyes. "The Sage sets a powerful seal."

She groped for adequate words of thanks—did he truly realize the precious gift he had given her?—but Tullis did not need to hear them. "A small number of wizards came back to Sare to recover from injuries they sustained during the invasion. Without going into my reasons for doing so, I asked them about the Sage and his actions. The things they told me . . ." Tullis flinched at the mere memory. "His Grace was always an exacting lord, but never a brutal one; his viciousness in murdering the priesthood . . . it grieves me terribly. He may not agree with them about the nature of our gift—I certainly do not—but Caithe's priests serve the same God we do, though in an admittedly wrong-minded fashion. He could have given them a quick and honorable end."

Athaya was tempted to observe that men like Lukin and his Tribunal of Justices doled out little enough mercy—why should they be granted any in return? But she also knew that just as all wizards did not believe their power endowed them with inborn supremacy, not every priest shared in the official opinion that the Lorngeld should be systematically hunted down and destroyed. Sadly, the Sage would not bother to discriminate between the two.

"I should have seen this coming," Tullis went on, sinking down on a cushioned stool at her bedside. His fingers absently followed the scalloped tracery on the bedcurtains. "I feared something like this might happen . . . months ago, after I released him from the sealing spell. His Grace was an ambitious man before, of course—no man without aspirations could attain the office of Sage—but he was always mindful of his proper place; God's chosen, but also His servant. He forgets that now, I think. He disavows his limitations and reaches for more than is his due."

"Should that surprise you?" Athaya asked. Try as she might, she could not envision the Sage in the more humble form Tullis described.

"It does, because such folly almost killed him once and not so long ago that he should have forgotten." Tullis looked to the oil lamp, idly watching the steady flame as he spoke. "It was at his last Challenge, over a year ago. His opponent, a wizard named Bressel, feigned weariness and defeat as the contest drew on. As a result—a result that Bressel anticipated and exploited to perfection—the Sage grew confident . . . and thus careless. Bressel then surprised him by lashing out at full strength with his deadliest spells. The Sage was the better magician, but it took every bit of his talent to save himself that day. Even so, he came away badly injured."

Tullis turned from the lamp, blinking away the afterglow that danced before his eyes. "But he is more powerful now than he was then, and it makes him feel invincible."

"But you knew he wanted more power all along," Athaya pointed out. "And you knew the sealing spell would give it to him. You even cast the seal yourself."

"Yes," Tullis admitted, without pride, "but only because he commanded me to do so. I never favored the plan, Princess, as Lady Drianna herself can tell you. In my mind, it is ungrateful for any wizard to deliberately try to gain more magic than God chose to grant. But his Grace did not care to listen to my reasoning—in fact, he rebuked me for it and caustically suggested that I tender my ethical complaints to the Circle of Masters. I had no choice but to obey his orders if I wished to retain my place in his household. And though he trusted me above all others, he still had me watched after that; Connor—the man you knew as Lady Drianna's husband—was put under a compulsion to kill me if I failed to release the Sage on the prearranged date."

Recounting the tale had made him restless, and Tullis rose from the stool with the dull snap of tendons. "Once his power was freed, the Sage began to search for the seeds of power among the household staff. After Lady Drianna left, destroyed by what he told her, I went to him again. I implored him not to use this new ability—to refrain, as you had done. Drianna's fate was proof of the harm it could do. And again, he censured me. And now he thinks not only to seek the seeds, but to plant them where he will? No," Tullis said firmly, "that I cannot allow. I had already seen the idea of obtaining more power begin to corrupt his judgment ... now that he possesses it, the corruption grows steadily worse. I can no longer serve a man who twists God's plan as he does."

Athaya studied the man before her, deeply impressed by his convictions and the risks he took to stand by them. "When the Sage learns that you have released me, you will certainly lose the position you sought to keep before ... if not your life as well."

"Only if you fail to stop him. And I have faith that you can. But do not mistake my motives, my Lady," he added, lifting up a crooked finger. "My father's family descends from Dameronne himself, and I affirm the Lorngeld's natural right to rule. But in payment for that right we must strive to make wise use of God's gifts; not for senseless domination, but for just and fair government. The Sage, I fear, has forgotten that distinction in pursuit of his own fame. You, your Highness, have not."

"But I don't want to govern anyone—I've told that to anyone who would listen for the past two years."

"Perhaps you do not. But he who will be the wizard king—I no longer think it was meant to be his Grace, the Sage—would do better to follow your leadership than his. I see that clearly now."

He glanced to the window, judging the time from the pattern of the stars. "It is almost morning; I will be expected in the storehouse soon. Go," he said, without turning around. The single word held all the solemnity of a formal commission from king to vassal. "Return to Caithe and stop his coronation. You must not let the Sage become king."

Athaya stepped behind the wardrobe screen and hastily changed from Drianna's robe and shift into her own gray gown. The worst wrinkles had softened after two days of disuse, and after dragging a comb through her hair and tossing on a lightweight traveling cloak, she looked almost presentable.

She went to the steward's side and took his hand. "Come with me," she urged him. "I can use you to help train the new students. You risk too much by staying."

Although visibly grateful for the offer, Tullis nonetheless refused it with a squeeze of his hand. "No. This island has been my home for over sixty years; I have no wish to uproot myself now. Curious," he added with a wry grin. "Generations of expectant Sarians have awaited the day of our return to Caithe, and now that it has come I find that I would much rather stay behind. But should you defeat the Sage," he added, "I will be glad to continue as caretaker here and serve you as his successor."

Athaya folded her brows inward. "Successor?"

"You will be so, should you win the Challenge."

"The—?"

Somehow, she had always known it would come down to that—a duel to the death between them—but the reality of it struck her like a cold slap in the face. Suddenly, her immediate future took on an entirely new—and deadly—aspect. She felt as if someone had thrust a sword into her hand, shoved her before an experienced soldier, and told her to survive as best she could. She had studied battle magic, of course—Master Hedric had not set her upon this crusade unprepared for the worst—but conceptual knowledge of killing spells was far different than hard experience in using them. Granted, her own abilities had often surprised her in the past—her talent for seeing futures, her discovery of translocation, her unexpected ability to discern the seeds of power—but a duel to the death was not the time to rely on something as intangible as luck. Not when Caithe's future—and her own life—was the price of miscalculation.

"But I only want to stop him—to drive him out of Caithe. How can I Challenge him?" she went on, aware that her nerves were making her ramble. "He's more powerful than I am . . . never mind that he's done this several times before and knows what he's doing."

"His spells are potent, yes, but his mastery is not what it was."

Athaya threw up her hands with a muffled curse. "A swordsman can have the finest technique in the world, Tullis, but it won't matter a whit if somebody fires a cannon at him."

"It must matter, Princess. He will be defeated only by his death—you know that as well as I. And if he is defeated by your hand, then you become Sage after him. It is the law."

"But I don't want to be Sage," she replied, ignoring for the moment the very real possibility that she would not defeat him and that her objection would be moot.

"Once he is crowned king," Tullis explained, "Dameronne's prophecy will have been fulfilled; the role of Sage will pass into obsolescence. His Grace will feel no obligation to accept your Challenge. And it is only victory by formal Challenge that will make you the sanctioned leader of the Lorngeld who follow him; you will never gain their obedience without first gaining that title. After that . . . well, I suppose you could simply command them all to go back to Sare and never return."

It was a tempting notion, but one that she could not allow to seduce her. "All right. I'll grant that the Sage has lost some of his edge. But I'm no Sarian; I don't know the first thing about the rite of Challenge."

"There is nothing to know; there are no rules or restrictions within the arena. It is quite simply a battle to the death with your inborn spells your only weapons. But beware of the

Sage's mind-magic," he added gravely. "It has been the downfall of every wizard who has opposed him."

Athaya pressed her fingers to her temples, sensing a growing headache; she was being pushed headlong into a confrontation for which she was in no way prepared. "Yes, mind-magic," she repeated absently. "I saw what it did to my brother Nicolas."

"No, that was a spell of compulsion," Tullis corrected. "Mind-magic is somewhat different—a more fragile kind of magic, but far more insidious. Compulsion wills the victim to perform a specific task; mind-magic deludes him into believing a thing is true and then acting accordingly. His actions, however, are all of his own choosing . . . more or less."

Tullis rested his hands on her shoulders, bracing her against the truth. "The Sage will attempt to use your own thoughts against you. He will pluck out your deepest fears and fashion them into weapons and cripple that part of your mind that discerns truth from falsehood. In the same way a wizard might steal a drop of your life's essence to create a likeness of you, the Sage will steal slivers of your mind to create an illusion of your own making and discourage you from questioning what you see. In this way, the enemy ultimately defeats himself. Mind-magic is not easy," Tullis finished, "but his Grace has had much practice at it."

Athaya was grateful for the steward's warning, but found herself far more apprehensive about the Challenge than she had been before receiving it. Her life was littered with fears and regrets and unpleasant memories; the notion that the dark secrets of her heart might be ripped from their hiding place and brandished before her in all their ugliness was more fearful than a battle of shields and fire spells could ever be.

Still, she forced herself to remember that she knew something that the Sage, as yet, did not. A precious pouch of corbal crystals was still in Jaren's possession. Granted, she had only used the gems to work magic that one time, but at least she had a chance to take the Sage completely by surprise, much as Bressel had done. It wasn't much, but it was a branch of hope to cling to in the flood that threatened to sweep her away. Athaya kept her secret from Tullis, however; he had proved himself trustworthy, but she feared the Sage might force the knowledge from him if he were caught before the Challenge— which now seemed her only option—could take place.

"Just one more thing before you go." Tullis moved away

from her to retrieve a weathered leather satchel left near the door. "His Grace planned to come back for these later—and the rest of his treasures—once his conquest was complete. If you do not object ..." The steward's words trailed off as he glanced meaningfully to the fireplace.

Athaya drew out the collection of books and papers, and pensively paged through them. The satchel's miniature library contained all of Rhodri's precious notes—everything he had learned and written about the forbidden rite of assumption in his twenty-odd years of study. She perused a coolly disinterested summary of the rite that had granted King Kelwyn his power, a catalog of the spells he could cast afterward, and a list of remarks on how well he performed each one. And last, she found a hastily written record of her own unexpected gift; and finally, a note about Kelwyn's equally unexpected death.

Her hands trembled with rage as she tucked the items back into the satchel. God, it would be gratifying to toss the whole lot into the fire, reducing Rhodri's life's work to nothing more than smoke and ash. Gratifying, perhaps ... but not right. Abhorrent as the ideas were to her, who was she to erase them from the earth? It went against all of Hedric's teachings—Rhodri's knowledge itself was not evil, but only what he had chosen to do with it. And the easiest way to expose that evil for what it was lay in careful study and not in suppression.

"I can't, Tullis. I'm not sure I can make you understand, but ... I can't destroy these notes. There are unique ideas here that shouldn't be destroyed simply because I happen to dislike them. That's no better than absolution—killing all wizards on the chance that a few of them might become dangerous. Let me send these papers to the library at Wizard's College; they can serve as a reminder of the danger that comes from dabbling in things we ought not—and provide fodder for many a long discussion over ale, I'm sure."

Tullis acceded to her wishes with a polite but baffled nod, unable to reason his way through the peculiarities of Reykan thinking.

Athaya looped the satchel strap over her shoulder and prepared to go. "Thank you for freeing me," she said, already withdrawing into the relaxed state of mind needed for a smooth translocation. Though still brilliant with stars, she could detect fingertips of dawn probing at the eastern sky. "You may have just freed us all."

Tullis went down on one knee before her in an unexpected

gesture of homage. "It has been a honor to serve the lady of the prophecy," he said, placing his right hand lightly over his heart.

Athaya winced through a smile at the steward's choice of phrase. "Please don't call me that. It makes me feel as if I ought to work a miracle or two before I leave, just for effect."

"Save your miracles for Caithe," he replied, glancing upward. "You have worked many there, though I suspect you do not see them yet."

It sounded like something Master Hedric would have said to her, and it took conscious effort to keep tears at bay. Athaya helped the aging steward to his feet and embraced him fondly, hoping that she would survive the Rite of Challenge to see him again . . . and trying not to think what it meant for all the Lorngeld in her homeland if she did not.

CHAPTER 17

✳✳

ATHAYA'S FEET MET THE FLOOR OF HER ROOM AT THE Kaiburn camp just before dawn. In a heartbeat, the rhythmic roll of the sea and the pungent smell of salt were transformed into the gentle murmur of windswept leaves and the scent of earth still damp from recent rain. The forlorn wail of a seagull changed mid-cry to the knowing hoot of an owl. She was home.

The translocation spell, cast so soon after her release from the Sage's seal, made Athaya woozier than usual; she collapsed beside the snoring bundle on her pallet, weary and light-headed. She groped in the dark for Jaren and shook him gently, and the bundle shifted in response as she rolled against him and brushed her fingertips across the bearded chin . . .

Bearded?

Durek jerked awake with a strangled gasp like a child breaking free of a nightmare, and Athaya barely kept herself from tumbling off the pallet onto the floor. Her brother's profile was limned by pale moonlight. "What are you doing here?" she demanded; her astonishment turned the question into an accusation.

"It was the biggest room, so Jaren let me have it," Durek snapped back defensively, as startled to discover an intruder in his room as Athaya had been to find him there. When his sister's flustered expression did not fade, he added imperiously, "I *am* the king, you know."

Only after this exchange did Durek realize what her presence meant. He sat bolt upright and threw the blankets aside, all traces of drowsiness gone from his eyes. "Where have you . . . I mean, how did you—"

"The Sage was holding me in his fortress on Sare, but his steward let me go. Lucky for me, Tullis doesn't hold with all of his master's lofty ambitions." Athaya refrained from mentioning the extent of those ambitions; Durek had enough to worry himself over without knowing that the Sage's plot to mastermind a dynasty of Lorngeld was far more diabolical than Rhodri's petty scheming had ever been.

"Where's Jaren?"

Durek cocked his head toward the adjoining room and then guided her footsteps—still wobbly as a fawn's—to Jaren's bedside. She leaned over and kissed him fervently back to consciousness—as fervently as was possible in his Majesty's presence—but instead of snapping back to consciousness as Durek had, Jaren roused more slowly, drowsily savoring the means of his awakening. He opened his eyes languidly, suspecting it all a pleasantly vivid dream, then swiftly realized his error and snatched her up in a powerful embrace of relief at seeing her safely home again.

Nesting in the blankets beside him, Athaya told both he and Durek of the tedious days of her confinement and of Tullis's hand in her freedom. She postponed all mention of the Sage's plans to sow the seeds of power in those of his own choosing until she and Jaren were alone—it was the only sure way to avoid blurting out the secret of Mailen's gift in front of Durek—and told them instead of the Sage's other plans, almost as repulsive, at least from her own perspective.

"The Sage wants to marry me and raise a new generation of adepts," she announced, brows arched. If the situation had been less dire, she would have laughed aloud at how closely Jaren's display of righteous indignation rivaled that of an affronted Archbishop Lukin. "He isn't too concerned what you'd have to say about that," she told Jaren dryly. "In fact, he didn't much care what *I* had to say about it either." Athaya pinched her lips together in disgust. "He has little interest in anyone's opinions but his own."

Durek's nostrils flared in outrage. "Of all the impudent, conceited—"

"You have to admit," Athaya broke in, cutting off his tirade before it spiraled out of hand, "it's a convenient way for me to get a crown. Assuming I wanted one."

Durek closed his eyes, expelling his breath slowly. "You don't have to keep trying to convince me of that, Athaya," he replied. His voice sounded drained rather than angry. "Lord help me for saying this, but I believe you."

Athaya touched his hand in a silent show of thanks. "So," she went on, eager to stow the notion of marriage to the Sage in the dustiest corner of her mind. "What have I missed during my unforeseen 'holiday' on Sare?"

Jaren and Durek passed the tale back and forth like a pair of bards alternating verses as they told her of the occupation of Delfar Castle, of their foiled attempt to spirit Nicolas to freedom, and of the Sage's intention of crowning himself king at the end of the week.

"End of the—" Athaya let out a low whistle. "Not much time."

"And to make it worse, he's sent messengers to every shire with the declaration that if I don't come to defend my crown, then I give it up by forfeit. But how am I supposed to defend it?" Durek cried, shaking a fist in frustration at the seemingly winless situation he was mired in. "If I set foot in Delfarham I'm as good as dead, but if I don't, my subjects will think I've abandoned them to this Sarian tyrant."

"You have to go back and confront him," Athaya said. "For your subjects ... and for yourself. But you won't be going alone or unprotected."

She frowned deeply, realizing how little time they had to prepare for what would easily be the most perilous—and perhaps the last—day of their lives. "Five days. Damn, I was hoping to get more practice with my corbals than that. You do still have them, don't you, Jaren?"

He pointed to a bundle in the corner, just beside his boots. "Good," she said with a nod. "Maybe I'll get a chance to use them in the Challenge."

Durek gazed at her blankly; she doubted he understood the full significance of her words as yet. But Jaren clearly did, and his face went pale as the moonlight streaming through the window. "The *what*? You're going to play by *his* rules?"

"What choice do I have? Like it or not, Jaren, it's the only game in town." She explained to them both what Tullis had ultimately proven to her: that only death would stop the Sage, and that death by Challenge was the only defeat his people would recognize, the outcome of such a contest being long-accepted by Sarian wizards as proof of the will of God.

"But you would become Sage if you win!" Durek blurted out, no less appalled at the prospect than Athaya herself.

"Better than being dead if I don't."

Jaren saw the logic in her reasoning but was in no way happy with it. "You're forgetting the possibility that *he* might win, Athaya. The Sage's magic is stronger than yours right now—you've admitted that yourself. And if I recall correctly, the loser of this contest doesn't walk away."

"No, Jaren," she replied solemnly. "I haven't forgotten. I'm just trying not to think about it much."

"Barbaric custom if you ask me," Durek grumbled under his breath. But behind the easy facade of disdain, Athaya detected a glimmer of respect in her brother's eyes—not begrudged this time—and his muted astonishment that despite all the bitterness between them in years past, she would freely enter into a duel to the death as his champion.

"Are you sure this is the only way?" Once, Durek would have rejoiced in the knowledge that she might soon be out of his life forever; now the notion clearly disturbed him.

Of course, the notion that he'd probably die within an hour after I did might have something to do with his distress.

"Until Brandegarth is crowned king, he is still the Sage of Sare. If someone Challenges him for that position, he is honor-bound to accept. Yes, I know," she murmured, seeing Durek roll his eyes at the word 'honor' being applied to the Sage in any context whatsoever. "But it has been over a year since his last Challenge—by his own laws he cannot refuse me. Master Hedric confirmed that much himself; it was in the documents he brought from the College archives."

The mention of the Master's name brought strained silence to the room. Jaren grasped her shoulders. "Athaya—"

"I know," she whispered in reply, feeling the pain afresh in the hollow of her heart. "I saw him, right before . . ." She shook her head, loath to say the words. "He said to ask you how it happened. Something about a charm . . . ?"

Jaren made his story brief, but Athaya could read the lingering grief in his eyes. He had known Master Hedric far longer than she and would doubtless feel the loss even more acutely—and with the added pain, Athaya realized, of knowing that the Master had given his life in payment for Jaren and Durek's freedom.

"No wonder the Sage was so shaken when he came for me," Athaya said when he was done, vividly recalling Brandegarth's powerful yet trembling hands. "He'd just had the scare of his life."

"If Master Hedric put the fear of God into him, then you can, too," Jaren told her. "You may not have any Circle charms, but you *do* have a pouch of corbal crystals. And the Sage only knows how to resist them, not use them."

"I'm not convinced I know how to use them, either," she observed. "I've only done it once. But Master Hedric died to keep my secret, and I'll do my best to see that his sacrifice wasn't made in vain."

Athaya turned to Durek with newfound resolve burning in her eyes. "The Sage dares you to come and claim your crown. Very well, then—you shall oblige him." She envisioned the stark astonishment that would surely grace the Sage's face, and the edges of her mouth curled up in spiteful satisfaction. "After that, leave the rest to me. I will submit a formal Challenge. If I win, then I will become the rightful Sage, and my first official act will be to disband the Sarian cult. And if I lose . . ."

She cast her eyes toward the pine trees swaying gently outside the window, reflecting on the possibility that she might not see them again. "Then may God help you all, for I won't be around to do it any longer."

The three of them left the next morning for Delfarham, charting a route that would keep them far from the main roads and away from the Sage's watchful allies. To conserve Athaya's strength for the Challenge to come—and to avoid popping into view before an unforeseen enemy—they opted to walk much of the way, hiring horses when they could, rather than traveling by translocation.

Along with a small satchel of food, two canvas tents, and a few silver coins, Athaya took with her the good wishes and prayers of everyone in camp, including Tonia, Gilda, and Girard—the latter among the handful who had survived the debacle in Delfarham. Girard was unable to believe that the three of them were going back to the capital of their own free will after all the trouble he professed to have in getting out.

"Give him hell, your Highness," he murmured, offering her a chaste kiss on the cheek. Athaya couldn't stop a chuckle from bubbling to the surface at the look of mild consternation with which Durek regarded the man's simply worded sentiment.

"We'll be praying for you," Gilda added, valiantly trying to keep her lower lip from trembling. "All of you."

Tonia pushed a well-stuffed basket of bread and muffins into Athaya's arms. "Hedric would be proud." She turned aside with a sniffle, muttering a feeble complaint that a mote of dust had lodged in her eye.

Athaya plucked out a still-warm corn muffin and bit into it. "He'll be prouder of me if I win."

Dozens of hands waved farewell from the dormitory windows as Athaya walked slowly out of the clearing, following the red glow of the rune trail through the Forest of Else for what she sincerely hoped was not the last time.

By that evening, however, the relatively optimistic spirit in which she had left the forest camp had badly dissipated.

After pitching their tents for the night and securing the tiny encampment with wards, Athaya promptly went to work with her collection of corbals; she hoped to channel a simple spell at first and work up to increasingly more difficult ones on each successive night until their arrival in Delfarham. At Jaren's instruction, Durek stood watch over her, prepared to break her concentration should she become irrevocably snared by the corbal's power and incapable of stanching the flow of her magic. In the meantime, Jaren distanced himself from the painful disturbances of the corbals and set off to catch some trout for their evening meal.

But despite these careful preparations, when Athaya drew a crystal from its pouch and held it before the campfire, she found that she could not attain the needed focus to tune herself to the crystal, to shift her perceptions into alignment with the gem so as to perceive its secret paths—the necessary preamble to sending her power hurtling through them. As she attempted to reach the corbal's source by countering its voice with her own, all she heard was the din of her inner thoughts—not the disciplined recitation she needed, but a perpetual and disjointed babble of anxiety about the outcome of the Challenge and the future of Caithe. In the end, it was all she could do to keep the crystal's heated blades of pain at bay, and after a third botched attempt at reaching the sanctuary of the crystal's heart, she failed at even that.

"I can't do it!" she cried, angrily thrusting the gem back inside its pouch. "Damn it all, I just *can't*!" Her temples were already throbbing badly, a condition only worsened by the shrill, keening sound that lanced through her ears.

"You're flustered, Athaya," Durek told her, dutifully offering the words that Jaren had instructed him to say if the need arose. "You just need to relax. If you don't, you'll never be able to do it."

"How can I possibly relax when I'm terrified I'll never be able to do it again?" she shot back. "And I have to, Durek—channeling magic through these crystals is the only real chance I have of getting out of this Challenge alive!"

And so it went for the next four nights. Each failure made her more agitated, and the more agitated she became, the more complete was each failure.

On the last day of their journey before reaching the capital, Durek went out of his way to be kind to her, acutely aware of how badly the pressure was fraying both her nerves and her spirit. It was a glorious summer day in early August, and as they strolled through the rolling hills east of Delfarham, the gentle breezes and featherlike clouds, combined with his Majesty's surprising dose of good-naturedness, helped to ease Athaya's misery a bit.

"Remember when we all went to Nadiera the first summer after Father and Dagara were married?" he remarked. He picked a stalk of wild grass and began to shred it absently. "It was a day much like this. You and Nicolas spent hours lying in the grass fancying that the clouds looked like dragons or lions or whatnot . . . I thought you were both being ridiculous."

"I was only six," Athaya reminded him, "and Nicolas not quite eight."

"I know. But I was fourteen, and young men of fourteen do *not* go about seeing dragons in the clouds." Lifting his face to the sky, Durek lazily watched the clouds drift by overhead as if trying to make up for his past omission by imagining what the cottony shapes resembled most.

"Then you wanted to bring home a litter of kittens you'd found in the barn," he went on, shifting his gaze back to the ground beneath his feet. "You cried for hours when Dagara said no. Funny," he added archly, "how she found a pair of mice in her bed that same night."

Athaya grinned broadly at the long-forgotten incident; at the tender age of six, she'd considered it a stroke of tactical genius. "If she'd let me have the kittens, they would have found the mice first."

Durek glanced at her sidelong. "Yes, you probably would have put them there regardless, wouldn't you?" The trace of a smile betrayed his approval of the prank—and perhaps a belated wish that he had thought of it first.

They spent their last night camped in a copse of pines a few miles west of the abbey of Evarshot. Although Durek trusted that the good monks would offer them a roof for the night, Athaya and Jaren advised against it; for all any of them knew, the Sage's men had already visited the abbey to wreak vengeance and absolve the clergy of Caithe for their myriad crimes against wizardry. Still, Athaya would have liked to see the place again, if only to marvel at how completely her life had been transformed since her last visit, when her seed of power was only beginning to bloom and Jaren was no more to her than a suspicious Reykan wizard sent to fetch her to Ath Luaine for what she and Tyler Graylen both assumed were quite sinister purposes.

Durek's wistful excursions into the past gave her a brighter frame of mind for her last session with her crystals, and Athaya set about her nightly task far less rattled than she had been since leaving Kaiburn. Jaren left her as he did each evening, but this time Athaya sensed that he did so with great reluctance. He had done his best to hide the depth of his concern these last five days, knowing it would only add to the intense pressures already upon her, but Athaya knew—as did they all—that if he returned to find that she had failed yet again, then it was all too likely that tomorrow's Challenge would not provide the triumph they were hoping for, and that the Sage would find himself king of Caithe when the moon rose once again.

"I'll do better tonight," she called to him, as he passed beyond the golden circle of the campfire and into the starry darkness.

"I know you will," he replied over his shoulder, but Athaya did not overlook the quiet urgency in his tone that rendered the words as much a desperate prayer as a vote of confidence.

Durek spread out a tattered brown blanket near the fire, and she settled cross-legged onto it and began to breathe deeply. The night was still and serene, and here, miles from the nearest village, the turmoil in Delfarham seemed unreal—as distant as that long-age summer afternoon when she and Nicolas had watched the clouds sail over Nadiera.

When the worst of the day's tensions had receded and her

mind was free of distractions, Athaya reached into the leather pouch and drew out a small corbal crystal, cupping it gingerly in her palm. She refused to listen to the gem's messages of pain, instead sending out her own stream of defiances as she focused on its center—the source of the corbal's voice. She examined the crystal's sharply angled facets, spied its inner flaws, and admired its subtle shades of indigo, reaching out to it as she would to another wizard, touching its mind—more certain than ever that it indeed possessed one—in search of its most hidden secrets.

The fragrant pines around her, the bright campfire, and even Durek's silent presence all melted into shadow; she knew only the crystal—all else was irrelevant. Then, some time later, she touched upon the corbal's heart and her perception shifted just *so*; as if a veil had been lifted from her eyes, she passed beyond the pain and beheld within the gem its glittering paths of power—not simple facets in a purple stone, but an array of channels through which her magic could be cast.

With the crystal cupped in one hand, she willed a simple witchlight to appear in the other. The globe came to life in an instant and blinding flash. Athaya had forgotten how drastically the crystal augmented a wizard's power, and instead of a palm-sized lamp, she found herself bearing a fiery red orb nearly ten times that size. It was magnificent, burning with rare intensity as it drew power out of her to feed itself. The corbal crystal gave off a pearly white glow in her left hand, but its gentle, starry radiance was all but engulfed by the vibrant swell of reddish fire in her right.

"Athaya, that's long enough," she heard a man's voice say from somewhere very far away, but the swollen witchlight was far too mesmerizing to pay the voice any mind. She felt her limbs begin to tingle with exhaustion, but could not bear to disperse her spell just yet—could not bear to still the enthralling rush of power gushing through her veins and spurting through the corbal's facets, making the witchlight ten times as strong and giving her the powers of the angels . . .

"*Athaya!*"

The voice was more distant now, receding into the distance like sunset. Then, abrupt as a slap in the face, the crystal was wrested from her hand; the heady flow of power was squelched, her communion with the crystal severed. Her trance shattered like fine glass and the witchlight likewise blew apart in a dazzling explosion of orange, its fragments showering down around her feet like a thousand falling stars. The sparks bobbed on the earth for a time like beads of grease on a hot griddle until eventually they burned out one by one with gentle hissing sounds, leaving only the steady glow of the campfire behind.

The pounding inside her skull started almost immediately, blurring her vision with the pain. It took only a quick glance to Durek—who had stuffed the crystal safely back inside the pouch—to tell her what had happened. Athaya slouched down with her face tucked between her palms, exhausted, sore, and hopelessly discouraged.

"What's the matter?" Durek asked her, genuinely puzzled. "It was rough going towards the end, but you did it. You sent your magic through the crystal."

"Yes . . . but only after concentrating a great deal more than the Sage will ever give me time to do in a formal Challenge," she pointed out. "And I couldn't control the spell once I cast it. The coils of fire I used against Lukin's hired assassin were one thing . . . that's a difficult spell, so I'm not surprised that I had trouble controlling them under a corbal's influence—especially that of three corbals at once. But a *witchlight*? Durek, it's one of the simplest spells there is and I still couldn't control it. The corbal's influence is just too strong. It's like being swept away in a river . . . you can dive in easily enough, but the river has more power in the end; it takes you along whether you want to continue or not. An exhilarating ride," she finished wryly, "until you eventually get tired and drown."

Durek frowned worriedly at her. "What are you saying?"

"I'm saying that if I don't use this talent, the Sage will likely kill me, but if I do, I'll most certainly kill myself. How's that for a mixed blessing?" Mouthing a curse, she picked up a stone and hurled it deep into the moonlit woods. "And they say God doesn't have a sense of humor."

"Don't give up yet," Durek said, leaning in closer to her. "You only tried it the one time; you can master it. All you need is some more practice . . . and maybe a little confidence."

Athaya glowered at him bitterly. "Now I know you're getting desperate—that was the first time in living memory that you've ever encouraged me to have confidence in myself." She picked up another stone, but balked before throwing it. "I didn't mean that. It's just . . . I've got a beastly headache and I'm—" She threw up her hands; why bother to hide what both of them already knew? "Frankly, I'm scared to death. Everyone is depending on me and now my secret weapon is proving to be worthless."

"But you almost got it," he persisted.

" 'Almost' isn't going to win the Challenge, Durek." She sighed heavily as she sought the counsel of the stars twinkling serenely overhead. "I hate to say this, but maybe my luck is finally starting to run out. After surviving my *mekahn*, six months of exile, arrest, imprisonment, and a heresy trial, maybe I've used it all up."

Durek didn't answer right away, as if afraid she had just brought up a very valid point. Neither of them bothered to observe that Caithe's king had been the cause of all those trials but one. When he next spoke, Durek's voice was barely above a whisper. "You can win, can't you . . . I mean, even without the crystals?"

A strained silence fell over the encampment, broken only by the tranquil crackling of the campfire.

"I don't know, Durek. Honestly, I just don't know." She tossed a twig into the fire and watched the flames devour it hungrily, like corbals feeding on a wizard's power. "Just for argument's sake, let's assume that by some miracle, I did figure out how to channel my spells through a corbal—and learn to stop them—by noon tomorrow. I could take the Sage by surprise, but unless I got in a killing blow right away, who's to say he won't figure out what I'm doing and pick up the technique as quickly as I did? And if he channels *his* power though the corbals, enhanced as it's been by the seal, then I don't have a chance in heaven of beating him. Granted, he'd end up dead if he couldn't manage to break free of the crystal's grip, but that doesn't make me feel a whole lot better since I'd already be dead myself by then."

A chill breeze swirled about them, making her shiver, and Durek unclasped his cloak and handed it to her. She settled it over her shoulders with a silent nod of thanks at the unexpected gallantry. "If anything good has come out of this whole mess," she observed, offering him a beleaguered half smile, "I suppose it's that the two of us have finally learned how to have a conversation that didn't turn into a fight."

Durek met her gaze for a moment, then awkwardly looked away. He squinted into the woods, clearly hoping Jaren would choose that moment to emerge from them and eliminate the need for him to reply, then turned back to face her when he realized that no such salvation was imminent.

"We never have liked each other much, have we?"

Under any other circumstances, Athaya would have laughed aloud at this exquisite measure of understatement. As it was, she merely shrugged and pulled the thin cloak tighter around her shoulders. "No, I don't think we have. But I've never hated you, Durek," she hastened to add, feeling an urgent need that the words be said—now, while there was still time. "I've thought you were a pigheaded ass about some things," she confessed, "but I've never hated you."

To her surprise, Durek simply cracked an absent smile and nodded. "Hedric told me that once. Strange how I believed him without even questioning it."

"He had that effect on people." Then, emboldened by his show of trust, Athaya reached out and clasped her brother's hand. He regarded her curiously, old impulses quick to suspect her motives, but he did not pull away. "We're just too different, you and I," she said through a sigh. "Or maybe we're too much alike. Stubborn and temperamental, neither one wanting to back down from a fight. It's a wonder Nicolas can stand either one of us." With her free hand, she picked up a twig and prodded the dwindling campfire to stir it back to life. "He's never going to believe any of this when he recovers, you know. He can sense something's not right between us—or rather that something *is*. I think he'd be confused by this alliance even if he didn't have the Sage's spell cluttering up his brain."

"No doubt," Durek said. "It confuses me enough as it is." He stamped out a wandering ember with his boot. "Nicholas' part in all this surprised me, that I will admit. His willingness to risk everything to join you . . ." Durek shook his head in profound disbelief. "I never dreamed he had that kind of mettle."

"We all have it, I think," she told him quietly. "If we let it out. Most people never do."

In the silence that followed, Athaya could sense Durek grasping for words, mentally framing them, judging them, and casting them aside. He had never been a man given to intimate conversation, but Athaya could see him attempting it now, struggling to express things left unsaid for too long.

"I've learned from you," he said at last, shifting nervously as he spoke. He drew his hand away, as if physical contact made his words that much more difficult to say. "Things I probably should have learned from Father but never did. For one, you don't just lead people by ordering them about—you inspire them . . . and then they follow on their own."

It was the finest compliment he had ever given her—not that there were a great many to choose from, but she cherished it nonetheless. "You're doing better than you think, Durek. I won't sing praises for everything you've done, God knows, but you had the courage to approach my people and ask for help without offering up a host of hollow promises you never intended to keep. Caithe has had more than enough kings who would sooner die—and take the rest of us down with them—than suffer such a perceived blow to their precious pride. Faltil was certainly one of them."

"It was hard; I'll admit it. You were—and still are—asking me to turn my whole world upside-down, to accept things I've always believed are wrong—and still do, to an extent. I don't know if I can change that," he confessed, turning his palms upward, "or even if I should." He turned his face to the sky, asking a boon of the stars. "I just want Caithe to be at peace—total peace, without wizards going about doing unexpected and inexplicable things all the time."

Athaya smiled wryly at him. "You want your world to be controlled and predictable . . . but life just isn't like that. It's messy—"

"I know! But magic just makes it worse."

"The weather is unpredictable, too," Athaya observed, "but do you plot to get rid of it because you can't live without knowing whether the morrow will bring sun or rain? No. You take what you get. What else can you do?"

Durek glanced to her dubiously, but did not protest her reasoning. "At least you're questioning your beliefs instead of blindly accepting what someone else taught you to think," she went on. "That's not an easy thing to do. It certainly wasn't easy for me. I wasn't sure I believed in the sanctity of magic myself until Tyler managed to convince me of it. He said that magic couldn't possibly be evil if it was a part of me. And he was right. It wasn't my choice. It's just what I was."

Durek stiffened as she spoke, awaiting a bitter diatribe on the subject of Captain Graylen's fate; his muscles relaxed when he realized he wasn't going to get one. "I thought I was doing the right thing at the time, Athaya. Now I'm . . . not so sure. I'm not sure about anything anymore. But you are . . ."

He lanced her to the soul with a penetrating stare. "You really believe in this crusade of yours, don't you? It's not just some rebellious game you've been playing simply to annoy me?" The words came out with a gruff edge, but behind the facade Athaya could discern her brother's genuine desire to *know*.

"I've never believed in much of anything, Durek—you know that. But my work ... it's my whole life. Haven't you ever wanted anything so passionately that it didn't matter what stood in your way?"

Durek took a long time to answer—long enough for Athaya to realize that he was truly struggling with the question. "Not many things stand in the way of what a king wants," he said at last. "But I never bothered to think about what I wanted for myself. Why should I? It was all decided before I was ever born; the king's eldest son doesn't get those sorts of choices. You're fortunate in that, even if you don't realize it. Whether or not I happen to agree with them, at least you've been able to make your own choices in life."

"Have I?" she replied with a mild arch to her brows, slow to believe that she had heard such words from the mouth of her ever-dutiful brother. "I was informed over supper one night that I was to marry Felgin of Reyka. I don't recall Father ever asking my opinion about it. The only reason the marriage never took place is that my magic came to me—and I didn't have much choice about that, either. So you see, Durek? We've both been fitted into our respective slots quite snugly, without either of us having much to say in the matter."

Athaya continued to poke absently at the fire while Durek stared intently into it, as if seeing visions of the past amid the dancing tongues of flame. "I knew what my future would be from the time I was old enough to speak—and I accepted it willingly enough. But somehow ... I always thought it would be easier; Father made it all look so effortless. It's hard when everyone is looking to you, expecting you to have all the answers and never make mistakes."

"I know how you feel. Especially now. Everyone is counting on me to defeat the Sage, but they don't realize how badly the odds are stacked against me. I've never been that diligent about practicing my battle magic; it was always more important to me to teach other wizards the spells they needed to survive—not to perfect my own. The Sage has been casting mind-magic and killing spells for over twenty years. Me? I'm working on theory I read in books. I've never deliberately tried to kill anyone with my magic," she said, wondering if Durek could possibly believe her after what had happened to Kelwyn. "It goes against everything I was taught. I'm not sure I can do it."

She could not tell if Durek's silence stemmed from a diligent effort to understand or a judicious attempt to keep his skepticism to himself. In the days since their alliance was forged, only one thing remained unsaid between them; one thing she desperately wished to hear and as yet had not.

Please, Durek . . . tell me you forgive me for what happened to Father. Tell me you understand.

She did not want to spoil the rare moment of closeness by asking it outright; if Durek forgave her, he would have to tell her so unprompted. And if he did not . . . then she didn't want to hear it.

"I know I have a chance, Durek," she said, after a moment of waiting for words that never came. "I just wish the odds were better."

Behind them, Jaren's footsteps crackled on dry pinecones, announcing his return to camp. He knew without asking that her spellwork had not been a complete success, but he said nothing, aware that even the most well-chosen words would only make her feel worse. Still, Athaya told him about her witchlight—and Durek's intervention—as she tossed the last of the twigs into the fire.

Bidding her brother a melancholy good-night, Athaya took Jaren's hand and walked silently to their tent. As he drew back the flap for her to enter, Jaren glanced back at Durek's hunched silhouette against the campfire.

"You made peace with him."

Athaya nodded slowly. "Shriven on the eve of battle, more or less. But yes," she said, only belatedly realizing what a rare and remarkable conversation she and her brother had just shared, "I think we healed a lot of old wounds tonight. Most of them, anyway," she amended, regretting that he had said nothing of Kelwyn. "I only hope it's part of a new beginning for us and not . . ." She forced down a swallow; her throat had suddenly gone dry. "Not an epilogue."

Her eyes met Jaren's with a palpable spark like flint on steel, and there, in the privacy of their tent, during the last fragile hours of peace before morning, the unspoken fears that had for days been gathering like stormclouds clashed in the air between them, shattering any vestige of composure either had managed to sustain. The ferocity with which they clung to one another, tumbling down onto the blankets with desperate passion, betrayed what neither dared to say aloud—that were she to lose the Challenge, this night would be their epilogue as well.

"I'm so afraid," Athaya said, each word coming out in a sickly, ragged gasp. She didn't loosen her embrace for even an instant, drinking in the scent of earth and pine and woodsmoke clinging to his skin as if it were the headiest of wines. "I know I'm supposed to be brave, but I'm so terribly, desperately afraid. And worst of all is knowing that the Sage isn't afraid of anything—except maybe God, and I'm not so sure he fears even *Him* anymore." She choked back an angry sob. "How am I supposed to defeat someone like that?"

"I know," Jaren murmured, stroking her hair as he whispered kisses into it. "I know how frightened you are. Just remember what Master Hedric always told you; try to have as much faith in yourself as the rest of us have in you. If you can do that, then no one will be able to stop you—not even the Sage."

"But what if I lose?" she cried out, yearning to hear his promises that everything would be all right, that her victory was assured even though she knew full well that it was not. "What will happen to you? To all of you?"

It was a prospect that Jaren clearly did not wish to dwell upon, but he would be foolish to deny the possibility and knew Athaya was entitled to an answer. "We'll keep trying," he said after a time, drawing back to gaze deep into her eyes. "We'll keep fighting for what we believe in, just like you did after Kelwyn and Tyler died. We'll keep fighting for what's right so that your sacrifice would always be remembered."

A breath of tension went out of her limbs. At least the work would go on; at least someone would raise the fallen banner from the battlefield and deny the Sage full victory.

Athaya burrowed impossibly close to him, wishing she could hide in the shelter of his arms forever. "Our journal," she said, barely above a strained whisper. "If something happens to me . . . take care of it. Finish it. Write the last chapter."

"There won't *be* a last chapter," he told her, forcing a semblance of certainty into his voice. "There can't be . . . not yet. Not for years to come . . ."

Then she slid easily beneath him, drowning her fears in a

sea of bliss and blinding her senses to everything but the tattered canvas above her, the coarse blanket against her back, and the sweat-soaked heat of Jaren's body against hers, torturing her with the ecstasy of what she might never have again.

CHAPTER 18

ATHAYA WAS HAUNTED BY AN EERIE SENSE OF FAMILIARITY as she slipped into Saint Adriel's Cathedral under the guise of a cloaking spell and waited for the Sage's coronation to begin. She tucked herself behind the mundane shelter of a tapestry in the chapel of some long-dead king, banishing the cloaking spell to conserve every last drop of power for the contest to come. Unlike the day of Kelwyn's funeral, however, Athaya passed the tedious hours alone; Jaren remained at Durek's side to keep him safely out of sight until the prearranged time for his arrival.

It had been hard to part from them, she thought as she leaned back against the cool stone wall, arms hugging her chest. Harder than she ever expected it to be. Although their mouths offered her comforting assurances of triumph, it was all to easy to read the unspoken anguish behind the joint facade. *We haven't had enough time,* Jaren's gaze told her. *I want to have children and grow old with you; I want to watch our children's children's eyes go round when we tell them what you did today.* And in Durek's eyes, more of the profound confusion that had graced them so often of late; he studied her as if only just noticing the similarities in her features that linked her, by blood, to him. *I've trusted you precious little in the past, little sister, but today I must trust my entire future to you . . . and the futures of us all.* He had even kissed her cheek before departing, though the act was quickly done as if he feared someone might catch him at it.

Now, only minutes before the coronation was scheduled to begin, Durek's trust—both as brother and as king—weighed heavy upon her shoulders. It was a burden she hoped she could bear; a commission she prayed she could fulfill.

Had she not known it for Delfarham, Athaya would have guessed herself in a Reykan city when she, Jaren, and Durek passed through the east gate earlier that morning. It was not the crowded streets and mood of boisterous celebration that struck her—though such merriment was rarely seen during the dark days of the Tribunal—but the wildly abundant displays of magic everywhere she turned, like a riot of roses bursting forth in joyous unison after a long and bitter winter. Lively music poured from otherwise-empty jugs placed at each streetcorner, autumn-colored witchlights dispersed every scrap of shade and shadow in the city, and dozens of loyal Sarians clad in their most extravagant attire spaced themselves along the main thoroughfare joining castle to cathedral, together sustaining the illusion that the cobbled streets upon which the Sage would walk were paved with solid gold. This was the Sarians' prophesied day of triumph, Athaya realized as she passed inconspicuously among the revelers, and they had two centuries' worth of celebrating to do.

As if proof that God's blessings were upon the Sage at his crowning, the day was all an August morning should be. A gentle breeze swept in from the Sea of Wedane to clear off the haze and keep the populace cool, and the sky was crystal blue but for a handful of clouds artfully arranged to provide the Sage the ideal background for the procession to come. From her hiding place in the chapel, Athaya would miss the Sage's triumphant approach to the cathedral, but she knew it would only sicken her to behold such a spectacle. She could picture it all quite vividly in her mind—the Sage and his closest adherents astride Durek's finest horses, his Grace clad in costly robes and jewels of state that only her brother had the right to wear, all of them like children playing with their parents' treasures as if they were but toys, lacking any appreciation for their value or significance.

Athaya had never witnessed a coronation—she was in exile at the time of Durek's crowning and was not yet born when her father became king—but knew the general order of the liturgy. After walking down the center aisle, the would-be king was ritually halted at an ornamental gate before the choir screen and asked to prove his claim upon the crown. When the Archbishop of Delfarham accepted the claim and formally declared the candidate to be the true heir—a thing never known *not* to occur in all of Caithe's history, despite the inevitable suspense of the moment—the soon-to-be king was escorted through the choir to the high altar; there he would make his solemn vows to both his God and subjects, after which he was anointed and crowned. Peeking out from behind the chapel tapestry, Athaya could glimpse the ancient wooden throne placed in front of the altar to await its new occupant, and on the altar itself, amid the gleaming plates, chalices, and candlesticks set upon a white cloth shot with gold, was a large box draped in crimson silk—the Caithan crown of state.

Few of the faces in the expectant congregation were familiar to her; with rare exceptions, attendance was restricted to those long of the Sage's following and the higher-ranking of Caithe's citizenry who had recently sworn—with varying degrees of zeal, Athaya was sure—their oaths of fealty. Much to her visible displeasure, Drianna sat in a box near the front, neatly pinned between a pair of black-liveried Sarian guardsmen. Athaya did not doubt that the poor girl's presence was forced upon her by the Sage, if for no other reason than to pointedly remind her that she had joined the wrong side of the Caithan conflict.

Then, shifting her gaze, Athaya's heart blazed with rage as she caught sight of Nicolas seated in the same box, likewise well-guarded and looking pitifully lonely and confused. Without Master Hedric's painstaking care, Nicolas had lapsed back into illness; he fidgeted like an anxious child, absently picking at the pearls embedded in the sleeves of his stiff, formal garments. *The Sage exploits his captive well,* Athaya thought bitterly; Nicolas' presence at this ceremony would be construed as condoning his brother's usurpation, allowing the Sage's grip on Caithe to tighten ever further. And to those who still believed that Nicolas attempted to murder the king at Athaya's behest this past winter, his presence here would only set them more firmly in their opinions.

The piercing flurry of trumpets from the gallery, each gleaming horn draped in silken banners of white and gold, broke Athaya out of her reverie with a start. In dutiful response to the clarion call, the great double doors opened at the west end of the nave, admitting a golden slant of brilliant noon sunlight. The bells that had been joyously chiming since dawn fell silent.

Athaya wetted her lips. Her hand went to the pouch of corbal crystals at her belt, assuring herself they were still there. It wouldn't be long now.

The procession was striking in its simplicity. Instead of being preceded by an endless stream of priests chanting solemn hymns of duty and stewardship, the Sage walked unescorted down the lengthy aisle, the air above him lightly graced by jubilant strains of organ music. Despite the formality of the occasion, scattered applause broke out among the assembly the instant the Sage's shadow crossed the threshold of the nave; as he passed by them, many among the congregation conjured witchlights in their palms and raised them aloft in glittering tribute.

"Dameronne's prophecy is fulfilled!" one woman cried, tossing a rose on the carpet for the Sage to tread upon. "Long live Brandegarth, the wizard king!"

Athaya hated to admit it, but the Sage of Sare was breathtaking to behold. Every inch of him was clad in snowy white silk, from mantle and tunic to hose and boots. His rich expanse of black hair was expertly combed over his shoulders, and he dazzled the congregation with each step as golden earrings, rings, necklaces, and buckles exchanged the colored reflections of the sun streaming through the stained-glass windows. Not even on his wedding day had Durek looked so splendid—he lacked the Sage's imposing stature and innate aplomb that turned majesty into divinity. No, not since the day of Kelwyn's own coronation, the glory of which Athaya had only heard tales about, had Saint Adriel's been graced with such spectacle.

The approving noises of the crowd quieted as the Sage reached the ornamental gate where Archbishop Lukin awaited him, quietly aglitter in his most formal ecclesiastical vestments. Lukin seemed unperturbed at his role in the day's drama, though he scanned the assembly intently from time to time during the processional, as if expecting someone who had not yet arrived. Behind him, just beyond the gate, marble statues of the saints lined the choir screen like a jury, silently assessing the merit of the white-clad aspirant now standing before them.

Archbishop Lukin lowered his crozier across the aisle, ritually barring the Sage's path. "Who comes into this hallowed place to claim the crown of Caithe and serve as her rightful king?"

"I do," Brandegarth replied, his voice ringing out like a great bronze bell to echo in the vaulted ceiling above them. Again, scattered applause broke the hush. The Sage's lips curled up in pleasure at this unprompted show of praise.

"By what right do you claim this title?"

"By right of the gifts God has bestowed upon me, making me most high among His people."

It was not the liturgy's traditional response—"by right of blood succession"—but Lukin balked only slightly before lifting the crozier. "Then approach God's altar," he intoned, "where you shall be anointed and crowned in accordance with your right." She wasn't sure, but Athaya thought she sensed a hint of malice lacing Lukin's words.

The archbishop opened the ornamental gate leading through the choir, but just before the Sage stepped through the delicate swirls of brass, a rustle of rapidly exchanged whispers moved through the crowd like a gust of wind through a wheatfield. One by one, the witchlights of homage winked out.

"I'm afraid I'll have to object."

The Sage whirled around in a blur of white silk to see Durek poised in the center of the aisle at the rear of the nave, with Jaren standing watchfully beside him. Durek was modestly garbed in a tunic and cap of Trelane crimson edged with gold—an intentional choice of colors made even more effective by his understated elegance in the face of the Sage's opulent display. Durek faced his enemy with cool composure, looking as much a king, Athaya thought, as she had ever seen him.

"Your Majesty!" Lukin exclaimed, as astonished as he would have been if God Himself had deigned to attend the day's festivities. The crozier slid from his nerveless grip and clattered against the brass gate before striking the floor.

Durek flatly ignored his recalcitrant bishop, outraged that the once-loyal prelate had sold his soul to the Sage by agreeing to preside over this travesty. Instead, he stared unflinchingly into the Sage's sea-green eyes, as if facing a boar in the wood and daring it to charge. "You bade me come and claim my crown, thinking I would lack the courage to do so. Yet here I am. I am Caithe's rightful sovereign, Brandegarth of Crewe," he declared, his voice steady and sure in spite of the dread

Athaya knew he felt inside. "You are not, no matter what you may think God has told you."

Although the sanctuary was uncannily still, Athaya could sense the intense emotions roiling just beneath the surface. Those forced into the Sage's service were elated at Durek's bold appearance, while those long of his following shook their heads and mutely ridiculed Durek's foolishness at walking so blindly to his own death.

The Sage was likewise amused, though Athaya detected a healthy dose of displeasure simmering beneath it. "And how do you propose to stop me?" he asked, in a placating manner that Durek was not meant to overlook.

"You have a custom on Sare called Challenge, do you not?" Durek replied, striding up the aisle in a well-crafted show of confidence. "A contest, I am told, in which it is determined to whom God has granted a larger measure of His grace."

"That is our law," the Sage agreed cautiously, wondering where Durek was leading him.

"As I understand it, should some other wizard prove to be your superior, then he proves worthy to succeed you as Sage and, as you apparently believe," he added, gesturing toward the high altar, "to inherit Caithe's crown."

The Sage inclined his head just enough so that a ray of sunlight glinted from one earring. "That is so. But you are no wizard. You have none of His grace at all." His tone rendered the words more an insult than a mere observation.

"No. But surely I could name a champion; someone to Challenge you on my behalf."

The Sage glanced idly over Durek's shoulder and let out a roar of laughter, deep from the belly. "This?" he said, stabbing a jeweled finger at Jaren. Sneering, the Sage scraped Jaren up and down with his gaze, seeing little reason to waste his time and talent in such a one-sided endeavor. "You make a poor choice of champions, my misguided friend. He is no adept."

"No," came the unexpected woman's voice behind him, "but *I* am."

The Sage spun around just as Athaya dispersed the cloaking spell that had shielded her approach and shimmered into view directly behind him. His eyes bulged like a hanged man's, and Athaya did not have to scan the congregation to know that the same expression graced many a Sarian face. From somewhere behind her, Drianna's squeal of triumph pierced the silence.

Ah, you were wrong that day in the council chamber, Athaya told herself, vaguely smug. This *was indeed the most dramatic entrance of your life.*

"I grew bored on your island and decided to leave," Athaya said before the Sage could regain use of his tongue. "And how could I bear to miss such a spectacle as this?" She stretched out her arms to encompass the trumpets and roses and riches around her. "It was rude of you not to invite me."

Although he hid it well, the Sage was livid as well as stunned by her appearance. He knew who had set her free and Athaya could sense his mind rapidly sorting through the many varieties of physical torment at his disposal, trying to select the most agonizing method by which to punish his steward's heinous betrayal.

"I, Athaya Trelane, wizard by the grace of God," she began, formally reciting the ritual words as Tullis had instructed her, "do hereby Challenge you for the office of Sage, acting on behalf of my brother." She paused until the swell of murmurs, both of outrage and delight, quieted around her. "Over a year has passed since your last Challenge; by your own law, you must accept mine." *Not that you would think of refusing,* she added, the curve of a brow conveying the thought to the Sage. *Your loyal following might suspect you fearful of losing, less certain of your power and thus less worthy to wear the crown you seek so badly.*

The Sage glared down at her like an angry god ready to strike her dead. In the face of his regal splendor, and amidst all of those who had donned their most extravagant finery on this day of victory, Athaya looked little better than an upstart peasant. For luck, she had clothed herself in the same forest green kirtle she had worn to her wedding; her hair was simply but neatly bound with a silver clasp. She suspected she made an absurd picture to the congregation, standing defiantly before this jeweled would-be king like an insolent serving girl, challenging him to battle.

Archbishop Lukin inserted himself between them, wringing his hands and looking as befuddled as Athaya had ever seen him in her life. "Er—Your Grace, what is this? Surely this . . . this 'duel' can wait until after you are crowned!"

"If you will ask the lady," the Sage replied, blanketing his wrath under a mask of poise, "she will surely claim it cannot wait. It is my crowning that she seeks to stop."

Lukin flashed her a singularly damning glare—worse than most of the glares he customarily shot at her—and Athaya frowned back at him, wondering what possible objection he could have to her interference in this unlawful and unholy coronation.

Then, shaking off the last vestiges of startled rage, the Sage sidled next to her, whispering to her alone. "I urge you to reconsider, Athaya. There is only one possible outcome of such a contest and we both know it. Truthfully, your Highness," he added with a leer intended to beguile her, "I would rather marry you than kill you."

Athaya's smile had as much warmth to it as the Sarian highlands in winter. "Truthfully, your Grace, I would rather die."

The Sage's eyes narrowed viciously at her; it was not what he had wished to hear. She was spoiling his day of triumph, but he knew it could be salvaged—if not enhanced—by proving himself superior in battle. "Very well, Athaya Trelane," he shouted so that all assembled could hear. He flipped back his cloak in a showy gesture of bravery. "I accept your Challenge."

As the surge of cheers and protests rose around them, Archbishop Lukin glanced worriedly back toward the gold-shrouded high altar like a host whose dinner guests have suddenly decided to depart, leaving him with a banquet hall of food. "Your Grace, you need not humor her this way," he said. Athaya would never have guessed the archbishop capable of injecting quite so much obsequiousness into his voice. "You are only moments away from your hour of triumph. Finish the ceremony and deal with the princess afterward."

"Silence, Jon!" Durek barked at him, glowering at his archbishop with all the rancor once reserved for his sister. "You have betrayed me as well as Caithe herself by sanctioning this ceremony with your presence. Once this Challenge is done, and Athaya is victorious, I will petition the Curia to strip you of your office, your titles, and your lands. Perhaps I shall give your estates to my sister as a belated wedding gift," he added, twisting the knife of his fury with every word, "and let her build magic schools on them."

The ploy worked to perfection. The archbishop's cheeks flushed to match his wine-colored chasuble, and he stared at his king stupidly, unable to believe Durek would make such threats even in jest.

"I hate to interrupt," the Sage said mildly, turning a dry gaze to Durek, "but before you start making plans for tomorrow, perhaps we should determine whether you or your dear sister

will have a tomorrow to plan for. I have accepted Athaya's
Challenge, and thus by proxy, yours. Let us get this done as
soon as possible."

Durek nodded tersely. "Agreed."

Athaya paused only slightly before echoing her brother's response; now there was truly no way out. "Agreed."

"Then let us step out to the square," the Sage remarked, extending his arm toward the west doors through which he had
so recently entered. "We shall require more space for the
arena."

With his black-liveried guardsmen clearing the way, the
Sage led Athaya, Durek, and Jaren to the plaza fronting the cathedral. As the assembly surged toward the doors in their
wake, Archbishop Lukin retreated in the opposite direction and
vanished into the choir, apparently uninterested in attending the
duel. With any luck, Athaya thought, he would hie himself off
to some remote corner of the globe and never be heard from
again.

Athaya squinted into the noonday sun as she emerged from
the nave and went to stand where the Sage bade her, Durek
and Jaren flanking her like bookends. "Once the blood-wards
are cast," the Sage informed her, absently watching his guardsmen demarcate a circular ring roughly twenty yards in diame-
ter, "they will remain in force until only one of the combatants
remains alive. The wards will protect the witnesses from harm
and keep any external spellwork from disturbing us."

Athaya's eyes skimmed over the hundreds of eager spectators jostling for a place from which to view the contest. "Witnesses . . . then everyone else will be able to see us?"

"And hear us as well. But we will be unable to see or hear
anything that transpires outside of the arena—rather like gazing into a panel that is closed on the other end. An illusion of
privacy to lessen distractions."

"And no one can pass in or out?"

"You and I will become part of the wards themselves; our
blood binds our lives inside. However, like traditional wards,
the blood-wards cannot physically restrict others from entering
or leaving the arena. But crossing the wards would be quite
foolish in any case," he pointed out with a shrug. "Should
someone rush in and attempt to aid either one of us, he would
very likely be killed in the crossfire before ever reaching our
side. Should either of *us* step outside the boundary, however,

the Challenge would be forfeited. A logical consequence, of course," he added, "as the transgressor would be dead.

"There are no rules inside the wards," he continued, "as I am sure you have been informed." His gaze darkened slightly as he reflected on Tullis' perfidy. "But before we begin, there must be an understanding between us. You fight as your brother's champion; therefore, if you lose the contest, I may freely claim his life as well as your own. He will surrender to me willingly and submit to whatever fate I choose."

"No, this is my—"

"She agrees," Durek said, his voice severing her objection like a blade.

Athaya whirled to face him, but before she could protest such an open-ended concession, Jaren's voice echoed in her mind, reminding her of unpleasant realities. *If anything happens to you, the Sage will kill him anyway. This way, at least he'd be able to salvage some dignity from it. Not that he'll have to,* Jaren was quick to add, *since you're planning to win, right?*

She knew Jaren was right, but sought confirmation in her brother's eyes nonetheless. She expected to see dread looming there—and perhaps a sting of resentment that he had so little control over his destiny—but to her surprise, she read nothing but stalwart resolve. He had given his life over to her in trust and looked strangely calm at having done so. Calm, she thought . . . and almost a little proud.

Durek gave her an imperceptible nod.

"Agreed," she said, close to choking on the word.

"And as for your beloved brother Nicolas," the Sage added airily, anticipating her next question, "I will see that he is cared for. It will be my memorial to you both, in lieu of having psalters sung."

Athaya and Durek glowered at him in wordless concord.

"Oh, one last thing," the Sage informed her as he pulled off his earrings and handed them to a waiting guardsman, "you must leave all of your possessions behind. Nothing may be brought into the blood-wards."

Athaya sucked in a gasp of dismay; the Challenge was not yet started and already she had been dealt the first blow. "What—"

"Your jewelry, your purse," he clarified, even as he began stripping off all but his most basic garments.

No, not my corbals! she thought frantically. *It may well kill me to use them, but if it comes to that, at least I can take you down with me . . .*

The Sage paused as he lifted off a heavy collar of gold links. "It is the law, Athaya. If you do not wish to Challenge by the law, then I have no obligation to honor your request. If you do not believe me, then take the word of someone you trust." He muttered something to one of his guardsmen, and Drianna was hastily shoved into the circle.

"Tell the princess the rules of Challenge, Drianna."

The glare she shot at him was poisonous. "He's telling the truth," she admitted; the pained look in her eyes betrayed her suspicion of what Athaya's small purse contained. "The Challenge is invalid if either magician brings anything into the wards that can possibly be used as a weapon. Only clothing is permitted. The Challenge is to be a contest of magic alone."

Athaya felt her stomach tighten as Drianna extended her hands to take the purse of gems away. She even asked for the simple clasp that bound Athaya's hair.

My only real weapon, Athaya thought as Drianna passed the precious pouch to Jaren. *My only real hope. Gone.* Jaren masked his emotions as best he could—to betray even a trace of despair would only embolden their enemy—but his face was bloodless. He gazed at the purse cupped in his hands as if it were her stilled heart, given to him as undeniable proof of her death.

Athaya stole a glance at Durek; he sustained an iron facade of courage for the benefit of his subjects, but like Jaren, he knew what the loss of the crystals meant.

At the Sage's signal, Sir Couric came forward bearing a pair of slender knives on a black velvet pillow. "Couric will act as my second in the blooding. Since you are your brother's champion, Princess, then he will act as yours."

Without knowing exactly what he was to do, Durek took the blade the Sage's deputy proffered. The blade trembled in his grasp; it was all he could do not to thrust it deep into the Sage's heart, consequences be damned.

The Sage extended his palm to him. "Take care with your cut," he advised, sensing the tenor of Durek's thoughts. "Couric will match its depth in your sister's tender hand."

Struggling to keep his anger checked, Durek took the Sage's wrist and made a shallow slice across the skin of his palm. The Sage cupped his hand so that none of the blood welling within it would be wasted on the ground. He gave a subtle nod to

Couric, and Athaya winced only slightly as the man carved a narrow slit into her palm, leaving a thin trail of red liquid in the blade's wake.

"Clear the arena."

Couric and Durek backed away at the Sage's command, each clutching a blade stained with the blood of his enemy. Jaren trailed them reluctantly, walking sidelong so as not to lose sight of Athaya for an instant.

The Sage approached, towering over her. "Now take my hand, Athaya Trelane, and let us bind ourselves within the arena until such time as only one of us remains."

He gripped her hand with inhuman strength, but she fought back the urge to cry out. Hot Sarian blood mingled with her own, oozing between her fingers and trickling down the back of her hand.

"Now repeat the words of the binding: *Aut vincere aut mori.*" His eyes burned into hers as he spoke; the game was being played in earnest now.

Athaya's throat was dry as dust. *"Aut vincere aut mori."*

She felt subtle pressure on her chest as the arena began to take shape. Tendrils of cloud-colored fog flowed from their joined hands, rising like smoke on a windless day. When the column of mist rose to the height of the nave's rooftop, it slowly arced back to shower down around them like a fountain, with she and the Sage the statues at the source of the water's flow. Like traditional wards, the blood-wards appeared as a sheer white curtain, barely visible. But then the curtain grew thicker and more opaque, the fluid white membrane shot through with red veins that pulsed in time with their heartbeats. Gradually, like being spun into a spider's meal, the wards thickened around her; the veil was going down, cutting her off from the world, and Athaya looked back just in time to see the faces of friends and enemies alike fade out of sight as if drifting away on a fog-shrouded lake.

Jaren. Durek. All of you . . . by God, let me see you again.

It was silent now and perfectly still; all sight and sound was absent, as if they had stepped out of the world into a place unaffected by time. It was the antithesis of the between-place of translocation—the divine realm, as she knew it now—all color and noise and vibrancy of life. This was a dead place that only the beating of their hearts sustained.

"It is just the two of us now," the Sage murmured, drawing Athaya's full attention to the matter at hand. They were not truly alone—outside the wards, hundreds of unseen witnesses eagerly awaited the outcome of the contest—but all Athaya could see was the Sage himself and the pulsating red-veined shell that encased their lives; a womb from which she would be born again or a cocoon from which she would never emerge.

They circled one another slowly, each assessing the other. Athaya tried not to distract herself by the obvious advantage of his physical size. This was a matter of magic alone; such things were irrelevant. Her only weapons were her spells and her only advantage the disciplines and techniques that Jaren and Hedric had painstakingly taught her.

For all our sakes, she prayed, *let them be enough.*

"Nothing is quite so sad as the sight of a lovely woman dead," the Sage remarked with an artful sigh. "I will regret this Challenge more than the others, I think."

He punctuated his words with a graceful arc of copper-colored fire—a spell to test the waters but not to kill. With a whisper, Athaya deftly caught the blaze between her palms and blew it out like a candle.

She let out the air trapped inside her lungs, unexpectedly relieved. Tension eased from her muscles as she readied herself to strike back. The first shot had been fired.

The Challenge was under way.

CHAPTER 19

✳✳✳

THEY TOOK EACH OTHER'S MEASURE FOR THE NEXT QUARter hour, each striking tentative blows in an effort to uncover the other's weaknesses. Once, Athaya found herself instinctively swatting at illusory wasps buzzing before her eyes and the brief distraction was enough to open her to the sting of an invisible lash across her cheek, drawing a delicate trickle of blood.

"I could be caressing you with kisses instead of with my lash," he observed. Athaya grimaced; he sounded like an inept bard attempting poetry. With blatant intimacy, the Sage raked his eyes down the length of her body and up again—a tactic doubtless planned to keep her angry and unfocused. "Surely you would find that more pleasing?"

To his acute irritation, the Sage promptly fell victim to his own trick while he awaited her reply, though Athaya conjured honeybees instead of wasps. Now each of them sported a battle wound, a fine trail of salty red liquid dripping from each of their chins.

She lashed out next with ice: *"Glaciem suffunde corpori!"* she cried, commanding white blasts of frigid fog to stream from her fingertips like the mist from a vision sphere. In seconds, her opponent was encased in a coffin of frozen water like a beetle set in amber. But the spell gave her only the briefest of respites; a moment later, an orange pinprick of light began to glow just over the Sage's heart, quickly blossoming over his entire body. The prison of ice melted into a harmless puddle at his feet.

"Ah, how refreshing!" he remarked, shaking droplets of water from his hair. A shiver rattled his limbs once, but he appeared otherwise unaffected by the ordeal. "Thank you, your Highness. I feel more invigorated than ever."

A witchlight sprang to life in his hand with a sharp twist of one wrist. With a whisper, he infused the orb with hellish heat and flung it at her face. She barely called her shielding spell in time, sending the globe ricocheting away in a cloud of blue sparks; it hit the ward boundary with a hiss like hot iron in cold water and shattered into tiny fragments that drifted to the ground like cinders.

The witchlight could have wounded her badly, but Athaya was encouraged rather than rattled; she recalled something crucial in the act of repelling it. As with his spell of translocation, the Sage's magics were frighteningly potent, yet lacked the technique that would have rendered them unbeatable. Just as pulling a thread unravels loose-woven cloth, so could she seek out and exploit the frayed edges of his spells to rob them of deadly force.

He launched another fireball at her, hoping to catch her off guard by using the same trick twice, but this time Athaya spied the flaw in the spell; the loose link in the chain of magics holding it together. The globe broke apart in midair before it reached her, showering down like fireworks. The Sage flinched at the sting of his shattered spell and then glowered darkly at her, irritated that she had countered his magic rather than simply deflecting it.

"You cannot defeat me," he said, hoping to rob her of any pride in her accomplishment. He circled her with deliberate care, like a cat carefully studying his prey before pouncing on it. "Why do you even try? Do you wish to be a martyr? Yes, I believe you do. I've an idea!" he cried with a theatrical snap of his fingers. Green eyes blazed maliciously as he gestured in the general direction of Saint Adriel's. "This fine cathedral is in urgent need of rechristening; as king, I will not tolerate it to bear the name of the man who concocted the obscenity known as absolution. Shall we rename it Saint Athaya's after your death?" he asked, taunting her with a smile. "Would it not be a fitting memorial to you? You, who has long yearned to be Caithe's savior and deliver her people from the ravages of false religion?"

Athaya knew his words were deliberately chosen to provoke a reaction, but could not keep the fires of rage from burning hotter in her heart.

"Shall we carve your image alongside the gargoyles over the door," he pressed on, "or would you prefer to be immortalized in colored glass? A more fragile medium, the latter, yet far more lovely to look upon. And tell me, Princess, what would you like the pilgrims to bring to your numerous shrines? Coins? Charms, perhaps? No," he added with a nasty little laugh, "I think you'd rather have them bring carefully prepared treatises on the ethics of magic, written in their own crabbed hand. Will you perform miracles for them if they thus solicit you? Yes, of course you will. Blessed Athaya, the patron saint of philosophers!"

Then, without a second's pause, he shouted the words of his next command: *"Opprime nocte corpus eius!"* Instantly, in dark parody of a vision sphere, black mist flooded from his fingertips to encircle her. The sticky cloud of darkness clung to her like molasses, striking her blind and fouling her movements. The air grew thin as the shroud choked off her breath; her lungs began to scream for air, straining within her chest as if ready to explode.

The flaw! she reminded herself, stamping down the urge to panic. *Look for the flaw!*

Sightless and disoriented, Athaya staggered dangerously close to the ward boundary; an iron fist clenched her heart in warning. Although she was blind to it, she sensed the red-veined membrane of the blood-wards grow more frenzied in its pulsing to match her racing heart. *Don't panic,* she admonished herself, cautiously easing away from the boundary. *That's just what he wants you to do. Keep your focus.*

She extended her senses into the darkness around her, seeking the fault in his spell. It was there; a pinprick of light in the stygian murk. She extended a finger and ripped open a hole in the sticky fabric, sucking in precious air. In her next breath, she commanded the blackness to disperse. It curled away from her body like smoke rising from a campfire to settle gently against the upper bounds of the arena.

The Sage tossed an idle glance at his now-ruined creation. "Scared of the dark, are you?"

Athaya was given no time to answer; she doubled over in the next instant, stunned by a stabbing pain cutting into her belly like the thrust of a cold sword. Before she could cry out, she heard the Sage murmur a second time; in brutal response, her stomach rebelled against her, spilling up what little she had managed to keep down for breakfast that morning.

"You will notice I have enough regard for your dignity not to cast any spells of incontinence," he informed her, mockingly awaiting words of gratitude.

Athaya tasted bitter bile as she formed the words of a counterspell. She had studied the various kinds of sickness spells but never actually cast them; like the spell of compulsion that bound Nicolas, such magics were considered highly unethical to those of traditional training. Unfortunately, the Sage would not adhere to such moral guidelines; as he and Tullis had warned her, there were no rules within the bloodwards. To honor her training would be her death. The Sage was casting spells faster now and with more force; she had little choice but to lower herself to his level or take her ethics to her grave.

"Ulceribus cutem afflige," she whispered. Red blotches broke out across every inch of the Sage's skin, growing into ugly blisters filled with pus. Another murmured spell robbed the moisture from his mouth and assailed his mind with thoughts of scorching sunlight, thirst, and salt. She willed him to believe that his bones were growing hot, like glowing iron rods set in his flesh; rods that would quickly burn to ash and leave him a formless hulk of clay, helpless and all but dead.

She hurt him that time; she could see the pain in his eyes even while he struggled to hide it. Sweat covered his body in a pungent sheen, soaking his once-fine silk garments.

"This is all very amusing," he said with greatly forced indifference. The boils on his skin popped one by one in response to his counterspell, each expelling a drop of sickly yellow liquid before vanishing. Athaya caught the subtle change in his manner; the Sage had grown tired of sparring, eager for the real contest to begin. "But we cannot be about this much longer; I have a coronation to attend."

Athaya went down hard onto the blunt-edged cobblestones, her knees buckling under her as the world tipped to one side, the ground a carpet that had been roughly yanked from beneath her feet. Ridiculously, the first thought that entered her head was that her wedding clothes were ruined, torn and bloodied beyond repair. *Better the dress than your own skin,* she reminded herself, and blearily labored to rise.

"Athaya, are you all right?"

It was not the Sage's voice. Sucking in a gasp of terrified disbelief, she turned her head to see Jaren kneeling beside her, reaching to help her up.

"What are you—" She waved wildly toward the boundary of the arena. "Hurry! Get out of—"

She realized her error just as the blast of raw power hit her broadside, like the ball of a mace striking square upon her temple. The next thing she knew, she was facedown on the ground, frantically gasping for breath and struggling to sustain a shielding spell against further assault. Jaren's wraith had already vanished back to the depths of her memory whence it had been plucked and the Sage chuckled at the success of his deception as Athaya scrambled to her feet, ignoring badly scraped knees and elbows and hastily piecing together the fragments of her concentration.

Beware the Sage's mind-magic. Tullis had done well to warn her. The illusion had been masterful, capturing the very essence of Jaren's eyes, the line of his chin, the sweep of unruly hair. Athaya had not doubted the truth of what she saw for an instant.

And that lack of doubt would kill her if she was not meticulously careful from now on.

Remember your disciplines. Don't let him muddle your thinking. Her harried senses began to relax as she repeated a few lines of the litany that Hedric had taught her: *Credony, lord of the first Circle, twenty-six years; Sidra, lord of the second.* . . . Athaya regarded her enemy with newfound wariness. *He's brandished his best weapon,* she reflected, sobered by how easily she had been duped. *Now he's playing to win.*

It was more difficult than she had ever anticipated to deliberately try to kill him. She didn't care to witness another bloody explosion of flesh like Rhodri's, a horror that haunted her nightmares to this day, but feared that only something so violent and powerful would destroy him. She cast a spell of sickness on his heart, commanding it to still its beating, but the Sage unraveled her spellwork as easily as a time-rotted tapestry. Then she tried to pierce his innards, to drain him of blood from inside so that she would not have to see her gruesome work, but again, after an initial grunt of pain, he turned her spell aside.

Worse, she grappled with the knowledge that she was not casting the most potent spell in her arsenal. She knew the crackling green fire coils could kill him, but balked at loosing them. Every time she drew herself up to strike with deadly force, she saw Kelwyn's phantom rise up before her, writhing in agony and begging for mercy, his final screams echoing for all eternity in her ears. Logically, she knew such fears should not hinder her—unlike Kelwyn in his last hours, the man she now faced was sane and more than able to defend himself— but logic alone gave her scant solace.

Think of what he's done, she reminded herself, trying to stoke the fires of revenge. *Think of all the lies he's told, the lands he's stolen, the priests he's murdered.*

Dear God, think of Nicolas!

But pure hatred—the steady, burning flame of loathing required to kill without pause—was alien to her. And worse, she sensed that the Sage knew it also and was emboldened by it.

Nevertheless, she had to try something—and soon.

The solution flitted across her mind and settled there. Why not use her opponent's expectations against him? Why not use the Sage's own strategy and let the enemy defeat himself?

She backed away from him with averted eyes, putting on her most convincing mask of humility even as she sent out probing tendrils of mind-magic. It was a technique she had seldom used before; the closest she had ever come to actual mind-magic was lulling an inconvenient guardsman to sleep—an extremely mild form of the spell and one generally deemed acceptable in times of self-endangerment—but the general principles were the same, just applied with far more force. This time, Athaya took care to err on the side of subtlety; too much force and the Sage would sense her hostile presence in his thoughts and unravel her spell before it could take hold. *But it shouldn't take much power,* she told herself. *And he's arrogant enough. It shouldn't be too hard to convince him. . . .*

"I've made a horrible mistake. I know it's too late now, but—" She allowed her lower lip to tremble for effect. "I can see now that you are a far better wizard than I. I was a fool to have Challenged you."

Crede omnino, came the potent undercurrent of her words, left to echo in the deepest chasms of his mind. *Crede omnino quae audis.* Believe. Believe everything you hear. . . .

"I only wish," she added with a delicate touch of melodrama, "that I had agreed to marry you before. It could have been so different." She sniffled miserably. "So wonderful."

His self-assured smile told her that he believed her—or

more accurately, that it did not occur to him to doubt what he was being told. His eyes were slightly glazed, his words vaguely stilted. "Would that you had. But we are irrevocably bound here; only one of us will ever leave the wards."

Athaya sniffled again even as she cautiously increased the power of her subconscious persuasions. "All my life I've realized important things too late. But if I have to die, then ... might I have a simple kiss? A small taste of what I might have had in greater measure?"

The Sage moved toward her with desire in his eyes, and Athaya fought the urge to shrink back in disgust. *At least I've already lost my breakfast,* she mused, stealing a glance at the puddle of sour-smelling bile near her feet.

She wrapped her arms around his waist even as she wrapped her spell more snugly around his mind. "I do desire you," she murmured. "What woman would not?" But just as their lips were about to touch, Athaya thrust her next spell through the breach in his awareness like a sword.

"Laqueum spinosum mihi fac!" she cried, swiftly encasing his throat in an invisible noose of nettles; the spell with which Kelwyn had attacked her that fateful night. She knew what the Sage endured as he crumpled to his knees on the cobbles—the world going black, lungs shrieking for air, the fuzzy sensation of melting consciousness as the unseen necklace of thorns ripped holes in tender flesh. She only hoped that he would not strike back with the deadly green fire coils as she had done, killing her as she had killed Kelwyn and providing a morbidly fitting finish to her life.

She fed as much magic as she could into the rope of thorns, pulling them as tight as her adept power would allow, but it was not enough. With a bestial grunt, the Sage tore the invisible bindings from his throat as if freeing himself from a slave's iron collar. A backlash of pain sliced through Athaya's skull as the rope of thorns was severed and destroyed.

The Sage glared at her as he choked down mouthfuls of air; he was not pleased at being made a fool, his dignity insulted by falling victim to her seductive devices.

"You will not deceive me again."

In the back of her mind, Athaya continued to recite the Succession of Circles, fighting to maintain her concentration and not be duped by what would surely be another attempt at mind-magic. *Malcon, lord of the third Circle, seven years; Kyria, lord of the fourth, one year ...*

Then she felt a hand upon her shoulder—or did she?—and when she turned to look, though somehow knowing she should not, she drew in her breath and held it, too shocked to let it out again.

No, it can't be!

And it isn't, she caught herself, shielding her eyes from the illusion. *Sacret, lord of the fifth.* . . . But her mind was already snared, entangled in the silky skein of mind-magic. She tried to peel the fabric back, but the layers of deception mounted too quickly, smothering her struggles. Defiance was soon forgotten as the blanket of the Sage's magic extinguished her thoughts and replaced them with those of his choosing.

The man's boots were strangely silent on the cobbles as he circled around to face her. Boots—the kind worn by Durek's guardsmen. It couldn't be . . . but it *was*. She was certain of it now.

"Tyler?"

He was garbed in crimson livery, just as she had seen him last, but without the captain's collar of rank that had for so long graced his shoulders. His once-blond hair was tarnished with gray, and green eyes that had in life gazed upon her with warmth and affection now burned her with wrath. Athaya reached out to him but he pushed her hand aside; his skin felt cold and dead to the touch.

Without a word, he opened the high collar of his shirt to reveal a puffed and swollen red streak around his throat—the place where the ax had struck, an impossible scar from a mortal blow. "After all I did for you, this was my reward," he said bitterly, skinning her with his gaze. "Don't ever let them say it doesn't hurt, Athaya. That's just a lie they tell so they won't feel so guilty about doing it." Leaving the collar open, he pointed an accusing finger at her. "You spoke love for me, yet all you wanted was someone to protect you from your brother's soldiers so that you could escape and marry someone else!"

The words lanced through her heart like a heated blade. "You know that isn't true—"

"Then prove it," he challenged. "Let the Sage win this petty contest. Join me in the world that I now inhabit; we can be together as you always claimed you wished. If you ever loved me, you must do as I ask. I died for you once, to prove my love. Now it is your turn."

Athaya's thoughts spun drunkenly inside her head, crashing

into one another like birds against a pane of glass. *No, this is wrong!* came a shriek from the abyss of her soul. *Tyler would never say such a thing. He would say. . . .*

I want you to live and be what you were born to be. She heard the words as clearly as when he had spoken them the night of Kelwyn's death. She had never doubted the truth of those words then.

And she would not be duped into doubting them now.

The Sage's spell snapped its hold on her in that moment of epiphany, but so immersed was he in sustaining his illusion that he did not yet realize it. *No, your Grace, you got it wrong. Tyler and I parted at peace. He gave his life for me willingly; his death gave me strength, not frailty and guilt.* And if the Sage assumed she had married Jaren simply to stanch a sense of loss, then she would do her best to make it a fatal miscalculation.

"I never meant it to happen!" she wailed at the phantom, grabbing fistfuls of hair and hoping the gesture was not overly theatrical. Summoning tears, she fell to her knees in bitter remorse. "I did love you, truly I did. Please, Tyler, you must believe me!"

The Sage let out a low roll of laughter, certain of his power over her. The illusion blurred a bit as he grew careless at his work; Tyler's image was clouded now, as if seen through dirty glass. In that unguarded moment, Athaya gathered all her power for one massive and final blow. She hadn't the leisure of squeamishness; it was time for the fatal strike. And she knew which spell would do it.

She ripped a gaping hole in the fabric of his illusion, sending Tyler's ghost shearing off into pieces like a tattered piece of cloth. Then she sent her killing spell hurtling through the void—*"Ignis confestim sit!"*—the Sage too startled to stop her.

The coils of fire sprang to life at her fingertips, angry green flames crackling with deadly rage. They closed around the Sage like hissing snakes, searing clothes and flesh alike as they drove him to his knees and squeezed the life from his lungs. As he grappled with the coils, Athaya scanned the exposed niches of his mind for past regrets and fears—anything that could be used as a weapon to dilute his strength from inside and thus make her assault more powerful.

To her dismay, she found surprisingly little. This was clearly a man who believed that everything he had done in his life was right—or at the very least, totally justifiable under the circumstances of the time. If the friends of his youth now despised him, it was because they were jealous of his position and power; if a lover complained he neglected her, it was because she demanded too much of a very busy man. He did not even bear the smallest scrap of regret for all those wizards he had killed in past Challenges—Athaya even picked up traces of contempt for some, supremely comfortable with the notion that they had simply gotten what they deserved for daring to supplant him.

Only one incident seemed to disturb him more than the rest—his last Challenge with the wizard Bressel, which he'd come dangerously close to losing. Pouncing on the opportunity, Athaya flooded his mind with memories of that day, relentless in her attack. *Bressel almost killed you and he was not as powerful as I!* She willed him to feel the terror of that day—to remember how close he had come to death and know that he was in graver danger now. *It is hopeless,* she persisted, dismantling the walls of his resistance brick by brick. *Do not bother to struggle. You are bested now.*

"But he lost to me," she heard him growl, deep from the throat, "and I am stronger than I was . . ."

Although flat on his back, laboring for breath and in undeniable pain, the Sage nonetheless fought back. Disregarding the stench of burned flesh, his hands clamped down hard on the crackling ropes of fire, the skin of his palms seared off by the heat of the power Athaya was pumping through them; he pulled the coils from his body with a piercing war cry, then flung them to the ground at his side. The fire coils writhed awkwardly on the cobbles for a moment, like fish hurled onto the shore, then quickly sputtered and died, leaving nothing but an errant afterglow behind.

He had not destroyed them gracefully, but with raw strength alone. As he scrambled quickly to his feet, unwilling to leave himself open to a second attack, Athaya met his gaze and tried to hide the growing terror in her heart.

The Sage was tired, burned, and bloodied, but he was alive. Alive, despite her best effort to destroy him. He let out a breathy laugh, weak but triumphant. "The spell that killed your father," he observed with a nebulous air of respect. "The deadliest one you know. And yet . . . here I am." He winced as he extended his arms, unable to conceal all the injury she had done him. "But enough of this. I grow weary and wish to see

this done. Farewell, Athaya Trelane," he said, offering her a
hastily sketched salute. "We shall not meet again."

She felt the grip of his mind-magic again, this time no seductive shroud of silk but an iron vise around her skull; trying
to repel it was like trying to hold back the king's army with a
slingshot. *No! Fione, lord of the sixth Circle, eighteen years,*
she rambled, desperate to maintain dominion over her wits.
Beviste, lord of the seventh. . . . But with the full brunt of his
skills behind him, the Sage overwhelmed her with brutal effi-
ciency, raping her defenses until there was nothing left of
them.

She no longer knew what compelled her to turn around just
then, but turn she did—and was struck immobile by the sight
before her. He stood not ten feet away, vital and alive, just as
she remembered him before his final descent into madness. His
powerful body was swathed in a mantle of royal purple and his
head crowned with a glittering circlet of gold, the white-
fletched hair beneath it curling neatly inward at his chin. As
they had done in life, his piercing eyes locked onto hers, demanding attention and obedience.

"Father—"

No! Arcaius, lord of the eighth. . . .

For a fleeting instant she remembered it was not real; remembered that all she had to do was look for the flaw in the
Sage's illusion and exploit it. But those thoughts were murdered even as they crossed her consciousness, the truth swept
away like a white cloud of dandelion seed in the wind. He was
here. She could not explain it, but he was. Somehow, for some
reason, her father had come back to her.

She took a cautious step toward him. "How can this be? I
thought . . . you were dead."

"And so I am," he replied in a voice she knew so well; a
voice she had last heard begging for her mercy in the face of
death. "But I was permitted to come to you at this critical
time, to warn you of the great mistake you are making."

Athaya felt as if someone had filled her head with honey; it
seemed an hour before she could stammer a reply. "Mistake?
I don't understand."

"You err in trying to win this contest," he replied, his tone
hypnotically soothing and yet touched with severity. "You
must not violate Dameronne's prophecy. The Sage of Sare
must be the next ruler of Caithe. He must emerge victorious
from this struggle and thus commence the long-awaited golden

age of the wizard king. It is Caithe's best destiny, my daughter, and one you endanger with your continued rebellion."

"No, that can't be—"

Kelwyn shook his head, pitying her ignorance. "Ever have you misunderstood me, child. After I accepted the powers Rhodri gave to me, I realized that magic was the key to Caithe's future; magic would be the cornerstone of a dynasty that could never be broken by civil war such as had plagued our land for centuries. Caithe could be at peace forever—you know as well as I that such was always my vision."

"Peace, yes, but not—"

Again, he did not let her finish. "You have played out your role in history, Athaya. Your work here is done. You have made way for the Sage as you were meant to do, just as my death made way for you."

Athaya backed away, utterly bewildered.

"Where I reside now, daughter, I see many truths that are as yet invisible to you. You must not succeed in this Challenge; it is God's own design that you do not. To disobey me in this is to disobey Him. If you truly wish to do His will, as you have long asserted, then you must not live out this day. Join me, Athaya. Join me in the kingdom that is now my home. There I shall answer your questions and we is can come to peace with one another at last."

Athaya's heart ached with the desire; a resolution to their years of discord was something she desperately wanted but never dreamed she could attain this side of the veil. Was he truly willing to forgive all that she had done? It was a temptation more enticing than any she had ever known.

"Then what I've done . . . the crusade . . . it was right?" she asked haltingly, yearning to hear words of approval rarely given while he had lived. "I did what I thought you would have wanted . . . what you would have done."

"The task is not quite finished; the most important step yet remains. Come with me now." He began to walk toward the ward curtain, then turned to offer his hand. "My time here is short, Athaya. Let us leave this place. Follow me through the boundary that separates us. All will be made clear to you on the other side."

She reached out to take his hand, but other faces crowded into her memory and she dazedly jerked it back, hindered by the links still binding her to the world. "But the others . . . how can I leave them? Jaren and Durek and—"

"A true leader must make harsh choices at times," he said sternly. "You must set aside selfish wants to do what is best for all. Your husband has long prepared himself to lose you in the fight for the Lorngeld's future; he would wish you to obey me, could he understand as I do the benefits Caithe will reap from it. And Durek cannot remain as king. He is my son, but remains unequal to this task—his feelings are still too mixed about the Lorngeld. The time is right for this transition of power. His children are too young to feel any loss for the crowns they might have worn."

"Wait—what about Mailen?" Athaya's heart fluttered with hope; perhaps Kelwyn truly did not know. "Mailen has the power—I've seen it myself."

Kelwyn's spirit flickered wildly like candles dancing in a draft, and Athaya rubbed her eyes, thinking the fault lay there. Oddly, her father did not look as delighted by the news as she would have expected.

"Does he?" her father murmured meaningfully, as if the news further complicated their problem rather than solved it.

"If I can win today," she persisted, "then in time, *he* will become the wizard king of the prophecy and not the Sage of Sare. So you see? The Sage is not the only choice. The crown passes on as it should—from you to Durek to Mailen—and Dameronne's words still become true."

Though the explanation was entirely logical, he flatly refused to consider it. "No. That is not as it is meant to be." His words were clipped and terse—almost angry. "Come. My time here is almost done. I must go and you must accompany me. I cannot return again."

Athaya followed without question, then froze as she neared the boundary of the wards. Something about that pulsing red-veined shell was dangerous, but try as she might, she could not remember precisely what. She only knew that she did not wish to cross it.

She placed a hand upon her chest, conscious of a growing pressure on her heart. "I . . . can't."

Kelwyn's eyes closed slowly as he drew breath, and Athaya shrank back, well-schooled in the warning signs of rage. "Will you ruin everything? Now, when we are only moments from victory? Always have you been thus," he accused, his earlier compassion dissolving into hostility. "Defiant and willful and the rest of us be damned. You fought against marrying every suitor I chose for you, and now—insolent girl!—you defy me again even though it means disaster for Caithe's entire future!"

"Oh, could I have but done it all myself," he groaned, shaking a fist at the unseen sky. "I could have made a treaty with the Sarians and avoided this destructive conflict. But no ... you had to take your petty childhood grudges out on me and see that I never lived to do it!"

Athaya's throat constricted with anguish. His words were more painful than any of the Sage's magic blows, meant to kill the spirit and not the body. "No, it wasn't like that! Your magic made you mad—you lashed out at *me*! I was only trying to defend myself, but I wasn't trained, and I couldn't stop in time. I never meant to hurt you. Surely you know that now, don't you? *Don't you?*"

His expression did not waver. "Would that you had never been born, Athaya," he said, cold and unforgiving. "Would that this prophecy could have been fulfilled without you. Caithe would have been better off—*I* would have been better off! Perhaps I would have lived to see my grandchildren grow up ... perhaps they would have come to love me as my daughter never did."

"How *dare* you say that!" Athaya shrieked at him, poised on the fragile edge between fury and hysteria. "I loved you—I *worshiped* you as a child. But every time I tried to talk to you, you pushed me away and told me to be still. The only time you ever spoke to me was to scold me. Nothing I ever did was ever good enough to please you!"

Kelwyn was unmoved by her display, as if enduring yet another pointless childhood tantrum. "Whatever has passed between us can be resolved. But not here—not now. There is no more time. You must follow me. It is the only way and the only chance you will have. Obey me, and all will be forgiven. Defy me, and you will never see my face again."

His forbidding gaze bored into her, and as she met it, something tightened inside her skull like the last twist of a thumbscrew. The fragile remains of her resistance crumbled to nothingness like dead and brittle leaves. Athaya would obey him. She had to ... there was no other choice. Why had she ever thought there was?

"You're right, Father," she said, tears of defeat stinging her eyes. "I have always been a trial to you. But I won't be any longer."

The look in Kelwyn's eyes at that moment was unlike anything she remembered dwelling there before—triumph laced with malice; heady victory poisoned with evil.

"Be glad, Athaya," he murmured through a loveless smile. "The Lorngeld will flourish because of your sacrifice."

She nodded in miserable silence. It would be difficult to follow him, but she had done difficult things before. The others would understand. It was the price she must pay for what she had done to him, and if Caithe would be the better for it, how could she possibly be so selfish as to refuse? She folded her slender fingers into his hand; the spirit-flesh was cold and unmarked by veins or scars. Slowly, he led her toward the perimeter of the wards; her heart convulsed in terror, thrashing within her chest like a caged bird.

"Only a moment, Athaya," Kelwyn assured her, the soothing words tainted with a curiously threatening edge. He urged her closer to that threshold from which there was no return. "A moment, and it will all be over."

CHAPTER 20

ATHAYA BRACED HERSELF WITH A PRAYER, PREPARING FOR her heart to burst in sacrifice as she stepped through the ward curtain and into her father's realm.

But at the fateful moment of crossing, she was snatched back by a pair of strong hands—warm hands pulsing with blood, unlike Kelwyn's lifeless spirit-flesh. One of those hands whipped across her face, stinging with reality. "Athaya, snap out of this! It's a trick, damn it all—a trick!"

The peach-colored blur slowly focused into a face. She blinked at it stupidly. "Durek?" Another moment's confusion, and then she twisted away from him, realizing his intent. "No, don't try to stop me. I have to go. Please . . . it's best for everyone." She looked to Kelwyn's image, now flickering and fading like sheet lightning. "It's the only way he'll ever forgive me. Please, let go . . . he's leaving without me—"

Durek shook her hard by the shoulders, then spat out a curse and slapped her again; his signet ring bit her cheek, drawing a trickle of blood. "Athaya, listen to me! Listen to me now, even if you never do so again." She gazed drunkenly into his eyes and mused how much they resembled Kelwyn's at that moment; alike, but not so murderous. "What happened to Father wasn't your fault. Do you hear me? It was an accident. A terrible, awful accident. You couldn't help it—your power was just too strong, and you didn't know how to control it." The words spewed out like a ruptured boil, expelling their poison so that the flesh beneath could finally start to heal. "Tyler tried to tell me that you were only defending yourself but I didn't want to listen to him. I was sure . . . even when I knew Father was going crazy, I was so damned sure of myself. I never bothered to give you benefit of the doubt."

Athaya stared at him, uncomprehending. *No, this is trickery; this can't be Durek talking . . .*

"Let him go, Athaya," her brother implored. "Stop idolizing him—don't give his memory that kind of power over you! He was a good man but he wasn't a god. He never saw you for what you were but only for what you were not—and couldn't possibly be."

"But what I did—"

"No, Athaya!" he shouted in staunch denial. His face was mere inches from hers, his breath hot upon her cheeks. *"What happened to Kelwyn he did to himself!"*

The Sage's enchantment shattered in a epiphanous instant; Kelwyn's ghost guttered out and died, the foundation on which it had been built now irreparably cracked. Athaya's senses came flooding back to her in a dizzying rush like magic freed from a sealing spell, painful in its intensity but blessedly welcome all the same. But there was no time for words of gratitude; no time to tell him what a priceless gift he had given her. She looked at her brother, then at the wards, and realized—as he did not—the dire peril he was in. *Or maybe he did know,* she considered. *Maybe he thought it was a price worth paying.*

Robbed of his near victory, the Sage glowered at the king of Caithe like a fallen angel ousted from paradise. "Foolish man," he snarled, every syllable a malediction. "Didn't I say that crossing the wards was dangerous?" He lifted his right hand, offering benediction.

"You will not interfere again."

King or no, Athaya roughly shoved her brother away. "Durek, go—get out *now!*"

Satisfied that she was free of the Sage's thrall, Durek started back—safety was but a few yards away. But he had only taken a single step when he doubled over as if kicked by a horse, clutching his abdomen and gasping savagely for breath.

"Intus sanguinet!" the Sage spoke again, and when Durek opened his mouth to cry out, Athaya saw that it was full of blood, staining both teeth and tongue a vivid and deadly red.

"Stop it! This isn't his fight. Leave him alone!"

The Sage's voice was devoid of compassion, his lips barely

moving as he spoke. "He is already a dead man. He knew that the moment he entered the arena."

Durek's stomach turned over, spraying a sickly mixture of blood and spittle on the cobbles at his feet. Despite the horror gnawing at her innards, Athaya took care to keep her defenses up. It would be a fine time for the Sage to strike her down—if far from an honorable one—but curiously he chose not to, content to watch her brother suffer. She tried to push Durek to safety, but the blow he'd taken was too great; he crumpled to the ground in torment, unable to rise. His face had gone a hideous shade of gray, and he spewed up another mouthful of blood—royal blood—that ran in tiny rivers between the cobblestones.

"Durek, why?" she beseeched him, bracing his shoulders against the convulsions wracking his body. "This was my battle. Why did you interfere?"

His words came in short and ragged scraps. "I had to. I didn't think . . . I just couldn't—" His body shuddered with another violent seizure. "I couldn't bear for you to lose that way. Not that way."

Athaya knelt beside him, extending her senses to try to heal his wounds. It took only the briefest of probes to learn that the damage inflicted by the Sage's spell was irreparable; the blow—like a sword through the belly—had ripped through vital organs, bleeding out his life from the inside. *God, no . . . not him, too. Not now, when we've only just become friends.*

"Durek? Can you still hear me?"

Her brother had always been one to bear physical pain well; once, as a boy, he had dislodged his shoulder after falling from his horse and stoically refused to cry when the castle physician popped the joint back into place with a sickly crunch. Kelwyn had been so proud of his heir's bravery that he'd neglected to scold him for carelessly forgetting to cinch the saddle before setting his gelding off on a dead gallop.

Durek struggled to be just as courageous now, but he was losing the battle badly. He grabbed onto her for support, crying out in anguish at the effort. "Athaya, do something—" His breath bubbled with fluid. "Tell Cecile . . ." He gagged on the liquid clogging his throat; another wellspring of blood and spittle gurgled out, staining both his tunic and the front of Athaya's kirtle. "Tell Cecile and the children that I loved them."

It was the first time he had ever admitted such sentiment in his life, and Athaya knew then that he was certain of his death.

With the last of his strength, he pulled off his heavy gold signet ring and pressed it into her palm; it was slick with blood but she did not wipe it away, too awed by the import of the gesture. "Take it. You're the only one who can bring Caithe to peace again. I think . . . now . . . that you were the only one who ever could . . ."

He gazed at her strangely then, thinking it curious perhaps, that of all people he had expected to attend him upon his death, she would most surely be the last. Then, at peace with what he saw, confident that earthly matters were in the proper hands, his eyelids fluttered closed. A final sputtering gasp for life and his body went limp upon the ground.

Athaya brushed her hand across the sparse brown beard tinted with gray. Gently, she wiped away the blood from his lips with the sleeve of her gown. *Good-bye, Durek.*

The Sage circled to stand before her, carefully stepping over the deepening puddles of blood so as not to sully his fine white shoes. "He was nothing more than a man," he said, as if that excused what he had done. "A king must be much more than that."

Athaya wiped her eyes with hands still sticky with blood, leaving a pair of dark red smears across her cheeks. Slowly, she rose to face her brother's murderer. "You are less than that, Brandegarth. Less than a man and much less than a king if you strike down an enemy without giving him a chance to defend himself."

The Sage shrugged indifferently. "How many of our people did he kill thus, he and his Tribunal?"

That doesn't make it right! Athaya wanted to scream at him, but knew her fury would descend upon deaf ears. A tide of grief threatened to engulf her, but the pulsing shell of the blood-wards was stark reminder that she had no time to mourn; not here, not now. Not while the Sage could use any lapse in her defenses to cast his killing blow.

But it was not so easy to simply will her anger away; anger and regret for what might have grown between herself and Durek, given time. Her soul shrieked for release from the tumble of emotions churning inside her, like spells trapped too long by a sealing spell. To keep it all caged inside would be another kind of madness, and she feared she might explode if she did not find some channel for the raw violence waxing within her, yearning for salvation from its prison.

And salvation did come; paradoxically, from the source Athaya would have least expected.

"Now, Athaya, shall we finish—"

The Sage broke off midsentence as Archbishop Lukin strode purposefully into the arena, still draped in the formal red and white vestments of the coronation rite. His gaze lighted only briefly on Durek's lifeless body before scalding her with sublime malice—such malice as she had not seen since her heresy trial, when the sentence of death was read. Lukin carried a strongbox in his arms; a familiar box, Athaya thought. One that she had seen before . . .

"Oh, dear God—"

Athaya backed away instinctively, but the icy grip upon her heart as she edged too close to the wards was rude reminder of how securely she was bound. *You've slithered out of my reach once too often,* Lukin's eyes spoke to her, glittering with inviolate hatred. *But you cannot escape me now. Your own sorcery entraps you.*

The archbishop bowed low to the Sage as he set the box upon the ground. "King Durek is dead," he said, contorting his visage into a seldom-used guise of submissiveness. "Long live Brandegarth, king of Caithe and lord of the Isle of Sare."

Unaware of the danger lurking inside the strongbox, the Sage barked out a colorful string of Sarian expletives at yet another interruption in his quest for the crown. "Leave us!" he bellowed, sweeping his arms outward in majestic rage. "This is not yet done!"

"No, but it will be," Lukin said with subtle spite. "Very shortly."

Athaya gaped at the archbishop with dreadful respect for his cunning. No wonder he had been so quick to consent to officiate at the coronation! In the act of crowning the Sage—with the Caithan crown of state conveniently exchanged for Faltil's deadly wreath of corbals, somehow stolen from her camp—Lukin would assure his death . . . and the death of every wizard who had come to witness the ceremony. What was to be the Sage's moment of triumph would instead become the archbishop's; he would make himself the savior of Caithe—God's greatest servant, delivering the land from the blight of wizardry for now and years to come. For without the Sage and Athaya to lead them, the Lorngeld would be scattered and vulnerable, easy prey for the Tribunal. And once again, as in Faltil's time, Caithe would no longer be troubled by sorcerers.

"I have brought your crown, Majesty," Lukin purred, pressing his palms together as if praying for the success of his endeavor. "Here, let me show you."

The Sage was about to erupt with fury at the archbishop's continued presence, but a vagrant glance to Athaya effectively silenced him; he read in her face that something was very wrong and glared at the strongbox with refreshed suspicion.

As Lukin knelt to unfasten the leather bindings, Athaya whispered the most urgent appeal of her life that Jaren had likewise recognized the strongbox and was even now dashing headlong to safety. Then, with the cool composure that comes from embracing the inevitable, Athaya prepared herself to face the only choice left open to her.

A feather of concern wafted across her awareness—*You had trouble enough casting a witchlight through a single corbal last night; how can you possibly channel something far more powerful through dozens of them now?*—but the doubt was quickly gone. She was too consumed by purpose, too swollen with a maelstrom of emotion crying for release, utterly focused on the task at hand—the sole remaining duty to be discharged. It would mean her death, of course; if one crystal could drain away her life and leave her helpless to stanch the flow, then Faltil's crown would feed on her at an alarmingly rapid rate. All she could do was pray that she would not falter in her disciplines before her work was done. After that . . . well, it didn't really matter. If the Sage was dead, it would be enough.

Great magic commands a great price. It was among the first lessons Master Hedric had taught her, and one she had learned the truth of very young and very well. *If this is the price of Caithe's future, then I will pay it so that none need do so again.*

Any remnant fears she had of death evaporated in that one apocalyptic moment. Vitality surged through her flesh; not directionless energy, but fueled to a single purpose and doubly powerful because of it. She relaxed into her mental preparations, bracing her mind against the crown to hold back its mind-breaking pain until such time as she could align with it and turn its massive and terrible potentials back upon itself, and aim them directly at the Sage. A Circle charm of sorts, she reflected—a weapon of last resort that would save the day only by destroying them both.

Athaya almost smiled as the archbishop sprang open the last brass latch; what he assumed would be his own victory would—with luck—be hers instead. *She will obtain aid in her endeavor from an unexpected quarter,* Dameronne's prophecy had said. And he had been twice correct.

Lukin cracked open the strongbox and reached inside.

I'll miss you, Jaren, one last, random thought came. *But I'll be waiting. Write the last chapter for me; it looks as if you'll have to now.*

Athaya's mental shield was up and ready, waiting for the enemy to strike; thus, it was with eerie calm that she watched Archbishop Lukin raise the priceless crown from the strongbox, purple gems sparkling softly in the diffuse light within the wards. Lacking bright light, the corbals also lacked full strength, and some idle sliver of Athaya's mind whispered gratitude that Kale had pried many of the larger stones from the crown's base months before. But it was still a ruthless weapon; one balk, one break in her focus, would be her death—something she now expected, but not before she took the Sage down with her.

She waited, hoping to hear her enemy's shrieks of pain pierce the silence, but the Sage had not been taken by surprise; her reaction to the strongbox had convinced him that Lukin was plotting something—and what would a wizard have to fear but corbals? He was ready for the blow when it came, though both wizards reeled backward as the first swells of the crown's influences crashed over them. Both she and the Sage struggled mightily to oppose the crystals' power, taut with the knowledge that their psychic shields were fragile as blown glass, and madness and death were but a single misstep away.

"What is the matter, your Grace? Your Highness?" Lukin taunted, inching closer. "Do you not find it beautiful?"

Each of the corbals wailed with its own voice, and together the crown clamored in keening, deafening discord. But strangely, Athaya found the din to her advantage. Like focusing on a single voice amid a shouting crowd, she targeted one of the larger gems near the crown's base and directed her well-honed energies onto it, leaving the others to fade into an indistinct blur, their words and meaning lost. Though the other crystals assailed her with a barrage of psychic messages, she calmly elected not to hear them, opening herself only to the gem she had chosen. *Pain, pain, pain!* it screamed in warning. *Flee!* it commanded.

No, Athaya replied, countering the crystal's admonitions with her own. *Your illusion of pain is but a trick to keep away; to keep me from using you; to keep me sane and alive. I thank you for your protection, but I no longer have need of it. I know what I am doing.*

"I was told you have a way of resisting the gems," Lukin said, dividing his gaze between them. "But so many? And for how long? I have no other engagements today . . . I can remain as long as it takes."

Beside her, the Sage trembled and perspired from the effort, barely able to hold his footing much less retaliate physically against the archbishop. He looked like a man attempting to lift a drawbridge by brute force, knowing that it would fall back and crush him if relief did not come soon. Athaya felt the building strain as well, but fueled by purpose and with nothing left to lose, her concentration was honed as it had never been before—not even when she doggedly fought the ravages of the sealing spell. Her resistance was strong as tempered steel; thoughts of failure died before they reached her awareness and she was possessed by a single-mindedness that she had not known since fleeing Delfarham that night in Tyler's headless shadow, making promises to whoever might be listening that she would change the evils in the world that had led him to such a fate.

Then, her focus sharp as a dagger's edge, she spied the corbal's source and plunged her presence into it. And in that place of crystalline silence, her perceptions shifted just *so*; she slipped into magical rapport with the gem and was suddenly privy to a dazzling array of paths open to whatever form of magic she chose to pump through them.

Athaya looked to the Sage, mindlessly howling defiance to the crown, and instantly discerned the key to his destruction. It was simple; the Sage's greatest flaw was that he thought he had no flaws at all. No one on this earth could convince him of anything he did not already believe to be the truth.

But perhaps, she reasoned, *he will heed one he believes to be* not *of this earth . . .*

Her own magic tingled inside her, sensing affinity for the corbal and yearning to couple with it. Athaya stretched her arms to the sides as if readying to catch the wind and soar into the clouds, kin to the eagles.

"Figuram visionibus praesta!"

In one magnificent surge, her full measure of adept magic

spiraled in and through the gem, spilling into those around it, and those around those, until her power ran like an electric river through the disparate stones, growing on itself as it gushed through every path and facet, and swept over the crown in glistening, hoarfrost patterns. Her spell multiplied upon itself a hundredfold, reflections upon reflections like a voice in a chain of caverns, its echo never dying out but passed on and on and on. Faltil's crown began to glow in response to the energies whirling within it, turning each gem from indigo to pearly white until the crown itself pulsed with inner light. Just as her brother's blood branched into new rivulets with every incline and shallow in the cobbles on which he lay, so did her power flow into every open crevice in every crystal in the crown, exploiting them to full and deadly advantage.

When the Sage lifted his face to her, he clutched his heart and staggered backward, green eyes glazed with awe. For he no longer saw Athaya Trelane, but only the apparition she willed him to believe was real—and believe he would, for she had plucked the image directly from his own fantastic dreams. But hers was more than a grand illusion born of mind-magic; like the vestige of life she had once given the fire coils, turning them to snakes to torment Lukin's hired assassin, she bestowed a breath of reality upon her present conjuration, becoming the vision even as she created it.

The world shrank down around her. Athaya rose to one, two, three times her height; her black tresses were spun into gold locks shot with moonlight, and her tattered kirtle transformed into a gown of snowy samite with billowed sleeves, belted by a ring of stars; a corona encircled her head, shining golden as the sun; her flesh was translucent as fine porcelain, glowing as if candlelight flowed through her veins instead of blood; and last, a pair of huge feathery wings, delicate as lace, rose up behind her, extending outward as far as the blood-•wards would permit. The wings pumped once, whipping the Sage's hair and garments back in an awesome gust of rose-scented wind.

"*Crede omnino,*" she commanded, looking down on his now-puny form. "*Crede omnino quae vides, quae audis.*" Believe. Believe all that you see and hear . . .

The Sage dropped to his knees in terrified homage; his mind was so occupied keeping the impossible pain of the crystals at bay that he had little left with which to fight her deceptions. It was madness and death should he allow the crown's pain to reach him; he had no strength to question what he saw—no powers of reason to doubt that this was anything other than the divine visitation it seemed. Even Archbishop Lukin, though not the target of her mind-magic, was stupefied by the spectacle before him. His eyes spoke what bloodless, sputtering lips could not: it was not possible to work magic in the presence of God's holy crystals ... could this somehow be *real*?

The Sage ventured a glance upward. "W-who ... who are you?"

Athaya studied him silently for a moment before replying, as if needing to translate his clumsy human speech into a more celestial form. "I am a servant of God. Not His greatest," she added, darkly wry. "None among my kind would dare dub ourselves so."

Athaya no longer had to consciously pour power into the spell; the crown took more than she could ever willingly give. Already it was feasting on her, using her magic—and her life—to sustain the fabric of her spell. And how could she prevent it? Resistance was as unthinkable as it was unattainable. She felt the forces of the tides move within her veins; felt the gusts of a stormswept ocean rage inside her lungs—powers too vast for her flesh to repel. All she could do was submit to their awesome beauty and let herself be borne away on a raging river that she could not even begin to comprehend or control and savor this tempting measure of true angelic might.

"Why have you come?" the Sage asked. He began to rise, but Athaya gestured sharply for him to remain on his knees. Her fingers were as long as tapers, candlelight gently streaming from each tip.

"I come to remind you of your place. You dare to take that which it was never meant for you to have. You are not worthy to be ruler of this or any land!" Athaya tossed her head in rebuke, masses of golden hair sluggishly tracing the motion as if slowed by water. "Your ambitions shame He who made you."

The Sage recoiled as if he had been struck. "No, no ... you do not understand! It was my destiny. Dameronne—"

"Foresaw an age of a great wizard king. Nothing more. He did not speak your name, though you act to all the world as if he had." Athaya glared at him with pewter-colored eyes. "Are you so certain of your worthiness?"

"I—" The Sage shuddered violently; unlike her, he still waged constant war against the crown. But while he was able to block out much of the pain, his resistance was fast growing threadbare; tendrils of the crown's painful influences seeped past his guards to poison his mind. His eyes went glassy as he tried even harder to oppose them, but the tighter he clung to his sanity the more deeply he was mired in her bindings.

Crede omnino. Believe that all is as it seems . . .

"I seek only to establish His kingdom here," he said, turning his palms upward in supplication.

"Your desires have ever been for your own selfish purposes—not His. Never has it been His will for any of His children to use their gifts to dominate others."

The Sage balled his hands into tight fists. "No, that cannot be! You lie!"

"*LIE?* Impudence!" she shouted, beating her wings with magnificent force. "I cannot lie. It is not my nature." She moved closer to him, shedding radiance with every step. "You dare to reveal His secrets by seeking out who amongst you are Lorngeld before their time; and you further plot to mold my Master's will to your own purposes and scatter seeds where you choose instead of where He has planted them. Do you seek to be a godling? Do you presume yourself God's *peer*? Your judgment will be harsh, indeed," she warned with narrowed eyes, "unless you prove your worth."

"Prove . . . ? But I have already—" The Sage shook his head in wild denial. "No, no . . . I cannot be so wrong! Let me see Him. Let me—"

"*See* Him?" Athaya's illusory body rippled with silent laughter. "No one sees Him until their life is done and they come before Him to be judged. Until that time you must be satisfied dealing with me."

The Sage's brows wrinkled inward; he was dissatisfied with her answer. "What do you want of me?"

Athaya struggled to hold back a tideswell of exhaustion; the spell was draining her badly. Her limbs felt taut as bowstrings stretched to impossible new lengths; her heart fluttered wildly; her knees began to quiver, threatening to buckle under her. But a few more minutes was all she required . . . a few minutes in which to entrap him utterly.

"I offer you one chance to prove that you are indeed as worthy as you claim." She slowly extended a finger to point to the glowing crown in Lukin's trembling hands. "These are truly God's crystals, little Sage—in that alone, the archbishop is indeed correct. But my Master has not shared with you the full extent of their secrets, and only His most favored can discern it."

"Then *I* shall be able to do so." The Sage's mouth formed a stubborn line of resolve. "What must I do?"

"Merge with them," she said simply. "There is peace amid their pain. You think the gems an enemy, but they are also a hidden ally. They are a source of great power; far greater than any you have ever known—far greater than the paltry tricks the sealing spell has granted you." As she expected, the Sage's eyes flashed greedily at that. "If you can discover the key to that power, then I will relent; I will accede you the homage that you seek. You will become king of Caithe and the most powerful magician in all the world, and you will have my blessings on you always."

"But ... the corbals are deadly. They bring agony and madness—"

Athaya shrugged gracefully. "So did your *mekahn*," she reminded him. "And yet that you survived. This is but another time of trial." Her eyes took on a subtly mocking cast. "Will you brave it, then? Or will you forfeit the Challenge?"

Athaya waited while the Sage mulled his answer. In his frazzled state of mind, she sincerely doubted the Sage's ability to scry the secret of the corbal's heart. The crown pressed down upon him cruelly; it was only a matter of time before his shield collapsed beneath its weight and, like Father Aldus, he would be so tortured by the crown's terrible pain that he would take his own life to escape it. It would save Athaya the grisly task of taking that life herself.

And if, by some chance, he won? If he learned to do as she had done? Then he would grasp at what was offered him like a greedy child snatching at a sweet, and send his adept powers spiraling through the corbals, working great magic in a glorious and unwitting suicide. Either way, he would be dead. Athaya only hoped that she would live long enough to see it and know her work was done.

"You wanted a crown so badly," she told him, when he still did not answer, "and here is one before you. Take it. But take all of it, in all its many aspects. A crown is more than a mere emblem of power and wealth; it demands responsibility and risk ... and death, if need be," she added with a meaningful glance to Durek's lifeless form. "If you cannot embrace it utterly, in all its many facets, then you are unworthy to hold it."

But the Sage was no longer listening; no longer in such awe

of her. His reverence had changed to dark suspicion, and he leapt to his feet and jabbed an accusing finger at her, defiant to the last. "No! I shall not meet your challenge. It is a trick, do you hear? A *trick*! You tell me there is power in that crown, but you only wish me to lower my defenses and walk blindly to my death! You are jealous of me! *Jealous!* I am destined to sit at God's right hand and you come to me with lies, bidding me to turn back at the brink of my greatest success—God's greatest victory upon this earth!"

Athaya drew back, mighty wings flinching inward in genuine astonishment. *Truly, your Grace, you bring new meaning to pride and vanity. If God Himself denies you, will you still mewl like a spoiled child, demanding to see* His *superior?*

By now the crown was glowing like a harvest moon in the archbishop's hands, and only then did Lukin's muddled senses piece together what was happening—that his precious weapon, meant to kill, was somehow the cause of all this pageantry; the locus of Athaya's power. As if it carried pestilence, he hastily dropped the crown into the strongbox and slammed the lid closed, locking it in impotent darkness.

The psychic shock ripped through Athaya like a severed limb. The delirious intoxication of power surging in her veins was gone in an instant, leaving an empty husk of flesh. The swift descent from one extreme to the other rendered her mute and paralyzed, as if the rhythmic pulses of love had suddenly been twisted into agonizing convulsions of death. Without the crown, her creation shattered like stained glass in an explosion of sharp and blinding color—a little death that returned her to human form. Her wings dropped away like autumn leaves; her flesh lost its lustrous glow; her gown turned once again to simple wool; her hair was once more night instead of day.

The spell was broken, but the Sage was beyond comprehension now, his mind irreversibly contaminated by both Athaya's magic and the residue of the crown. "Are you afraid of me, then?" he shrieked, ignoring Athaya's battered mortal presence and whirling around like a madman in the dark for signs of the now-vanished archangel. "Have you gone back to carry false tales of me to God?" He shook a fist at the sky, damning it and all that it contained. "You all conspire against me! I will speak to Him without your aid. I need no intercessors! He will see *me*!"

Clutching the strongbox by a leather strap, Lukin bolted toward the arena's edge and freedom, but the Sage snatched his arm with unholy strength and held him back. "Give me the crown! I *will* see Him . . . and this crown shall be my gift to Him. And if the crystals do have secrets, then He will tell me what they are!"

Lukin's face was waxen and his lips convulsed several times before any sound came out of them. "See Him? A gift? What are you—"

"Give it to me!" The Sage clamped a fist over one of the leather straps and wrenched the strongbox from the archbishop's arms.

"No! The crown is priceless! It's Caithe's only hope against—"

Heedless of Lukin's protests, the Sage threw his head back and shouted at the heavens, a herald proudly announcing his own arrival. *"HINC LIBERA ME!"*

But Lukin was unwilling to give up his prize so easily; he made one last leap at the strongbox—and his body touched the Sage's own the instant the spell was cast. Their forms began to shimmer in unison, ebbing from the world like morning mist. *Translocation,* Athaya breathed in wonder. But this time the Sage intended not merely to pass through the between-place; what he had once called heaven. This time it was his destination—a destination from which his human form could never return.

The Sage was badly weakened by his battle against the crown and the spell was poorly cast. Time and again, he and Archbishop Lukin drifted in and out of the world like the moon slipping out from behind one cloud only to be quickly obscured by another. Lukin's face was frozen in a mindless scream of terror, while beside him, the Sage's eyes gleamed with reckless expectation, certain of the reward and vindication that would surely be his.

After several uncertain seconds, the Sage and his captive vanished completely, and from somewhere very close, Athaya heard Lukin's wails of terror echo in her ears like a half-remembered nightmare. He gained no more respite from his pain than he had granted to any of the Tribunal's prisoners; his wails transformed to tormented shrieks as his flesh was rent from him piece by piece, leaving nothing but the soul behind—if, Athaya mused, he had one. Would that soul be permitted to stay? she wondered. Or would it be cast down into a realm far less forgiving, reserved for those who had done great evil in the world?

Then she heard the Sage's voice as well, more distant than Lukin's but no less anguished. But the voice was swiftly gone, spiraling into nothingness beyond human pain, and silence once more settled over the arena. Whatever they endured was over now. And where there had been two heartbeats sustaining the blood-wards, there now remained only one.

With the Sage dead to this world, the blood-wards began to dissolve, melting like wax in summer heat and leaving pools of sticky whiteness on the ground. Through Athaya's black-edged vision came a badly blurred image of hundreds of bodies lying prone upon the cobblestones, some still writhing in the last paroxysms of death. Couric's form she recognized, now staring sightlessly up to God; and another—was it Nicolas?—stood near him, with someone just behind, watching in fearful expectation. And around them was a city in chaos, as fires and sickness and madness raged, the work of those struck down by the crown who had not yet been granted the mercy of death.

Athaya dropped to one knee, no more than a bruised and bloodied woman in a tattered dress, her heart straining to keep its rhythm—pitiable, she thought, compared to what she had been only moments before.

Though she knew the sun shone bright above her, twilight soon descended on her vision. Her body was ready to collapse from the strain it had suffered—the weariness of translocation multiplied a hundredfold—and ached for endless sleep. She felt no pain; only a mellow and hazy fading away, like death from cold, too far gone to be afraid of the shadows overtaking her. Tired . . . so tired. She felt plunged into a sea of lukewarm water fully garbed in wool, the fabric's sodden weight slowly dragging her down into the cold and murky depths.

I have done my duty, as I once pledged to do. Please, she implored, to whatever Power held sway over the fates of men. *Please, let it be enough.*

Just one thing more remained to be said; one thing more, before she could rest. And with the arena now dissolved, those still able paused to hear the words of the victor.

"I am the Sage of Sare," she said aloud, though her awareness was drifting beyond the sound of her own splintered voice. "But none will follow after me. I renounce this office and dissolve it for all time, its purpose ended." She drew a breath . . . oh God, so hard. "And I declare the rightful king of Caithe to be Mailen Trelane, first son of my late brother."

The wizard king, though none save Jaren knew it.

Then the world spun crazily, and she hit the cobbles hard, collapsing over Durek's still-warm body in motionless embrace. She heard the clatter of footsteps approaching and felt warm hands upon her face, but consciousness spilled out of her as quickly as had her magic to mingle with her brother's blood upon the stones.

CHAPTER 21

✹✹

"**H**AS A DATE BEEN SET FOR THE FUNERAL YET?**"** Jaren asked, gingerly breaking the silence.

With the quiet creak of hinges, Nicolas opened the shutters to admit a mellow beam of sunlight. "No," he replied, his voice incongruously weary in the bright face of morning. "But we can't wait much longer. Your preservation spell will keep the body intact well enough, of course, but . . ." The prince shuddered as if something small and furry had just skittered across his boots. "There's something eerie about it— leaving him like that, I mean. And now that Cecile and the children are back, we don't have much cause to delay. As for Athaya . . ." Nicolas surrendered to a sigh. "I know she'd want to be there, but who's to say when she'll be up to it?"

The mention of her name, combined with the hint of morning chill that snaked beneath her coverlet, gradually roused Athaya from the soft weight of sleep that pressed her down. She cracked opened her eyes, half expecting to find herself ringed by clouds and stars and winged things, but her surroundings were nothing so grand as that; it was only her bedchamber in Delfarham with its aging blue coverlets and pleasingly weathered furnishings. Her journal lay open on the bedstand beside her, the creamy pages filled with Jaren's graceful script. The restless murmur of voices drifted in from the outer sitting chamber.

She moved only slightly, but the rustle of bedsheets brought

Jaren and Nicolas to her side as if drawn in by a fisherman's line. She glanced past them for an instant, thinking to see Durek as well, and her throat tightened as she recalled that she had seen her eldest brother for the last time on the day of the Challenge. If Durek remained at Delfar at all, then it was in a grandly fitted casket, awaiting burial in the crypt at Saint Adriel's.

"Good morning," she breathed to Jaren, her voice stubbornly refusing to rouse itself as quickly as the rest of her. Though too drowsy yet to lift her arms, she accepted his embrace with a contented sigh. Then she turned to Nicolas and smiled; for the first time in months she gazed into eyes unclouded by magic. He was whole and healthy, the Sage's poisons cleansed forever from his blood.

"Nicolas . . . you're back."

He squeezed her hand. "So are you." His tone revealed that until now, the latter occurrence had by far been the more uncertain of the two. He studied her eyes like a worried physician. "Are you going to stay with us this time?"

"What? Where would I be going?"

Nicolas continued to inspect her for a moment, then glanced hopefully to Jaren. "I think she's finally shaken it off. Her eyes are clearer than they were yesterday."

"I think you're right. And she's not slurring her words as badly—"

"Would the two of you kindly stop talking about me as if I wasn't here?" Athaya scolded, rolling her eyes toward the brocade canopy. "Next you'll start spelling things out to one another as if I were a child."

Nicolas arched a chestnut-colored brow. "Yes, I'd say she's back to normal."

With Jaren's help, Athaya propped herself up against the pillows and took in a glorious taste of tangy salt air, relishing the luxury not only of being alive—miracle enough in itself, she realized—but of waking to the splendor of such a morning. Sunlight turned the rushes on the floor to polished brass and the sea was calm, its waves gently murmuring their promises that all was once more set aright, Caithe's long-awaited peace duly paid for by both her magics and Durek's blood.

Jaren laid a palm on her forehead to check for vestiges of fever. "You've been coming and going for a few days now," he told her, "once you were strong enough to wake up at all, that is. You haven't been ill, exactly—not like the time Tonia and

I released you from the sealing spell—but in a sense, this was worse. The seal made you delirious and feverish—something we could understand and help to soothe. This time . . ." He ran his fingers through a tousled shock of blond hair. "You slept constantly—you didn't move at all except to breathe—and the few times you did wake . . . it wasn't you. You were somewhere else, far away."

Nicolas' face temporarily lost its usual merriment. "You had us scared to death, Athaya. Ranulf, Mason, and Jaren have been taking turns sitting with you; I left instructions that you were never to be left alone. We almost lost you once," he added quietly, his face paling to match his ivory-colored tunic. "You stopped breathing one night about a week after it happened, but Ranulf was there to help you through it—apparently he learned some healing spells in his mercenary days. Damned good thing, too." He shivered at the unpleasant memory.

Athaya suddenly felt cold, mirroring her brother's shudders. "Wait—a week after I . . . how long have I—?" She scooped up the journal from the bedstand with a shallow gasp. After a lengthy entry consisting of Jaren's detailed report of what he had witnessed at the Challenge—something she would read with rapt attention later, as the events of that day seemed little more than a fading nightmare to her now—there were a series of brief notes about her condition, the last written—

"This can't be right," she protested. "The Challenge was in the middle of August. This entry is dated a full month after that."

Jaren's eyes skimmed over the page. "I wrote that four days ago. You've been away a long time."

"A *month*?"

"Considering how quickly that crown was pulling the life out of you, Athaya," he said soberly, returning the journal to the bedstand, "you're lucky you came back at all."

Lapsing into boyhood habits, Nicolas settled cross-legged on the linen trunk at the foot of his sister's bed, looking in spite of princely garb as if the years between had never passed. "I know it's unsettling, but if it makes you feel any better, the Sage's compulsion spell made me lose *eight* months. I can remember bits and pieces of it, but in feelings, mostly—not actual events. The first week was a little rough, but I eventually came back to my senses."

Though the tale was a serious one, his final words brought

a grin to Athaya's face. "There are those who would claim that has yet to happen."

"Not so many who would say it aloud now that I'm running things around here." Nicolas cast a sardonic glance at Jaren. "See? I told you she was fine; well enough to go about insulting me again. In any event," he went on, "I was more than a little confused the day the Sage . . . well, 'died' I suppose you'd call it—like I'd been jolted awake from sleepwalking. There I was, standing in the middle of a riot, totally ignorant of how I'd gotten there or why you and Durek were lying on the ground in what looked like puddles of melted wax. Somehow, Jaren found me in the commotion and kept me from getting killed by demented wizards while we got you out of the square."

Nicolas averted his eyes, suddenly pensive. "I never thought Durek . . ." He abandoned the thought and slumped forward, forearms resting on his knees as he grappled with the knowledge that the brother he had lost was not the same man he remembered. "I guess neither one of us knew him very well."

"Has there been any trouble from the Sage's men?" Athaya asked, eager to set aside the melancholy subject for a later time.

"Not really," Jaren answered dryly, "since most of them are dead. And the few that aren't probably will be shortly. When I saw that strongbox in Lukin's hands, I realized what he was doing and tried to keep him from entering the arena, but our friend Couric thought it was a trick and had the Sage's guardsmen hold me back—he assumed Lukin would walk to his death the same way Durek did and save the Sage the trouble of killing him later. I screamed at them to run for their lives, but they just laughed at me. They didn't even bother to use sealing spells."

"Is that how you—"

"I had no choice. I wasn't going to leave without knowing what happened to you. I thought I'd have to make a quick trip back to Kaiburn so Tonia could release me, but she arrived at the castle a few days later. As for the city itself," he continued, shaking his head, "you were lucky you couldn't see anything from within the wards. If I hadn't seen it myself, I couldn't have imagined hundreds of wizards all stricken mad at the same time. The area around the cathedral is almost entirely gutted by fire—it's a miracle the church itself is still standing. Most of the wizards simply killed themselves to escape the crown's pain, but the ones that didn't . . . well, if they weren't torn apart by the mob in retribution for the Sage's invasion, then they're hopelessly insane and locked away so that their spells won't harm anyone. Fortunately, Ranulf and Mason and the other wizards in the castle dungeons were far enough from the cathedral to get nothing worse than a mild headache."

Athaya twirled a lock of hair thoughtfully around one finger. "If Lukin hadn't put that crown back into the box when he did, I'd be dead, too. Funny, but it seems that I have Archbishop Lukin to thank for saving my life." Laughter bubbled up from deep within. "If he wasn't dead already, that fact alone would kill him."

"Nice of him to take that blasted crown with him, too— wherever he's gone to," Nicolas remarked with a snort. "Neither he or it will trouble anyone again."

"No. But Lukin did have allies."

"Oh, I'll grant you that our problems are far from over," Nicolas conceded, "but whether we agree with his tactics or not, the Sage didn't leave too many Adrielite Justices alive to make trouble for us—not that they have a legal commission anymore, since I've disbanded the Tribunal permanently. And the Curia is remarkably less antagonistic these days. They're still reeling from the Sage's ability to seize most of Caithe in the span of three months, and like it or not they have you to thank for saving her. Just don't be surprised if some people walk in wide circles around you for a while," he added. "Not everyone is convinced that what they saw that afternoon was only an illusion."

Athaya's brows curled inward. "How absurd. What else could it have been?"

"Divine intervention, maybe?" Nicolas flipped his hands over, palms up. "A little outside help to make sure you won the Challenge? After all, you were able to turn aside the power of that crown. And the way I hear it, you made a fairly convincing archangel."

Athaya stiffened skeptically at the compliment. "Better than being called a Devil's Child, I suppose. At the very least, maybe my enemies will assume I have friends in both places from now on."

She asked for a glass of watered wine—speaking so much after four weeks of silence was making her throat raw—and sipped at it leisurely while she listened to Jaren and Nicolas recount all that she had missed during the past month.

"Cecile and the children are back from Reyka," Nicolas told her. "Mosel's with them—and Prince Felgin, too." He tossed a knowing look to Jaren; the news clearly had more significance than she knew.

"I imagine Cecile and Felgin became good friends," Athaya ventured, "what with all the unsolicited 'help' Hedric said she was giving him in selecting a wife."

Jaren's nod was meaningful. "Her help paid off—in a sense. He hasn't come right out and said it, but I think Felgin has finally decided who he wants to marry."

Still somewhat drowsy, it took a moment for her to realize just what Jaren was saying. "What?" she exclaimed, sloshing a few drops of wine onto the coverlets. "You think Felgin is in love with Cecile?"

"I know he is—although it took three tankards of ale for me to get him to admit it. He adores Mailen and Lillian, too; he dotes on them constantly and gives them sweets when Cecile isn't looking. But he hasn't told her how he feels—he'd never tell her at all if Durek was still alive. Felgin is quite honorable for a scoundrel, you know. As it is, I think he'll wait a proper amount of time for her to adjust to Durek's death, then start dropping hints—if she hasn't sensed it already. I've seen the easy way they are with one another; I'm sure she'll accept him when she feels the time is right."

"If she isn't put off by the idea of taking one of your rejected suitors," Nicolas observed.

Athaya threw a spare pillow at him. "Yet another wizard in the family. I can only imagine what Dagara will have to say about that."

"Dagara isn't saying much of anything at the moment; she's still at Saint Gillian's where the Sage sent her. I'd been debating whether or not to bring her back, but realized that I had to send for her to attend Durek's funeral, if nothing else. I sent Captain Elison to fetch her back—being in a coach with Dagara for ten days takes the sturdiest of men."

"Wait . . . who's Elison?"

"You remember Paul Elison, don't you? Good man—and a loyal one. He was posted at the postern gate on the night Rhodri died and the two of you needed a quick way out of here."

"Yes, but what about Parr?"

Nicolas's face reflected an odd mixture of dutifully solemnity and private satisfaction. "Hung himself in the dungeon six weeks ago. Kale was in the cell across the hall. He tried to stop Parr from doing it—God only knows why—but Parr went ahead with it anyway. Apparently he wasn't too happy with the Sage's prediction about his future."

Athaya's jaw dropped open and despite the tragic circumstances came dangerously close to laughing. "Parr . . . a *wizard*?"

"Poetic justice if you ask me," Nicolas murmured with an air of dismissal. "I offered Kale the captaincy, but he turned me down—very graciously, of course. Said something about retiring from soldiering. Frankly, I think he's had quite enough of all this."

Athaya commiserated with a sigh. "So have I, Nicolas. So have I."

Nicolas slid off the linen trunk and went to stand beside Jaren, prodding his shoulder. "Shall you tell her the rest or shall I?"

"Tell me what?"

Jaren poured himself a goblet of the watered wine and leaned back into the pillows next to Athaya. "Nicolas has decided to appoint a High Wizard to the King. Someone to advise him on issues affecting the Lorngeld, just as Hedric did with Osfonin." His eyes flashed back to Nicolas with a secretive glint of delight. "You see, the Caithan court is in desperate need of such an office now that absolution has been declared a strictly voluntary observance and it's perfectly legal to teach magic again."

It was fortunate that Jaren took the goblet from her hand just then, for Athaya surely would have dropped it. Her tongue suddenly went numb, unable to form anything but disjointed noises of disbelief. "It . . . you . . ."

Nicolas grinned broadly. "I signed the order myself. I can do that now, you know, what with being regent and all. And considering how close the Sage came to being king and his proclivity for executing priests, the Curia wasn't of a mood to fight me on it." He picked up a rolled sheet of parchment from the bedstand and handed it to her—almost reverently, she thought. "I had a copy made for you."

Athaya took the gilt-edged paper as if it were a dry leaf that would crumble if grasped too hard. She uncurled the paper and skimmed it with speechless awe, her eyes resting at last on Nicolas's swirling signature—and the seal of Durek's signet ring—at the bottom of the page.

The future of Caithe was right here between her fingers; everything she had struggled for, done with a few simple lines scribbled in black ink.

Athaya sank back against the pillows. It was done. Finished. "Thank you, Nicolas."

"No, Athaya," he said, his eyes suddenly serious as he took the paper gently from her grasp and set it on the bedstand. "Thank *you*."

Athaya savored the silence for a moment, none of them inclined to break it, and then looked up toward the canopy, envisioning the myriad tasks to come in the swirls of blue brocade. "Do you know what this means? It means we have schools to build and tutors to train and . . ." She let out a pleasured groan at the staggering amount of work to be done. "You do need a High Wizard to advise you, but I just can't imagine when I'd find the time. And I'm not cut out for a council post anyway. You know that."

Nicolas shifted his weight to his other foot. "As a matter of fact I do; that's why I didn't appoint you to it. And you'll be far too busy—more so than you realize," he added, mildly evasive.

"Then who—?"

Abruptly, she realized that Jaren had been taking great pains to look inconspicuous. "So I appointed your husband instead," Nicolas concluded, "who was good enough to accept after a full . . . oh, fifteen seconds of deep consideration."

"I didn't think we'd be living in the forest any longer," Jaren reasoned, "so I had to find something useful to do around here. You don't mind, do you?"

"Mind? Of course not! You were Hedric's secretary for five years; you know all about what a High Wizard is supposed to do. And besides, you tend to think *before* you talk, unlike me. And you have a much higher tolerance for bureaucrats—I'd just end up shouting at the council every other day for wasting time arguing instead of getting things done."

A twinkle of amusement lit up her brother's eyes. "Speaking of bureaucrats," he ventured, "if you're feeling up to it, there's someone waiting in the other room who's quite anxious to see you. A few someones, to be exact."

Athaya spent a few hasty moments combing the tangles from her hair, and after judging her presentable, Nicolas slipped out to fetch her visitors. The bedchamber soon rang with the merry voices of Ranulf, Mason, Master Tonia, and—to her complete surprise—Overlord Basil.

Tonia was first to bustle to her side, clad in a flowing gown of embroidered silk more sumptuous than anything Athaya had seen her wear before. "Good to see you still all in a piece, my girl. Gilda and Girard wanted to come, but somebody had to stay behind and keep an eye on the camp and this time it damned well wasn't going to be me."

Likewise dressed as befitting a king's court—and nigh unrecognizable because of it—Ranulf and Mason each greeted her with a chaste kiss on the cheek, neither looking the worse for their brief imprisonment in the dungeons. But as Mason was quick to observe, "Sharing a cell with Ranulf was the worst part of it. I never heard a man snore so."

"It was damp down there an' it gave me a cold," Ranulf retorted. "You don't hear me bellyaching about your habits, now, do ye? Grinding yer teeth all night like they was a pair o' damned millstones."

Laughing at the welcome sounds of their good-natured banter, Athaya extended her hand to the overlord, resplendent in a summerweight robe of sapphire blue. "Lord Basil, welcome." She cast a glance of mock wariness through her lashes. "I'm not in trouble again, am I?"

"Not this time, no," he said; his lean face wore a smile, but Athaya sensed the sadness lingering just behind it. "When I saw Hedric's image fade from the register in the Circle Chamber, I knew that he was gone. I came to Delfarham to take his body back to Reyka, knowing it his wish.

"But I came for another reason as well."

A spell of expectant silence fell over the room. At a subtle signal from Basil, the others drew back a step, their faces settling into reverence. Even Ranulf put on a mask of dignified respect, which only increased Athaya's suspicions. The knowing gleam in Nicolas' eyes, however, proved that whatever was happening, it was nothing too sinister.

Overlord Basil clasped his hands together, priestlike. "Athaya Theia Chandice Trelane, Princess of Caithe," he began, ignoring the arch of her eyebrows at being hailed so ceremoniously, "you have done our people great service in Caithe, and in so doing, have been a worthy servant to He who bestowed your gifts upon you. In light of your efforts, your talent, and your veneration of our ways, it is my pleasure to inform your name has been entered into nomination to serve on

the Circle of Masters, to take the place left vacant by Master
Hedric in his passing, may God shelter his soul in peace."

If anyone but Overlord Basil had delivered the words,
Athaya might have thought herself the victim of a peculiar sort
of joke. But the glow of pride in the eyes of family and friends
was not feigned, and she looked from one to the other and
back again in wordless shock, unable to fathom what she had
heard.

"Who . . . me?"

In spite of the formality of the occasion, Basil expelled a
merry chuckle; it was the first time she had ever heard him so
utterly amused. "He told me you would say that very thing.
We spoke of this months ago, Hedric and I." The light on Basil's face dimmed slightly. "When he left Ath Luaine last
spring, I do not think he expected to return."

Then Basil extracted a plain silver ring from his robe and
extended it to her, awaiting her answer.

"You'd best accept," Tonia advised her with mock gravity.
"No one's ever turned it down before, and the Circle has been
nominating candidates through eighty-nine overlords."

"And I'm painfully aware of each and every one of them,"
Athaya replied, as the Succession of Circles came unbidden
into her brain. *Credony, lord of the first Circle, twenty-six
years; Sidra, lord of the second* . . .

She looked to Overlord Basil with all the dignity she could
gather, considering she was lying in bed clad only in a linen
dressing gown. "I'll be honored to accept, my Lord. And I'll
try to be a worthy successor to him."

As Basil nodded his satisfaction at her answer, Jaren came
forward to brush her lips with a kiss. "Just keep doing as you
have been," he whispered softly, "and you'll be the best there
ever was."

Basil slipped the ring onto her finger to conclude the for-
malities. Afterward, Athaya sank into the pillows and laughed.
"Rhodri would die all over again if he knew about this," she
remarked to Jaren, admiring the play of light across the simple
band of silver on her hand. "Being on the Circle was all he
ever wanted." Then she glanced sidelong to Basil. "And I
don't imagine the idea would have sat too well with you either,
if you'd known this would happen when we first met."

"I probably would have resigned in disgust," Basil admitted.
"But now I can't imagine anyone more capable of filling
Hedric's place."

"Savor that, my dear," Tonia broke in. "It's the only compliment from this old mule that you'll ever get."

As Nicolas passed out congratulatory glasses of wine, Mason came forward and bestowed his own good wishes on her future. "I imagine we'll be reading your works in a future *Book of Sages*," he said, a kindly gleam of envy in his eye. "I shall have all the students of my College study your essays diligently."

"My—" Athaya chuckled dryly. "I'd guess I'd better write some, then, hadn't I?" Despite Jaren's lengthy entry about the Challenge, the journal at her bedside was still painfully thin, waiting for her wisdom—if she could devise any—to grace its empty pages.

"Master Athaya," Nicolas said, trying out the phrase on his tongue as if sampling a new vintage of wine. "Sounds a bit pompous to me."

"Then you'd better hope she doesn't become overlord one day," Ranulf remarked. "Aye, there's a pompous title for ye. No offense, o' course," he added to Basil.

The overlord pursed his lips, silently debating whether to reproach him or not, and decided to forgo it in light of the happy occasion. "We can take care of the details later," he told Athaya. "Your formal investiture and so forth. The ceremony will be held in the Circle Chamber, preferably before the year's end—though I don't imagine getting there at any time of year will be a problem for a wizard so adept at translocation."

"I suppose this means you'll have to tell me the rest of the Circle spells," she said lightly.

Basil replied with an eloquently martyred sigh.

Drowsy from both the watered wine and her recent illness, Athaya soon began to yawn noticeably. Jaren quietly suggested to the others that she be left alone to rest.

"Well, I'd best go make some edicts or command somebody to do something," Nicolas said as he set his wineglass aside and moved toward the door. "People will think I'm not doing my job."

"Mailen doesn't come of age for what . . . ten years?" Athaya mused, battling to suppress another yawn. "I'm not sure Caithe is ready for a decade of government under the regency of Prince Nicolas."

Nicolas tossed a smirk over his shoulder. "If nothing else, I'll see to it that we have plenty of good parties." Then, more seriously, he added, "The council is urging Durek's funeral to take place as soon as possible, Athaya. They're nervous at the delay—as if somehow all those dead Sarian wizards are going to rise up and start fomenting rebellion again. Still, I think they have a point. We need to put a proper end to this; to Durek's reign . . . to all of it. If you're well enough, I'd like to make the arrangements for week's end."

"I'll be there, Nicolas." It was the last thing she could do on her brother's behalf; she would attend even if she had to be borne there on an invalid's litter. "I have to be."

King Durek's funeral was held on the morning of the equinox marking the passage of summer into fall. Although most of Delfarham was crowded into the cathedral, the congregation kept eerily silent—a striking change from the jubilant atmosphere of the Sage's aborted coronation. The fragrance of roses lining the galleries was diminished by the tang of smoke still lingering from last months' debacle, and even the slender white tapers adorning the altar seemed to glow less radiantly out of respect for the dead.

Athaya felt oddly detached from the world that morning, as if watching the events through a hazy distance of a vision sphere. She felt it was some other woman that walked down the aisle on her husband's arm; some other woman that was honored with solemn bows by the citizens of Caithe, many of whom had doubtless cried out for her death but a year ago. *A pleasing change,* Athaya thought as she watched herself incline her head in acknowledgment of another proffered bow; secretly, however, she knew that some rebellious part of her would miss being an outlaw and renegade.

Another pleasing change—and one she could accept without any reservation—was that after almost two centuries, Saint Adriel's Cathedral was Saint Adriel's no more. During her month-long slumber, Nicolas had ordered the great church rechristened. The Cathedral of the Innocents. *Yes, most suitable,* she thought as her gaze swept up the massive limestone pillars toward the great rose window in the east. A fitting memorial by which to remember all those thousands upon thousands of Lorngeld led to the slaughter out of the senseless fear their gifts inspired.

The choir opened the service with a doleful hymn of invocation that wished the dead a just and merciful hearing in the court of God. Athaya was tucked comfortably in the royal box between Jaren and Nicolas; to Jaren's right were Lord Basil, Master Tonia, Mason, and Ranulf and Drianna—the latter pair sitting with hands clasped, Athaya noted, while taking great pains to avoid it being noticed—and to Nicolas' left were Dagara and her brother Mosel, Felgin of Reyka, Cecile, and the two youngest Trelanes. At just over a year old, Princess Lillian dozed through much of the gloomy affair, but at four, Prince Mailen was old enough to realize that this would be the last he ever saw of his father; he whimpered pitiably throughout the service despite Cecile's gentle murmurs that he was king now and should try his best to be brave for his subjects.

The bishop who delivered Durek's eulogy was unknown to Athaya—and to most of Delfarham. Nicolas and the Curia had not yet had time to agree on who was to be Lukin's successor, so an unknown priest from a remote eastern shire was granted the honor. He had also been granted the honor or revoking Athaya's decree of excommunication, thus restoring privileges she had not truly missed, but was nonetheless glad to have back again. *Perhaps now that all of us are welcome here,* she thought, *this will be more a church of God and less a one of those who fancy themselves His mouthpieces.*

When the service was finally done, solemn-faced Caithans trickled from the sanctuary while the royal family approached the bier for a more intimate farewell. When it was Athaya's turn, she noticed that the others drew back as she stepped forward, perhaps sensing that she had private things to say to him that none could truly understand. Her Circle ring gleamed in the candlelight as Athaya laid her hands upon the jeweled cloth draped over her brother's casket.

"I wish we'd had more time," she said simply. She had never expected to weep at Durek's passing, but raised a square of white linen to her eyes to blot away the tears, mourning not only his loss but the loss of what might have grown between them. "Strange as it might have sounded once, I think we could have been friends."

Then Athaya broke away from the others and headed for the south ambulatory. "I'll be back shortly. There's something I need to do before we go." Jaren moved to join her, but she gently waved him back.

Alone, she followed the narrow passage behind the high altar, walking past statues of saints and tombs of long-dead kings until she came to an isolated chapel in the easternmost corner of the cathedral. It was the first time she had ever been to Kelwyn's tomb; she hoped she would be welcome there.

A gleaming bronze plaque was newly set into the flagstones just outside the threshold. On it was only one word: Graylen. Nicolas had seen to that, bless him—a permanent reminder of the captain's loyal service to his lord. Smiling wistfully, Athaya kissed her fingers and then knelt down and brushed them across the cool square of bronze; though Tyler's body did not rest there, its spirit surely did. Ever Kelwyn's guardian, even now.

Slowly, Athaya entered the chapel and approached the marble tomb. She leaned against the polished brass railing surrounding it, quietly studying her father's face. It was a good likeness, she thought, gazing upon the broad shoulders and stern jaw etched forever in the gray-veined stone. His arms were crossed over his chest, the left hand bearing a sword and the right left empty, slightly raised and cupped as if ready to accept some proffered gift. Sunlight streamed through an arched stained glass window to her right, spotting the floor in red and gold and green like a field of wildflowers in summer. Somehow, Athaya felt unduly somber in her mourning gown of black silk.

"I'm sorry I didn't come before," she said, curling up on the floor at his feet like a child eager to hear a tale be told. "But I probably would have been arrested if I'd tried."

Tendrils of incense drifted into the chapel from the sanctuary, accompanied by the gentle strains of organ music. "It's over now. You already know that, I think, but I wanted to come and tell you myself." And then, as if he were in the flesh beside her, she told him the tale of the Sage and her Challenge, of the secret power hidden within Faltil's crown, and of her brother's final act of heroism.

"You'd have been so proud of him, Father. He did what he had to do to keep Caithe safe, even if it meant making peace with me. He learned that sense of duty from you. After all, you assumed magic powers in an effort to understand the Lorngeld, even if it meant risking your soul."

Athaya paused as if expecting an answer, and then smiled at her childish fancy. "Nicolas tells me there's to be a formal alliance with Reyka," she went on, "just as you always wanted. Felgin is acting as ambassador for his father, so it shouldn't be long before Reyka and Caithe are friendly neighbors again. In fact, I'd not be surprised if the alliance isn't sealed by a marriage—though not precisely the one you intended," she added, briefly telling him of Felgin and Cecile's friendship. "I hope it's not awful of me to be telling you that at Durek's funeral, but it's comforting to think that something good might come out of this one day."

Athaya tapped her chin, pondering other developments that might be of interest to him. "Jaren is to have a council post, so perhaps that distinguished assembly will actually get something done for a change. And Mosel Gessinger has agreed to serve as Lord Marshall of Sare—I think the island will be very quiet for a while, and quiet is just what he wants in his last years. He and Tullis should get on well ... they both have gentle souls.

"And don't worry about Nicolas," she added, as if he had moved to voice a concern. "The thought might have scared me to death a few years ago, but I think he'll make a fine regent. Oh, he jokes a lot, but he's bared his teeth to the world when he's had to. All of your children have a stubborn streak, I'm afraid," she observed wanly. "And being close friends with the overlord of the Circle doesn't hurt his cause. Now that the study of magic is legal again, the Circle's influence will start to be felt here before long, and neither the council or the Curia want seven powerful wizards angry at them. And I'm to be one of them, did I tell you? It will keep me busy, when I'm not keeping Nicolas out of trouble and setting up magic schools. Mason's already drawing up plans to turn our little sheepfold into a Wizard's College just like the one in Reyka."

After a moment's silence, Athaya got to her feet and smoothed the wrinkles from her skirts. The time for trivial chatter had past; the others were waiting and it was time to get to the real purpose of her visit. She drew closer to the tomb, stepping gingerly as if somehow afraid of waking him.

"I wish we could have liked each other better," she said, grasping the brass railings around the tomb. "I know I wasn't exactly what you wanted ... but I never could have been. No one could have taken Chandice's place in your heart. I simply wasn't born to be like her, delicate and tranquil and fully content to care for a husband and children. I was too restless for that ... too unsettled. In truth, I was more like you," she observed, a slight waver creeping into her voice, "though neither of us saw it then. I just needed a focus—a direction like you had in wanting to end the civil wars and make Caithe whole again. My magic gave me that direction; now I have wizard's work to do. Neither of us were perfect," she finished, gazing upon her father's cool and sculpted likeness. "It's sad that we didn't accept that when we had the chance."

Then her wistful gaze turned to something more beseeching, and Athaya's grip tightened on the rail. "You must know I never meant to hurt you. That day has haunted my dreams ever since. My mind knows it was an accident, but my heart can't always accept that. At least that kind of tragedy won't ever need to happen again; no one has to hide their magic from the world anymore. They can seek a teacher and learn their craft, and not let their *mekahn* make them a danger to anyone. And that's partly because of you. I only did what I thought you would have done—or we could have done together, given time. I just hope," she whispered, "that wherever you are . . . that you are pleased."

The organ music had stopped; now the silence in the chapel was complete. "I should go soon. Jaren and the others will be waiting. Oh, but shall I tell you a secret first? I haven't even told Jaren yet; I want to be certain, but . . ." She set one hand atop her belly. "I think that come the spring you're going to have another grandchild." She smiled at the tomb, returning the imagined beam of pleasure in Kelwyn's marble eyes. "Sometimes I wonder if the child will have the power . . . but it won't really matter. Now the child can grow up to be anything it's born to be."

She heard the squeak of a boot behind her as Jaren reluctantly stepped inside. "Athaya?" He didn't approach her, loath to violate the sacred space around father and daughter. "The coach is waiting."

Athaya nodded over her shoulder. "I'll be right there."

When he was gone, she looked one last time upon her father's likeness. "I have to go now. But I'll come back again soon—I promise. I just . . ." She swallowed hard; even alone, the words were difficult to say. "I just hope everything is all right between us now."

She was answered by utter stillness, broken only by the sound of her own breathing and the susurration of silk skirts as she turned to go. She chided herself with a smile; *Come now, Athaya, did you really think he would answer you?*

She paused at the threshold, her eyes smiling once more upon the bronze plaque on the floor. But then the plaque began to gleam with orange light, as if it reflected a nearby torch. Curious, she turned . . . and there, poised above Kelwyn's cupped right hand, was the faint glow of a witchlight, dim as a lantern spied across a misty lake. It was a hazy blur of distant color; a beacon through a veil of fog that cast a radiant sheen of life upon her father's marble face.

Athaya's heart began to hammer in her chest until a far more rational explanation came to her. "Jaren?" she called out, thinking to catch him at this kindly bit of magic. But a quick inspection of the corridor proved it empty; Jaren was no longer there. She and Kelwyn were quite alone.

By the time she turned back to the tomb, the errant glow was gone, faded back whence it had come. Had it been there at all, she wondered with a frown, or was it only a reflection from the window, a random glint of the sun that tricked her eyes into believing she had obtained the answer she sought?

But from the well of her soul, she already knew. Athaya departed the chapel in newborn serenity, secure in the knowledge that she was absolved at last.